Stephen Leather is one of the UK's most successful thriller writers. Before becoming a novelist he was a journalist for more than ten years on newspapers such as *The Times*, the *Daily Mirror*, the *Glasgow Herald*, the *Daily Mail* and the *South China Morning Post* in Hong Kong. His titles have topped the Amazon Kindle charts in the UK and the US. His bestsellers have been translated into fifteen languages and he has also written for television.

Also by Stephen Leather

Pay Off	The Bombmaker
The Fireman	The Stretch
Hungry Ghost	Tango One
The Chinaman	The Eyewitness
The Vets	First Response
The Long Shot	Takedown
The Birthday Girl	The Shout
The Double Tap	The Solitary Man
The Runner	The Tunnel Rats
The Hunting	

Spider Shepherd thrillers

Hard Landing, Soft Target, Cold Kill, Hot Blood, Dead Men, Live Fire, Rough Justice, Fair Game, False Friends, True Colours, White Lies, Black Ops, Dark Forces, Light Touch, Tall Order, Short Range, Slow Burn, Fast Track, Dirty War, Clean Kill, First Strike, Last Chance

STEPHEN LEATHER

LAST CHANCE

HODDER &
STOUGHTON

First published in Great Britain in 2025 by Hodder & Stoughton Limited
An Hachette UK company

The authorised representative in the EEA is Hachette Ireland,
8 Castlecourt Centre, Dublin 15, D15 XTP3, Ireland
(email: info@hbgi.ie)

1

A CIP catalogue record for this title
is available from the British Library

Hardback ISBN 978 1 399 74959 6
Trade Paperback ISBN 978 1 399 74960 2
ebook ISBN 978 1 399 74963 3

Typeset in Plantin Light by
Palimpsest Book Production Ltd, Falkirk, Stirlingshire

Printed and bound in Great Britain by Clays Ltd, Elcograf S.p.A.

Hodder & Stoughton policy is to use papers that are natural, renewable
and recyclable products and made from wood grown in sustainable forests.
The logging and manufacturing processes are expected to conform
to the environmental regulations of the country of origin.

Hodder & Stoughton Limited
Carmelite House
50 Victoria Embankment
London EC4Y 0DZ

www.hodder.co.uk

CHAPTER 1

As graves go, it wasn't much of one. Two feet wide and a little over six feet long, it was barely big enough to contain the body. It wasn't deep, either, four feet at most, just deep enough so that the body wouldn't be disturbed by one of the hundreds of foxes that roamed the New Forest. The soil from the grave was in a neat pile beside it with a spade stuck in to it.

There were three men standing at the side of the grave, looking down at the body.

'Looks like he's sleeping,' said one of the men. His name was Paul Dutch, a professional killer with more than a dozen contracts to his credit. He was a Geordie, though his accent had been smoothed over by a quarter of a century living in London. In the trade he was known as The Dutchman, though none of his clients ever dealt with him directly. Before he became a professional killer, he had made his living from robbing banks and post offices, and had the quiet authority that came from years of waving a sawn-off shotgun in people's faces. He was in his late forties and his hair was greying, but he was heavyset and well-muscled from daily workouts in the gym and an hour a day in his own pool.

'Looks dead enough to me,' said the man standing on Dutch's left. Jimmy 'Razor' Sharpe had a strong Glaswegian accent though, like Dutch, he had spent decades away from the city of his birth. He was an inch or two shorter than Dutch but weighed about the same, though the weight he carried was mainly fat, and most of it was distributed around his gut. His black hair was swept back tied into a small ponytail and he had his hands thrust deep into the pockets of his overcoat.

'Jimmy's right,' said the third man. 'You can see the three bullet holes clear enough.' His brown hair was greying at the temples but other than that he looked a good ten years younger than his true age, with a runner's build and an alertness to his eyes that suggested he was used to nipping problems in the bud. He was wearing a black leather jacket over a grey polo neck sweater and was holding a smartphone, busy taking a couple of pictures. 'Everyone keep schtum while I take a video. We wouldn't want a confession caught on tape, would we?' He was using the name Darren Griffiths, but that was an alias. His real name was Dan Shepherd, and his friends called him Spider.

'I'm ready for my close up, Mr DeMille,' said Sharpe.

Shepherd pressed the button to stop recording. 'For fuck's sake, Jimmy, what part of "keep schtum" didn't you understand?'

Sharpe mimed a silent apology and Shepherd took another video, just three seconds showing the grave, the body, and the pile of earth. He stopped recording and nodded at Dutch. 'Are we good?'

Dutch took a long look around before nodding. 'Yeah, we're good to go.'

Shepherd put the phone into his jacket pocket and leaned over the grave. 'All right, Ricky, you can get out now.'

The man lying in the grave opened his eyes. 'About fucking

time,' he said. 'It's fucking freezing down here and something has crawled into my ear.'

Ricky Lewis got unsteadily to his feet and Sharpe helped him out of the grave.

'This is fucking ridiculous,' said Lewis, using his hands to brush soil off his trousers.

'Ridiculous or not, it's keeping you alive, Ricky,' said Shepherd.

'My suit's ruined. Are you gonna pay for a new one?'

'Me personally, no. But I suppose the NCA might run to picking up the dry-cleaning bill.' He looked over at Jimmy Sharpe. Sharpe had been with the National Crime Agency for more than ten years, and prior to that had worked for the Serious Organised Crime Agency's undercover unit.

Sharpe grinned. 'About as much chance as hell freezing over,' he said. 'Come on, let's get you back to the safe house.'

'Yeah, about that. The safe house sucks. Can't I just check into a decent hotel? I'll pay.'

'You need to be in a safe house, Ricky,' said Sharpe. 'The clue is in the name: safe. We can protect you in a safe house. Any man and his dog can walk into a hotel.'

'There's bed bugs in the bed.'

'Well sleep on the bloody sofa then,' said Sharpe. 'Ricky, mate, if it wasn't for us, you'd be lying in that grave for real.'

Ricky wiped his nose with the back of his hand. 'And yet you still won't tell me who took the contract out on me.'

'We don't know who it was,' said Sharpe.

'I've got a lot of enemies,' said Ricky.

'Yeah, well in your line of business, that's to be expected,' replied Sharpe.

Ricky Lewis was a major player in the UK cocaine trade,

shipping it in from Colombia and dispersing it to several criminal gangs across the south of England. There were always disputes about supplies, pricing and competition, and someone had felt aggrieved enough to put out a hundred grand contract on his life. The contract had been taken up by The Dutchman, who hadn't realised that the NCA had bugged his phones, car and house. The NCA had pulled him in immediately and given him a choice: cooperate or face a lengthy prison sentence. Dutch had agreed, albeit reluctantly.

Sharpe put a hand on Ricky's shoulder. 'Come on, let's get out of here.'

'I want a steak.'

'Through the heart?'

'Did anyone ever tell you that you're a very funny Scotch prick?'

'All the time,' said Sharpe. He ushered Lewis away from the grave. He had parked his Jaguar a hundred yards away on a track that led through the trees.

'There goes a hundred grand,' muttered Dutch. 'What a waste.'

'You'd rather spend the rest of your life behind bars?' asked Shepherd. Shepherd was an officer with MI5, the United Kingdom's domestic counter-intelligence and security agency. MI5 and the NCA were running a joint operation to find out who was handing out assassination contracts across the UK. The Dutchman was their way in.

'I'm not sure that a lifetime in witness protection is going to be any better,' said Dutch.

'I've been in prison, and I can tell you that it's no fun,' said Shepherd. 'You're better off on the out.' Shepherd pulled the spade out of the pile of soil and handed it to Dutch. Dutch held up his hands.

'Fuck the fuck off.'

'We can't leave it like this. If somebody finds out and the papers print it then The Office will know that Ricky isn't dead.'

'I dug the bloody hole, didn't I?'

'You did. And now you need to fill it in.'

Dutch took the spade from Shepherd and hefted it in both hands as if trying to decide whether to bring it crashing down on Shepherd's head.

'You wouldn't get far,' said Shepherd.

Dutch chuckled. 'I'd get further than you.'

Shepherd stood with his arms at his sides. If Dutch did decide to have a go, Shepherd was reasonably sure he'd be able to take the spade off him. But the last thing he wanted was to fight the man. He wanted – and needed – his cooperation. He grinned. 'Just fill in the hole and I'll take you for a pint,' he said. 'On me.'

Dutch stared at Shepherd for a couple of seconds, then he shrugged and began shovelling soil into the grave.

CHAPTER 2

The safe house was on the outskirts of Reading, a nonde-script new build detached home that was one of almost fifty identical boxes. Ricky Lewis had no connection with the town, and neither did Jimmy Sharpe, so it was the perfect place to stay below the radar. Lewis hadn't been impressed with the lodgings, claiming that it was a tenth the size of his house in Beckenham, south London. He had taken the main bedroom, which had an en-suite shower room, while Sharpe slept on the sofa in the living room. There were two other perfectly acceptable – albeit small – bedrooms upstairs, but Sharpe knew that if they did ever get visitors, it would be unlikely they'd be coming in through an upstairs window.

'Fancy a fry-up?' asked Sharpe, placing a mug of coffee in front of Lewis. Lewis was sitting at a small circular table over-looking a garden the size of a badminton court. Beyond it was a six-foot-high wooden fence, and beyond the fence was another house, a mirror image of the one they were in.

'Yeah, I guess.' He sighed. 'Jimmy, mate, seriously, this is going to do my head in.'

'I hear your pain, Ricky. But if anyone finds out you're alive and kicking, the shit will well and truly hit the fan.'

'All you've got to do is tell me who placed the hit on me and I'll take care of it.'

'We need to take out the organisation that's carrying out the hits, not the person who's got a hard-on for you,' said Sharpe. 'Once we've shut down the organisation, we'll arrest anyone who's used them and you'll be home free.'

'I'll kill him, whoever it is. And it won't be quick.'

'Yeah, you don't want to be telling me that, Ricky.' He opened the fridge and took out eggs, bacon, sausages and black pudding slices.

'What, you'd grass me up?'

'My job here is to keep you safe, not help you take out your competition.' He closed the fridge door and took the food over to the counter by the cooker.

'So, it *is* one of my competitors? I fucking knew it.'

'I'm not saying that, Ricky. I don't know who placed the contract, hand on heart, that's the truth. What I do know is that so long as everyone thinks you're dead, you're safe.'

'Except no one knows I'm dead, do they? My kids will think I've just fucked off, my crew won't have a clue where I am. The only people who'll think I'm dead are the ones you sent the video to.'

Sharpe set two of the burners going and pulled two frying pans out of a cupboard. 'Fair point.'

'I mean my ex-wife would probably be happy enough if I was dead, but my kids will be devastated. Can't I even get word to them?'

'Sorry, Ricky, no.'

'And this is costing me money, too. A lot of money. I've got a consignment coming in from Colombia next week, and if I'm not there to arrange the money transfer and the handover it could all turn to shit. Can't I at least use a phone? A burner will do.'

Sharpe sighed. 'Ricky, if you don't stop complaining I'll put a bullet in your head myself.' Sharpe had a Glock 19 in an underarm holster, though he had no intention of using it on the man he was protecting. He dropped bacon into one of the frying pans, the sausages and black pudding into the other.

Lewis laughed. 'You've never killed anyone, Jimmy, don't kid a kidder.'

'Why do you say that?'

'It's in the eyes, Jimmy, it's in the eyes. You're a tough guy all right, I'll give you that, but you've never taken a life.'

'What about you, Ricky?'

'You asking if I've killed a man? I'd hardly be likely to tell you if I had. But no. I haven't. I've shot a few guys over the years but only in the leg or the arse to teach them a lesson. Taking a life is a big thing, Jimmy. The biggest. It's not something you just do and forget about. It changes you.' He sipped his coffee. 'Those guys this morning, that Darren and the other one, now *they're* killers.'

'I suppose the grave was a clue, was it?'

Lewis shook his head. 'Like I said, it's in the eyes. They've both taken lives. It's not that they're trying to be hard the way that the guys on the doors pretend to be tough, all cold stares and gritted teeth. Those guys were smiling and cracking the odd joke, but when you look them in the eyes there's something there.' He grimaced. 'Nah, I take that back. It's not that there's something there, there's something missing. A lack of something. A coldness.'

Sharpe looked over his shoulder and grinned. 'I didn't realise you were such a philosopher.'

'In my line of work, you have to be able to read people,' said Lewis. 'You have to know who you can trust, who'll rip you off first chance they get, who'll have your back when the shit hits the fan. If you can't read people, you might as well pack it in and go and stack shelves in Tesco.'

'And what do you get when you read me?' Sharpe turned back to the stove and began turning the sausages.

'You're NCA, but even if you hadn't told me that I'd have pegged you as a copper right away. You're straight as an arrow, I don't see you ever bending the rules or taking a bribe. I know I'd have a problem if you were on my case because I'd know I couldn't pay you off.'

'You paying off a lot of cops?'

Lewis laughed. 'Jimmy, you don't know the half of it.'

CHAPTER 3

Shepherd put a pint of lager on the table in front of Paul Dutch. 'They only had Foster's,' he said. They were in a pub ten miles away from the gravesite. They had ended up taking it in turns to fill the hole and the spade was in the back of the Range Rover that Shepherd was using. It had been thirsty work.

'I'm not prejudiced,' said Dutch, taking the glass from him.

Shepherd sat down at a right angle to Dutch so that they both had their backs to the wall with a view of the bar and the entrance. Shepherd was drinking Jameson with ice and soda, heavy on the soda. 'What normally happens now, after the video's been sent?' he asked.

'The rest of the money gets transferred into my Caymans account,' said Dutch. He frowned. 'I get to keep the cash, right?'

'No one's told me otherwise,' said Shepherd. 'Treat it as a perk of the job.'

Dutch sipped his lager. 'I'm still not sure I can trust you, Darren.'

'How can you say that? You've seen what we have on tape, more than enough to put you away here and now. We might not know all your bank accounts but we know most of them, and with the Proceeds of Crime legislation we could have scooped up any assets you have. This way, you get to keep your ill-gotten gains and you keep your freedom. That sounds like a good deal to me.'

'Yes, but what about when this is over, when you've pulled The Office apart. How do I know you won't renege on our deal? It's not as if we've got anything in writing, is it?'

'My bosses aren't interested in you, Paul. But then, we haven't looked that closely at you, have we?' He smiled at the look of disgust that flashed across Dutch's face. 'And we won't, not if you carry on helping us.'

'Helping who, exactly?'

'What do you mean?' asked Shepherd.

'Well Jimmy is NCA, I know that much. But you, you're not a cop. And you said you'd been in prison.'

'I was a warder.'

Dutch chuckled. 'Like fuck you were. And you told me to tell The Office that you'd done a three-stretch for GBH. Was that true?'

Shepherd grimaced. 'Not really.'

Dutch shook his head. 'Look, it doesn't matter who you are or who you work for, just as long as you keep your word.'

'I will. I'd be a fool not to.'

Dutch took another long pull from his lager. 'Why are you so hot for The Office? Most of the contracts they issue are for villains. It's very rare for civilians to be involved.'

'Yeah, well that might be changing,' said Shepherd. 'I asked you before how many other contractors you've met, and you said none. Are you sticking with that?'

'It's the truth. Scout's honour.'

'Were you ever a scout?'

'I was a cub. Yabba-Dabba-Doo.'

Shepherd grinned. 'That was Fred Flintstone. The cubs say "dyb, dyb, dyb".'

'Dyb, dyb, dyb?'

'Do Your Best, D-Y-B.'

'So, you were a cub?'

Shepherd smiled. No, he'd never been a cub, but his son Liam had. But there was no way he was going to share personal information with a contract killer like Dutch. He wasn't even prepared to give the man his real name. 'A lifetime ago,' he said. 'I'm especially proud of my knot-tying and fire lighting badges.'

'But not gravedigging, right?' Dutch laughed and had more of his drink.

'And when do I get to meet Kingsley?' Neville Kingsley was Dutch's contact at The Office, the man that he had sent the video to. Unfortunately, all that MI5 knew about the man was his name and a description that Dutch had given them. Balding, sixty-something, with a Black Country accent. Dutch had met him just once, otherwise all communication was through email drop boxes or Telegram Messenger, the cloud-based, cross-platform, encrypted instant messaging service that guaranteed anonymity.

'That's up to him.'

'You've introduced people to him before. Twice, you said.'

'Yeah, they're always looking for freelancers and it's not as if they can advertise in the *Guardian*, is it? It has to be word of mouth.'

'And the previous guys, how long before they were called in for a meeting?'

'Couple of days after I took them on a job. They want proof that the applicants can do the work.'

'They won't take your word for it?'

Dutch shook his head. 'Actions speak louder than words,' he said.

'And you went along with the applicants?'

'No. You'll be on your own.' He gulped down more lager. 'And then I'm home free, right?'

'We won't need you any more. But you have to realise that when we bust them, they'll almost certainly know that I was involved, and that you introduced me to them. You'll be a marked man, Paul.'

Dutch shrugged. 'I've got more than enough put by to disappear forever,' he said. 'New name, new passport, new everything. I'm told that Costa Rica is nice.'

Shepherd raised his glass. 'I wish you luck.'

'You think I'll need it?'

'I think you know what you need to do, Paul.'

'You know they'll be checking you out, big time?'

'I've got that covered.'

'So, you really were in the Paras?'

Shepherd smiled. 'A lifetime ago.' As Dan 'Spider' Shepherd, he had indeed served with the Paras, and the SAS, but it was his Darren Griffiths legend that The Office would be checking out. Griffiths had served with 2 Para, with distinction. During a fifteen-year Army career he had served in Macedonia and done three tours in Iraq and four in Afghanistan. He had left the Paras in 2012 after which he had worked for a number of security companies. The Darren Griffiths military record would stand up to any scrutiny, and the security companies were all in some way connected to MI5 or MI6. It was a perfect legend.

'Kingsley thinks you did three years for GBH. What if he checks?'

'He can check all he wants.'

'So did you really do a three stretch?'

'Best you don't worry about that, Paul.'

'You're the one who'll need to worry, mate. If there's anything wrong with your CV, anything at all, The Office will find it. And it won't be a rejection letter they'll send you, it'll be a bullet to the back of your head.'

'It'll be fine,' said Shepherd. The backroom boys – and girls – at MI5 were experts at creating legends, backstories that would stand up to any scrutiny. He had a passport and a driving licence in the name of Darren Griffiths, he lived in a two-bedroom flat in Wapping, and he drove a black Range Rover registered in Griffiths' name. Utility bills, rent and car payments were all taken care of by MI5 footies, whose job was to maintain the digital footprints of legends used by MI5 officers working undercover. Money went in and out of the Darren Griffiths bank accounts, his credit cards were used to pay for tickets and meals, and Amazon made regular deliveries to his flat. The Police National Computer had a record of offences that he had been charged with, and intelligence reports suggesting that he had been involved in several murders but nothing that could be proved.

'You're a strange one,' said Dutch. He took another chug.

'Why do you say that?'

'I've met my fair share of villains over the years, and I've crossed paths with a lot of cops. But I've never met anyone like you.'

'They broke the mould.'

'Yeah, maybe they did. You're obviously some form of cop. Or a spook, maybe. The spooks are all over organised crime these days. But you don't look like a cop or talk like a cop.

Military, yes, I'm fairly sure you're not lying about your military background. That's where you've killed people, right? In the army?'

'That's not something I talk about.'

'Got any medals?'

Shepherd grinned. 'No. No medals. Just cub badges.' He sipped his Jameson. 'What about you, Paul? How many contracts have you carried out for The Office?'

'A few.'

'A dozen?'

'Probably more.'

'Probably? You don't keep count?'

Dutch's eyes hardened. 'I keep count, but like you, it's not something I talk about.'

'And how did you get into it?'

'Friend of a friend heard that I was looking for work. I'd run about a few debts and the people I owed money to weren't the sort to take me to the small claims court. The friend of a friend took me with him on one of his jobs and had me do the dirty, they checked me out and I had an interview with Kingsley and I was put on the payroll.'

'And you never had any reservations?'

'About killing people?' He shrugged. 'Not really.'

'Not really?'

Dutch flashed him a tight smile. 'You're starting to sound like a therapist, trying to get me in touch with my inner feelings.'

'Just curious.'

'Yeah, well you know what curiosity did to the cat.'

'Forget I asked.'

Both men sipped their drinks. Dutch was watching Shepherd

carefully over the top of his glass. It was a look that Shepherd had seen many times over the years, he was being weighed up. Evaluated.

Dutch put down his glass. 'Why do you want to know? Just curiosity?'

'You're right, Paul. It's none of my business. Forget I asked.'

'You killed people when you were a Para?'

'That's what soldiers do.'

'And do you feel guilty? About the lives you took?'

'That's not the same,' said Shepherd. 'When you're a soldier, you're told who to fight. And more often than not, it's kill or be killed. And if it's kill or be killed, guilt doesn't really come into it.'

Dutch nodded. 'Yeah, I can see that. Okay, well to answer your question, yes. A bit. Sometimes. I mean, usually the contract is for an out and out crim. A guy like Ricky Lewis. He's had people killed. Maybe not pulled the trigger himself, but he's made the decision and people have died. If I'd killed him today for real, I wouldn't feel in the least bit sorry.'

'What about if it's not a villain?'

'I wouldn't know. All you get is a name and a photograph and a location. Sometimes it's a face I'd know, but if it's not, I don't ask questions.'

'So you don't need a reason?'

Dutch chuckled. 'It doesn't work like that. You don't get to pick and choose with The Office. You get an envelope and that's it.'

'What if it was a woman? Or a child?'

'Hasn't happened so far,' said Dutch.

'But if it did?'

Dutch frowned. 'I don't know.' His frown deepened. 'I really don't know. Have you ever killed a woman?'

Shepherd took a long slow breath. He had, yes, but that wasn't information he was prepared to share with The Dutchman. 'It'd be a tough call, wouldn't it? Because I'm sure there'd be problems if you didn't carry out the contract.'

Dutch chuckled again. 'That's for sure.'

Shepherd drained his glass and looked at his watch. 'Do you want another before we head back to London?'

'Are you buying?'

'Sure.'

'Yeah, go on then,' said Dutch.

CHAPTER 4

There were two men on the high-powered Yamaha motorcycle, both wearing white full-face helmets with tinted visors. The driver wore black racing leathers reinforced at the knees and elbows and boots with toecaps. His gloves were black leather with steel armoured knuckles. The passenger was wearing a brown leather bomber jacket, zipped up at the front, blue jeans and Timberland boots. Like the driver, the passenger was wearing black leather gloves, but his were thin lamb's leather that moulded to his hands like a second skin.

They had parked on a side road that overlooked the target's home, a small white-painted terraced house a short walk from Plaistow Underground Station. The house had probably once had a small patch of grass in front of it, but the grass had long since been paved over and it was now home to wheelie bins and litter blown in from the street. The house had been converted into two flats but they shared the front door.

The target arrived home at the same time each day, give or take ten minutes, except for Fridays when he usually went for an after-work drink with his colleagues. Today was Wednesday.

'Here he comes,' said the driver.

The passenger looked to his right. The target was a small portly man, Asian, with glistening black hair and a neatly-trimmed beard. He was wearing a dark blue raincoat over a tweed jacket and brown corduroy trousers. 'You sure?' said the passenger. 'They all look the same to me.'

'That's racist.'

The passenger chuckled. 'Why would you say that? Black, brown, yellow, white, makes no difference to me. I'm all for diversity. I'll slot anyone if the price is right.'

'It's him.'

The target had a bulging brown leather briefcase in his left hand and he had a slight lean to the right as he walked, as if compensating for the weight. The target's name was Ali Khatib, but the men on the bike knew nothing else about him other than his name and address. They had studied several photographs of the man but had no idea what he did for a living or why they were being paid £60,000 to kill him. If he had been a heart surgeon or the father of five or the world's greatest humanitarian, it would have made no difference to them. A job was a job, and they were never going to turn down £60,000 for a few hours work.

The passenger climbed off the back of the bike. The target was forty yards from them, walking at a brisk pace. The passenger turned to face the driver, as if they were having a conversation. The driver watched the target. 'Thirty. Twenty-five. Twenty.' The driver was counting off the distance between the target and his house. Timing was everything. The best place to shoot the target was in front of the door. At that point he wouldn't be seen from the street and the passenger could shoot him in the back of the head. The passenger had shot plenty of people face-to-face, and he wasn't in the least bit worried about looking into a man's eyes as he died, but a back of the head shot was easier and quieter.

'Ten,' said the driver and he nodded. 'Now.'

The passenger turned and walked across the road. He looked left and right. The road was clear. There was a woman pushing a stroller about sixty yards to his left, and an old couple walking arm in arm to his right. Witnesses were never a problem. All they ever remembered was the crash helmet and the gun. Sometimes the clothes, but the clothes would be burning in an old oil drum within the hour.

Quickening his pace, he unzipped his jacket, slipping his gloved hand around the butt of the Smith & Wesson J-Frame that nestled in its nylon underarm holster. It was a 340 PD model, chambered for five .357 Magnum cartridges. It weighed less than twelve ounces and was just over six inches long, making it the perfect concealed weapon. The gun retailed for about eleven hundred dollars in the United States, but the passenger had paid his regular Brixton supplier three times that figure.

A Glock would hold more than twice as many cartridges, and revolvers couldn't be suppressed, but in the passenger's line of work two shots were all that was needed and silence wasn't a prerequisite. Two loud bangs and he was gone. And unlike a semi-automatic, the 340 PD didn't spew cartridges all over the place, they stayed in the cylinder. The J-Frame wasn't a gun for amateurs. It had a heavy double-action-only trigger with a long pull and it needed firm handling. But it was always the passenger's gun of choice for close-up hits.

The target reached his front door and fumbled in his pocket for his keys. He heard the rapid footfall of the Timberland boots but before he could turn, the first round smacked into the back of his head and blood and brain matter splattered across the door. The target's legs buckled and as he fell, a second round hit him in the base of the neck.

The passenger turned and walked away from the house. The bike pulled up at the side of the road and the passenger climbed on the back. The driver twisted the throttle and the bike roared away.

CHAPTER 5

Giles Pritchard was on a conference call and Shepherd had to spend the best part of half an hour sitting in the outer office with the man's secretary making small talk. Amy Miller was in her sixties, a former MI6 officer who had been active in Berlin before and after the wall came down. Pritchard had brought her out of retirement in Surrey where she had been a keen beekeeper, selling her honey at farmers' markets across the county; her hives produced some of the best honey that Shepherd had ever tasted. Shepherd would have loved to have heard her war stories, but all she would talk about was the weather and her bees. Eventually, Pritchard came off his call and Amy ushered him in.

The MI5 director was sitting behind his desk, his shirt sleeves rolled up and his club tie loose around his neck. He looked flustered and waved Shepherd to one of the two wooden chairs facing his desk as he picked up a bottle of Fiji water.

'Is everything okay?' asked Shepherd, sitting down.

'I just hate dealing with Americans sometimes,' said Pritchard. He gulped water from the bottle. 'They want access to our intel on a daily basis, but they don't seem to have heard of quid pro quo.'

'I don't think they speak Latin, do they?'

Pritchard grinned. 'Probably not, but I think they're aware

of "share and share alike". But it's a one-way street with them. It's the same with extraditions. They expect us to hand over Brits to face trial in the US, but getting them to extradite an American to the UK is like getting blood out of a stone.' He took off his metal-framed spectacles and polished them with a blue handkerchief. 'So, how did it go with The Dutchman?'

'All good. Ricky Lewis is tucked away in an NCA safe house and Dutch has sent the video to Neville Kingsley.'

'We still don't have anything on this Kingsley character,' said Pritchard. 'I'm pretty sure it's a fake name. We've had GCHQ on the email drop boxes and the Telegram accounts but they've got nowhere. And they've had no luck following the money trail.'

'An organisation like The Office couldn't survive without secrecy,' said Shepherd. 'They've had a lot of experience of operating below the radar.'

'Which is why your meeting with Kingsley, when it happens, is so important,' said Pritchard. 'All the signs are that we'll only get the one bite at the cherry.'

Shepherd nodded. 'I'm here to pick up the tracking gear from Amar Singh, and Donna will be on the case.' Donna Walsh headed up MI5's London surveillance operations and she had been tasked with following Shepherd to and from the meeting with Kingsley, when it eventually took place. She had already put surveillance in place on Paul Dutch, just in case he decided to make a run for it.

'The clock is ticking on this, Dan. We had another killing today. A lecturer at the School of Oriental and African Studies who had been very critical of the Iranian Islamic regime. He ran a blog that has attracted attention because it highlights anti-Islamic behaviour of some well-known mullahs in Tehran.

He was shot arriving back at his house. The killer was waiting for him and put two bullets in his head before leaving on the back of a stolen motorcycle. The bike was abandoned and set on fire, the shooter and the driver wore full-face helmets with tinted visors. Lots of CCTV of them fleeing the scene but nothing that helps us identify them.'

'Pros, obviously.'

'Obviously. But an MO that's used by hitmen around the country. We're looking at the usual suspects but I'm not holding my breath.'

'Is it possible it was a contract through The Office?'

Pritchard grimaced. 'Your guess is as good as mine. If not The Office then it'll be another agency. But we're sure that the Iranians aren't dealing directly with criminal gangs, there's too great a risk of exposure.'

'How many of these agencies do we think there are?'

'There's no way of knowing. There are between six and seven hundred murders a year in the UK, a hundred or so of them in London. Most are domestics, and probably 90 per cent are solved. That's still sixty or seventy unsolved murders a year, plus there'll be other cases where the bodies aren't found. Our best guess – and it is a guess – is that there are close to a hundred contract killings a year. There's no way of knowing how many of those killings are booked directly with the killer and how many are done through agencies like The Office. But I think there must be several agencies, three or four. Five, maybe. It's all about economics. A gangland killing costs between ten and twenty thousand pounds. Cash in hand. But we know from Dutch that the minimum price of a hit brokered through The Office is fifty thousand, twenty to the agency and thirty to the operative. The average seems to be a hundred, with the agency taking forty. It wouldn't make financial sense if an agency only brokered a few killings a year. They'd need a dozen or so to get any sort of decent cash flow.'

Shepherd nodded. 'He does an average of four jobs a year for them, and he knows of at least two others that he helped recruit. So, if they all work at the same rate as Dutch, that'll be a dozen killings a year, minimum.'

'Hopefully we'll have a better idea of how things stand once you've met the elusive Kingsley.'

Pritchard looked at his watch, a not-so subtle hint that the meeting had come to an end. Shepherd got to his feet.

'I'll keep you posted,' he said, and headed for the door.

CHAPTER 6

Shepherd took the lift to the office of Amar Singh, one of MI5's top technical experts. When Shepherd eventually went for his interview with The Office he'd be very much on his own, so it was vital that he had some way of letting the rest of the team know where he was and what was happening. Singh was a wizard when it came to surveillance equipment and tracking beacons and he had been on the case for more than a week. Not long after joining MI5, Singh had gone through a phase of trying to get people to refer to him as Q – after the quartermaster character in the James Bond films – but the name hadn't stuck.

Singh's office was packed with equipment, most of it in cardboard or plastic boxes packed onto metal racks, though his more sensitive material was locked away in wooden cupboards. The really top-secret gear was kept in a six-foot tall safe against one wall, complete with a retinal scanner.

As Shepherd knocked and entered, Singh was bent over a soldering iron, wearing a white coat and protective goggles as he worked on some sort of circuit board. The smell of solder almost masked the scent of his favourite Dior Sauvage after-shave. Almost, but not quite. Singh was a big fan of aftershave, and expensive suits and footwear. Under the lab coat he was wearing a pale blue Hugo Boss suit and he had gleaming black Bally loafers on his feet.

He waved the soldering iron at a chair. 'Grab a pew, Spider, I won't be long.'

Shepherd slid onto a high-backed stool as Singh finished whatever he was doing. Eventually Singh put the soldering iron into its holder and shrugged off his white coat, hanging it on the back of the door.

'I've rigged up an iPhone 16 Pro Max for you, special order,' he said. Singh went over to a wooden cupboard, pulled open a drawer and took out the iPhone. 'From what you've told me the guys you are up against are professionals so they will almost certainly take the phone off you. But if they don't and all they do is ask you to switch it off, or even if they remove the SIM card, the phone will still broadcast your location to us. Switching off the phone or removing the SIM card will automatically activate the phone's recorder and recordings will be sent to us via the Cloud every fifteen minutes. Even if they were to break the phone open they wouldn't spot the modifications we made.' He grinned. 'I'm quite proud of this. I'd love to do a scientific paper on the work but obviously we have to keep it to ourselves. Do you want me to set it up for you?'

'Sure. Thanks.'

Shepherd handed over his own phone and Singh took out the SIM card and inserted it into the new phone. He tapped on the screen for a few seconds, then gave both phones back to Shepherd. 'You'll need to set up facial recognition,' he said.

As Shepherd set up facial recognition while Singh took a black Apple Watch from the cupboard. 'This watch is linked to the phone, but it has its own GPS and listening function.

The battery is obviously smaller than in the phone so it's set up to activate the GPS and the microphone when you activate the Heart Rate app.'

Shepherd finished setting up the phone, slid it into his pocket, and held out his hand for the Apple Watch. It had a black rubber strap and an analogue face. 'It has all the features of a regular Apple Watch so you can choose whatever face you like. And all the other apps will work just fine. The difference is that the GPS and tracking work independently of the phone.'

'If they're smart, they'll take the watch, too.'

'We have a GPS tracker wired into your car.'

'You do, but they'll probably pick me up in their own vehicle. So, let's assume they do, and let's assume they make me remove my phone and the watch, and just to add to the pressure, let's assume they run a metal detector over me or make me strip off all my clothes, what are my options then?'

'You're determined to make it difficult, aren't you?' said Singh. 'To be honest, if they strip off all your gear and make you wear clothes they provide, there *are* no options. I mean, we could give you a subcutaneous transmitter but it'd need a decent battery which means it would be at least a centimetre across and if they did strip you naked they'd see the incision.'

'That would be game over,' said Shepherd.

'I'm sure it would be,' said Singh. 'We could build something into your footwear, something they wouldn't find unless they took it apart. But if they do make you dump all your clothes then that wouldn't work. We do have a transmitter in what looks like a regular fifty pence piece but if they take your stuff, you'd lose it.'

'Might be worth trying,' said Shepherd. 'I could always swallow it.'

'Well I definitely wouldn't recommend that,' said Singh. 'I've no idea what the stomach acid would do to it. How dangerous are these guys, Dan?'

'On a scale of one to ten, probably twelve. They're in the contract killing business, they wouldn't think twice about slotting me if they realised I was a threat to them. If all goes to plan I'll be picked up for an interview and if I pass then I'll have the inside track.'

'And if you fail?'

'I'm trying really hard not to consider that possibility, Amar.'

Singh went over to his desk and slid out a drawer. He reached in and took out a small plastic bag containing several fifty pence pieces. He fished out one of the coins and put the bag back in the drawer before sitting down and tapping on his computer keyboard. He placed the coin on a white circular disc, peered at his computer and tapped on the keyboard again. Eventually, he picked up the coin, tossed it into the air and caught it. 'Heads or tails?' he asked.

'Heads,' said Shepherd.

Singh slapped the coin down on the back of his hand, looked at it, and grinned. 'Heads it is. That has to be a good sign.' He gave the coin to Shepherd.

Shepherd examined it. There was nothing at all unusual about it, it appeared to be a regular coin.

'You activate it by squeezing the two faces with your finger and thumb. You'll feel a click but probably won't hear anything. For about forty-eight hours it will transmit your GPS position. There's no microphone so we usually use it as a distress beacon, only to be activated when there's a problem. But you can work out whatever strategy you want with Donna. I'd recommend keeping it separate from any other change you're carrying.

They're impossible to tell from the real thing and it can be a real pain recovering them if they're spent by mistake.'

'You're a star, Amar, thanks.'

'Good luck,' said Singh. 'Or is it like the theatre, am I supposed to tell you to break a leg?'

'Good luck works for me.'

CHAPTER 7

Donna Walsh was sitting at her desk scrutinising three screens when Shepherd walked into her office. She removed her dark framed spectacles and flashed him a beaming smile. 'How's it going, Spider?'

'All good, Donna. I was just in to see Amar and thought I'd swing by to say hello.'

'Always a pleasure to see you.' She was wearing a dark blue dress and had clipped her brown hair away from her face. 'I gather that you're ready to move.'

Shepherd nodded. 'I've jumped the first hurdle, so I could get the call at any moment. That's why I was in with Amar.' He held up his left hand so she could see the Apple Watch on his wrist.

'When do you want the full monty?' she asked.

'That's a good question. In theory it could happen at any time. A car could pull up next to me and they could tell me to get in. Refusal wouldn't go down well.'

'Do you want us to start the surveillance now?'

'Hopefully they don't know I'm in Thames House. If they do, then it's game over before it even starts. I'll Uber it back to the flat and plan to spend most of the next few days there.'

'We have a place ready in the block opposite yours. And

we'll have two bikes – a courier and a Deliveroo – and a black cab stationed nearby.'

'The Apple Watch has a GPS tracker, as does the phone, so if they let me keep one or both, you'll be able to hang back.' He reached into his pocket and took out the fifty pence coin. 'Have you seen one of these before?'

Walsh grinned. 'Amar's pride and joy,' she said.

'Do they work?'

'They work just fine.'

'The plan is that if they take the phone and the watch then I have this to fall back on. Amar says they're usually used as distress beacons but the GPS function means you'll be able to follow it. I figure that if I can't use the phone or watch I can activate the coin and you can follow that.'

'We can get set up for that, sure. But what if they take everything from you? Do you want us to follow you line of sight?'

Shepherd scratched his chin. He would have preferred the safety net of an MI5 surveillance team but if they were made, then it would all be over. Plus, if he wasn't in radio contact he'd have no way of summoning help anyway.

A lot depended on where they took him for the interview. If it was somewhere in London, a black cab and motorbikes would be able to follow him without too much difficulty, but if they drove out of the city it wouldn't be long before they'd be spotted. But would they take him outside the city? The only reason he could see for taking him out of London would be if they wanted to take him to an out of the way place and put a bullet in his head, though they'd only do that if they found out who he was. And if they realised that he was working undercover, they had plenty of hitmen who'd happily take care of him without the necessity of an out of town ride. He sighed. 'I'm probably overthinking it, Donna,' he said. 'Any meeting is almost certainly going to be local, and if my cover is blown I don't think they'll bother taking me for a drive. In fact, safest thing would be for them to just cut all contact with me.'

'Unless they want to interrogate you,' said Walsh. She smiled when Shepherd grimaced. 'Sorry,' she said, 'just a thought.'

'No, it's a fair point. The problem is, if I don't have any transmitting devices then I won't be able to call for backup. You'll know where I am but you won't know if I need help or not.'

'We'd find your body quicker.'

'Well, yes, there is that, I suppose,' said Shepherd. 'How about this? We assume that they let me keep the Apple Watch, which means you can keep well away because you'll have sound and GPS. If they take the watch, I'll try to activate the fifty pence coin and again, you can keep well back. At least you'll know where they're taking me. And if for whatever reason I can't activate the coin, just use your best judgement as to how close your guys get. I know they're pros, but the people we're up against are professionals, too.'

'If we do have sound, what's your get-me-out phrase?'

'How about, "This isn't going the way I thought it would go"? That sounds banal enough.'

'Works for me,' said Walsh. If they heard Shepherd use the phrase it would mean that he was in trouble and needed to be extracted without delay.

'And if that doesn't work, I'll throw something heavy through a window.'

Walsh grinned. 'That's always a workable fall-back position.'

CHAPTER 8

Boris Reznikov wasn't a fan of Dubai. It wasn't just the heat, though that was definitely a good enough reason to dislike the place. It was more the fact that Dubai had no soul, no heart. There were glitzy hotels, huge shopping malls packed with anything a person could want to buy, and close to twenty Michelin star restaurants. But the city state was cold and soulless, depending on migrants to survive, with Pakistani and Bangladeshi construction workers, Filipino shop staff, French chefs, Indian nurses, American IT specialists, and British estate agents. It always seemed that no one was there because they actually wanted to be there, it was all about the money and the tax-free status.

Reznikov knew that many Russians felt differently, and since Vladimir Putin had invaded Ukraine more than seven hundred thousand of them had applied for residency in the United Arab Emirates. But they weren't there for the lifestyle, they were there to avoid conscription and a violent death in Ukraine. Reznikov had no fears about being given a rifle and being sent to the killing fields of Ukraine, he served Putin in other ways and was too valuable a resource to be squandered.

Reznikov hadn't booked himself a hotel. He'd flown in on one of the last flights of the day from London and would be on the first flight back. He would be able to sleep on the plane:

the Emirates First Class cabins were renowned for their comfort and luxury. The man he was meeting had to be dealt with face-to-face. Emails could be read, telephone conversations could be overheard, but two men talking in lowered voices in a busy bar could say what they wanted to with no fear of repercussions.

Reznikov was contemptuous of Dubai, but even more so of the man he was there to meet. Jafar Hosseini was an Iranian, a terrorism financier if not exactly a terrorist, a man who claimed to be a devout Muslim when in Iran but who happily paid for high-end hookers and expensive champagne while in Dubai. He had tried to entice Reznikov to play his little games, but while Reznikov was happy enough to drink, he had no time for hookers – especially Russian hookers – which is what Hosseini craved, usually in pairs.

Reznikov spotted the Iranian sitting on a sofa at the far end of the bar and he gritted his teeth when he saw that he already had two women with him. Most of the Russian hookers who worked in Dubai spoke reasonable English, but Hosseini would insist on using Reznikov to explain some of the kinky things he wanted the girls to do to him when they got back to his suite.

Hosseini was in his sixties, with three wives in Tehran. He was an ugly little man with beady eyes either side of a beaked nose, a straggly grey beard and thin, bloodless lips. Reznikov was sure that no woman had ever gone with Hosseini for any reason other than cold hard cash, though it was possible that he had acquired his wives from families who wanted to avail themselves of the man's undoubted political power. When he was in Iran, Hosseini always wore traditional Muslim dress, a long dark tunic over baggy trousers and a kufi – a small round cap – on his head. But in Dubai he favoured Hugo Boss suits and handmade loafers and wore a diamond-studded Rolex on his left wrist.

Hosseini noticed Reznikov and waved him over. Reznikov smiled and approached. Hosseini was a cockroach but Reznikov had a part to play and he played it well. His smile appeared warm and genuine as he sat down on the sofa next to one of the hookers.

'*As-salamu Alaykum*,' he said. Peace be upon you.

The Iranian grinned, showing two gold teeth in his lower jaw. '*Wa-Alaykum As-salaam*,' he said. And peace be upon you.

An Indian waiter took the bottle of champagne from ice bucket, but the Iranian wagged a finger at him. 'No, my friend will drink brandy. Remy Martin XO. A double.'

'On the rocks?' asked the waiter.

'Are you stupid?' snapped Hosseini. 'Only an animal would put ice in Remy Martin.' He waved the waiter away dismissively. 'I am sorry, my friend,' he said to Reznikov. 'The girls here are wonderful but the staff . . .' He shrugged.

'No problem,' said Reznikov.

'Are you hungry?'

'I ate on the plane,' said Reznikov. 'You have something for me?'

'I do.' The Iranian reached inside his jacket pocket.

Reznikov raised a hand to stop him. 'Ladies, you would do me a great service if you would pop to the lavatory for a few minutes,' he said in Russian. He slid them each a hundred-dollar bill and they giggled and hurried away, tottering on impossibly high heels. Reznikov smiled and nodded at the Iranian, letting him know he could proceed. Hosseini took a thick envelope from his jacket pocket and slid it along the sofa to Reznikov. Reznikov opened it. There was a thick wad of bills, and two photographs of a young woman. One of the pictures was a head and shoulders shot. She was in her twenties with smooth honey brown skin and large eyes with pupils of such a dark brown that they were almost black. In the second picture, she was jogging, her hair tied back. She was pretty. He turned the photograph over. On the back were the woman's details: her name, date of birth, home and office address. Everything they needed. At the bottom was a website address.

'This woman is a thorn in our side,' said the Iranian.

Reznikov smiled thinly. She looked more like a girl than a woman. He wanted to ask how such a young girl could possibly be a threat to the Islamic Republic of Iran, but that wasn't his business.

'We shall remove the thorn for you,' said Reznikov, slipping the photographs back into the envelope.

'She has a website, a website that prints lies about our government,' said Hosseini. 'We would like the website deleted. You can do that, right?'

'Of course,' said Reznikov.

'I have doubled your fee for this.'

Reznikov put the envelope into his inside pocket. He made a point of never counting the money that the Iranian gave to him. 'We will take care of this for you.'

'Soon?'

'As soon as I get back to London.'

Hosseini grinned and gulped down some champagne. The hookers were tottering back to their table and the Iranian's right foot was tapping on the tiled floor like a metronome. Reznikov looked at his watch. It was five hours before he could check in for his return flight. The Remy Martin XO would help dull some of the pain. He took no pleasure in working with Hosseini. The man was repulsive, a hypocrite who pretended to be a good Muslim when it suited him, but who showed his true colours when away from the Republic. The man was a whoremonger and a drunk who thought nothing of ordering the killing of girls for no other reason than that she was critical of his masters. And his masters were, if anything, worse. The Iranian mullahs were cowards, using terror groups to fight proxy wars against their enemies, pouring millions of dollars into the likes of Hamas and Hezbollah, backing the Houthis in Yemen and countless militias in Iraq, including the Islamic State. They were unwilling to face their enemies directly, but used their money to get others to fight their battles, and were the first to complain whenever they faced retribution.

Reznikov had nothing but contempt for the Iranian and his masters back in Tehran. But he was under orders to make sure that everything that Hosseini wanted, Hosseini got.

CHAPTER 9

Home for Darren Griffiths was a two-bedroom flat in Wapping, a warehouse conversion with floor-to-ceiling windows overlooking the River Thames. According to the lease, Griffiths had been a tenant for the best part of three years. He had Sky TV and an Amazon Prime account and in the block's underground car park was a black Range Rover. It wouldn't have been Shepherd's car of choice, he much preferred his own BMW X5 SUV, but the Range Rover was more in keeping with his hard man legend. Griffiths had owned the Range Rover for two years and had run up a number of speeding and parking fines over that period, and had three points on his licence.

The clothes hanging in the wardrobes were definitely not Shepherd's fashion choices, they had been chosen for him. Versace jeans, Armani suits, Gucci shoes. Shepherd never felt comfortable in the designer gear but it was camouflage, it allowed him to blend in. It was all about appearances. He had to look the part. And that meant eating in expensive restaurants and drinking Cristal champagne by the bottle when he was out with Dutch and Dutch's friends and associates.

There were half a dozen bottles of Cristal in the fridge, but Shepherd was sipping a bottle of lager as he looked out through the floor-to-ceiling windows. Far below a red rib boat was racing down the river, carrying tourists east to Canary Wharf and the Thames Barrier near Woolwich, rock music pounding from onboard speakers.

It had been three days since they had carried out the mock execution in the New Forest. Shepherd wasn't sure why it was taking so long for Kingsley to take it to the next level. It could be that The Office was carrying out more enquiries, or that Kingsley was busy on another contract. There was no way of knowing.

Shepherd had stayed in the flat most of the time, leaving only to get food from his local Waitrose and twice daily visits to the block's well-equipped gym. Donna Walsh's team were in the nearby building, ready to spring into action at a moment's notice.

His phone rang. He kept only one phone in the flat, his others stayed in his own flat in Battersea. It was Paul Dutch. 'It's on,' said Dutch. 'Kingsley is ready to see you.'

'Excellent,' said Shepherd. 'Where and when?'

'Someone will collect you at your place later today.'

'And what about you?'

'What about me? You're flying solo on this. I'm off to Costa Rica.'

'Not now you're not,' said Shepherd. 'If you disappear they'll know something is up. You have to carry on as if everything is normal until we're ready to move in.'

'But what if you blow the interview? They'll know for sure that I betrayed them.'

'That won't happen,' said Shepherd. 'But whatever happens, Paul, you're safe. They can't get near you.'

'You can't say that. You've no idea what they're capable of. They'll put a contract out on me and I'll be gone.'

'Relax, Paul. You've been under surveillance from the moment the NCA started looking at you. Just because you agreed to cooperate doesn't mean we called off the dogs.'

'I'm under surveillance? You're watching me?'

'Not me personally. But there's a team monitoring you twenty-four seven, and they will be until this is over. The good news is that no one can get near you, the bad news, so far as you're concerned, is that even if you so much as look as if you're about to do a runner, you'll be arrested and charged with multiple murders.'

There was a silence that stretched out for several seconds.

'When you say monitoring, what do you mean, exactly?' said Dutch eventually.

'I'm not going to go into specifics, Paul, but trust me, you're being watched.'

'Inside the house?'

'Everywhere. If someone breaks into your house, we need to know it before you do.'

'So you're watching me shit?'

'No, we're not watching you shit, Paul. I don't know for sure where the cameras are but they won't be in the bathroom or bedrooms. In the hallway probably, and covering points of entry. And there'll be cameras covering the front and back of the house.' They had also bugged Dutch's phone and car, but Shepherd didn't want him to know that. 'You should be grateful, Paul. It shows that we've got your best interests at heart.'

'This is out of order,' shouted Dutch. 'Bang out of order.'

'Paul, mate, you're looking at this the wrong way. You doing a runner doesn't help anyone, in fact it makes it more likely that Kingsley will realise you've set him up. Best bet is to stay put and ride it out. If we can put him away and shut down his operation, you're off the hook.'

'Until someone finds out that I'm a grass.'

'Mate, no one is going to put your name in the frame.'

'But I'm the one who introduced you to The Office. When they know you were undercover they'll know that I set them up.'

'They won't know I was undercover, I won't be giving evidence, Paul. That's the last thing I want. The day I appear in court is the day that my career is over. My bosses will do whatever's necessary to keep me out of it, and if my role stays secret then you're in the clear.'

Dutch said nothing, and Shepherd figured he was thinking things through.

'All you need to do is to sit tight,' said Shepherd. 'I'll take the meeting, I'll see what Kingsley has to say, and then we can put a case together to shut him and his organisation down. If at any point I even suspect it might go tits up, I'll warn you, I promise. And if it's necessary, you'll be offered witness protection and you'll get a way better deal than Costa Rica.'

'I don't want to spend the rest of my life in Milton Keynes or Hemel Hempstead.'

Shepherd chuckled. 'Who does?' he said. 'But it won't come to that. We have reciprocal arrangements with the CIA to put people in the States, and with the Australian Secret Intelligence Service. We can put you in Los Angeles or Miami, or Sydney or Brisbane, you'll have plenty of choice.'

'What about visas and stuff?'

'Under the deal we have, you'd get citizenship and a passport under whatever new name you're given. You wouldn't believe the number of Mafia hoods who now live in the UK, and there's two undercover Aussie cops who turned over the Comanchero biker group who are now running a very nice pub in Chiswick. You'll be well looked after, Paul. But if you run, all bets are off.'

'I wish I could believe you, Darren.'

'You can, mate. Look, there's no reason for me to lie. If anything happens to you, it makes me look bad. It's in my best interest to keep you alive, career-wise and trust-wise.'

'Trust-wise?'

'If word were to get out that I'd let a contact down, nobody would trust me ever again.'

'How would word get out?'

'It would, Paul. One way or another it would. But it won't come to that. We'll put Kingsley and his people away, we'll close down their operation, and you can carry on your merry way. Though obviously if you go back to killing for cash you run the risk of being arrested. Your get out of jail free card is only good for past offences. Once we're done, the clock will start ticking again.'

'Okay,' said Dutch. 'But I'm going to stay home with a loaded gun at my side until you tell me that you're in the clear.'

'That'll work,' said Shepherd. 'As soon as I'm back I'll call you.'

'Stay lucky.'

'I intend to,' said Shepherd, and he ended the call.

CHAPTER 10

Shepherd was on his second cup of black coffee when his intercom buzzed. He went over to the front door and looked at the screen by the handset. There were two men at the entrance, big men in leather jackets. He'd never met either of them but he recognised them from his briefing files. The one on the left was Stretko 'Stretch' Divak. He was a few years shy of forty but looked older with greying, unkempt hair and sun-damaged skin. He was a Serb who had worked for The Office for the last two years. He had never been in trouble in the UK and there was no information about him on the Police National Computer, and a search of Interpol and Europol databases had also drawn a blank.

Divak's companion was five years younger and almost six inches taller, a muscled redhead with a sprinkling of freckles across his snub nose. His name was Billy 'Donzo' Donnelly, and until 2023 he had been a leading light of the Real Ulster Freedom Fighters in Belfast, a loyalist paramilitary group that had split off from the Ulster Defence Association. To be fair, the splinter organisation was more about money and drugs than it was about politics and was ostracised by most of the loyalist movement because of its drug dealing activities. Donnelly became a marked man after it became known that he had done a deal with the New IRA to protect some of his

UFF colleagues who were behind bars, so he had left Belfast to start a new career with The Office.

It was Dutch who had identified the two men.

'I'll be right down,' said Shepherd.

'No, we're coming up,' barked Donnelly in his harsh Belfast accent. 'Buzz us in.'

'Sure,' said Shepherd. He pressed the button to open the door downstairs and hung up the handset. The men coming up to the flat was good news and bad news. The good news was that the flat was hard-wired for sound and vision, with everything recorded at the flat where Donna Walsh's team were holed up. The bad news was that Divak and Donnelly were Kingsley's enforcers, more than capable of beating him to a pulp and throwing him out of the window. Shepherd's SAS training meant that he was no slouch when it came to hand-to-hand combat, but Divak and Donnelly were younger, bigger, and probably armed. If they were there to give Shepherd the bad news, he doubted that Walsh's people would be able to get to him in time.

He looked up at the smoke detector, forced a smile and flashed it a thumbs up. 'Maybe they just need to use the bathroom,' he said. Hopefully someone was watching, he just hoped that whoever was on the other end hadn't popped into the bathroom.

Shepherd had two guns in the flat, a Glock 17 in his bedside table and Glock 19 that was taped to the underside of the coffee table in the main room. Picking up either weapon would be a red flag; he was expecting a visit from The Office so there would be no reason to greet them with a gun. Darren Griffiths had applied for a job, he wanted to work with them. He had to stay in character and greet the two men with smiles and enthusiasm.

The doorbell rang and Shepherd walked slowly over to the front door. He opened it, smiling broadly. 'Hi, guys,' he said. 'What's happening?'

'Just sit down and button it,' said Donnelly, looking around. He pointed at the sofa. 'Park yourself there.'

'Sure,' said Shepherd. 'Do you want a tea? Coffee? I've got some Cristal in the fridge if you fancy some bubbles.'

'Just sit the fuck down,' said Donnelly, pushing Shepherd in the chest.

Divak's jacket was open and Shepherd caught a glimpse of a gun in an underarm holster. The Serb walked over to the windows and looked out over the river.

Shepherd stared at Donnelly, his face a blank mask as his mind raced through his options. If they were there to kill him, they'd probably have done it already. It was more likely that they wanted to give his flat a going over, to make sure there was no cause for concern. The easiest thing to do would be to follow instructions and let them get on with it. But he was Darren Griffiths, a seasoned hard man and a cold-blooded killer. A man like Darren Griffiths wouldn't take that sort of disrespect from anybody, and Shepherd had to stay in character.

'Who the fuck are you, anyway?' said Shepherd. 'Who sent you?'

Donnelly walked over to Shepherd and stood just inches away from him, so close that he could smell the previous night's curry on the man's breath. 'Sit. The fuck. Down,' he said.

Shepherd smiled easily, refusing to be intimidated by the man. Donnelly was about an inch and a half taller than Shepherd and fifty pounds heavier, with bulging forearms that suggested a fair amount of gym time and a spreading midriff that meant he wasn't into counting calories. Close up, Shepherd could see that Donnelly didn't have a gun stuck in his belt or in an underarm holster, so if he was carrying it would be in the small of his back or in an ankle holster, no use at all if they were to start trading punches.

Donnelly had his head back and was staring at Shepherd down a nose that had been broken at least twice. There was a Union Jack tattoo on one side of his neck, and a spider's web on the other, both prison tattoos by the look of them. Donnelly's fists were clenched and he squared his shoulders, trying to intimidate Shepherd with his bulk. The man was a bully, clearly used to getting his own way, but he had a surprise coming. He was Darren Griffiths, hard man and hired killer, and he didn't back down to bullies.

'I think I'll stand,' said Shepherd boldly. He returned Donnelly's stare. The eyes would tell Shepherd if and when an attack was imminent, there would be a slight tightening before he moved. Donnelly was too close to throw a punch, but the distance was perfect for a knee in the groin or more likely a headbutt. Donnelly looked like the type who'd go for the latter, in which case there would almost certainly be a quick intake of breath followed by the head going back an inch or two before launching the attack. Headbutts could be debilitating if they weren't expected, but Shepherd was prepared and knew exactly what he had to do. He was shorter than Donnelly so he'd drop his chin once Donnelly was committed and move forward. Donnelly's nose would explode on the top of Shepherd's head. But the headbutt wasn't guaranteed so Shepherd had to keep all his options open. Donnelly might have some kickboxing experience in which case he'd be happy to use his elbows, or he might go for a regular pub fight shove in the chest to send Shepherd staggering back. Donnelly's upper lip curled back in a sneer and his chest expanded. Shepherd tensed. Timing was everything. If he moved too soon, Donnelly could change his attack.

Divak turned away from the window and put his fists on his hips. 'Why don't two of you just whip out dicks, slap on table and we measure them?' he said. He spoke his broken English in a heavy Serbian accent with a slight lisp.

Donnelly continued to glare at Shepherd, his nostrils flared.

'We are not here to break merchandise,' said Divak, once neither of them moved, taking a step towards them.

Donnelly took a deep breath, exhaled, and slowly nodded. 'Okay, but I just want him to sit down like I told him to.'

'He can make me coffee,' said Divak. 'Milk and three sugars.'

'Sure,' said Shepherd. 'Milk and three sugars it is.' He grinned at Donnelly. 'What about you? I'm guessing you like your coffee like you like your men? Black and hot?'

Donnelly frowned. 'What?'

'Do you want a coffee or not?'

'No, I don't want a fucking coffee.'

Shepherd shrugged and went over to the kitchen area to switch on the kettle. 'Have you got a gun?' asked Donnelly.

As they were clearly there to search the flat, Shepherd knew there was no point in lying. 'I've got two.'

'Where are they?'

'There's a Glock in the drawer of my bedside table, and another one under the coffee table.'

Donnelly frowned. 'Coffee table?' he repeated.

Shepherd pointed at it. 'The table that I put my coffee on.'

Donnelly bent down and peered under the table. 'There's nothing there.'

Shepherd stepped towards the coffee table and upended it so that Donnelly could see the Glock taped to the underside.

'Clever,' said Divak, nodding his approval.

Donnelly ripped the gun away from the table and stripped away the duct tape. 'Ever fired it?' he asked, sniffing the barrel.

'Not in the flat, no,' said Shepherd. 'Soundproofing isn't great and quite a few of the flats are Airbnb so you're never sure who's around.'

Donnelly ejected the magazine, checked that it was full, and slapped it back in.

Shepherd held up a hand. 'Just so you know, there's one in the chamber. I'd hate you to shoot me accidentally.' He took two mugs out of an overhead cupboard. 'I'm assuming that you both work for The Office, so is there any reason why you won't tell me your names?'

'We're here to check out your flat and deliver you to Mr Kingsley,' said Donnelly. 'You don't need to know our names.' He put the gun down on the coffee table. 'End of.'

Shepherd raised his hands in surrender. 'Sure, fine. It's not as if we're ever going to be friends, is it?'

Donnelly leaned towards the framed photographs on the wall above a polished pine sideboard. They had all been put together by MI5's legend experts, showing Shepherd in various war zones and carrying a range of weapons. He was in uniform in most of the pictures but there were several when he was supposed to have been working as a contractor, including one in front of the As-Salam Palace in Baghdad, former home of Saddam Hussein.

'You were in the Paras?' asked Donnelly.

Shepherd nodded. 'For my sins.'

Donnelly pointed at one of the photographs, six men in

fatigues gathered in front of a Warrior tracked armoured vehicle. 'Is that Afghanistan?'

'Yeah.'

'You were there for the invasion?'

Shepherd shook his head. 'Nah. I was in Macedonia then.'

'Macedonia? Where's that?'

'Former Yugoslavia,' said Shepherd.

'Next to Serbia,' said Divak. 'You were fighting Albanians?'

'Yeah.' British troops were sent into Macedonia in August 2001 as part of a NATO intervention called Operation Essential Harvest, fighting Albanian insurgents. The photo had been faked by MI5's experts, it was a nice bit of detail that added meat to the Darren Griffiths legend.

'Fucking Albanians,' said Divak. 'I hate Albanians.'

'So when were you in Afghanistan?' asked Donnelly, peering at the photographs.

'2002. It was still pretty hairy.'

'And Iraq?'

'Yeah, I was there for Operation Iraqi Freedom, and did two tours after that. What about you? Were you ever in the army?'

Shepherd knew the answer to that question: no, Donnelly had no military experience. He had served three sentences in HM Prison Maghaberry, near Lisburn, his first at eighteen, and when he wasn't behind bars he was claiming benefits and dealing drugs. So far as Shepherd knew, Donnelly had never killed anyone, which is presumably why The Office used him as an enforcer and not an assassin. 'Nah, no way could I follow orders. Yes sir, no sir, three bags full sir. No fucking way.'

'Why you leave army?' asked Divak.

'I was thirty-seven,' said Shepherd. 'Soldiering is a young man's game.'

'But you became a contractor, right?' said Donnelly.

Shepherd grinned. 'Yeah, same shit but a different pay grade. Basically running security in the likes of Afghanistan and Iraq, mainly for American companies.'

'Good money?' asked Donnelly.

'Very good, yeah. And tax free.'

'So why did you pack it in?'

'Well, the Yanks pulled out of Afghanistan and the margins in Iraq got whittled away year by year.'

The kettle boiled. Shepherd switched if off and poured water into two mugs before stirring in spoonfuls of Gold Blend.

Divak headed to the bedroom, presumably to check out the other Glock.

Donnelly walked into the kitchen area and opened the fridge-freezer. He peered inside. 'It might help if you told me what you were looking for,' said Shepherd.

'Just giving your crib the once over,' growled Donnelly.

'I get that, but what are you expecting to find? I don't keep my cash in the flat. And I don't take drugs.'

Donnelly took out a box of Findus fish fingers. He used a gnarled fingernail to pry open the box and he peered inside.

'Seriously?' said Shepherd.

Donnelly tossed the box back into the freezer and closed the door. 'A few years back, a guy was keen to work for The Office. Like you, he said he was former military. This was before my time, mind. Anyway, it turns out that the guy was an undercover cop from Manchester. The Office had carried out a contract on a drug dealer and the Manchester cops somehow got Mr Kingsley's name. They sent in the undercover agent and he got a face-to-face with Mr Kingsley. At some point Mr Kingsley realised that the guy was a bad 'un and he had him dealt with. But the two men who brought the guy to him, well, let's just say they were dealt with too. Seems unfair, right? But that's the way the cookie crumbles, so forgive me if I do a few checks before I deliver you.'

'Where are you going to be taking me?' asked Shepherd.

'That's for us to know,' said Donnelly.

'I get that, but if it's going to be an hour or so then I should probably take a piss now, and if it's going to be much longer than that then I'd probably be better taking a dump.' He grinned. 'Unless you're okay with me pissing in your car.'

'It's not far,' said Donnelly.

Shepherd nodded. 'Cool.' That was good news. From the sound of it, they wouldn't he leaving London. Donna Walsh's people would know that and could act accordingly. They would also be checking on the Manchester undercover cop who from what Donnelly had said had been murdered trying to penetrate Kingsley's organisation. That was the first Shepherd had heard of it. It could be that Donnelly was misinformed or simply lying, but the intelligence needed checking out.

Divak returned and he nodded at Donnelly. 'All good.' He looked over at Shepherd. 'No girlfriend?'

Shepherd shrugged. 'I do okay.'

'But you never have anyone stay over? There's only one toothbrush and no women's clothes.'

'What, you have to be celibate to work for The Office? Did you not see the condoms in the drawer with the Glock?'

'They're not keen on family men,' said Donnelly. 'Not for your job, anyway.'

'I get that, and no, there's no one close.'

'Never been married?'

'I was a soldier for fifteen years, then I travelled a lot as a contractor. I guess you reach a point where a wife is just unnecessary baggage.'

'No children?' asked Divak.

'You did see the condoms, right?'

'I have three children,' said Divak. 'Two boys, one girl.'

'Well done you,' said Shepherd. 'So are we ready to go?'

'Where's your phone?' asked Donnelly.

'In here,' said Shepherd, tapping his right jeans pocket. 'Or did you think I was pleased to see you?'

Donnelly held out his hand and Shepherd gave him the phone. Donnelly switched it off and put it on the coffee table next to the gun. Shepherd picked up his leather jacket and slung it over his right shoulder. He kept his left arm down so that the cuff of his shirt hid his Apple Watch.

'We're going to have to pat you down,' said Donnelly.

'No problem,' said Shepherd, holding his hands out to the side. Donnelly grabbed the jacket, pulled it from him and tossed it to Divak. Divak started to go through the pockets as Donnelly patted down Shepherd. He found a bulge in Shepherd's back pocket. 'My wallet,' said Shepherd.

'Let me have a look,' said Donnelly.

Shepherd gave him the wallet. Donnelly flicked through the notes, then took out the credit and debit cards and examined each one. Then he checked the Darren Griffiths driving licence, before slotting it back into the wallet and giving the wallet back to him. Divak finished examining the jacket and he threw it to Shepherd.

'Right, here's what's going to happen,' said Donnelly. 'We're parked outside. It's a van. We'll open the back and you climb in. There's a hood on the floor. You put the hood over your head as soon as you get into the van. You lie down on the floor and you stay on the floor until we tell you to get up. You got that?'

'Got it,' said Shepherd.

'Don't talk to us, don't say anything, don't do anything to attract attention to yourself.'

'I hear you.'

'You do anything to piss us off and your life changes for ever, and not in a good way.'

'I'll be a good boy,' said Shepherd.

CHAPTER 11

Donnelly walked ahead of Shepherd as they left the block of flats, and Divak followed a few steps behind. They had parked their van – a black Renault Master – across the road. From the awkward way that Donnelly walked, it was clear that he was carrying a gun in an ankle holster on his left leg. It wasn't the smartest place to carry a gun as any sort of quick draw was next to impossible.

Donnelly took a key fob from his pocket and unlocked the van. He reached for the side door handle and pulled the door back. 'In,' he said.

Shepherd stepped towards the van but Donnelly held up his hand. 'Wait,' he said. 'What's that?' He pointed at Shepherd's left hand.

Shepherd faked a frown as he looked at the Apple Watch. 'It's a watch.'

'Take it the fuck off.'

'What?'

'Take it off and give it to me.'

Divak came up behind Shepherd. 'What's going on?'

'He's got an Apple Watch.'

'Why you didn't see it in flat?' asked Divak.

'Why didn't you?'

'Guys, it's just a watch,' said Shepherd. 'If it's not connected to the phone, it just tells the time. And the phone is upstairs.'

Donnelly held out his hand and clicked his fingers.

Shepherd took the watch off and gave it to Donnelly. Donnelly looked at it, front and back, and then dropped it into a grid.

'That's a four hundred quid watch,' snapped Shepherd.

'You can fish it out when you get back,' said Donnelly. He gestured at the van door. 'Get in and put the hood on.'

'You owe me four hundred quid,' growled Shepherd. He climbed into the van and Donnelly slammed the door shut. Shepherd sat down on the floor and picked up the hood, then reached into his pocket and took out the fifty pence coin that Amar Singh had given him. He pressed it between his first finger and thumb and felt it click inside. The driver's door opened and Shepherd slipped the coin into his jacket pocket and pulled the hood over his head. Hopefully Donna Walsh's team would be able to track him through the coin.

The passenger door opened and Divak climbed in. 'Lie on floor, face down,' he said, and pulled his door shut. Shepherd did as he was told. The engine started and the van pulled away from the kerb.

Shepherd was blessed with a near perfect photographic memory and for the first few minutes it stood him in good stead. He knew that the van headed west along Lower Thames Street and took London Bridge and was fairly sure they went south on the A3 past Borough tube station, but no matter how focused he stayed he didn't know what speed they were travelling at and after about ten minutes he had lost all sense of where he was, other than that he was south of the river. He counted all the time they were moving, so he knew exactly how long it was before the van stopped: 1318 seconds, which was twenty-two minutes, give or take.

The passenger door opened and Divak climbed out and slammed it shut. Shepherd heard the rattle of a metal door being pulled up, then the van drove forward ten or twenty feet. Donnelly switched off the engine. Shepherd tensed, but it was doubtful that they would be going to all this trouble to simply kill him.

The metal door rattled down and Donnelly climbed out of the van. The side door opened and hands pulled Shepherd from the van. The hood was ripped from his head and he blinked under the overhead fluorescent lights. Divak was holding the hood. Shepherd looked around, still blinking. They were in a warehouse, with metal sides and thick metal beams running overhead. The floor was dusty concrete dotted with irregular patches, probably old oil stains.

There was a man standing with his back to the wall, vaping. The scent of vanilla and orange wafted over. The man was in his late twenties, square jawed with designer stubble, wearing a grey hoodie over baggy blue jeans. He had the hood up and a Covid mask was hanging around his neck. He put the vape away and positioned the mask over his mouth and nose. Shepherd figured he was doing it to hide his features rather than trying to avoid germs.

Shepherd looked over to his right and stiffened when he saw a man bound to a chair with duct tape. The man was in his late twenties, stick thin with gelled hair that glistened under the fluorescent lights. He was rocking from side to side but the duct tape was too strong. His face was bathed in sweat and there were dark patches under the arms of his T-shirt. He was naked other than the shirt and his boxer shorts, the rest of his clothes were in an untidy pile on the floor, next to a pair of Reebok training shoes. The man grunted but the duct tape around his mouth muffled most of the sound.

Shepherd looked over at Donnelly and Divak. 'What's going on? What's this about?'

'You passed the theory test,' said Donnelly. 'Now you get to sit the practical.'

The vaping man walked over, his boots crunching on the concrete. He reached behind his back and pulled out a revolver. It was a Glock 17. He handed it to Shepherd. Shepherd took it and looked down at it. 'You know what you have to do, Darren,' said Donnelly. He gestured at the bound man. 'One in the head, or the heart. Your choice.'

Shepherd weighed the gun in his hand. It felt as if the magazine was full. He'd been in a situation like this before, in Thailand, where British armed robbers had tested him, given him a gun and told him to kneecap a Thai guy they were holding prisoner. In that case Shepherd had recognised the man from surveillance photographs and knew he was a trusted member of the crew. Shepherd had pulled the trigger and been proven right – it was a test and there were blanks in the gun. But he didn't recognise the man bound and gagged in the chair in front of him, and the fear in the man's eyes seemed real enough.

'Come on, we don't have all day,' snarled Donnelly.

'This is not what I'm here for,' said Shepherd. 'I don't do freebies. I get paid for my work.'

'That's between you and Mr Kingsley,' said Donnelly.

'How do I even know that Kingsley wants me to off this guy?' asked Shepherd. 'For all I know you could be setting me up here.'

'Mr Kingsley says he wants you to shoot this guy. To show that you're serious.'

'What does that even mean?' said Shepherd.

Divak reached into his jacket and pulled out a gun. It was a SIG Sauer P320 semi-automatic pistol. The P320 came in a range of calibres but close up it didn't really matter if it was 9mm, .357 or .45. Divak gestured with the gun. 'Do it,' he said.

Shepherd kept his Glock pointed at the floor. He had no way of knowing where they were and if there were any neighbours that would hear a gun being fired. The warehouse was large and there were no windows so the sound probably wouldn't carry.

The prisoner was struggling against his bonds and his eyes were fearful. If he was acting, he was doing one hell of a job.

Shepherd's mind was racing as he ran through his options. He could just point the gun at the man and pull the trigger. But if the gun was loaded and the man died, Shepherd would be guilty of murder. The fact that he was on an MI5 operation wouldn't be a defence, murder was murder.

Shepherd could refuse to shoot the gun, but there was a real risk that Divak would shoot him. And even if Divak didn't shoot him, and they simply let him go, the operation would be over.

'I knew you were a wrong 'un,' said Donnelly. 'Too bloody smooth. Shoot him, Stretch.'

Divak glared at Donnelly. 'You use my name? Why do that?'

Donnelly sneered at him. 'It's a nickname. And who cares if he you knows your nickname, you're going to shoot him anyway aren't you?'

'No one is going to shoot anyone,' said Shepherd.

'You shoot him,' said Divak, gesturing with his gun, 'or I shoot you. You choose.'

Shepherd kept his gun pointing down at the floor. Divak's finger was on the trigger of his P320 but Shepherd didn't get the feeling that the Serb was committed to firing the weapon.

'Guys, listen to me. I'm here for a job interview, not to carry out a contract. Especially a contract where there doesn't seem to be any money forthcoming. I doubt that you guys are working for free, so why would you expect me to?'

'It's a test,' said Donnelly. 'And if you fail the test, you're leaving here in a body bag.'

'And Kingsley is okay with this?'

'It's his idea,' sneered Donnelly. 'Now shoot him, or Stretch here will shoot you.'

'Stop using my name!' hissed Divak.

Shepherd nodded at the bound man. 'Who is he?'

'It doesn't matter who he is. Mr Kingsley wants him dead so you have to shoot him.'

'Let me talk to him.'

'Who?'

'Kingsley. I want to talk to him because this isn't what we agreed.'

'He's not going to talk to you,' said Donnelly.

'If he wants me to kill this guy, I need to hear it from the organ grinder and not the monkey.'

'Who are you calling a monkey?' ground Donnelly, his cheeks reddening.

'Mate, if the cap fits, wear it. Call Kingsley and tell him I need to talk to him. Taking a life is a big thing, and I'm not prepared to do it on your say so.'

Divak looked over at Donnelly. 'Do it,' he said.

'Hey, I don't work for you, dipshit.' Divak's eyes narrowed menacingly and Donnelly sneered at him. 'Fine.' He took a mobile phone from his jacket pocket and tapped in a number. He held it to his ear. 'Yeah, Mr Kingsley, it's me. We're at the warehouse but he wants to speak to you.' Donnelly stopped speaking as he listened, and gritted his teeth. 'Yes, I told him that. Several times.' Donnelly gritted his teeth again, then he held out the phone.

Shepherd took the phone and looked at the screen. His trick memory automatically memorised the number. If nothing else he now had Kingsley's phone number and with any luck that would give up his location. He put the phone to his ear and opened his mouth to speak but Kingsley beat him to it.

'What the fuck's going on there?' The man had a definite Black Country accent. Wolverhampton, perhaps. Or Dudley. A Black Country accent had more of a sing-song quality than a basic Birmingham accent, with a more pronounced intonation.

'Nice to talk to you, too, Mr Kingsley. Look, there seems to be some sort of misunderstanding here. I thought I was coming to see you for a chat about job opportunities but your monkeys here want to me shoot a guy tied to a chair.'

'That's right. You put a bullet in his head and then we talk.' The voice was clipped. It was the voice of a man who expected to be obeyed.

'Who is he?'

'It doesn't matter who he is. If you work for me, you don't ask who or why, you ask where and when. You don't get to pick and choose your contracts. That's not how it works.'

'Yeah, well as I've already explained to Laurel and Hardy here, I don't work for free. I was happy enough to help Dutch with the Ricky Lewis thing because I was getting paid. Now they've brought me to a warehouse in the middle of nowhere and are telling me to shoot a guy tied to a chair. I don't know where we are or who'll hear the shot, my DNA and prints are on the gun and I've no idea what will happen to it. I dunno what the CCTV situation is or who is outside. This is not how

professionals work. The reason that guys like me and Dutch
are so good at this is because we plan, we consider all even-
tualities, we don't just pump bullets into the target and hope
for the best.'

Kingsley didn't reply and the silence stretched for so long
that Shepherd began to think that he'd lost the connection.
'There's a contract on the man in front of you,' said Kingsley
eventually. 'But as all the hard work was done getting him tied
to the chair, it seems that a fee of ten thousand pounds is
reasonable. Finalise the contract, then I will pay you, and we'll
talk. Feel free to clean the gun after you've used it.'

Kingsley ended the call. Shepherd gave the phone back to
Donnelly. He forced a smile. 'Now that's how you negotiate,'
he said. He raised the Glock. Killing the man wasn't an option.
It just wasn't. There was still an outside chance that this was
a test, and that there were blanks in the gun. Shepherd wasn't
generally a betting man, but if pushed he'd have said that there
was a one in ten chance that he would be firing blanks. He
aimed at the man's chest and tightened his finger on the trigger.
He took a breath. His could hear the blood pounding in his
ears. If there were blanks in the magazine then maybe, just
maybe, he'd get through this. But it wasn't a risk he could
take. He moved the gun slightly to the right and pulled the
trigger. He knew as soon as the Glock kicked in his hands that
he wasn't firing blanks and the round ricocheted off the floor
and buried itself in the wall.

Donnelly and Divak were both frowning at the man in the
chair, presumably confused by the fact that Shepherd had
missed despite firing at point blank range. Divak's gun was
still pointed at Shepherd, but his eyes were on the bound man.

Shepherd moved quickly, up on the balls of his feet, stepping to the side to get out of the line of fire, then rushing towards the Serb, twisting his grip on the Glock. Divak caught the movement out of the corner of his eye and started to turn but he was too slow, Shepherd reached him and slammed his gun against the side of Divak's head. The Serb slumped to his knees. Shepherd hit him again with the pistol, this time on the back of the neck, and Divak pitched forward and hit the ground hard, out for the count.

The man in the hoodie started to run for the exit but Shepherd twisted the gun around and fired a warning shot that screeched off the concrete a few feet ahead of him. The man stopped and raised his hands. 'On your knees, now!' Shepherd shouted. The man obeyed, keeping his hands in the air.

Shepherd heard a frustrated roar from behind him. He turned to see Donnelly bending down, groping for a handgun in his ankle holster. Shepherd swung the Glock around and pulled the trigger, sending a round smacking into the floor by Donnelly's foot. 'The next one goes into your leg, Donzo!' Shepherd barked. 'Hands in the air!'

Donnelly did as he was told. 'How do you know my name?' he scowled.

Shepherd ignored the question. He kept the Glock pointed at Donnelly's chest as he bent down and picked up Divak's SIG Sauer. 'Get down on your knees,' he said.

Donnelly slowly went down. Shepherd walked behind him and kicked him between the shoulder blades. Donnelly slammed into the ground with a grunt followed by a torrent of swear words. Shepherd tucked the SIG Sauer into his belt, then knelt down and pulled the gun out of Donnelly's holster. It was a Ruger LCP Lightweight Compact Pistol. It was a nice enough gun, a subcompact .380 pocket pistol, and at just over five inches long and weighing under ten ounces, it was easy to keep hidden. Many police officers in the United States used one as a backup weapon, but as Donnelly had shown, ankle holsters were often worse than useless in a firefight. 'You're a dead man,' growled Donnelly.

'Yeah, we'll see about that,' said Shepherd. He patted down the man's jeans and found his phone. He fished it out. It was an iPhone 16, similar to the one that Shepherd had been using. 'I need your PIN code, Donzo.'

'Fuck you.'

Shepherd kicked him in the ribs and Donnelly yelped.

'I'll hurt you as much as I have to,' said Shepherd. 'And if I have to knock you out and use facial ID, I will.'

'It won't work with my eyes closed,' Donnelly snarled.

'Then I'll cut your eyelids off,' said Shepherd. 'Mate, one way or another I'm going to be using this phone so you might as well make it easy for yourself. Capisce?'

'Capisce? What the fuck is *Capisce*?'

'It's Italian for understand.' He kicked him in the side again. 'Capisce?'

'I will fucking kill you,' grunted Donnelly.

'Yeah? Well I'll add that to the list of things I need to worry about,' said Shepherd. 'But it's a long list, so . . .' He kicked the man again, harder this time.

Donnelly cursed and gave him the PIN. Shepherd tapped the digits into the phone and then called Donna Walsh's number from memory. She answered almost immediately. 'Are you okay?' she asked.

'I'm okay but the operation is a washout,' he said. 'This definitely isn't going the way I thought it would go. Come and get me.'

'On the way,' said Walsh.

'Are you nearby?'

'Amar's spare change worked a treat.'

He ended the call. The man tied to the chair was lurching from side to side and making grunting noises. Shepherd kept the gun trained on Donnelly as he walked over to the prisoner and ripped the duct tape away from his mouth. The man gasped. 'Untie me. Quickly.' He had a Mancunian accent.

'Who are you?'

'It doesn't matter who I am, just bloody well untie me.'

'Why does Kingsley want you dead?'

The man frowned. 'Kingsley? Who the fuck is Kingsley?'

'Someone wants you dead, obviously. So who might that be?'

The man shook his head. 'I'm just an innocent bystander,' he said. 'I don't know who these guys are or what they want.'

'They want you dead, mate.' He gestured with the Glock. 'And I was the guy who was supposed to slot you. So you must have upset someone.'

The man shrugged. 'I dunno what's going on. I was minding my own business on the way home when I was hit over the head from behind. I woke up here. Now come on, untie me will you?'

'What do you do for a living, mate?'

The man frowned. 'What?'

'How do you earn money? Your daily bread?'

'What the fuck? Why do you care?'

'I don't. But the cops probably will.'

'Cops? What cops?'

There were loud bangs from the double doors at the far end of the warehouse. 'Those cops,' said Shepherd.

CHAPTER 12

Shepherd didn't have to wait to see Giles Pritchard this time, Amy Miller waved him straight through with a sympathetic smile. Pritchard was at his desk, wearing his jacket and with his White's club tie tight around his neck, so he was either just back from a meeting or about to head off to one. There was a cup of tea in front of him and two biscuits that looked as if they might be Hobnobs. Pritchard waved for Shepherd to sit and he dropped down onto one of the two wooden chairs that faced the desk. He looked at Shepherd over the top of his wire-framed spectacles. 'Are you, okay, Dan? I understand there was a bit of rough and tumble.'

'All good,' said Shepherd. 'But we've wasted three months. Three hard months.'

'You shouldn't beat yourself up about it. From what I was told, you were in an impossible position. If you had killed the guy you'd have been sent down for murder. There are some things we can sweep under the carpet, but shooting dead a man bound to a chair isn't one of them. Paul Dutch wasn't tested like that, was he?'

'He says not.'

'And you believe him?'

'I don't see any reason for him to lie. Donnelly told me that a while back The Office was approached by an undercover cop from Manchester and he managed to get a face-to-face with Kingsley. Kingsley discovered what was going on and had him killed. And the guys who brought the cop in were also killed. I guess they instituted a testing phase to weed out any more cops.' He shrugged. 'It's pretty foolproof, obviously.'

'It's not a complete loss. Both Divak and Donnelly are facing prison sentences for firearms possession.'

'What about the guy they kidnapped?'

'He's not talking and refused to give his DNA and finger-prints.' Pritchard grinned. 'Wasted his time refusing because his DNA was all over the duct tape they used to gag him. His name's Terry Edkins, big time Liverpool drugs dealer. He's obviously upset someone but he's sticking to "no comment" and the cops are going to have to release him eventually.'

Shepherd sighed in frustration. 'Without a kidnapping charge, Divak and Donnelly are going to get a slap on the wrist.'

'Well, maybe. I guess it depends how upset Kingsley is. If he blames them, I'm assuming retribution would be harsh and immediate.'

'They didn't seem the types who would be easily turned,' said Shepherd. 'What about Kingsley? Were we able to track him through the phone call?'

'Sadly not. It appears to have been a burner phone and cell tower pinging suggested the phone was in a vehicle on the M5 to the west of Birmingham.'

'So we're no closer to knowing who, or what, he is. We don't even know for sure that Kingsley is his real name. We have Paul Dutch's description but the artist's impression he came up with could be anyone.' He gritted his teeth and sighed. 'All that time and effort for nothing. Worse than nothing. We're now going to have to protect Paul Dutch – Kingsley's going to be after him, for sure. And at some point he's going to find out that Ricky Lewis isn't dead so we're going to have to do what we can to protect him, too. They're both going to be furious, obviously. Lewis in particular. Dutch really didn't have a choice, he either helped us or he went to prison for ever, but Lewis could have just walked away.'

'Well, yes, but he would have walked away knowing that The Office had taken a contract to kill him. A contract that is still in effect. There's every chance that if we hadn't approached him he'd be dead by now.'

'I'm not sure he'll see it that way,' said Shepherd.

Pritchard picked up his cup and sipped his tea. He clearly had no intention of offering Shepherd a beverage, but then he wasn't generally one for social niceties. Pritchard put it back down. 'I suppose the big question is, how do we move forward?'

'Well I'm a busted flush, obviously,' said Shepherd. 'They know what I look like, and while they perhaps don't realise I work for Five, they'll know I'm law enforcement. And I don't see we'll be able to get anyone else in undercover, not now they've instituted this final test. With one move they've made it impossible to get someone into the organisation.'

'So we need to turn someone who already works for them,' said Pritchard. 'With hindsight we could have done that with Paul Dutch, sent him in wired up.'

'I don't think he would have gone for that,' said Shepherd.

'He wouldn't have had a choice, though. As you said, we had enough evidence to put him away for ever. But no use crying over spilled milk. Sending you undercover seemed the best option at the time, but from here on in we need to be looking to turn an existing member of the organisation. What about those guys you took down, Billy Donnelly and Stretko Divak?'

'I don't think we have enough leverage,' said Shepherd. 'A few years for possession of firearms and ammunition at best.'

'Except that Kingsley isn't a man who suffers fools,' said Pritchard. 'As I said, he might well blame them for what happened and decide to punish them accordingly. They must realise that The Office can get to them in prison just as easily as they can outside. There's leverage there.'

Shepherd nodded. 'There is, yes. But I can't see we'd be able to send either one of them in undercover. They'd see them coming a mile away.'

'They would, of course. But Donnelly and Divak have presumably met Kingsley. And they will probably have met other applicants. We could get them to identify another of The Office's contract killers and we could pull them in and turn them.' He sipped his tea again. 'Of the two, who is the more likely to turn?'

'Divak has a family,' said Shepherd. 'They're in Belgrade. Families always provide the best leverage. Donnelly is single and frankly he's a moron. He'd constantly be trying to get one over on us so everything he said would have to be checked out. He's volatile, too, he'd kick off at the slightest thing. If Divak did agree to help us, albeit under duress, I think he'd remain professional.'

'How much do we know about him?'

'He's not on the PNC and there are no Interpol red notices on him. But now that we have his fingerprints and DNA, we can take a closer look.'

'Depending on what you find out, you might well convince him to help us.'

'Fingers crossed,' said Shepherd.

'And what about The Dutchman?'

'He's at home. Donna has him under surveillance. I'll go and see him now. What can I tell him? Is our deal to put him into witness protection still good?'

'I don't see how we can go back on that, do you?'

'He kept up his end of the bargain.'

'There's your answer, then. But let's try to do it as cheaply as possible, shall we? Fort William rather than Fort Lauderdale.'

Pritchard picked up a biscuit and looked at one of his screens, his way of letting Shepherd know that the meeting was over. Shepherd took the hint and left, getting a warm smile from Amy Miller as he walked by her desk.

'How are the bees?' he asked.

'Buzzing,' she said.

'Me too,' said Shepherd.

CHAPTER 13

Shepherd parked his black Range Rover in the driveway of Paul Dutch's detached house. Dutch lived in south London in one of the nicer parts of Croydon. His blue BMW Five Series was parked outside a double garage. An Openreach van was parked down the road. Shepherd figured that two of Donna Walsh's watchers would be in the back, monitoring the house, but it could just as easily have belonged to technicians working in the area. Owned by BT, Openreach maintained the country's telephone cables and broadband network, and with some thirty thousand vans on the road, their commercial fleet was the second largest in the country. Only the Royal Mail had more vans, but MI5 stopped using its livery after several cases of angry customers banging on surveillance vans demanding to know where their mail was.

Shepherd walked past the BMW and rang the doorbell. It was one of the video models and he flashed it a smile. Paul Dutch wasn't smiling when he opened the door and ushered Shepherd inside. 'What the fuck happened?' he asked.

'Yeah, nice to see you, Paul. And yeah, I'd love a coffee, thanks.'

'This isn't a social call,' said Dutch.

'I'm as unhappy as you about the way things went,' said Shepherd. 'But there's no use crying over spilled milk.'

'That's what I am? Spilled milk?'

'It's an expression,' said Shepherd, walking down the hall towards the kitchen. As he went by the sitting room he saw a bulging red and green leather overnight bag on the floor. 'Going anywhere nice?' he asked.

'I've booked a flight from Heathrow at six o'clock, checked in online, printed the boarding pass and everything.'

'Flight to where?' asked Shepherd. He walked into the kitchen. It was huge, easily large enough to feed a small restaurant, with a gleaming six burner gas stove that looked as if it had never been used and a massive double door stainless steel fridge-freezer that had a gizmo that delivered ice cubes without the need to open the door. There was a large island with six chrome and leather stools around it. Shepherd slid onto one.

'It doesn't matter to where because obviously I'm not going to Heathrow. I'll drive up to Manchester and get a flight to Belfast from there,' said Dutch. 'I'll buy the ticket at the airport. Then I'll get the train from Belfast to Dublin and when I'm at Dublin airport I'll buy a ticket to somewhere hot and sunny with pretty girls in bikinis.'

Shepherd pointed to a large Italian coffee maker on one of the counters. 'Can you make a flat white on that?'

Dutch snorted. 'I've never used it,' he said. 'It came with the house and all the furniture and fittings.' He shrugged. 'I can't be bothered, I've got instant.'

'Instant is fine,' said Shepherd. 'No sugar and a splash of milk.'

Dutch switched on a kettle and opened a cupboard to reveal a jar of Nescafé and a bag of sugar. He took the coffee out and placed it next to the kettle.

'So, you're running?' said Shepherd.

'Of course, I'm running. If you had any sense you'd be running, too.'

'This is my job, Paul. It's what I do.'

'I don't think that Kingsley will see it that way,' said Dutch, taking two white mugs off a mug tree. 'Not only did you try to bring him down, you arrested two of his main guys. He's going to want his pound of flesh.'

'This isn't over, Paul. We can still bring him down.'

'How? You're blown and he knows that I betrayed him. If he makes every recruit prove themself by shooting someone dead, then no undercover cop is going to be able to get near him. It's brilliant.'

'What if you'd faced a test like that, Paul? Would you have pulled the trigger?'

Dutch shrugged. 'Why not? I'd already done one murder for him, might as well do two. It wouldn't have been a problem for me, but for you, yeah, it put you in an impossible position, didn't it? And fucks up *my* life.'

'There was no way I could have pulled the trigger, that's true. I had to back off.'

'Even though by doing that you dropped me in the shit?'

'I'm sorry about that. But I had no choice.'

'We always have choices. You put your career ahead of my life, that's what you did.'

'He won't be able to get to you. And you were always going to start a new life, no matter how this panned out. Your killing days are over.'

'I was happy enough to get out of the contract killing business, but I didn't expect to have to spend the rest of my life looking over my shoulder.'

'Paul, mate, once the NCA had you in their sights, your only choices were to help bring The Office down or to spend the rest of your life behind bars. What's happened isn't great, there's no getting away from that, but we're still set on arresting Kingsley and closing down The Office. Nothing has changed on that front.'

'What's changed is that now he knows I betrayed him. I'm a dead man.'

'The deal you have is still on, Paul. We'll fix you up with a new identity, and help you move abroad if you want. The States. Australia. You have options.'

'Not while Kingsley is free, I don't. He can track anyone down, that's what he does. He puts the intel on his targets together and sets one of his hired killers to do the job. And that's what I am now, a target. They know where I live, they know what car I drive, what phones I use. I'm lucky that I don't have a family, but if I did they'd be at risk, too.'

'I did say before that if you run, all bets are off, but obviously what happened today changed all that. I understand that you need to get out of the country but you shouldn't rush into anything.'

'He knows where I live. It's a matter of time before he sends someone.' The kettle finished boiling and Dutch poured hot water into the mugs, then spooned in instant coffee.

'I get that, but we can find a place for you in London. A safe house. There's still useful intel that you can give us.'

'Nowhere is safe in London.' Dutch opened the right side of the fridge. There was a carton of milk and half a dozen bottles of champagne. Shepherd smiled when he saw they were all Cristal, the champagne of choice for gangsters and hookers it seemed. Dutch added a splash of milk to each mug and put the carton back in the fridge.

'I'm serious, Paul, your best bet is to continue working with us. If we can bring Kingsley and his people down, you'll be safe. Or at least safer. If you just run and he stays in business, that's when you've got a problem.'

Dutch put one of the mugs down in front of Shepherd. 'Where would the safe house be?'

'I'll ask, and see what our options are.' He smiled thinly. 'I did hear Fort William suggested, but that might have been a joke.'

Dutch's eyes hardened. 'You think this is funny? You think I want to hide out in fucking Haggis Land?'

'No, I don't. My bad, I was just trying to lighten the moment. Safe houses are usually fairly close to big cities, in the suburbs, detached houses with a fair bit of land, ideally with a wall or thick hedge around it. We'd find one suitable for you and there'd be armed bodyguards and state-of-the-art surveillance.'

'Armed bodyguards?'

'Probably armed cops. Team of six probably, working staggered shifts. You'd be protected, Paul. Better protected than you'd be on some South American beach. I'm serious, mate, we can still get Kingsley and his people. It's just that we can't go the undercover route. But we've got other irons in the fire and you can help us. If you want, we can move you in with Ricky Lewis.'

'Yeah, thanks but no thanks,' said Dutch. He sipped his coffee, watching Shepherd over the top of his mug. 'Okay,' he said eventually. 'But where will the safe house be?'

'Let me make a call.'

'But I can move today, right?' He looked at his watch. 'I should have been out of here already.'

Shepherd slid off his stool. 'Shouldn't be a problem.'

He headed towards the door that led to the back garden but Dutch held up his hand to stop him. 'Anything you need to say, you can say in front of me,' he said.

Shepherd shrugged. 'Sure.'

'On speaker.'

'You really have trust issues,' Shepherd said and chuckled. He called Giles Pritchard's mobile and the man answered immediately. 'I'm with Paul Dutch,' said Shepherd. 'He's agreed to going to a safe house and to cooperate with the ongoing investigation into The Office.'

'Speaker!' said Dutch, jabbing his finger at the phone.

Shepherd nodded. 'Paul wants this on speaker,' he said. He tapped on the screen. 'On speaker now.'

'All good,' said Pritchard. 'Can you hear me, Mr Dutch?'

'I can, yes.'

'Terrific. My name is Johnathan Cooper and I'm Darren's boss. I just want to thank you for all your help so far, and to assure you that despite the unfortunate events of today we'll be doing everything within our power to keep you safe.'

'That's good to hear,' said Dutch.

'Now I understand that we need to get you into a safe house. Do you have any preferences?'

'What do you mean?'

'Are there any places that wouldn't be good for you? Places where you might be recognised?'

'I'd rather stay clear of Sheffield,' said Dutch. 'And Birmingham.'

'Okay,' said Pritchard.

'In fact, I'd rather keep away from the Midlands and the North,' said Dutch. 'And Scotland. I don't want to be anywhere near Scotland.'

'Any parts of London out of bounds?'

'Not really, no.'

'Okay, let me have a look at what's available and I'll get back to Darren. And again, thank you for your help and your patience.'

Shepherd ended the call and put his phone back in his pocket. 'Okay?' he asked.

'That's not his real name, is it?'

'Why do you say that?'

'It didn't sound right when he said it. Like it was the first time he'd said the words. I'm right, aren't I? His name isn't Johnathan Cooper, is it?'

Shepherd met Dutch's stare. He knew that he was being measured, that Dutch was waiting to see if Shepherd would lie or not. Shepherd was a good liar, it came with his job. And he was reasonably sure that if he did lie, Dutch wouldn't be able to tell. But the question was, did Shepherd have the right to lie to the man? Dutch had already put his life on the line when he first started to help Shepherd, and he was now in even more danger. Dutch had earned the right to the truth. To some of it, anyway. 'No, it's not. But don't take it personally, he's just following protocol.'

'He's a fucking spook, isn't he?'

Shepherd sighed. 'He is, yes.'

'MI5?'

'Dutch, mate, the cops don't have the skill set or the resources to take down a man like Kingsley.'

'So, what is his name?'

Shepherd grimaced. 'I can't tell you that, I'm afraid. At the level he operates, his name is never made public. But you should take that as a good sign. He has the clout to make things happen. If he says you'll be in a safe house, you will be. If he says you'll get a new identity, it'll happen.'

Dutch nodded. 'Okay. I trust you, Darren.' He smiled as he

looked at Shepherd and Shepherd knew exactly what the man was thinking: that Darren Griffiths wasn't his real name either. Shepherd smiled back, wondering if Dutch would ask the question and was relieved when he didn't.

Shepherd's phone buzzed to let him know that he had received a message. It was from Pritchard. Just an address, in Stanmore. 'We're sorted,' said Shepherd. 'It's in Stanmore, nice place with a snooker table in the basement and a hot tub. I've used it before. Are you ready to go?'

'How are we getting there?'

'My car's outside. I'll drive.'

'He knows about your car. And mine. Better call an Uber.'

'An Uber can be traced. But you're right, let me arrange a ride.'

He called Donna Walsh and she answered almost immediately. 'Pronto Cabs,' she said. Shepherd smiled. She was obviously listening in. Dutch's kitchen was wired for sound and vision, as were most of the rooms in his house.

'We'll need transport from Croydon to Stanmore for Mr Dutch and myself,' said Shepherd.

'Bodyguards,' said Dutch. 'This time of the day it could take two hours to get to Stanmore and we'll be stuck in traffic most of the way, we'll be driving right through the city.'

Shepherd nodded. The man had a point. 'Donna, can you see what we can have in the way of protection,' he said.

'An ARV, you mean?'

A police armed response vehicle was usually a specially modified BMW X5 SUV, painted with a distinctive blue and yellow Battenberg pattern. The fact that there were firearms on board was shown by a cricket-ball sized yellow sticker on each of the vehicle's windows. Using an ARV for protection meant there would be no way they could move across the capital without being noticed.

'We'll pass on the ARV,' said Shepherd. 'We need this to be low profile. Can you see if you can arrange a plain-clothes car with a couple of CTSFOs?'

Counter Terrorist Specialist Firearms Officers were the cream of the country's armed police, often training with the SAS at the Stirling Lines camp in Hereford. Their training involved using live rounds under close quarter combat conditions, and unlike regular armed police they often went into their operations knowing that they would be firing their weapons. There were seven CTSFO teams in the Met's Specialist Firearms Command, each with one sergeant and fifteen constables. They often worked in plain clothes and drove around in unmarked Toyota Land Cruisers, BMW X5s and Land Rover Discoveries.

'Will do,' said Walsh. She ended the call.

'Okay, so we'll hopefully have a couple of bodyguards and an unmarked vehicle,' said Shepherd.

'Yeah, I know what a CTSFO is,' said Dutch. He sipped his coffee. 'What about you?'

Shepherd frowned. 'What about me?'

'Will you be staying at the safe house?'

'I'll get you settled in, and I'll visit for briefings, but I won't be staying there.'

'They'll be coming for you,' said Dutch. 'They know where you live, they know what car you drive, they probably know your shoe size.'

'You don't have to worry about me, Paul. This isn't my first rodeo.'

Dutch forced a smile. 'I wish I had your confidence.'

CHAPTER 14

Two CTSFOs arrived at Dutch's house an hour after the phone call, Pritchard sent Shepherd a text message with the names of the two men – Mitch Flynn and Marc Robinson – and the registration number of a Toyota Land Cruiser, so he was expecting them. Robinson was driving and he stayed in the vehicle while Flynn walked down the drive and rang the doorbell. Shepherd opened the door. Flynn was wearing a pale green bomber jacket, the zip undone, and his right hand stayed loose, ready to pull out whatever gun was nestling in his underarm holster.

'Your chariot awaits,' he said. Shepherd had met the man several times over the past year. He was a tough no-nonsense Yorkshireman who had spent five years in the Paras before joining the Met.

'Thanks, Mitch,' said Shepherd. He turned and called out for Dutch, who was sitting in the kitchen.

Dutch picked up his bag, set the burglar alarm, and followed Shepherd out before closing and locking the door. The alarm console beeped and then went silent.

'I'm told we're to take you to Stanmore, we can cut through the city but the traffic is a bugger this time of day,' said Flynn. 'It's about twenty-three miles as the crow flies but we're looking at two hours. We can head south and follow the M25 around, which is closer to sixty-five miles but the time will be about the same. The difference is us being stuck in traffic and we're obviously safer with the wheels turning.'

'M25 it is,' said Shepherd.

Flynn nodded at the Range Rover as they walked down the drive. 'That yours?'

'It is, but we'll leave it here. The opposition know about it.'

'Robbo and I will sit up front, you two in the back. Are either of you carrying?'

'No,' said Shepherd.

'What's the story with the opposition?'

'We're not sure how imminent the threat is. But they're pros and not afraid to shoot in public.'

'Mob handed?'

'I'm really not sure. They're generally involved in single contract hits, but they have plenty of resources to draw on.'

They reached the Land Cruiser and Flynn opened the back. He held out his hand for Dutch's bag and Dutch gave it to him. Flynn put it in the back, then reached in and pulled out two Kevlar vests. 'Better safe than sorry,' he said.

Shepherd took one and pulled it on over his jacket, then helped Dutch put his on. Flynn stood looking around until the two men were sitting in the back of the Land Cruiser, then he walked quickly around to the passenger side and climbed in. Robinson immediately drove off, heading south towards the M25.

Dutch was looking around nervously. 'Relax, Paul,' said Shepherd.

'Easy for you to say,' said Dutch.

'Mate, I'm sitting right next to you,' said Shepherd. 'These guys are pros, they'll get us there in one piece.'

Dutch tapped the window. 'Is this bulletproof glass?'

Flynn twisted around in his seat. 'If it makes you feel better, you can lie on the floor,' he said.

'You're armed, right?'

Flynn patted his chest. 'Locked and loaded,' he said.

Dutch gritted his teeth and stared out of the window. Flynn winked at Shepherd and turned back.

They continued south, through Purley and Coulsdon. There was a lot of traffic in the built-up areas, and Shepherd kept checking the side mirrors. His photographic memory was useful for spotting tails but he didn't see anything to worry about.

The road cut through countryside but traffic was still heavy. There were four lanes and the Land Cruiser stuck to the outside. A black BMW was weaving from lane to lane behind them and Shepherd tensed but as it got closer they could see there was only the driver in the car, probably a sales rep late for an appointment. The BMW came up behind them and flashed its lights.

'Wanker,' muttered Robinson. There were plenty of vehicles ahead of them so he had every right to stay in the lane, but he indicated and moved over. The BMW roared by and began flashing its lights at the car ahead of him. Robinson sighed and moved back into the outside lane.

A high-powered motorcycle appeared behind them, and Shepherd tensed again when he saw that there were two figures on it, both dressed in black. The bike got closer. It was a blue Yamaha. Both the men on it were wearing full-face helmets with tinted visors. Dutch had seen the bike and he turned to look at Shepherd.

'Do you see that?' he asked.

'I see it,' said Shepherd.

Flynn twisted around in his seat to get a better look at the bike, but as he did, it accelerated and powered by them on the inside. Everybody relaxed.

The road began to curve to the left. They were about half a mile from joining the M25. The BMW was still trying to force its way through the traffic but a white van was refusing to move out of the way. The BMW driver began to pound on his horn.

Shepherd's eyes flicked to the left side mirror. Another big bike was coming up on their inside, this one red with a curved windshield. The driver was crouched low over the fuel tank, the passenger was bent over him. Both were wearing black full-face helmets.

Flynn turned to his left to get a better look, his right hand reaching inside his jacket.

The road was looping around to the right now. There were fields either side. The traffic was still heavy but there was some room to manoeuvre. Robinson's eyes were flicking between his rear-view mirror and the side mirror.

The pillion passenger was sitting up now. He was wearing a black motorcycle jacket and he didn't seem to be carrying anything in his gloved hands, but he was looking directly at the Land Cruiser.

'Paul, maybe lean down, away from the window,' suggested Shepherd.

Dutch didn't react, but he had started to shake.

Flynn's hand was inside his jacket now.

Robinson flicked on his indicator and moved into the next lane. The bike slowed, then matched their speed, about fifteen feet behind them.

The passenger's gloved hands were still visible.

Robinson was concentrating on his rear-view mirror now, clearly looking for any threat to materialise.

Shepherd put a hand on Dutch's shoulder, but as he did the bike accelerated and passed them on the outside. They went by in a flash of red and black.

Flynn sighed and relaxed. 'Jumping at shadows,' he muttered.

'Better than sleepwalking into problems,' said Shepherd.

'Satnav says we'll be there in ninety minutes,' said Robinson.

Shepherd smiled thinly. It was going to be a tiring hour and a half. They couldn't afford to let their guard down and there was a lot to keep their eyes on, front and back, left and right. He took his hand off Dutch's shoulder. The man's lower lip was trembling and Shepherd could see the fear in his eyes. Dutch was a professional killer but he wasn't reacting well to finding himself on the opposite end of a contract. Shepherd forced a smile.

'This'll be over soon and we'll be at the safe house having a cup of coffee,' he said.

'I hope so,' whispered Dutch.

Flynn was looking off to his left now. Shepherd moved so that he could see what he was looking at. The blue Yamaha bike was now in the inside lane, tucked in behind a Shell oil tanker trunk.

Shepherd squinted at the satnav. There was no turn off coming up so the manoeuvre made no sense.

'Where's the red bike?' he asked.

'A hundred yards ahead of us, indicating left,' said Robinson.

As they watched, the red bike moved into the inside lane and slowed. The blue bike accelerated past the oil tanker and caught up with the red bike. The two bikes drove in parallel, just a couple of feet between them. The passenger on the red bike twisted around and looked over at the Land Cruiser. 'Paul, get down,' said Shepherd.

'What's happening?' said Dutch.

Shepherd grabbed the back of his neck and pushed him down, moving to the right to give him more room. 'Just keep your head down,' said Shepherd. 'We've a couple of bikes behaving strangely.'

The two bikes kept pace with the Shell truck and the Land Cruiser drew level with them and then went by.

'They've probably got in-helmet radios,' said Robinson.

'Spider, are you carrying?' asked Flynn.

Shepherd winced at the use of his real name but Dutch was probably too scared to have picked up on it. Even if he had spotted it, they had bigger fish to fry.

'Sadly not,' said Shepherd.

'Maybe you could give him yours, Robbo, or are you planning on multitasking?'

Robinson chuckled and reached into his jacket. He took out a Glock 17 and passed it back to Shepherd. Shepherd ejected the magazine, checked it and slammed it back in.

'I'm thinking windows open,' said Flynn. 'They're not bullet-proof and glass will go everywhere.'

'Makes sense,' said Shepherd.

'We'll wait until they're committed,' said Flynn. 'Rules of engagement are that we can fire if we see a weapon and it's pointed in our direction, we don't have to wait until shots are fired.'

Shepherd nodded. 'Got you.' He looked over his shoulder. The two bikes had moved out of the inside lane and were now drawing level with the oil tanker truck, about a hundred yards behind them.

'What's happening?' asked Dutch.

'The bikes appear hostile,' said Shepherd. 'Just stay down.'

He scanned the area for any other threats but none presented themselves. More than two would be overkill. In all probability, the shooters would approach from the same direction. If they were either side of the Land Cruiser, they risked catching themselves in the crossfire.

If Shepherd had been a betting man, he'd have staked money on the two bikes coming up on the passenger side. The initial passes had been surveillance runs, and the fact they had followed them from Croydon meant that it was Dutch who was the target rather than Shepherd. There was always the possibility that they were going for two birds with one stone, but Shepherd figured that was unlikely.

The bikes were now about fifty feet behind the Land Cruiser, separated from them by three vehicles.

Shepherd lost sight of them in the side mirror so he twisted around in his seat. He saw the blue bike, moving closer. Now it was just two cars behind.

'I'm moving into the outside lane,' said Robinson.

'Roger that,' said Shepherd.

Having no vehicles to their right would make their life easier, but the worry was that any stray rounds might well fly across the dual carriageway and hit traffic coming the other way.

Robinson indicated and moved over. The blue bike followed. Then the red bike was with it, riding in parallel, just a yard apart.

The passenger on the red bike sat up and unzipped his jacket. His hand reappeared, holding what looked like an Uzi.

'Gun!' Shepherd shouted. 'Gun, gun, gun!'

It wasn't an Uzi, he realised, it was an Ingram. Not that it mattered, both machine pistols were lethal up close. The Ingram was a MAC-10, which could be chambered in either 9mm or

.45 ACP. Damage-wise there wasn't much difference between them, but there was definitely more recoil with the .45 ACP and that was the last thing you needed when firing from the back of a moving bike. The MAC-10 often came with a Sionics suppressor but it was bulky and not the sort of thing you could hide under a motorcycle jacket. And noise wouldn't be a consideration seeing as how they were carrying out the attack on a crowded motorway.

The MAC-10 was heavy – almost three kilograms even without a suppressor – so it really needed two hands on it for the shooter to have any sort of control. But even in the hands of a pro, its twelve hundred rounds a minute rate of fire made it more suitable for 'spray and pray' than targeted shooting. The 9mm version had thirty-two rounds in the magazine, the .45 ACP just thirty, but either way a two-second burst on fully automatic would empty the weapon. The shooter would more likely have the gun set to semi-automatic which would give him more control and more time to aim, but Shepherd thought it was still a strange choice of gun for a motorcycle shooting.

Robinson pressed the button to lower the windows and the slipstream immediately whipped at Shepherd's hair and assaulted his ears. He pushed Dutch again. 'Stay down, Paul!' he shouted.

Robinson accelerated and flashed his lights but the white van ahead of them refused to move.

Flynn had twisted around in his seat and had both hands on his Glock. The red bike was moving closer. To their left was a red Tesla being driven by a grey-haired woman who was either muttering to herself or having a hands-free conversation. Ahead of them was the white van, still refusing to get out of the way.

Shepherd caught a glimpse of the blue bike. The pillion

passenger also had a gun out now. It looked like a handgun. A revolver. A big one. Shepherd gritted his teeth. It looked like a 500 Smith & Wesson, and, if it was, it fired a round that was half an inch across and weighed almost an ounce.

'I see a MAC-10 on the red bike and 500 Smith & Wesson on the blue,' shouted Shepherd.

He looked over at the red Tesla. The grey-haired woman was oblivious to what was going on around her. Robinson was checking his mirrors. He flashed his lights again but the white van ahead of them wouldn't budge. Robinson accelerated and gently bumped the van and beeped his horn.

The white van accelerated and they pulled away from the red Tesla.

Both bikes came up behind the Land Cruiser.

'Brace yourselves,' said Robinson and a fraction of a second later he stamped his feet on the brake. The Tesla shot by them, the bikes split, the blue bike went to the right of the Land Cruiser and the red one went left. Flynn leaned out of the window and fired two quick shots but the rider braked and both shots went wide and smacked into the side of a DHL truck. Flynn cursed.

Robinson accelerated again. The white van had pulled over to the left and they swept by it. The driver was ashen, his mouth and eyes open wide in terror.

Shepherd twisted around in his seat trying to get the red bike in his sights but it was in his blind spot and the only way he'd get a clearer look was to stick his head out of the window. The decision was taken for him when a shot shattered the side mirror. The bike moved out and Shepherd heard two shots behind them.

'Bastard is going for our tyres,' shouted Robinson.

He braked again and as the tyres squealed on the tarmac,

the red bike had to swerve to avoid a collision. Shepherd found himself looking at the rider and passenger. The rider had his head down and was curved over the handlebars, the passenger was swinging the MAC-10 around. Shepherd wasn't sure if the man was wearing a Kevlar vest under his jacket and had no idea of how bulletproof the helmet and visor were so he had to choose his target carefully. He aimed at the man's neck but as he pulled the trigger Robinson accelerated and Shepherd's shot went low and hit the passenger in his chest. The passenger jerked but the gun stayed in his hands, so a vest looked to be on the cards. The MAC-10 fired but the man's aim was off and the round whizzed by Shepherd's ear and out of the car. Shepherd's heart was pounding now but he was breathing slowly and deeply, willing himself to stay calm. Shepherd aimed at the man's neck and squeezed the trigger but the Land Cruiser accelerated and the shot missed.

The red bike dropped back. Shepherd turned his attention to the blue bike. He fired a double tap and both shots hit the passenger in the chest. The man's gun went up but there was no blood and he remained upright. He was clearly wearing a vest. Flynn aimed at the driver of the blue bike and fired twice. One of his shots hit the driver in the neck.

Shepherd aimed at the passenger who had regained his composure and had both hands on his gun. They fired at the same time. The passenger's shot missed Shepherd but Dutch grunted in pain. Shepherd's shot caught the passenger in the neck and blood spurted down his jacket.

Flynn continued to fire. The handlebars started to jerk back and forth, then the bike turned to the side and span through the air, throwing off the rider and passenger before crashing into the tarmac.

Shepherd's ears were ringing from the explosions in the confined space and his eyes were watering. He blinked to clear his vision as he turned towards the nearside window. The red bike had dropped back. Robinson braked, hard. The bike braked too and moved to the next lane. The passenger fired and almost immediately the Land Cruiser bucked and the rear end slid to the side. 'Tyre's gone!' shouted Robinson.

The Land Cruiser slowed and the bike came up on the driver's side. Flynn leant out of the window and fired but their vehicle was rocking up and down, throwing his aim off. His shot went high, as did the next one he fired.

Shepherd brought his gun up and steadied his hands but before he could pull the trigger the passenger fired his MAC-10 and three rounds into Shepherd's chest. His breath exploded from his lungs and he felt as if he had been kicked by a horse.

The passenger continued to fire as Shepherd fought to breathe. Rounds slammed into the door and Dutch screamed in pain. The shooter was firing through the door.

Shepherd tried to raise his Glock but all the strength had gone from his arms. His chest was on fire and he could barely breathe. His mind was racing but he fought to stay calm. Panic under fire never ended well.

The Land Cruiser was slowing and lurching from side to side as Robinson fought to control the steering wheel.

Flynn fired and the round hit the driver in the chest. A second shot ricocheted off the man's helmet.

Cars were pulling over now, many with their hazard flashers on.

The passenger fired at the door again and Dutch twitched and went still.

Shepherd tried again to raise his gun but his arms had gone numb. The Land Cruiser came to a halt on the hard shoulder.

The passenger fired again and then the bike accelerated. Flynn managed to get off another shot, hitting the passenger in the middle of the back as the bike roared away.

'Dutch is hit!' shouted Shepherd. 'We need to get him to hospital.'

'Caterham Dene is the nearest but they don't have an A&E department,' said Robinson. 'We'd be better heading for the Mayday.' The Mayday was Croydon University Hospital in Thornton Heath, it had undergone several name changes during its one hundred year life but locals always referred to it as The Mayday, the name of the road that led to the nineteen-acre site. 'But that's going to take twenty to twenty-five minutes and we'll never get there in this.'

'I'll get us another ride,' said Flynn, putting his gun away and pulling out a warrant card. He threw open the door and climbed out.

Shepherd pushed Dutch upright. Two of the rounds had gone into the vest, but he was bleeding from the neck. Dutch's eyes were closed and he was breathing shallowly and rapidly. 'Have you got a cloth, something I can use to stop the bleeding?' he asked Robinson.

Robinson leaned over and popped the glove compartment open. He reached inside and took out a green and white first-aid kit. He unzipped it and took out a pack containing a large abdominal gauze pad. He ripped it open and handed the pad to Shepherd. Shepherd slapped the pad on the wound and pressed down on it.

'You're going to be all right, Paul,' said Shepherd. He tried to sound confident, but it was a bad wound.

Dutch's eyes were closed and he didn't react. He was breathing, but fast and shallowly, like a dog panting.

Flynn appeared at the window. There was a woman behind him, her grey hair cut short. She was looking anxiously over Flynn's shoulder.

'As luck would have it, there's a nurse here,' he said. 'We can use her car to drive to The Mayday.'

Shepherd nodded at her. 'I've got a gunshot wound to the neck, the wound is deep but I think the round passed through. It's bleeding heavily but I'm applying pressure.'

Flynn opened the door and stepped to the side.

'Can you sit him up and we'll get him into my car,' she said. 'I'd suggest waiting for an ambulance but the way the traffic has backed up it'd take them ages to get here.' She forced a smile. 'I'm Christina, by the way.'

'Darren,' said Shepherd. 'This is Paul.'

Christina leaned towards Dutch. 'Hello, Paul. Can you hear me? My name is Christina and we're going to get you to hospital.'

Dutch didn't say anything and his eyes stayed closed.

'Help me get him up,' said Christina, taking hold of Dutch's left arm.

Shepherd kept the dressing on the wound with his right hand and pushed Dutch up with his left. As Dutch sat up, Shepherd could see that his shirt below the Kevlar vest was soaked in blood.

'There's another wound,' said Shepherd. 'His stomach.'

'Lie him down,' said Christina quickly.

Shepherd opened the car door and got out, allowing Dutch to fall back onto the seat. His shirt and trousers were soaked in blood. Shepherd gritted his teeth. It was bad. Very bad. He looked at Christina and it was clear from her face that she was thinking the same. It would be touch and go for them to get him to hospital before he bled out. She took a deep breath, then nodded. 'Right, get him into the back of my car, now,' she said, moving out of the way to let Flynn get to the injured man. 'I'll get a blanket to stop the blood.'

'Who's going to drive?' asked Flynn.

'I'll drive,' said Robinson.

'We can't leave the car here,' said Shepherd. He looked over his shoulder. Traffic was backed up as far as he could see, and traffic on the other side of the carriageway had slowed to a crawl as drivers sought to get a better look at what was going on.

'I'll leave the keys,' said Robinson.

Flynn began to pull Dutch out of the Land Cruiser. Shepherd walked around the back of the vehicle to help. Robinson climbed out and looked around. 'Which is your car, Christina?' he asked.

'The Fiesta.'

There was a blue Ford Fiesta on the hard shoulder, its hazard lights flashing.

'We're not all going to get into it,' said Robinson.

'I'll drive,' said Flynn. 'Best you stay to talk to Plod when they finally get here.'

Shepherd and Flynn got Dutch out of the Land Cruiser and carried him over to the Fiesta. Christina ran ahead of them and opened the rear door. Blood trickled onto the tarmac but Dutch was still breathing, just about.

Shepherd and Flynn eased Dutch onto the back seat and Christina climbed in next to him.

Flynn closed the door. 'What do you think?' he asked.

'Not good,' said Shepherd.

CHAPTER 15

Flynn kept the Fiesta's hazard lights on and banged on the horn during the frantic drive to the Croydon hospital. Shepherd sat in the front seat, while Christina stayed in the back, cradling Dutch's head and keeping a tartan blanket pressed against his stomach. She had Shepherd call ahead to the hospital's accident and emergency department and there was a team waiting for them when they arrived.

Dutch was unconscious but still breathing. Four nurses in pale blue scrubs lifted him onto a gurney while a white-coated doctor shone a small flashlight into Dutch's eyes.

'Gunshot wounds, two I can see, a through and through in his neck and the major one in his stomach,' said Christina.

One of the nurses lifted the tartan blanket, winced and replaced it. She pressed down on it with both hands.

Another nurse attached an IV and then they wheeled the gurney into the building.

'I'll stay with him,' said Flynn. 'I'll call Robbo and see how he's getting on. If he's tied up with Plod I'll get a replacement.'

'I'll call my boss and see what we do next. Though a lot depends on how bad Dutch is.'

Flynn hurried after the gurney. Shepherd turned to look at Christina. 'Thank you, so much,' he said.

'All part of the service,' she said.

'I think Paul bled quite a bit, we'll make good any damage to your car.'

'The police, you mean?'

'Police or Home Office,' he said. 'If you give me your name and contact details someone will get in touch.'

'Christina Fulcher,' she said. She gestured at the hospital. 'I work here.'

'In the A&E?'

'Paediatrics,' she said. 'Who are you? And what happened back there?'

'It's complicated.'

'Your colleague showed me a warrant card but I've never seen a policeman like him before.'

'He's a specialist firearms officer,' said Shepherd. 'They are . . . special.'

'And Paul?'

'He was the guy we were protecting.'

She smiled ruefully. 'Well that didn't work out so well, did it?'

Shepherd grimaced. 'Yeah, that's putting it mildly.'

'It was like a movie, guys on motorbikes firing guns. What is the world coming to?'

Shepherd flashed her a tight smile. 'That's not a question I can answer, Christina. I'm just grateful that you were on hand to help. Thank you.'

She nodded and headed into the building. Shepherd phoned Pritchard and quickly brought him up to speed.

'Will Dutch pull through?'

'It's not looking good,' said Shepherd.

'And you're okay?'

'Yes, thanks to Kevlar. Two of the attackers are still at the scene, I'm pretty sure they're dead. They were on a blue Yamaha. Two more were on a red Suzuki. Both took hits but they were wearing vests and got away. The shooter had a MAC-10.'

'You got the registration number?'

'Of course,' said Shepherd. His photographic memory kicked in and he reeled off the number. 'But the bike was almost certainly stolen and will probably be on fire by now.'

'Sure, but we might get lucky with CCTV and ANPR. What about security?'

'There's a CTSFO with Dutch now and another on the way. They'll be with him twenty-four seven until we decide if we can move him.'

'I meant for you, Dan. This was obviously a revenge hit which means you're almost certainly in the frame, too.'

'I'll be fine,' said Shepherd. 'They'll be after Darren Griffiths, and he never existed.'

'If you change your mind, let me know.'

'I really don't need babysitting,' said Shepherd. 'But your concern is appreciated. What's happening with Donnelly and Divak?'

'We're holding them under anti-terrorism legislation, so zero phone contact and no lawyers. But obviously we can now assume The Office knows that we've got them in custody. One interesting thing we've turned up is that Stretko Divak isn't Stretko Divak.'

'Now that *is* interesting,' said Shepherd.

Christina walked down the corridor towards him and it was clear from the look on her face that it was bad news. She walked slowly over to him, shaking her head. 'I'm sorry,' she said.

Shepherd nodded and thanked her. She walked away.

'Dutch didn't make it,' he said to Pritchard.

'I'm sorry.'

'We let him down,' said Shepherd. 'We said we'd protect him and we didn't.'

'Dan, Paul Dutch was a professional hitman who has killed God knows how many people.'

'What are you saying, live by the sword, die by the sword? He was helping us. He was our best hope of bringing The Office down. And if he hadn't been in that car, he'd be alive now.'

'We were moving him to a safe house,' said Pritchard. 'We had his best interests at heart.'

'I should have seen it coming.'

'Dan, you have some amazing skills that always stand you in good stead, but psychic ability isn't one of them. You're not a mind reader.'

Shepherd knew that Pritchard was right, but it didn't make him feel any better. Paul Dutch had been his responsibility, and now he was dead. He ended the call.

CHAPTER 16

Jimmy Sharpe's phone rang and he put down his coffee mug and picked it up. It was Darren, AKA Spider Shepherd. Shepherd got straight to the point and briefed Sharpe on what had happened to Paul Dutch and what he planned to do next. Sharpe listened without interruption.

'Ricky's not going to be a happy bunny,' he said once Shepherd had finished.

'Do what you can, damage limitation-wise,' said Shepherd, and ended the call.

Sharpe put his phone away and walked to the gym. It was at the rear of the house, overlooking the garden. It was well equipped with a range of machines and a free weight area complete with a large mirror. Lewis was wearing a purple Nike tracksuit, pedalling on an exercise bike with a towel around his neck. He waved at Sharpe. 'You wanna join, Jimmy?' he called.

'Why would I want to pedal like fuck to get nowhere?' he said. He walked over to the bike. 'So, I've got good news and bad news, which do you want first?'

'Oh shit. The bad news, I suppose.' He slowed but continued to pedal.

'Someone killed Dutch earlier today. It was four guys on two bikes, one of them had a MAC-10 Ingram. They shot up the car that was taking him to a safe house.'

Lewis stopped pedalling. 'Was it The Office?'

'Presumably.'

'How did they find out he was working with you?'

'We're not sure,' lied Sharpe. Shepherd had explained exactly what had gone wrong.

'But you were moving him to a safe house, so you must have thought there was a problem?' He climbed off the exercise bike and wiped his face with the towel.

'I wasn't involved,' said Sharpe. 'My brief is to keep you safe, and to be honest I'm doing a better job than the guys who were supposed to be looking after The Dutchman.'

Lewis grinned. 'Don't kid a kidder, Jimmy. Reading people is what I do.'

'I don't know what you want me to say, Ricky.'

'The truth would be a start. Look, you're a copper, and all coppers are bastards, that's a given, but as far as I know you've always been straight with me so let's keep it that way, shall we? I agreed to help you, so I deserve some credit for that.'

'Let's not forget that if we hadn't approached you, you'd be buried for real somewhere in the New Forest.'

'There's a quid pro quo. You scratch my cock and I'll scratch yours.'

'I'll be honest, Ricky, I've never thought of you that way.'

'Right back at ya,' said Lewis. 'Just be honest with me, Jimmy. You owe me that much.'

Sharpe sighed. The man had a point, he deserved the truth. Besides, a gangster like Ricky Lewis wouldn't take kindly to being lied to. 'Maybe we should have a drink,' he said.

'Why not, the sun's above the yardarm.' Lewis headed to the kitchen and pulled open the fridge. 'Bubbles?' he asked, surveying a rack filled with champagne bottles.

'Hell no,' said Sharpe. 'I'll have a Scotch.' He reached for a bottle of Glenfiddich and a tumbler.

'Yeah, go on,' said Lewis. 'Do you want ice?'

Sharpe scowled. 'What sort of blasphemous heathen puts ice in whisky?'

Lewis grinned and closed the fridge door. 'I guess not.'

Sharpe grabbed a second glass and poured large measures of whisky into both. He handed one to Lewis. They clinked glasses and drank. 'Is this the condemned man's last drink?' asked Lewis.

Sharpe chuckled. 'It's not that bad, Ricky. It's just got . . . complicated.' He took another sip of whisky. 'Kingsley found out that Darren was using Dutch to penetrate his organisation. Presumably he's taken out contracts on both of them.'

'Oh shit. So they know that I'm involved?'

'I'm sorry, yes. They know Darren was a plant and that Dutch was helping him, and as they sent photographs of you lying in a grave I think we can assume he'll know that you were part of it. Obviously, Darren couldn't be involved in a real murder so you can't be dead . . .'

'There's probably a contract out on me, too?'

'To be fair, there's always been a contract out on you, nothing's changed.'

'Shit.' Lewis drained his glass and held it out. Sharpe refilled it for him. 'I can't stay here forever, Jimmy. This was supposed to be a short-term gig.'

'I hear you.'

'No, I'm serious. I can't stay away from my family like this. They need me.'

'You said your ex-wife wouldn't care.'

'Maybe not, but there's the kids.'

'They're both at university, Ricky, doing whatever it is that students do these days. Your phone's being monitored and neither of them have texted or phoned.'

Lewis grimaced. 'Yeah, I only hear from them when they're short of readies. But let's be honest, we won't be able to hide like this for ever.'

'No one's talking about forever. But we need to put another operation in play. And we're working on that as we speak.'

'So, what's the plan?'

'We're trying for another way in.'

Lewis sneered and shook his head. 'These people aren't stupid, Jimmy. They won't fall for it a second time, they'll see you coming.'

'We have to try.'

'Yeah, but the emphasis there is on the "we" and I'm not involved in that. You gave it your best shot, it didn't work out, now it's time for me to get back to business. My absence is costing me money, Jimmy. Literally thousands a day.'

'You're a marked man, Ricky.'

'I've always been a marked man, it's the nature of the business. There's always someone who wants to take your place or move onto your turf. Okay, this was a little different, I'll give you that, but they know I'm alive and I know they're after me, so I'll do whatever's necessary to protect myself.'

'We're better placed to do that.'

Lewis laughed scornfully. 'The fact that The Dutchman got shot suggests otherwise, doesn't it? Seriously, I have more faith in my guys. And while my house isn't exactly a fortress, it's better protected than this place. And I have a safe room.'

'Seriously, a safe room?'

'Explosive resistant, protected communication system, its

own air supply, and enough food and water to last a week. Any sign of trouble and I'm in there while my guys do whatever they have to. I'm going to go, Jimmy. My time here is done.'

'At least give me one more day. Until I know for sure what happens next. And I have two very large T-bone steaks in the fridge. Aberdeen Angus.'

Lewis nodded. 'I'm out first thing tomorrow morning,' he said.

'Fair enough,' said Sharpe.

Lewis took another sip of his whisky. 'What was the good news, then?'

Sharpe grinned apologetically. 'Yeah, I lied about that,' he said. 'There is no good news.'

CHAPTER 17

Billy Donnelly and Stretko Divak were being held at Lewisham Police Station. It had the distinction of being the largest purpose-built police station in Europe, and it included the Metropolitan Police's largest custody suite, stabling for thirty-six police horses, and a multi-storey car park filled with taxpayer-funded cars for middle management officers who hadn't walked a beat in years, if ever. The complex looked like a regular brick-built nondescript office block, though the fact that it was shielded from the road by steel bollards and security barriers was a clue to the fact that it had been the police station of choice for holding and questioning terrorists since Paddington Green had closed in 2018.

As an MI5 officer, Shepherd didn't have a warrant card, had no powers of arrest, and certainly didn't have the authority to walk into a police station and demand to interview suspects. That wasn't how MI5 operated. Instead he arrived at reception at just after nine o'clock in the morning and was met by a plain-clothes sergeant from SO15, the Counter Terrorism Command. His name was Martin Williams and Shepherd had crossed paths with him several times over the years and had always found him to be a safe pair of hands. He was in his mid-thirties, which meant that Shepherd was old enough to be his father, though that tended to be the case with most of the cops that he met these days. He was an inch or two taller than Shepherd and probably twenty pounds heavier, wearing a dark blue pinstripe suit, a starched white shirt, and gleaming black shoes. He grinned as he shook hands with Shepherd.

'Welcome to Lewisham,' he said.

'I'm glad to see a friendly face, Martin,' said Shepherd. Generally, MI5 officers didn't have a great working relationship with regular cops. Often, they resented the fact that MI5 officers didn't have to follow the confines of the Police and Criminal Evidence Act and felt that sometimes the agency would disrupt long-running police investigations to further its own – often secretive – aims. The problem was that often MI5 wasn't able to explain the bigger picture to the police and that sometimes procedure had to be sacrificed for the greater good. But SO15 officers – and there were more than one and a half thousand of them in the Met – had a better understanding of the fight against terrorism and tended to regard MI5's people as collaborators rather than competitors.

Williams walked him through security and took him along to a lift which they took down to the basement, making small talk about football. When the lift doors opened Williams took Shepherd along a corridor with metal doors left and right. Ahead of them stood a bored constable in shirt sleeves and a stab vest, his arms folded. He turned to look in their direction, then unfolded his arms and had a reasonable attempt at standing to attention.

The sergeant stopped and nodded at the door. 'The suspect is in there, alone. He hasn't requested a solicitor, though our instructions were to ignore any such request. He has been denied access to a phone, but again he hasn't requested such. The cameras are off and no recordings will be made. The constable will remain outside the door, just let yourself out when you're done. He'll call me and I'll walk you out.'

'I can see myself out, Martin,' said Shepherd. 'I don't want to be a bother.'

'It's no bother,' said Williams. 'It's protocol that you're escorted in and out.'

'Thank you,' said Shepherd.

'Glad to be of service,' he replied. He walked away, his shoes squeaking on the tiled floor.

Shepherd smiled at the constable. 'Sorry about this,' he said. 'Can't be much fun guarding a door.'

'That's all right, sir. I'm on overtime and the wife is after a new kitchen.'

'It's an ill wind that blows nobody good,' said Shepherd, opening the door. The Serb was sitting at a table set against the far wall. There was a chrome rail in the middle of the table and the man's right wrist was handcuffed to it. There were video cameras in the ceiling left and right and a double tape recorder on a shelf next to the table. A plastic strip ran around the walls. If pressed, it would in theory summon urgent help, though that help would probably consist of the constable in the corridor.

Shepherd closed the door. 'Can I get you a coffee or a tea? Water?'

The Serb shook his head.

'Sorry I can't offer you any Šljivovica,' said Shepherd. Šljivovica was one of Serbia's most popular drinks, a 40 per cent proof spirit made from fermented and distilled plums.

The Serb shook his head again and stared at the chrome bar in front of him.

Shepherd pulled back one of the two plastic chairs on his

side of the table and sat down. 'Funny that you gave Donzo grief for calling you Stretch,' said Shepherd. 'I mean, Stretch isn't your nickname and Divak isn't your real name.'

The man's eyes hardened and his knuckles widened.

'Oh, come on, you can't be surprised that we found out who you really are, surely? We don't take fingerprints and DNA for fun. We know that you are Sasha Zlatnar and that you were born on 12 April 1986 which makes you an Aries, and a tiger under the Chinese horoscope system.'

'No comment,' muttered Zlatnar.

'You don't have to say "no comment" with me,' said Shepherd. 'This isn't an interview and the cameras aren't on and nothing you do or don't say is going to be used in court. This is just by way of a chat, and if after you've heard what I have to say you want to tell me to jog on, then I will.'

Zlatnar frowned and looked at Shepherd for the first time. 'Jog on?'

'It means I'll be on my way. I'll leave you with the cops. They'll be charging you with possession of a gun, and possibly kidnapping.'

Zlatnar's frown deepened. 'You're not a cop?'

'No, Sasha, I'm not a cop. So, here's what we know. You're a former member of the Serbian mafia clan known as the Principi group. You fled Belgrade after the leader of the Principi Group – Veljko Belivuk – and his henchmen were arrested on charges of murder, kidnapping and drug trafficking. You were Belivuk's torturer-in-chief but somehow managed to escape the raids that snapped up Belivuk and his henchmen. For some reason, the Serb authorities had never issued an arrest warrant for you and you surfaced a year later in London, working for The Office.'

Zlatnar sat back in his chair and folded his arms.

'At first we thought that maybe you were just lucky, that you'd managed to avoid the police operation. Tipped off, maybe, and you did a runner in the nick of time. But then we made a few inquiries and it seemed the police never issued a European Arrest Warrant for you, or put you on an Interpol's most wanted list. Interpol publishes a list of Red Notices identifying and describing fugitives who are being sought internationally for capture and extradition and there is no Red Notice for you, as Divak or as Zlatnar.'

Zlatnar's knuckles had turned white and his jaw was tense. He obviously knew where the conversation was heading, but Shepherd took his time.

'That got us thinking. Why aren't the cops after you? And we had a good look at your passport and your Serbian driving licence. They're the real McCoy, even though they don't use your real name or date of birth. They're not forgeries, they're genuine government-issued documents. It's doubtful that even the cops could provide documents like the ones you have.' He smiled thinly. 'But the BIA could. It'd be the easiest thing in the world for them. If they wanted to.'

The BIA's was Serbia's intelligence agency – the *Bezbednosno-Informativna Agencija* – the equivalent of the UK's MI5 and MI6, responsible for Serbia's national security and for collecting intelligence and conducting counter-intelligence operations. The BIA even had its own patron saint, Saint Michael the Archangel.

'What if you'd been working for the BIA, feeding them intel to take down Belivuk and his people? And what if as part of that deal the BIA had promised you a new identity? They couldn't really offer you witness protection in the UK, not after all the nasty stuff you've done, but they could give you a new identity and let you keep your ill-gotten gains. Getting into the UK is easy enough and staying here is even easier. I'm not sure how thrilled they were that you went to work for The Office, but so long as you were out of the country, maybe they didn't care.'

'You can't prove any of this,' hissed Zlatnar.

'Well, we've proved that you're Sasha Zlatnar and not Stretko Divak. The rest of it, well we got the intel from a former BIA agent who now works on our Balkans Desk and he got it off the record from his uncle who still works for the BIA. So yes, you're right, the bit about you snitching on Veljko Belivuk probably isn't provable, not in a court of law, but then it doesn't have to be, does it?' He leaned towards the Serb and lowered his voice to a whisper. 'The thing is, Sasha, we don't have to prove anything, do we? Veljko Belivuk is in Sremska Mitrovica Prison and he'll probably die there, but he's still pulling strings, not exactly running things, but he does exert influence. If he even thought that you'd sold him out to the BIA, well, we both know how he'd react, don't we?'

Zlatnar glared at Shepherd as he gritted his teeth.

'He'd have no problem getting to you in London. They reckon that more than seventy thousand Serbs live here, did you know that? But for you, they'd probably fly in a specialist. And what about Andrea? And the kids? Luka, Bogdan, Marko, and Sofija? I'm sure that at the moment Belivuk assumes you're on the run and wishes you well. But that'll change when he finds out you betrayed him. And from what I know of Belivuk, he's likely to lash out at your nearest and dearest. Tell me, Sasha, what do you think his men will do to your children before he kills them?'

Zlatnar lurched towards Shepherd, his hands balled into fists, but Shepherd didn't flinch. The two men stared at each other for several seconds, then the Serb sat back in his chair. 'Now you threaten women and children?' he said. 'Are you proud of yourself?'

Shepherd shrugged. 'I'm just telling you the way things are, Sasha.'

'Are you a father?'

'This isn't about me.'

'What would you do to man who threatened child of yours?'

Shepherd smiled thinly. It was a good question. Shepherd would do whatever he had to in order to protect his son. He had done so in the past, and would do so again without hesitation if ever it became necessary. And yes, that would include killing anyone who threatened the life of his boy. He was sure that Sasha felt exactly the same, and that if the Serb had been holding a weapon he'd happily have used it there and then. Shepherd wasn't proud of himself, that was true, but he would do whatever was necessary to get Zlatnar to help him. If the Serb refused, would Shepherd actually betray him to Belivuk? Almost certainly not, but it was vital that Zlatnar believed that he would. 'I would do everything I could to make sure that nothing happened to my family,' he said. 'And I'm sure that you feel the same. Family is important, Sasha. At the end of the day, it's really all that matters. Family and friends.'

Zlatnar continued to glare at Shepherd. 'What is it you want?' he asked quietly.

'We need your help to penetrate The Office,' he said. 'We want to shut down their operation.'

The Serb nodded slowly. 'And what is carrot?'

'Carrot?' Shepherd repeated.

'You have shown me stick,' said Zlatnar. 'Rape and murder of my wife and my children. So, what is carrot? What will I gain if I help you?'

'What do you want?'

'I want my family to join me in England. And I want passports for them.'

'Citizenship?'

Zlatnar nodded. 'Yes. Citizenship. Under new names. And new name for me.'

'And then what?'

'We will live somewhere, somewhere safe. We will start new life. With proper English papers I can set up company, go into business myself.'

'What sort of business?'

'I like to bake. Pazarske mantije, krofne, bundevara, krapfen, my mother taught me to bake when I was child. I will open cafe, near sea, and I will sell my own cakes. You fix up papers for my family, and then we disappear. You never see me again. Do we have deal?'

Shepherd nodded. 'Yes. We have a deal.'

CHAPTER 18

B oris Reznikov knocked on the front door and stood back. He always preferred a knock to ringing a doorbell. A bell sounded courteous, polite, almost deferential. There was a brass door knocker in the shape of a lion's head, but Reznikov didn't use that either. A knock, especially a hard knock with the knuckles or the flat of the hand, demanded respect, especially when delivered in the early hours. Reznikov's visit wasn't at dawn, though he had been parked in the road opposite the house since seven thirty, waiting for Mrs Wheeler to pile her four children into the family people carrier and take them off to school.

He pounded on the door again, even harder this time. It opened and Max Wheeler peered out. His jaw tightened when he saw Reznikov, and his eyes widened. Reznikov resisted the urge to smile.

'Boris, I wasn't expecting you,' said Wheeler. 'You should have called.'

'This is urgent,' said Reznikov.

'Sure, yes, not a problem. Come in, come in.' He opened the door wider and ushered Reznikov inside. Wheeler was a big man but had run to fat. He had tried to hide the fact by wearing his pink linen shirt loose over his cord trousers but there was no disguising the fact that he was carrying more than fifty kilograms of excess lard, most of it around his waist. Reznikov had nothing but contempt for men who did not look after their bodies. He was the same age as Wheeler – fifty-two – but daily workouts in the gym and regular runs around Vauxhall Park meant that he was still in good shape, helped by regular steroid injections to help bulk out his shoulders and forearms.

Wheeler's greying hair was tied back in a ponytail and he had wire-framed spectacles on the end of his nose. He closed the front door. 'Do you want a coffee? Something stronger?'

Reznikov took an envelope from his jacket pocket and handed it to Wheeler. Wheeler walked down the hallway and into his sitting room. He dropped down onto one of the two overstuffed leather sofas that were facing each other either side of a chest-high Victorian fireplace. He opened the envelope and took out a stack of hundred-dollar bills, which he placed on the coffee table in front of him. It was half the money that Hosseini had given Reznikov in Dubai. Wheeler took out the two photographs of the target and studied them.

'This needs to be done quickly,' said Reznikov.

'I hear you. But it's difficult.'

'Difficult why?'

Wheeler waved the photographs in front of Reznikov's face. 'She's a kid.'

'She's a *target*.'

'She's a pretty girl and a lot of the guys who work for me draw the line at shooting kids.'

'She's twenty-six.'

'She looks younger.'

'It doesn't matter how young she looks or how pretty she is. You're being paid to take care of her so that's what you'll do.' Reznikov made no move to sit down. Standing gave him authority and he took advantage of it, stepping forward so that he loomed over Wheeler.

Wheeler grimaced. 'I'm not saying it won't get done, it's just that not every one of our people will take on a job like this. Some of them have . . . scruples.'

'Scruples?'

'They have rules. Some won't kill women or children, some won't kill civilians.'

Reznikov sneered at him. 'You should not give them the choice. They either work for you, or they don't. And if they don't, and if they know about you and your operation, then they are liabilities and need to be taken care of.'

Wheeler frowned. 'Kill my own people, is that what you're saying? Are you crazy?'

Reznikov reached inside his jacket and pulled out a Glock. Wheeler blanched and pushed himself backwards as if he was trying to disappear into the sofa.

'If they are truly your people, they would obey you,' said Reznikov. 'They would do as they were told. If they are picking and choosing their contracts they are not your people. And if they are not your people, they are a liability.'

Wheeler put his hands up, trying to placate the Russian. 'Boris, it'll be done, I promise you.'

'It needs to be done now. Today or tomorrow.'

'I'll arrange it. I promise. There's no need for this.'

Reznikov sneered at him again. 'There is every need for this, my friend. Would you prefer I put you under pressure? Perhaps put a bullet in the leg of your oldest son? Would that help concentrate your mind? Or remove a few fingers from your youngest daughter?'

'Please, Boris . . .'

'Shall I make a call and get a few men over here and let them have fun with your wife when she returns? Perhaps if you saw your wife being raped, you might realise that we are in a serious business. A business where people need to do what they're told.'

Wheeler was shaking now, physically shaking, and all the colour had faded from his face. 'I'm sorry,' he whispered.

'I don't want your apology, Max,' said Reznikov. 'I just want you to do as you're told.'

Wheeler nodded enthusiastically, a fixed smile on his face that did nothing to disguise the fear in his eyes. 'I will, Boris. You know I will.' He waved the photographs above his head. 'Consider it done.'

Reznikov slid his gun back into its holster. 'That is more like it,' he said.

CHAPTER 19

Shepherd decided against driving to Reading in his own car, and the Range Rover that Darren Griffths had been driving had been returned to the MI5 car pool where it would be issued with a new registration number. He walked from his flat to the Thames, then through Battersea Park to make sure that he wasn't being tailed, before calling an Uber. It picked him up within five minutes, a grey Prius that smelled of pine driven by a cheerful chap called Mo who asked him what sort of music he wanted to hear, whether the temperature was to his liking, and if he had a preferred route. Shepherd was neutral on all three questions and thankfully after that Mo didn't speak again until they had arrived in Reading. Shepherd got out of the car around the corner from the safe house, promised five stars and then walked around for a few minutes to reassure himself that he still wasn't being followed.

Before Shepherd approached the house he sent Sharpe a text message so that he'd be ready, and the Scotsman had the front door open for him when he walked down the drive.

'Fancy a full Scottish?' asked Sharpe as he headed to the kitchen. Shepherd caught the aroma of frying bacon and heard the sizzle of sausages cooking as he walked down the hallway.

'I think you'll find that it's called a full English,' said Shepherd.

Sharpe snorted. 'The English have black pudding and fried bread, we have tattie scones and haggis.'

'And throw in a deep-fried Mars bar for good luck.'

'That's crazy talk,' said Sharpe. 'No one eats a delicacy like a battered Mars bar for breakfast.'

They reached the kitchen and Sharpe went over to the stove where he had two frying pans going. There was a clock on the wall above the fridge. It was just before ten. 'Where's Ricky?' he asked.

'He's a late riser,' said Sharpe. 'But I went up and told him you were on your way.' He began cracking eggs into one of the frying pans. 'We had a long chat last night, over a couple of very nice steaks and a superb bottle of Nuits-Saint-Georges.'

'Date night, was it?'

'More like an official break-up. He wants out. Today.' He picked up a spatula that had been lying next to a Glock. The gun was SO15 issue, NCA officers didn't carry firearms.

'That's not a good idea, Razor.'

'I told him that. But he says his business is going to pot – no pun intended. And I think he's worried that he might lose his crew. He's got a point. He's not just lying low, he's vanished and the assumption is that he's dead.'

Sharpe served up the breakfasts and Shepherd had to admit that it looked good. 'Did you make the potato scones?' he asked.

'Sainsbury's. Got the haggis there, too.'

They tucked in and were halfway through their food when the door opened and Lewis appeared, wrapped in an oversized fluffy white bathrobe. He looked at their plates and shook his head. 'What must your arteries be like?' he said. He opened the fridge door and took out a large pot of Greek yogurt, and packs of blueberries and raspberries.

'Last check-up I had, the doc said I had the heart of a thirty year old,' said Sharpe. He grinned. 'I just hope he never asks for it back.' He nodded at a cafetière by the kettle. 'I just made coffee.'

Lewis poured himself a mug of black coffee, then busied himself mixing the berries into the yogurt.

'Jimmy says you want to go home,' said Shepherd.

'I am going home,' said Lewis. 'Cat's out of the bag, so I'm achieving nothing by sitting on my arse here.'

'We can't guarantee your safety if you do go back,' said Shepherd.

'Like you guaranteed the safety of The Dutchman?' said Lewis. 'That didn't work out too well, did it?'

'They shot Dutch for revenge,' said Shepherd. 'But you've got a live contract out on you. Dutch was paid a third up front but now that they know he's betrayed them, the contract will be offered elsewhere so we have no idea who'll be coming after you.'

'As I told Jimmy, there's always a risk that someone's going to take a pop at me. Welcome to my life.'

'It's not the same, Ricky. These are pros. And they'll keep on coming until the job's done.'

'So I have to stay hiding like a bitch for the rest of my life?' He shook his head. 'That's not going to happen. I'm going home – today.' He took a spoonful of yogurt and berries, but it was clear from the look on his face that he wasn't enamoured with the taste.

'I've got spare bacon in the pan, Ricky,' said Sharpe. 'How about I fix you up a bacon butty?'

Lewis looked at his bowl of yogurt and berries, then over at the bacon in the frying pan. 'Yeah, go on,' he said.

He put the bowl down, picked up his coffee and sat down opposite Shepherd as Sharpe went over to the stove. 'I gain nothing being stuck here, and I stand to lose a whole lot,' he said. 'I was okay helping you out before, because I owed you one, what with The Dutchman lined up to put a bullet in my head. But your little ploy didn't work so now I need to go back to the way things were.'

'Ricky, I hear you, but as I keep saying, there's a live contract out on you. A hundred grand. And so long as that contract is out there, your life is on the line. And if you're back to business as usual, there's no way we can have our people protecting you.'

Lewis laughed out loud. 'The last thing I want is cops looking over my shoulder,' he said. 'Look, I'm not going to be out every night partying. I told Jimmy, my house is well protected with a safe room and everything. My guys will be carrying and they know what they're doing.'

Shepherd held up his hands. 'I don't need to hear that, Ricky. If your guys are armed, that's down to you. But if you get caught, that's prison time right there. If you're on your own, we can't protect you.'

'My guys are always armed and it's never a problem,' said Lewis. 'They're subtle.'

'Have you given any thought as to who might have taken the contract out on you?' said Shepherd. 'Presumably one of your competitors.'

'When it comes to importing the gear, there really isn't any competition,' said Lewis. 'We tend to work together. Help each other out, even. On the distribution side here in the UK, sure, that tends to be competitive and there can be issues, but if it did get nasty it'd be kept in-house. I can't see any of the local gangs bringing in an outsider. There'd be no need. We've all got firepower.'

'Sure, but to get to a guy like you, they'd probably need a pro. As you say, you're well protected. Have you had any recent run-ins with anyone? Anyone who might be prepared to take out a contract rather than handle it themselves?'

'You asked that the first time we met.'

'And you said no. But things have moved on since then. If there is anyone you can think of, now would be a good time to tell me.'

'You think you can stop them?'

'It's not them we have to stop, Ricky. Once they've paid for the contract, they're done. But if we know who placed the contract, maybe we can force them to tell us who they paid. And if we can follow that trail and shut down The Office, that would put an end to it. Nobody's going to kill you if they know they won't be paid.'

Sharpe put a plate down in front of Lewis. Lewis picked up the sandwich, took a large bite, and chewed thoughtfully. Eventually he swallowed and grinned. 'Bloody yogurt,' he said.

'Yeah, can't beat a bacon butty,' said Sharpe.

'Have you got any names we can look at?' said Shepherd.

'I had a bit of a ruckus with some Colombians earlier this year,' said Lewis. 'But I thought that had been smoothed over.'

'What sort of ruckus?' asked Shepherd.

'It was a storm in a teacup. I lost a consignment of coke that we were bringing in from St Lucia. One of those things. We were using a yacht and they ran into a storm and lost their mast and the coastguard turned up to help. Ended up about a hundred kilos short and we'd promised firms across the country that we'd be delivering and already taken deposits.'

He took a swig of coffee. 'Anyway, I put out some feelers and met up with a couple of Colombians based in Marbella. They had a hundred kilos going spare, arriving in Gijón on a freighter. Their buyer had fallen through so they offered it to me at a bargain price, five grand a kilo. Half a mil. A bargain. Half in advance, half on delivery. Street price in the UK at the moment is about thirty, thirty-five grand a kilo, getting it in from Spain is easy-peasy, so I did the deal and handed over a quarter of a mil.' He grimaced. 'The freighter arrived but the Spanish cops busted it and I never got my drugs. Then it all went a bit nasty. I told the Colombians I wanted my deposit back, they said that as the freighter had moored in Spain the drugs were my responsibility and they wanted the rest of the money.' He shrugged. 'That was about three months ago and since then it's been a stalemate, pretty much.'

'But they've got your money, why would they want to kill you?'

Lewis pulled a face. 'I might have said a few things that ruffled their feathers.'

Shepherd chuckled. 'To them?'

'To people I know. I put the word out that they weren't to be trusted. And I know a lot of people. Serves them right, trying to rip me off like that. I'd paid for delivery in Spain and that means on land, not on the boat. Everyone knows that. They were trying it on.'

'So you put the word out that they'd stolen from you, and refused to pay?'

'No one would pay. That's not how it works. You pay for delivery to whatever location you agree on. Prior to delivery, the consignment is the responsibility of the shipper. That's drug smuggling 101. They owe me two hundred and fifty grand. I'm the one that should be pissed off.'

'But assuming they don't see it from your point of view, would they be pissed off enough to put out a contract on you?'

Lewis sighed. 'Yeah. I guess.'

'They wouldn't try to carry out the hit themselves?'

'In Spain, sure. But in the UK, probably not.'

Shepherd looked over at Sharpe. 'What do you think, Jimmy?'

'Colombians? They can be vicious bastards. But I haven't heard of them using contract killers before.'

'They don't have a full crew in Marbella,' said Lewis. 'They probably figured it was easier than flying someone in from Bogotá.'

'Anyone else?' asked Shepherd.

Lewis grimaced. 'I don't set out to win any popularity contests,' he said. 'People's noses get put out of joint, feathers get ruffled. But I can't think of anyone who'd be upset enough with me to take out a contract.'

'These Colombians, who are they?'

'Carlos Blanco and Diego Florez. They own a club called Casa de Los Angeles, just outside Marbella. The House of Angels.' He grinned. 'Well, I say club, it's a knocking shop really.'

'Are they with a cartel?'

'They always claimed they were affiliated to the Clan del Golfo, the Gulf Clan, which is Colombia's biggest cartel. But I think they were just blowing smoke. And a hundred kilos would be nothing to the Gulf Clan. I think they're just middle men but they've definitely got connections.'

'And they'd spend a hundred grand just because you bad-mouthed them?'

Lewis shrugged. 'I cost them money. A couple of their deals fell through after I spoke up. Could be they wanted to teach me a lesson.'

'Okay, I'll take a look at them.'

'But that doesn't help me, does it?' said Lewis.

'It might if I can find out from them who they placed the contract with. That could well help us to put The Office out of business, and that would help you.'

'Blanco and Florez aren't going to cooperate with you.'

Shepherd smiled. 'I can be persuasive.'

'They'll eat you alive,' said Lewis. He took another bite of his bacon sandwich.

'Ricky, I don't think we can provide you with protection if you leave.'

'My own people will take care of me.' He waved his sandwich in the air. 'But I'll miss Jimmy's cooking.'

'If you're not under our protection, all bets are off,' said Sharpe. 'While you're in the fold, no one is looking at you or your operation. If you go it alone . . .' He shrugged.

'How many times have I been inside, Jimmy? How many times have I even appeared in court?'

Sharpe didn't reply.

'I'll tell you,' said Lewis. 'Zero times inside, three times in the dock, one not guilty and two hung juries followed by the CPS throwing in the towel. And that was what, nine, ten years ago? I'm pretty much untouchable these days.' He grinned. 'I even pay my taxes, just in case they ever think of trying the Al Capone route.'

'It's not the cops or the NCA I'd be worried about,' said Shepherd.

'What about you? If they're coming for me they're as sure as hell going to be coming for you.'

'I can take care of myself, Ricky.'

'Yeah, well so can I. Look, I appreciate your concern, really I do, but I'll be fine. And let's face it, I'm no more use to you. You'd be wasting your time and money protecting me. Especially when I don't need your protection.'

'How about this, Ricky?' said Shepherd. 'Just give me a few days to sort the Colombians. I'm going to send someone to Spain, and I'll make sure that the contract is taken down. Then you'll be free to do whatever it is that you want to do.'

'A few days?'

'Four.'

'Two.'

Shepherd smiled. 'Let's split the difference and call it three. I'll have everything sorted within three days and we'll call it quits.'

'Can I order in some hookers?'

'Of course not.' Shepherd sighed. 'This isn't a joke, Ricky.'

'That's exactly what it was,' said Lewis. 'I was joking.' He looked over at Sharpe. 'This is one hell of a bacon butty, Jimmy.'

'I'll give you the recipe,' said Sharpe.

'And I'll miss your sense of humour. When I eventually get out of here.'

CHAPTER 20

Shepherd took an Uber to Thames House, though as usual he had the driver drop him outside the Burberry HQ building in Thorney Street and walked around to the entrance on Millbank.

He went up to Amar Singh's office to drop off the rigged phone and the fifty pence coin. 'The watch is in a drain in Wapping,' said Shepherd. 'Sorry.'

'I'd be more upset if you'd lost the coin,' said Singh. 'Donna says it worked like a treat.'

'Yeah, she was able to track me with it with no issues at all. You should patent it, wives could use them to keep an eye on unfaithful husbands.'

'Nah, if one was ever found and taken apart, there'd be hell to pay,' said Singh. 'Besides, Five owns everything I come up with. It's in my contract. But I'm glad I was able to pull your nuts out of the fire.' He grinned. 'Again.'

Shepherd headed to Giles Pritchard's office and his secretary waved him straight through. Pritchard was looking back and forth between the two screens on his desk, frowning. He took off his wire-framed spectacles and sat back in his high-backed executive chair, raising his eyebrows expectantly.

'I wanted to run something by you,' said Shepherd.

Pritchard waved him to a chair. 'Go ahead,' he said.

Shepherd sat down and crossed his legs. 'I was thinking that I could do with some backup, just until we finish The Office thing.'

'Backup in what way?'

'Protection. Kingsley is clearly out for revenge and there's a chance he'll have me in his sights.'

'You want some sort of protection detail? Sure, I don't think that'd be a problem, I can get a couple of CTSFOs assigned to you.'

'I'd rather it was someone from outside,' said Shepherd. 'The CTSFOs are good guys and they're well trained, but at the end of the day they still think like cops. I need a poacher rather than a gamekeeper.'

Pritchard frowned. 'You have someone in mind?'

'I do. Lex Harper.' Shepherd had known Lex Harper since his time in the SAS. Harper had been a young paratrooper on attachment to the Regiment. It had been clear from the start that Harper wasn't SAS material. He didn't have the mental toughness to be a special forces soldier, but he was a more than competent paratrooper and the two men had clicked the first time they met. Harper had left the Paras not long after and spent a few years in Spain moving commodities in fast boats before relocating to Thailand.

Pritchard grimaced. 'Well, he's definitely poacher material.'

'He sees things from a different perspective,' said Shepherd.

'As a hitman rather than a bodyguard? Yes, I'll give you that.'

'Hitman is a bit strong,' said Shepherd.

'Just because he carries out his contracts for The Pool, doesn't make him any less of a hitman,' said Pritchard.

The Pool was a group of contractors who carried out assignments for the intelligence agencies, jobs that were too murky to be done first-hand. No one knew for sure if the group got its name because they formed a pool of talent, or because so many of its operatives came from Liverpool. A large number were former special forces but others were simply criminals or common or garden psychopaths. Horses for courses. The Pool was run by Shepherd's former boss at MI5, Charlotte Button. These days she acted as a conduit for MI5 and MI6's less than official operations, and also carried out work for the private sector.

A sudden thought struck Shepherd and he opened his mouth but Pritchard beat him to it and he held up his hand. 'Yes, I have spoken to Ms Button, at length. And I have her word that there are absolutely no connections between The Pool and The Office. She keeps a close eye on her people and she is sure that there is no crossover. She is equally adamant that The Pool has not taken on any contracts from the Iranian government or anyone acting on their behalf. And while of course she would say that, she'd have to be pretty stupid to start carrying out political assassinations on UK soil. She does have some protection, obviously, but that would be crossing a line that would result in . . . well, we both know what that would result in. But as to getting Lex Harper on board, yes, I don't see why not. Just make sure he doesn't do anything . . . controversial.'

'He'll be fine,' said Shepherd. 'And are you okay paying his fee?'

Pritchard sighed. 'Yes, I suppose so. I'll probably put it through as consulting services and I'll need a receipt.'

'And his flight? First Class?'

'Business,' said Pritchard. 'And again, receipts.' He rubbed his chin. 'How's Zlatnar coming along?'

'Can't shut the guy up. I don't think he's holding anything back, but most of the intel he has is regarding the operatives who work for The Office. He's never met Kingsley and doesn't even know what he looks like. That's what he says, anyway. I'm going to have another talk with him after this.'

'Are we wasting our time with him?'

'No. He's already told us about three men that Kingsley hired – two men and one woman, actually – and we're looking at them as we speak.'

'What about the Iranians, does he know anything on that front?' said Pritchard.

'No, but he was involved in the periphery of one of the Iranian hits last year and he's given us the details of the two men involved, Joey and Axel Farrel. Brothers, and neither of them are on our radar. He was also involved in their preliminary check so he knows where they live, their backgrounds etcetera. We're still gathering intel, but the hope is that we get enough to charge them and get them to turn on Kingsley. Have the cops identified the two guys who died at the scene?'

Pritchard nodded. 'The driver broke his neck. Marlon Crighton. Used to be in the Peckham Boys gang but realised that he could make more money freelancing. The shooter was another Peckham Boys alumnus, Javari Madden. He used to carry out supermarket robberies for the gang but after doing a three-year stretch in Pentonville he linked up with Crighton.'

'What about the red Yamaha?'

'It was found burned out on the outskirts of Dorking. No CCTV at the location so we don't know what vehicle they switched to.'

'They were pros. They knew they could get Dutch by shooting through the car door. Most professional killers go with a 9mm semi-automatic for a close-up hit but Madden had a big revolver. The 500 Smith & Wesson packs a punch, so he might have chosen it figuring that he'd be shooting through the car. But if he used that model of gun all the time, there might be evidence at previous assassination crime scenes. It fires the .500 S&W cartridge, which is the most powerful production handgun cartridge you can buy.'

'I'll get that checked,' said Pritchard. He nodded and put his spectacles back on. Shepherd stood up and left.

It was just after midday and Thailand was six hours ahead of London but Lex Harper was a creature of the night so Shepherd left it until he was back in his Battersea flat before making the call. Harper answered almost immediately.

'What do you need?' Harper asked. He had a strong Liverpool accent, even though it had been close to twenty-five years since he had lived in the city.

'How do you know I need anything, Lex?'

'Because you're not really one for social skills, Spider, the only time I ever hear from you is when you want something.'

'I was going to see if you fancied afternoon tea at the Dorchester,' said Shepherd, 'and then maybe we could catch a film after.' He laughed. 'Yeah, you got me. Are you in Thailand?'

'I am. Pattaya. Just about to head out for poker night.'

'Is that a euphemism or are you playing cards?'

Harper laughed. 'The latter. Wish you were here, your trick memory would come in handy.'

'Sadly, I'm stuck in London. And you're right, I need your help.'

'Officially or off the books?'

'It'll be a paid job. I need someone to watch my back for a

few days. And do a few other things for me. How soon can you get here?'

'I can get a flight out first thing tomorrow. What's the story?'

'I'll fill you in when you get here.'

'Do I need to bring anything?'

'Just yourself, mate. Text me with your flight number and I'll meet you at the airport.'

CHAPTER 21

Sasha Zlatnar had been moved to a safe house in Maida Vale. Truth be told it was a safe flat, a two-bedroom in a mansion block overlooking Paddington Recreation Ground, where Roger Bannister had trained prior to breaking the four-minute mile. There were eight flats in the block, with a single entrance that was monitored by CCTV. The windows of the flat had been replaced with bulletproof glass and the front door had been reinforced with metal sheets and bolts that embedded it into a steel frame. The flat was on the second floor, and there was a small balcony off the kitchen that looked down on to the rear communal gardens.

Zlatnar was being protected by a single CTSFO, an experienced guy by the name of Gary Moore who sported a striking horseshoe moustache and whose bulging forearms suggested long sessions in the gym lifting weights. He buzzed Shepherd in and checked him through the peephole before opening the door. Moore was wearing a tight Lonsdale T-shirt over which he had a nylon shoulder holster with a Glock 17. 'He's in the front room,' said Moore.

'How's he been?'

'Good as gold. Hardly a peep out of him. He spends most of the time watching TV. Cookery shows, mainly. He loves *Hell's Kitchen*.'

'What about you? Are you on a twelve-hour shift?'

'I wish. We're stretched at the moment so my guv says that I'm here for the duration.'

'Sorry about that.'

Moore shrugged. 'It is what it is. Any idea on a time frame?'

'I'm sorry, no. We have to keep him off the radar for the foreseeable future. He's a marked man and the guys after him are pros.'

'I heard,' said Moore. 'No problem. He's low maintenance.'

'Glad to hear it.' He held up the carton of Rothmans he was carrying. 'I've got his smokes.'

Shepherd went through to the sitting room. The wooden blinds were down and Zlatnar was sitting on a leather sofa watching television, his bare feet up on a coffee table. He was watching a cookery show and he used the remote to mute the sound when Shepherd walked in. Shepherd tossed him the carton of Rothmans and the Serb thanked him.

'Anything else you need?' Shepherd asked, dropping into a leather armchair that matched the sofa.

'My family in England,' said Zlatnar. He ripped open the carton and pulled out a pack of cigarettes. 'I want my family with me.'

'Your family are safer in Belgrade,' said Shepherd. 'If we pull them out now, The Office will know that you're helping us and they'll become targets.'

'I can protect them,' said Zlatnar. He opened the pack, took out a cigarette and lit it with a disposable lighter.

'This way they don't need protection,' said Shepherd.

'How long?'

Shepherd shrugged. 'We don't know. Once we've taken down The Office we can move you on to your new life and bring your family over. But until then, you need to stay in hiding.'

'What about Donnelly? Where is he?'

'In police custody. He'll be charged with conspiracy to murder.'

'He will have lawyer. And lawyer will talk to The Office.'

'We're holding him under the 2006 Terrorism Act which means we can keep him under wraps for twenty-eight days.'

'But he can still talk to lawyer, yes?'

'That's a grey area,' said Shepherd. 'So far he hasn't spoken to a lawyer and we intend to keep it that way.'

'He will know his rights,' said Zlatnar. 'Eventually he will talk to lawyer and lawyer will talk to The Office and they will want to know where I am and when they can't find me they will know I am talking to you and they will kill my family.'

'As I said, he hasn't spoken to anyone yet. As soon as it looks as if he's going to talk to a lawyer, we'll pull your family out.'

'It will be too late.'

Shepherd took a deep breath and held it as he looked at the Serb with unblinking eyes. Zlatnar had a point. The Office would have known that something had gone wrong, but with Donnelly and Zlatnar out of circulation they could only guess at what that was. They would almost certainly have realised that Shepherd had been trying to penetrate their organisation and that Donnelly and Zlatnar had been taken into custody. But if The Office could contact Donnelly and not Zlatnar, they would assume, correctly, that at the very least the Serb was assisting the police with their inquiries. And that would be a death sentence for Zlatnar's family.

Zlatnar blew smoke up at the ceiling. 'I have plan,' he said.

CHAPTER 22

The girl's name was Layla Latifi and she had a schedule that you could set your watch to. She woke at dawn each morning, whether it was a work day or not. She would leave her flat in Richmond, wearing either a pink or a purple tracksuit. She wore earbuds connected to an iPhone that was strapped to her left arm. She ran for forty minutes, always the same route through the park, then stopped at a coffee shop on her way home, picking up a decaf latte and a chocolate croissant. Bremner knew that because one morning he had sat in the coffee shop and listened to her place and collect her order. He could have killed her there and then, but there was CCTV in the shop and on the traffic lights of the main road. Latifi would return home, shower and change into her office clothes. Bremner had seen her leave her flat on six occasions and she had never worn the same outfit twice.

She worked in an office in Kensington. She took two buses to get there, the 190 and the 27. He had travelled the route himself, but never with her. The buses had CCTV. She left the office promptly at five thirty. Sometimes she went straight home, on the bus, and sometimes she would go to a wine bar with colleagues. Bremner had seen her go into the wine bar but he hadn't followed her inside. CCTV.

It was a no-brainer where to intercept her. There were no

CCTV cameras in the park, at least none where Latifi did her running. And there were few other people in the park at that time of the morning.

The crack of an automatic being fired in the open air wouldn't carry far, but Bremner would be using a suppressor. Not a silencer – silencers were for movies and trashy thrillers. No matter what you screwed into the barrel of a gun you could never silence it, suppression was the best you could hope for.

Bremner was wearing a high-vis jacket over blue overalls, and he had a bright yellow hard hat on his head. In the unlikely event that anyone saw him carrying out the kill, it was the outfit they would remember. That and the fake moustache. He had a black North Face backpack which contained a change of clothing, and a second gun, just in case. He had three possible evacuation routes mapped out and committed to memory. All were on foot. The first thing the cops would do would be to check all the nearby car parks and CCTV cameras covering the roads. He would walk from the park to the centre of Richmond, where he'd change his clothes in a public toilet, and then make his way to the Paradise Road multi-storey car park where he'd left the Honda Civic that he'd rented with a cloned driving licence and credit card.

Right on time, Latifi let herself out of the front of the block. She was wearing her pink tracksuit and had her long curly black hair tied back. Even without make-up she was a very pretty girl, with large almond-shaped eyes and razor sharp cheekbones. She jogged on the spot as she tapped on the screen of her phone, then headed towards the park.

Bremner followed. He had no idea who wanted the girl dead, but he assumed it was a spurned lover. Obviously a spurned

lover with money to burn because Bremner was being paid
£80,000 for the hit. He entered the park.

Latifi had, as usual, turned right. She was running freely
now, her arms pumping and her hair swinging from side to
side. Bremner went right, following the path, walking at a
steady pace. There were several dog walkers on the path, and
a few runners, and off in the distance a small group of elderly
men performing Tai Chi exercises. They were there every day,
but they weren't a problem. He was planning to carry out the
hit in a clump of trees about ten minutes' walk away. Providing
he timed it right – and he was sure that he would – he would
arrive there shortly before Latifi.

He walked briskly, like a man on his way to work. He looked
around, staying aware of who else was in the vicinity. A dog
barked excitedly off to his left. A man shouted for the dog to
come to heel but he was clearly being ignored.

Bremner checked his watch. He had walked the route the
previous day. A dress rehearsal. At his current pace he'd reach
the trees in seven minutes.

He breathed slowly and evenly. If he'd taken his pulse it
would have been between 78 and 82 beats a minute. His blood
pressure would have been close to 120/80. He wasn't relaxed,
he had to stay focused on everything that he needed to do,
but his body wasn't in the least bit stressed. He smiled to
himself. It was a literal walk in the park.

By the time he reached the clump of trees, his heart rate
was nudging 85 beats a minute. He walked to a spreading
chestnut tree that he'd earmarked the previous day. He stood
with his back to it and checked his surroundings. He looked
at his watch. She was about a minute away. He reached inside
his high-vis jacket and took out his Glock 17, as reliable a gun

as had ever been manufactured. It weighed a little over two pounds, was just eight inches long and had seventeen rounds in the magazine with another in the barrel. The gun was brand new, supplied by an arms dealer in Surrey, and after the hit, Bremner planned to dissemble it and drop the pieces in skips across the city. He never used the same gun twice.

He took the suppressor from his jacket pocket and screwed it into the barrel of the gun. He never used the same suppressor twice, either. It wasn't that the suppressor could be identified, it was that possession alone was a criminal offence. He would dispose of the suppressor at the same time as the gun.

He held the gun down at his side and stepped around the tree. Latifi was about a hundred yards away. She was running at a steady pace and her movements were fluid and relaxed. Bremner took another quick look around but there was no one within earshot. He walked to the path, the gun pressed against the back of his right leg. She saw him but the high-vis jacket and hard hat put her at ease. She moved to the right to give him plenty of room, but avoided eye contact.

Sixty yards. Forty yards. Thirty yards. He took a deep breath and prepared himself. Twenty yards. He stopped walking, spread his legs shoulder width apart, and brought up the gun. As he levelled the Glock at her chest he slipped his finger over the trigger.

For the first time she looked at him and her mouth fell open in surprise. She slowed, then stopped, her brow furrowed. He pulled the trigger and a red rose appeared in the centre of her chest. He fired again and a second rose blossomed a couple of inches above the first. She staggered backwards and then hit the ground with a dull thud. One of her earbuds fell out and rolled across the path.

Bremner walked up to her. Her chest was still moving but the life was fading from her eyes. She was as good as dead but it always paid to make sure so he fired a third time, this time at the centre of her face. It imploded into a bloody mess and her chest stopped moving. Her blood was pooling over the path as Bremner walked away. Job done.

CHAPTER 23

Shepherd left the Maida Vale mansion block and walked over to Paddington Recreation Ground to use his mobile. He called Pritchard on his direct line. A group of dogwalkers were standing in the middle of the park, chatting as their dogs romped together. Several joggers were running along the path that circled the park, and mothers with toddlers sat on benches and gossiped. Pritchard answered.

'I've been talking to our Serbian friend,' said Shepherd.

'How is he?'

The hairs on the back of Shepherd's neck stood up and he wrinkled his nose. 'Actually, I'll come in and talk to you face-to-face, if that's okay.'

'Not a problem, I'm here till late.'

Shepherd ended the call. He opened the Uber app but again had second thoughts. Whoever they were up against seemed to have no problems tracking people and they could well be doing that through phones. He was going to have to raise his game. As John le Carré always used to say in his books: Moscow Rules.

He walked up Elgin Avenue to Edgware Road and hailed a black cab. He had the driver drop him at the Burberry HQ building again, where he paid in cash and asked for a receipt. He walked around to Thames House and went straight up to

Pritchard's office. Amy Miller greeted him with a smile. 'We're seeing a lot of you these days,' she said.

'Not by choice, Amy,' he said. 'You know I'm not a fan of offices.'

'Me neither,' she said. 'I'd much rather be at home with my bees.' She waved at Prichard's office, multi-coloured bracelets rattling on her wrist. 'You can go straight in.'

Pritchard was sitting on the sofa by the window, with two files on the coffee table in front of him. He flicked them both closed as Shepherd walked in, and waved at the other side of the sofa. Shepherd sat down. 'Sorry about this, I'm starting to worry about our phones.'

'By that you mean *your* phones?'

'Just phones in general. I'm going to get a couple of burners from Amar and I'll use them until someone can convince me that they're not tracking phones.'

'Duly noted,' said Pritchard. 'So, what's the story with Zlatnar?'

'He's come up with a suggestion that I think we should consider. He wants us to release him and he'll work as an informer for us, he even offered to wear a wire.'

'And why is he being so supportive all of a sudden?'

'He's realised that it's going to take time, and he's worried about his family.'

'Or he could be looking to do a runner. Our Serbian contacts aren't the best, if he gets back to Belgrade we might never see him again.'

'He knows we know where his family is. He'd be looking over his shoulder for the rest of his life. I think it's a genuine offer. He knows that we can't hold Donnelly for ever, and at some point he's going to contact The Office. If Donnelly makes contact and Zlatnar doesn't, they'll put two and two together. But if we allow both of them to talk to lawyers and see to it that they get bail, then both men can go back. All the bad stuff gets dumped on me and if anything, Donnelly and Zlatnar come out as heroes. They stopped an undercover agent infiltrating the organisation. If we're really lucky they'll be debriefed by Kingsley himself.'

'There's a fair few ifs there. And there are risks. The Office might just decide to cut ties with Donnelly and Zlatnar. Permanently.'

'I'll be keeping an eye on him.'

Pritchard nodded. 'What do you think?'

'I think it could fast track the operation. If Zlatnar can win their trust, we have what we wanted, a man on the inside. And as I said, he's up for wearing a wire. The alternative is that we keep debriefing him but all he has is low-level intel and at some point we'll have to pull his family out. If we use him proactively we can speed up the investigation.'

'There are risks, obviously.'

'Zlatnar's aware of that. But he knows that the moment Donnelly contacts The Office and he doesn't, he and his family are in the firing line.'

'And family is important to him?'

Shepherd nodded. 'Definitely.'

Pritchard rubbed his chin. 'Okay, well I'm up for it if you are. What do you need?'

'I'll have to brief Zlatnar. And fix him up with a bugged phone. Maybe get his place and car wired up. Then we need to get him transferred back to Lewisham Police Station, which is where Donnelly is being held. Once he's in place, we allow access to solicitors and, assuming we fudge any objection to bail, they could both be released in a couple of days.'

'What about the guy they were going to kill? Terry Edkins?'

'Edkins has lawyered up and is saying no comment. We're going to have to release him soon because there's no way we can hold him on terrorism charges. That'll be to our advantage now because without his evidence there isn't much we can do to bring kidnapping or conspiracy to murder charges against Donnelly or Zlatnar, so bail becomes a lot more likely.'

'If Edkins is released he becomes a target again, surely. Presumably there's still a contract out on him.'

'I'll have a word with him. But I doubt he'll want police protection.'

'I think we have to give him the option, but if he wants to go it alone that's his choice. One less criminal for us to be taking care of. What's your time frame on this?'

'The sooner the better,' said Shepherd. 'I'll go up and see Amar now, and assuming he has kit I can use then I can brief Zlatnar tonight and get him transferred to Hammersmith in the early hours. Then we have to let things run their course. We have to make it look as if we're being forced to release them.'

'And you're happy to run Zlatnar?"

Shepherd nodded. 'I think I have a rapport with him.'

'Do you trust him?'

'He's not helping us out of the goodness of his heart, he's helping us because it's the only way he can guarantee that his family will be safe. He knows what's at stake. It's his last chance and he can't afford to screw it up.'

'If you need any additional resources, let me know. At the moment it looks as if he's our best shot at getting to The Office.'

CHAPTER 24

Lex Harper's EVA Air flight from Bangkok was early and, as usual, the man was travelling light so he walked into the arrivals area twenty-five minutes after the plane had landed, swinging a red Liverpool sports bag. His sandy hair was hidden under a green Chang Beer baseball cap and he was wearing a leather bomber jacket, weathered black Diesel jeans, and gleaming white Nikes. He spotted Shepherd, waved, then hurried over. He dropped the bag and the two men hugged. Harper was almost as tall as Shepherd, but a few kilos lighter, with a slightly crooked nose, the result of being punched in the face at least once. 'Good to see you, Spider.'

'And you, Lex.'

Harper picked up his bag and looked around. 'Anyone else on your security detail?'

'Just your good self.'

'And who's after you?

'Professionals,' said Shepherd.

'So where am I staying tonight? The Savoy? The Ritz? Claridge's?'

'My spare bedroom.'

'Terrific.'

'Don't worry, I changed the sheets.'

They took a black cab back to Battersea and both men checked behind them as they headed along the M40. Any conversation was limited to the weather and football until they were safely inside Shepherd's flat and sitting on the sofa with bottles of lager.

Harper listened in silence as Shepherd ran though the operation, starting with the realisation that the Iranian government was using British criminal organisations to assassinate critics of their regime, and ending with the failed attempt to penetrate The Office.

'Have you heard of The Office, or this guy Neville Kingsley?' Shepherd asked.

'I've heard talk of The Office, sure. But the name is new to me. You're sure that the fragrant Charlotte Button isn't involved in this?'

'Pritchard says no. And she's smart enough to know that working for the Iranians could mess up her CV, big time.'

'And she can guarantee that no one in The Pool is involved?'

'Guarantee is probably too strong, but so far as she knows no one from The Pool is working for The Office.'

'You seen her recently?'

'It's been a while. You?'

'Did a thing for her last year.' He shrugged. 'She pays well.' He sipped his lager. 'I know Ricky Lewis, by the way. I've met him a few times. Who placed the contract to have him offed?'

'A couple of Colombians by the name of Carlos Blanco and Diego Florez.'

Harper chuckled. 'Them I definitely know,' he said. 'Charlie White and Dirty Diego. They arrived in Spain not long before I left for Thailand.'

'Were the two events connected?'

'No, they never gave me any problems. But I wouldn't touch them with the proverbial barge pole.'

'Are they serious players?'

'If by that do you mean are they cartel-connected, then no, not really. They have a small crew and the Gulf Clan throws them a bone every now and again, but no one would trust them with a seriously big deal.'

'Well the Colombians took out a hit on Lewis. They placed the contract with The Office, and The Office lined up The Dutchman, which is where we came in. What we'd really like to know is how Blanco and Florez placed the contract but we can hardly pull them in for questioning.'

'I could maybe help you there.'

Shepherd frowned. 'Are you serious?'

'I've still got lots of connections in Spain. And Ricky Lewis is an okay guy. I could go over and ask them a few questions.'

'Would they talk to you?

Harper grinned. 'If I asked nicely, maybe.'

'It's probably too late to fly to Malaga tonight, but maybe first thing in the morning?'

'I'll make a few calls. I'll need backup.'

'Of course you will.'

'They'll need paying.'

'No problem. I told Giles Pritchard I needed you for protection, but we can expand your brief. And I need something else. A message delivered to Blanco and Florez.'

'Think of me as FedEx,' said Harper.

CHAPTER 25

Harper took an Uber to Heathrow Airport first thing, and Shepherd used two black cabs, changing at Charing Cross station, to get to Maida Vale. While carrying out counter-surveillance around the station he popped into an off-licence. They didn't have any Šljivovica but he was able to buy a bottle of Vilijamovka, another popular Serbian spirit which was made from Williams pears and which came with a complete pear in the bottle.

Gary Moore opened the door and let Shepherd in. There was a sweet buttery smell wafting down the hall. 'He's in the kitchen,' Moore said as he closed the door. 'Did you know he can cook?'

'Yeah, he wants to be a baker.'

'He's amazing,' said Moore. 'He does these pastry things that just melt in your mouth.' He patted his stomach. 'I'm going to put on twenty pounds if he carries on like this.'

'Did you go out shopping?'

'Nah, Ocado delivered everything he needs. Are you okay if I grab a shave and a shower?'

'I'll be here for a few hours, so if you want to pop home that'd work,' said Shepherd.

'Seriously?'

'Sure. Are you okay to leave your gun?'

Moore shook his head. 'No can do,' he said.

'I'll get my boss to call your boss. We're not issued with weapons so I tend to borrow from SO15 if I need one. I just don't want to be caught without a gun if it kicks off while you're away. Not that I think it will, I just want to err on the side of caution.'

Moore rubbed his chin, then nodded. 'Okay, why not? It's not as if you're exactly unfamiliar with a gun, is it? You're a bit of a legend around SO15. I'll leave it when I go. Just don't fire it.'

Shepherd chuckled. 'I'll do my best.'

Moore headed off to the bathroom. Shepherd went into the kitchen. Zlatnar was standing over the stove. He had stripped down to his T-shirt, boxer shorts and socks, and was wearing a shower cap on his head. The oven was on and he had two frying pans on the go. On the kitchen table were four plates of pastries that he had already cooked. Zlatnar waved his spatula at a plate of doughnuts that had been drizzled with chocolate. 'You must try my krapfen,' he said.

Shepherd picked one up and bit into it. It had been deep-fried until golden and crispy on the outside, but it was soft, light, and airy on the inside and had been filled with a delicious chocolate custard. 'Oh, that's good,' said Shepherd.

'And those, try those,' said Zlatnar, pointing at a plate of small balls of pastry. 'They are pazarske mantije. You dip in yoghurt.' He jabbed his spatula at a bowl filled with creamy white yoghurt.

Shepherd picked one up, dipped it into the yoghurt and popped it into his mouth. He chewed and swallowed and immediately picked up another. 'Amazing,' he asked. 'What's in them?'

'Ground beef, salt, pepper, onions, and a bit of oil. They are better cooked in an old furnace, but this cooker will do.' He unscrewed the cap off the bottle and poured out two measures of the pear brandy. He picked up his glass and toasted Shepherd. 'I hope you make my dream come true,' he said.

'So do I,' said Shepherd. He clinked his glass against Zlatnar's and both men drank. The brandy was fiery but smooth and its warmth spread across Shepherd's chest. Zlatnar went to pour him another but Shepherd moved the glass out of reach. 'I can't, Sasha, I have to go into the office later.'

Zlatnar grunted and poured himself a large measure. 'I don't,' he said. He drained his glass again. 'This is good,' he said. 'Everything okay at office?'

'Everything is good.'

'My family, they can come?'

'It's all been agreed, Sasha. The documentation is being processed.'

Zlatnar refilled his glass. 'Can I trust you?'

Shepherd nodded. 'Yes, you can.'

'Good,' he said. He raised his glass. '*Živeli!*' Good health.

'*Živeli,*' repeated Shepherd.

The Serb scowled at him. 'Is bad luck to say "*Živeli*" with no drink.' He filled Shepherd's glass almost to the brim, then clinked his against it and both men drank.

Shepherd spent the morning watching the Serb cook, sampling his pastries and drinking coffee. Moore went out soon after Shepherd had arrived, and left his gun – a Glock 19 – behind. Shepherd kept it tucked into the back of his trousers. As Zlatnar cooked, Shepherd talked to him about his time with The Office.

Zlatnar had been teamed with Donnelly early on. Zlatnar

insisted that he only worked as hired muscle and that he and Donnelly had never killed for the organisation, but Shepherd wasn't convinced. If he had failed the test in the warehouse, they were ready and apparently willing to shoot him on the spot. According to Zlatnar, The Office fulfilled contracts across the country and in Ireland, and had even sent people to the States. Some of the killings were reported in the press but the majority weren't and, more often than not, the victims simply disappeared without trace.

During his time with The Office, Zlatnar had met more than a dozen hired killers and he was happy to tell Shepherd everything he knew about them. Cooking relaxed him and the fact that Shepherd never wrote anything down also seemed to put him at ease. Shepherd was happy to let him talk. Much of what Zlatnar said was opinion or gossip, but there were nuggets of intel that were useful and his trick memory filed everything away for future use.

CHAPTER 26

Pritchard's secretary phoned Shepherd in the early afternoon. Moore was back and Zlatnar had drunk half the bottle of pear brandy. Ocado had delivered more ingredients and the kitchen table and working surfaces were now covered with plates of delicious cakes and pastries, all of which Shepherd and Moore had sampled. Pritchard wanted to see Shepherd at Thames House, no rush but the sooner the better.

Zlatnar insisted that Shepherd take some pastries with him, and he filled two Ocado carrier bags with goodies. Shepherd walked through Paddington Recreation Ground to reassure himself that he wasn't being followed, and hailed a black cab on Kilburn Park Road.

He had the cab drop him at Burberry HQ and he walked around to Thames House. He left one of the bags with a girl at reception and gave the other one to Amy Miller. She opened the bag and sniffed. Her face broke into a grin. 'That smells amazing,' she said.

'Wait until you taste them,' he said. 'There are some croissants in there that will go great with your honey.'

He headed into Pritchard's office. Pritchard had taken off his jacket and rolled up his sleeves, always a sign that he was under pressure. He waved Shepherd to one of the chairs facing his desk.

'Another Iranian dissident was killed this morning,' said Pritchard. He pushed a photograph across his desk and Shepherd picked it up. It was a head and shoulders shot of a pretty dark-eyed girl with shoulder length curly black hair. 'Layla Latifi. She came to Britain in 2010 with her mother, who was part of the Iranian Green Movement demanding political change at the time. The regime cracked down and thousands of demonstrators were arrested, tortured and abused. Many were killed, including Latifi's father. The rest of the family fled to London and were granted asylum and eventually citizenship. Layla was twelve years old when she fled Iran. As a teenager she got involved with various protest groups and for the last two years she's run a successful podcast interviewing dissidents and opposition leaders, here and in Iran. She was shot this morning as she jogged in Richmond Park. Killed instantly.'

Shepherd winced. She wasn't much older than Liam, his son. What sort of people would order the death of a young woman for no other reason than they didn't like what she had to say? 'Do we have any idea who carried out the contract?'

'A lone shooter, wearing a high-vis jacket and a hard hat. A witness saw him leaving Richmond Park on foot after the shooting. Nothing useable by way of a description and no CCTV. A professional, clearly.' He sighed. 'This can't go on, Dan. Every Tom, Dick and Harry seems to think they can assassinate their enemies here with impunity.'

'The problem is, they're right, aren't they? We never caught the Russians who poisoned Alexander Litvinenko, even though we knew who they were. Ditto the Salisbury poisonings.' He shrugged. 'If you want to carry out a contract killing, London is the place to do it. Next to no coppers on the beat and a

Border Force that gave up the ghost years ago. Sure, we've got more CCTV cameras per head of population than most of Europe, but a full-face motorbike helmet or even a face mask renders that pretty much useless. We've banned guns across the country but criminals have no problems getting them, we ban knives and we have fatal stabbings every week in London. It's just crazy. If the police were doing their job . . .' He shrugged and smiled when he saw the look of amusement on Pritchard's face. 'I'm ranting, right?'

'A bit,' said Pritchard. 'But I understand your frustration.'

'I'm frustrated because I can see what needs to be done. We need more cops on the street, walking the beat and not driving around or sitting behind their computers. These killers know that they can shoot someone in broad daylight and that no one will see them, let alone stop them. What's the first things that cops do when they arrive at a crime scene? They check CCTV and ANPR. But it's always after the event, after the damage has been done. If there were cops in Richmond Park, this wouldn't have happened.'

'Strictly speaking, the policing of Richmond Park is in the hands of the Royal Parks Police.'

'They're still part of the Met. And come on, when was the last time you saw cops in the park? In any park?' He wrinkled his nose. 'I'll tell you when: back in the Covid days. They were all over the parks then, hassling dog walkers and telling people to wear their masks. There were plenty of resources then to put bobbies on the beat, and they find the manpower these days to track down people who say shady things on social media. But when a guy can walk into a London park and gun down an innocent girl with no repercussions, there's something wrong with the system. It's all down to numbers. In the UK, there are about two hundred cops for each 100,000 population. The EU average is 330, and countries like Spain and Italy have more than four hundred. And those countries have their cops on the street, visible and there when needed. Most of ours are sitting behind desks, or even working from home.'

'You were a cop, Dan. An undercover cop, and then you were with SOCA, you know that resources are always an issue. We have a similar problem, there are financial limits on what we can do.'

'Yeah, well we get the money we need because when we fail, bombs go off and the government looks bad.' He held up his hands. 'Rant over,' he said. 'Sorry.'

'As I said, I understand your frustration,' said Pritchard. 'But we need to stay focused on the matter in hand. What about Zlatnar? Have you briefed him yet?'

'I've run through what's expected of him. At the moment he's still in the safe house. I'm waiting for Amar to produce the bugged phone. He says he'll be a couple of hours yet. Once I've got the phone, I'll go back to see Zlatnar and, assuming he's still good to go, I'll get him into the cells at Lewisham before dawn.'

'Anything else I should be aware of?'

'We're chasing up a Spanish connection. It looks like two Colombians based in Spain ordered the hit on Ricky Lewis. We're trying to find out how they got in touch with The Office.'

'We?'

'Lex Harper is on the case. He used to live in Spain so he knows his way around.'

Pritchard grimaced. 'You need to keep a close eye on Mr Harper,' he said. 'He has a tendency to go maverick.'

'He gets the job done.'

'I'm sure he does. But there are rules we have to follow, and if he's on our payroll those rules apply to him.'

'I'm aware of the 2012 Covert Human Intelligence Sources code of practice,' said Shepherd.

'With your memory, I'm sure you are. And I'm sure you're aware of what does and what doesn't have to be signed off.'

'I am, yes.'

'I would prefer that there was no paper trail, do you get my drift?'

'Off the books?'

'I'm not saying that officially, I'm just saying that I don't want a paper trail.'

'I hear you. And I've told Lex to tread carefully.'

'I hope he listens to you,' said Pritchard. 'Right, best I don't ask any more questions. Just make sure he behaves himself.'

CHAPTER 27

The phone in Harper's lap vibrated to let him know that he'd received a text message. He picked it up and looked at the screen. 'On way'. The text came with a photograph of Carlos Blanco and Diego Florez climbing into a Mercedes G-Wagen, the size of a small tank. The text was from Peter 'Echo' Chambers, an old Marbella friend who had agreed to sit outside the Casa de Los Angeles and keep an eye on Blanco and Florez. The Colombians had arrived at the club as the sun went down and Chambers had sent regular updates throughout the night. It was now half past five in the morning and dawn was two hours away.

Harper tapped out a reply. 'Cheers, Echo. You can stand down.'

He sent the message and after a few seconds he received one in return. 'Let me know if you need me.'

Harper smiled. He had known Chambers for the best part of ten years and the man had never let him down. But Harper wouldn't be needing him for what lay ahead, the two men with him in the white Mercedes would be more than enough. John 'Marsbar' Marsden and Andrew 'Wally' Wallace were Liverpudlians like Harper but long-time residents of Fuengirola, a tourist city on the Costa del Sol, a thirty-minute drive from Marbella. Harper had gone to the same Liverpool secondary school as the two men, but their paths had never crossed there.

It was only when Harper had left the Paras and begun his career as a transporter of illicit substances that he had been introduced to them. They had done business together several dozen times over the years and he had absolute faith in them.

Marsden was driving the Mercedes S-Class and Wallace was in the back seat. The villa where Blanco and Florez lived was halfway up a hill overlooking Marbella and the sea beyond. Marsden had parked close to the top of the hill and from their vantage point they had a clear view of the rear of the villa and its large swimming pool, and they could also see the road that wound its way up from the town.

So far as they could tell, the villa was empty. In the early morning, two Spaniards had arrived in a pickup truck and worked on the grounds and in an orange grove at the edge of the property. They had left at midday. A plump woman wearing a headscarf had arrived on a Vespa scooter at nine, and they had caught glimpses of her throughout the day. Including serving lunch to Blanco and Florez on the pool terrace. She had left on her scooter as the sun went down. The only other visitor was a young man who came to clean the pool in the early afternoon, not long after the pickup truck had driven away. The pool man arrived in a white Renault van and stayed there for less than half an hour.

Lights came on in the villa and on the wall surrounding it at six o'clock precisely, presumably activated by a timer.

The three men sat in silence. There were no street lights on the hill so they tensed each time they saw headlights moving along the road, relaxing when it became clear that they weren't driving to the villa.

It was a twenty-minute drive from Casa de Los Angeles – Marsden had driven the route the previous day – and the

Mercedes had obviously been speeding because just fifteen minutes after the text message, headlights stopped in front of the villa and the main gate opened.

'Here we go,' said Marsden.

The G-Wagen drove up to the front door as the gate closed behind it. They couldn't see the Colombians get out of the vehicle, but after a few minutes they saw them through the floor-to-ceiling windows that overlooked the pool.

Harper surveyed the villa with a pair of high-powered binoculars. Both men were wearing suits. Blanco's was dark blue, Florez's was white. Blanco was holding a bottle of what looked like tequila, and Florez had a beer. They were laughing and Blanco did a soft-shoe shuffle over the tiled floor.

'Okay, let's do this,' said Harper.

Marsden put the Mercedes in gear and he drove slowly down the hill. They had scouted the area earlier and earmarked a place where they could leave the car, a lay-by that was tucked away. Marsden parked and switched off the engine. The three men pulled on gloves and black ski masks. They were already wearing beige overalls that Harper thought made them look like the Ghostbusters.

They climbed out of the car. Wallace opened the rear of the Mercedes and took out a red petrol can. It sloshed as they walked towards the waist-high stone wall that ran along the side of the road. On the other side of a stone wall there was patchy scrubland and a site where the foundations of a new villa had been built.

They climbed over the wall, blinking to get their eyes accustomed to the gloom. There was a quarter moon overhead and enough light to see by. A ramshackle chicken wire fence ran around the building work and the three men skirted it. They reached the orange orchard next to Blanco and Florez's villa and crouched down behind one of the larger trees. The Colombians had sprawled on overstuffed sofas with their feet up on coffee tables. Harper was reasonably sure that they wouldn't be able to see much through the windows, but to be on the safe side they kept behind the tree as they checked their weapons. They were sporting holstered Glocks, but the idea wasn't to kill anybody, not that night. They also had stun guns clipped to their belts, two apiece.

Once they were satisfied that they were locked and loaded, they made their way through the orchard at the side of the house. They bent double and jogged across the scrubland before flattening themselves against the brickwork, working their way around to the front of the house.

Harper moved up the stone steps and tried the front door, smiling when he realised it wasn't locked. He slipped inside and Wallace and Marsden followed him.

They stopped in the tiled hallway, moving their heads from side to side, listening intently. They could hear voices from the room at the back of the house. And music. Spanish music. Harper nodded. Wallace put the petrol can down and pulled his Glock from its holster. They moved silently across the tiles. There were dark wooden doors leading off the hallway, all of them closed. Above their heads was a spreading brass chandelier filled with flickering electric candles.

They reached a door that led to the rear of the house and Harper eased it open. He pulled one of the tasers from his belt and flicked off the safety. Marsden did the same. The Spanish music increased in volume as Harper opened the door wider.

Blanco was standing by the window, looking out over the

pool. Florez was lying back with his feet on the coffee table, waving his bottle of beer in time with the music. Harper stepped in the room, his finger on the trigger of the taser. The plan was to incapacitate the two men straight away, they'd be much easier to deal with if they were comatose. Guys like Blanco and Florez would have weapons all over the place, so the sooner they were securely tied up, the better.

Marsden moved to the right behind Harper, up on his tiptoes. Wallace stood in the doorway, his Glock at the ready. They didn't want to shoot anyone with lead but the Colombians were nasty pieces of work and Wallace would do what was necessary.

Blanco jerked and Harper realised he had caught their reflection in the window. Harper moved quickly. The stun gun fired two barbed electrodes that would incapacitate a bull, with a range of a little over fifteen feet. Blanco was about thirty feet away from Harper, so he moved quickly.

Florez saw the movement from the corner of his eye and his head began to turn. Harper ignored him. The taser only fired one shot and Harper had already committed to his target.

Marsden moved towards Florez, holding his taser with both hands. Blanco raised his bottle of tequila but before he could throw it, Harper squeezed the trigger. The two wires shot out and the barbs embedded themselves in the Colombian's chest. Harper kept his finger on the trigger and Blanco convulsed and pitched to the side, slamming into a coffee table and rolling onto the tiled floor.

Harper heard a roar behind him. Florez had got to his feet and was glaring at Marsden. Marsden pulled the trigger but he was too far away and the barbs buried themselves in the sofa. Florez hurled his beer bottle at Marsden and he ducked.

The bottle missed his head by inches and smashed against the wall.

Wallace aimed his Glock at Florez's chest.

'I've got this,' said Harper. He rushed towards Florez. The Colombian raised his fists and threw a jab at Harper's face but Harper ducked to avoid it and planted two quick punches on the man's solar plexus, left and right. The right had his full body weight behind it and the air exploded from Florez's mouth. He bent double, coughing and spluttering, and Harper had all the time in the world to punch him on the side of the head and put him out for the count.

CHAPTER 28

Z latnar took the phone from Shepherd and looked at it. It was switched on and he flicked through his contacts list. 'This is my phone,' he said. They were sitting in the front room, overlooking Paddington Recreation Ground. Gary Moore was in the spare bedroom, napping. It was three o'clock in the morning and the street lamps were on outside.

'Yes, but we've done some work on it,' said Shepherd. 'Now, you need to remember my number. You mustn't put it in your phone's contact list.'

'I'm not good at remembering numbers.'

'We've taken care of that,' said Shepherd. 'We've set up a phone for me that starts 078 followed by your date of birth – date followed by month followed by the year in full. You can remember that, right? You're the only one who has that number. You can call or send a message, whichever suits. I'll have the phone with me twenty-four seven, so if you need help, you'll have it.'

The Serb nodded. 'That's clever. What about wire?'

'The phone is the wire,' said Shepherd.

Zlatnar frowned. 'Phone is wire?'

'Anything said within six feet or so of the phone is recorded and sent to us. It doesn't matter if the phone is switched on or not, we'll hear everything.'

'What if they check phone?'

'They can check all they want. It looks no different from a regular phone. Now, if at any time you feel you are in danger, I will give you a rescue phrase, something that you can say that will let us know that you need rescuing.'

Zlatnar shook his head. 'I don't understand.'

'Suppose they are questioning you and you realise that they are going to hurt you. You can say the phrase – the words – without them realising. Then you keep them talking until we get there. Something like "I wish I'd never come to England" would work.'

'I say that and you rescue me?'

'That's the idea, yes.'

'What if nobody is listening?'

'Somebody will be.'

'You?'

'No, not me,' said Shepherd. 'But there will be somebody listening and they will contact me right away.'

Zlatnar looked at the phone and nodded. 'Okay,' he said, but Shepherd could hear the uncertainty in his voice. The Serb was wearing the clothes he'd had on when he was arrested.

'What we really want, Sasha, is for you to have a face-to-face with Neville Kingsley.'

'Then you will arrest him?'

'Not immediately. We just need to know who he is so that we can investigate him in full.'

'Because now you have no evidence?'

'He's very careful. We need to know who he deals with, who his contacts are, where he keeps his money.'

'You have a lot of questions.'

'Yes, we do.'

'So how long do I have to wait until you bring my family to London? If I have to wait until Kingsley is in prison, I wait for ever.'

'Once we know we have enough evidence to convict him, then we can pull you out.'

'I have your word?'

'Yes. You do.'

Zlatnar smiled thinly. 'The word of a man whose name I do not know.'

'My name doesn't matter, Sasha. I'm part of a team and the entire team knows what you have done. My boss is the one who will arrange for your family to join you and for you to start your new life.'

'I want to meet your boss.'

'You will. At some point. Once you have shown that you are committed.'

'You do not trust me?'

Shepherd smiled. 'I know who you are and I know what you are, what you are now and what you were in the past. So you have to earn my trust.'

'I understand. What do I have to do?'

'We'll take you to Lewisham Police Station now and you'll be put in a cell. That's where Donnelly is being held. Donnelly has been asking to see a lawyer and we'll allow that to happen. We'll also arrange it so that Donnelly knows for sure that you are being held there. The assumption is that he'll then get his lawyer to contact you. The lawyer will press for bail and our people will allow that to happen.'

'So they will release me?'

'That's the idea, yes.'

Zlatnar nodded thoughtfully. 'Can I ask you a question?'

'You can. I can't promise I'll be able to answer it, but go ahead.'

'When we took you to the warehouse, we took your phone off you. Did you have a rescue plan then?'

'I did, yes.'

'What were you to say?'

Shepherd smiled. 'Well this isn't going the way I thought it would go.'

Zlatnar chuckled. 'That's funny. But we took your phone so you couldn't use it, right?'

'That's right.'

'And I have another question.'

'Sure.'

'When we tested you, did you ever think about shooting the man there? The man we had tied up.'

'No. Of course not.'

'But you have killed before, haven't you?'

'Why do you say that?'

'I can see it in your eyes. You have killed. You have the look.'

'I'm a policeman, Sasha. The British police don't kill people. Not without good reason, anyway.'

'I know what I know,' said Zlatnar. 'You have the eyes of a man who has taken lives. But our test worked, didn't it? You couldn't pull the trigger because you are police. You would have problem.'

'A big problem, yes.'

'And that is why our test works, yes?'

'Yes.'

'So this is my third and my last question. When I am released, what if The Office asks me to do something, something illegal. Will I have problem?'

Shepherd forced a tight smile. It was a very good question. Zlatnar had almost certainly killed for The Office in the past, even though he had denied it, and he could be offered immunity for those crimes in exchange for his cooperation. But once he was actively working for MI5 as an informer, any crimes he committed would automatically involve the agency. And as Zlatnar's controller, Shepherd himself would be involved. In fact, such lawbreaking was covered by the Covert Human Intelligence Sources Act, and providing the operation was approved at the top, a CHIS could break the law with impunity. So yes, Zlatnar would actually have a licence to kill, but it was probably preferable that he didn't know that. 'It'd be best if you told me in advance what you planned to do,' said Shepherd.

'That might not be possible,' said Zlatnar.

'I hear you. But remember we'll be listening in so we'll hear if they ask you to do something illegal. If we don't move to stop you, you can assume that you have approval.'

'And what if it all goes wrong and they try to kill me? Can I protect myself?'

'Of course you can.'

Zlatnar smiled grimly. 'Then we are good.'

CHAPTER 29

'You can drop me anywhere here,' said Ricky Lewis. The safe house was about a hundred yards away but he wasn't sure how deep a sleeper Jimmy Sharpe was and he didn't want to risk waking him up. They had shared a bottle of red wine with their dinner and Sharpe had fallen asleep on the sofa. Lewis had pocketed Sharpe's phone and slipped out of the kitchen door. Sharpe hadn't trusted him with a key so he had left the door on the latch. Assuming Sharpe was still in the land of nod, he'd be able to slip upstairs and the cop would be none the wiser.

'You sure?' said the driver, twisting around in his seat.

'Yeah, we're good,' said Lewis. He was dog tired and the last thing he wanted was a walk but needs must.

The driver brought the Prius to a halt and Lewis climbed out. 'Five stars?' said the driver, hopefully.

'Definitely,' said Lewis, and he slammed the door shut. As the Prius drove away, Lewis looked around but the street was deserted. He thrust his hands in his pockets and started walking to the house. It was a cold night and he hadn't taken a coat with him so he shivered as he turned the corner and saw the safe house ahead of him. He heard the sound of a motorbike engine and he froze, his breath catching in his throat. He turned around, his eyes narrowing, but he relaxed when he saw it was a Deliveroo moped, the driver crouched low over the handlebars trying to squeeze as much speed as he could from the 50cc engine. Lewis waited until the moped was out of sight before walking up to the safe house. All the lights were off, which was a good sign.

He walked around Sharpe's Jaguar, and slipped around to the rear of the house. He stopped and listened but heard nothing but the far-off barking of a dog.

He put his hand on the kitchen door, saying a silent prayer that it wasn't locked, then smiled as the handle turned and the door eased open. He stepped into the kitchen, holding his breath, then pulled the door closed behind him. As the lock clicked, something hard jammed under his neck and forced his head back. Lewis tried to push whatever it was away but the pressure increased and he staggered to the side, then his feet were kicked out from underneath him and he fell to the floor so hard that the impact knocked the breath out of him.

'I should put a bullet in your head myself.'

Lewis rolled over onto his back, gasping. Jimmy Sharpe was standing over him, aiming a Glock with both hands.

'Calm the fuck down,' said Lewis.

'Where did you go?' asked Sharpe.

'It doesn't matter.'

'It does.'

Lewis sighed and got up onto his knees. 'If you must know, I went to see a bird.'

'What bird?'

Lewis got to his feet, still gasping for breath. 'Just a bird I know. She lives in Reading. Fit as fuck and tits out to here. Maddy her name is, not that it's any of your business. I've known her for years.' Sharpe gritted his teeth and Lewis held up his hands. 'Mate, it's all good. She doesn't know any of my friends, she hadn't heard what had happened, just two ships passing in the night.'

'How did you get there?' Sharpe tucked the gun into his belt.

'Just relax will you. I walked down the road and called an Uber.'

'How? You don't have a phone.'

Lewis grinned shamefacedly and pulled a smartphone from his pocket. 'I used one of yours.'

Sharpe snatched it from him. He stared at the screen. 'How did you use it?'

'You're careless when you tap in your pin,' said Lewis. 'Is it your birthday? You're older than I thought.'

Sharpe's eyes hardened. 'You think this is funny?'

'No, I don't think it's funny. But you can't keep me locked up here like an animal. A man has needs. Especially a man like me. Have you any idea how often I used to get laid?'

'I don't care and I don't want to know.'

'A lot. Birds flock to me, they always have. And after I got divorced I took full advantage. And now you expect me to live like a monk?'

'You really don't get it, do you? These guys we're up against, they don't mess about. They kill people for money. That's their whole raison d'être.'

Lewis grinned. 'Didn't know you spoke French.'

Sharpe shook his head with contempt. 'Ricky, if it was up to me I'd just let you go home. I'd wash my hands of you and let you face the consequences.'

'I keep telling you, I've got security.'

'You've got a few meatheads who spent some time on the doors. You're up against professionals, with serious fire power, and with access to pretty much any intel they need. This organisation, The Office, they can track phones, cars, they seem to have access to all sorts of government databases.'

Lewis frowned. 'How's that possible? What about the Data Protection Act?'

'These guys are professional killers, I don't think the Data Protection Act is an issue.' He stared at his phone and wrinkled his nose. 'Wait . . . how did you say you got there? To the bird's place?'

'I told you, I called an Uber.'

Sharpe frowned. 'But I don't have an Uber account.'

'I downloaded the app. Don't worry, it's my account, I paid for it.'

Sharpe's jaw dropped. 'You did *what?*'

'I downloaded the app and signed in.'

Sharpe sneered at Lewis and grunted in frustration. 'Just how stupid are you?' he said. 'If they track you, the Uber fare will lead them straight here.'

'Come on, how would they know it was me?'

'It's your account, Ricky. If they are monitoring it . . .' He shook his head in frustration.

'Like I said, I had him pick me up and drop me around the corner. I didn't use this address. You're overthinking it.'

'And you're not thinking at all,' said Sharpe. 'You don't seem to understand how dangerous these people are. They're in the business of killing people worldwide, they don't care who they kill, all they care about is the fee. And your very existence threatens their business model. If you get away, how can anyone trust them to carry out contracts in the future? You being alive stands to cost them a lot of money.'

'Okay, okay!' said Lewis, holding up his hands. 'I'm sorry. All right?'

'I don't need you to be sorry, I need you to stay alive.'

'I hear what you're saying. Now I need my bed. I expended a lot of energy tonight, if you catch my drift.' He grabbed Sharpe's shoulders and leered at him. 'Let's not fall out over this, hey? I fucked up, I'm sorry, I won't do it again.' He pulled Sharpe close, planted a sloppy kiss on his cheek, then headed for the door. Sharpe glared at his back as he wiped his cheek with the back of his hand. As Lewis went upstairs, Sharpe phoned Shepherd and apologised for waking him.

'No sweat, Razor, I'm not asleep. I'm getting ready to take Zlatnar to the cop shop.' Sharpe ran through what had happened and Shepherd groaned. 'He's a moron.'

'No argument. But I'm to blame for falling asleep.'

'You can't stay awake twenty-four seven, Razor. And there's no way we could have expected him to sneak out like that. The question is, what do we do now?'

'We have to move him, right?'

'Better safe than sorry. Even if he did use the Uber away from the house, there's a chance that they'll stake out the area and find you. But I'm going to have to clear it with Giles Pritchard and I don't want to call him in the middle of the night. Can you keep a lid on things until the morning?'

'Lewis has gone up to bed. I'll stay on the sofa.'

'I'll call you once we've got a new safe house sorted. I'll help you with the move.'

'Just a thought, but what about letting him loose? He's clearly not happy being looked after and he's made the point several times that he can arrange his own security. He might be better off at home with half a dozen of his own people around him.'

'I hear you, but if The Office does make good on the contract then there'll be a pile of shit heading our way. Ricky agreed to cooperate so the onus is on us to protect him. If he dies on our watch, it makes us look bad.'

'So it's about image is, it? PR?'

'No, it's not that. Ricky has put his life on the line to help us. If he dies as a result of that, then it'll be that much harder to get any other thugs to cooperate with us.'

'Are we any closer to bringing these guys down?'

'We're working on it, as we speak.'

'You're still paying me overtime?'

'Until this is over.'

'I'll try to grin and bear it then.'

Sharpe ended the call. He went to the kitchen and opened the fridge. What he really wanted was a bottle of Irn-Bru, a renowned hangover cure north of the Border, but he hadn't seen any when he'd made a visit to the local supermarket so he made do with a can of Coke. He went back to the sitting room and dropped down onto the sofa and swung his feet up onto the coffee table. He leant over to put his Glock on the table, then popped the can and took a sip. He looked at his watch. It was three thirty in the morning so he probably had six uncomfortable hours ahead of him. He cursed Lewis under his breath and reached for the TV remote.

CHAPTER 30

Carlos Blanco blinked his eyes as he tried to focus. He tried to speak but the ball gag in his mouth muted any sound he made. He glared at Harper and his eyes narrowed as he grunted. Harper couldn't tell if it was English or Spanish but he was fairly sure that whatever he was saying, it wasn't complimentary. Florez was slumped in a chair to Blanco's right. Both men were tied to their chairs with grey duct tape.

Harper stepped forward and slapped Florez, left and right. 'Wakey, wakey, sleepyhead,' he said. Florez's eyes flickered open.

Wallace and Marsden were standing behind the Colombians, their arms folded. The jerrycan was at Wallace's feet.

They had dragged the two unconscious Colombians into the hall and closed all the doors before tying them to the chairs and gagging them. The chances were slim that anyone would be passing the villa at that time of the night, but better safe than sorry, and there were no windows in the hallway. It would also keep the noise down when the screaming started.

The two Colombians were both talking now, but it was impossible to make out what they were saying and Harper silenced them by raising a gloved hand. 'I need you to answer a few questions,' said Harper. 'The only way you're getting out of this alive is if you're truthful. Do you understand?'

The two men glared at him sullenly.

Harper nodded at Wallace who picked up the jerrycan, upended it and began pouring the fuel on the floor around Blanco. Blanco's screams were muffled by the ball gag and Harper took a few steps back to keep away from the torrent. After he had poured about half a gallon on the floor, Wallace stepped away and replaced the cap.

The two Colombians were trying to speak but Harper could hear only grunts. He reached into one of the pockets of his overalls and took out a battered brass Zippo lighter. He held it up and waggled it from side to side until the two men stopped struggling. 'I'll ask you again. Do you understand?'

The two men nodded fearfully.

'Excellent,' said Harper. He gestured at Marsden who stepped behind Blanco and untied the ball gag.

The Colombian coughed and spat after Marsden had pulled the glistening red ball from his mouth. 'Who the fuck are you?' he asked.

'Yeah, that would render the whole ski mask thing pointless, wouldn't it?' said Harper.

Marsden untied Florez's gag and pulled the red ball from his mouth. Florez immediately let loose a flurry of rapid Spanish and spat at Harper. A stream of phlegm splattered across the fuel-soaked floor.

Harper flicked the lighter and the two men winced at the sparks. 'Anything else you feel like sharing with me? Or are you going to forever hold your peace?'

'What do you want?' shouted Blanco. 'Money? Is that what you want? You're out of luck because we don't keep cash here.'

'In the words of the Spice Girls, God bless 'em, "what I

want, what I really, really, want," is for you to tell me about the contract you took out on Ricky Lewis.'

Blanco sneered at Harper. 'I don't know who you're talking about.'

Harper flicked the lighter again. 'I don't see any fire extinguishers around, so once you catch light there's no way to stop the fire.'

Blanco looked across at Florez. Florez was gritting his teeth together and the tendons in his neck were standing out like taut steel wires. Blanco said something in Spanish and Florez nodded.

'You're friends of his?' asked Blanco.

'Former colleagues,' said Harper. He flicked the lighter closed. 'But that's not the matter that's up for discussion here. Who did you place the contract with?'

'This is about revenge, is it?' said Florez. 'Lewis was a thief and a liar. He deserved what he got.'

'Yeah, again, the whys and wherefores aren't what we're talking about. It's the who we're concerned with. Who did you place the contract with?'

'If we tell you, what happens then?' asked Blanco.

'We're out of here,' said Harper. 'You'll have to clear up the mess, but at least you won't be a barbecue.' He looked over at Wallace. 'What's Spanish for barbecue?'

'*Barbacoa*,' said Wallace.

'It's not a difficult language, is it?' said Harper. He looked back at the two Colombians. 'So, if you don't want to end up as *barbacoa*, you need to start talking.' He held up the Zippo for emphasis.

'You must understand, it wasn't personal, it was just business. Shit happens,' said Florez

Harper gestured at Wallace who carried over the red petrol can and placed it on the floor in front of Blanco. He knelt down and unscrewed the cap of the jerrycan. Harper wrinkled his nose as the fumes rose into the air and flipped up the top of the Zippo lighter.

Florez began shouting at Harper in rapid Spanish. Harper shook his head. 'I'm not fluent in the old Spanish, Diego,' he said. 'And keep your voice down or I'll get one of the guys to gag you again.'

'You can't do this,' hissed Florez.

'Can't do what?' said Harper. 'Because from where I'm standing, I don't see that there's anything you can do to stop me.'

'We never did anything to you,' said Blanco.

'You don't even know who I am,' said Harper.

'Which means you're doing this for money,' said Blanco. 'You're hired hands. Professionals. Let's talk money. How much are you being paid to do this?'

'It's not about the money, Charlie.'

'It's always about the money. That's why we wanted Lewis dead. He was bad mouthing us around and hurting our business. We had to do something.'

'So you paid for a hit?'

'If Lewis had still been on the Costa then we'd have done it ourselves. But he was in London and I've never been. It was easier to bring in a contractor.'

'How much did the contract cost?' asked Harper.

Blanco sneered at Harper and muttered darkly under his breath.

Wallace splashed more of the fuel over Blanco's legs.

Marsden took out his phone and began videoing the two men as they struggled against their bonds.

'Okay, okay!' shouted Florez. 'We paid. Yes, we paid.'

'How much.'

'Two hundred k.'

'Dollars?'

'Euros.'

'Who did you pay?' asked Harper.

'It was crypto. I don't know who got the money.'

Harper shook his head. 'Bloody crypto. Whatever happened to good old carrier bags full of fifty-quid notes? So what did you do, pay a deposit and then the rest when you got the photographs?'

Blanco nodded. 'We paid 50k up front in Bitcoin and 150k when they'd done the job.'

'Who gave you the Bitcoin wallet? You must have met someone. I'm assuming you're not stupid enough to give someone fifty grand on the back of an email.'

'It was a guy,' said Blanco. 'Just some guy.'

Harper shook his head. 'You wouldn't give "some guy" fifty thousand euros. You'd need to know he was kosher. Where did you meet him?"

'Barcelona,' said Blanco.

'And what was his name?'

Blanco shrugged. 'I don't know his name.'

'But he must have told you who you were placing the contract with?'

'It's a gang in London.'

'A gang?' Harper shook his head again. 'Nah, it's not a gang. We both know it's not a gang.' He gestured at Wallace, who continued pouring fuel over Blanco's legs.

The Colombian started screaming. 'Okay, okay.'

Wallace lowered the can.

'Okay, what?' said Harper.

'It's a company. In London. But they operate worldwide. Killers for hire. You pay them and they arrange the contract.'

'What are they called?'

'The Office. That's all it's known as.'

'And who runs this Office?'

'I don't know. I only know the guy we met in Barcelona.'

'And what was his name?'

Blanco opened his mouth to reply, then he shut it and looked down at the floor.

'I don't have time to piss around,' said Harper. 'Give me the name or we'll go all Guy Fawkes on you.'

Blanco frowned, not getting the reference. Wallace began pouring again and this time he didn't stop as the two men screamed and strained against their bonds.

Harper flipped up the top of the Zippo. He flicked the striker and there was a shower of sparks and a flickering flame.

'Okay, okay, okay!' shouted Blanco. 'He's Danish, his name is Kurt Kristiansen. He runs a private detective firm in Barcelona with a couple of Spanish guys.'

'How do you know him?'

'Everyone knows him in Spain. If you want someone taken care of, he's the go-to guy. He has a direct line to The Office. I got an introduction through a friend of a friend and we met him in a cafe in Las Ramblas, around the corner from his office. We agreed a deal and I transferred the deposit. We gave him what we knew about Lewis and he said they'd do the rest. Ten days later we got the photographs and we paid the rest of the money.'

'Did you meet anyone who works for The Office?'

Blanco shook his head. 'Kristiansen is the middleman. It all went through him. All he said was that the job would be done and we'd be shown photographs. We got a video too.'

Harper grinned. 'See, now that wasn't difficult, was it?' He flicked the top of the lighter up and span the striker with his thumb. It sparked and the lighter flamed. He tossed the flaming lighter into the air and it clattered to the fuel-soaked floor. The Colombians screamed in terror, heaving at their bonds, rocking backwards and forwards in their chairs.

Harper laughed as the men struggled. 'Twats,' he said. The Colombians continued to scream for several seconds before they realised that the fuel hadn't caught fire. The Zippo continued to burn but the fuel just glistened wetly. Eventually they stopped screaming and stared at Harper in confusion.

'It's diesel,' said Harper. 'It doesn't burn until it's above 55 degrees Celsius, so a naked flame won't do anything to it. Don't they teach basic science in Colombia?' He bent down, picked up the still-burning Zippo, and flicked it shut.

The two Colombians stared at him in disbelief. Blanco swore at him, the words tumbling over each other so quickly that Harper barely caught the gist of it. Something about Harper's mother, definitely. He shrugged and grinned.

'Consider this a warning,' he said. 'But if we ever cross paths again, we'll bring petrol with us, not diesel. And you'll end up as a couple of kebabs. Am I making myself clear?' Both men nodded sullenly.

'I'm glad we've reached an amicable agreement,' said Harper. He nodded at Marsden and Wallace. 'We're out of here.'

'Can you at least untie us?' asked Blanco.

'Yeah, that's not going to happen,' said Harper.

'The maid is off now, she isn't here until Monday,' said Blanco. 'We could be dead by then.'

'Nah, you can go three days without water, no problem,' said Harper. 'Don't they teach the rule of three in Colombian schools? You can survive three minutes without air, three hours without shelter in a hostile environment, three days without water, and three weeks without food.'

'Today's Friday,' said Blanco. 'Monday will be three days.'

'It's Saturday morning now,' said Harper. 'And it's not a hard and fast rule. You'll be fine.'

'And I need to piss,' said Florez.

Harper put the lighter away. 'Fine. We'll make a call when we're well away from here.'

'Not the cops!' said Blanco hurriedly. 'They'll be looking for any way to get in here.'

'You telling me you keep drugs on the premises?' said Harper. 'That's a rookie mistake, right there.'

'Not drugs,' said Blanco. 'But guns. Enough to cause us problems. No cops. Call the bar, tell Enrique to come to the house, he's got keys.'

'What did your last servant die of?' said Harper. 'I'm not here to carry out your orders, Charlie.'

'*Por favor,*' said Blanco. He flashed Harper a sarcastic smile. '*Por favor, por favorcito, con una cereza arriba.*'

Harper grinned. 'That's more like it. And one other thing. After we've gone, you might start thinking about telling Kristiansen that we're after him. But I'd caution you against having any thoughts along those lines.' He jerked his thumb at Marsden, who was still holding his phone. 'We've got you on video, singing like a songbird, and if I even think that you've tipped them off, they'll get a copy of the video. Kristiansen and The Office. Snitches get stitches, remember?' He looked over at Marsden. 'How do the Spanish say that?'

'*Los chivatos reciben su merecido*,' said Marsden.

'Yeah,' said Harper. He looked back at the two Colombians. 'Except it'll be more than stitches coming your way. Mum's the word. *Entiendes?*'

The two men nodded fearfully. Yeah, they understood.

CHAPTER 31

Shepherd drove Zlatnar to Lewisham Police Station in a Nissan Qashqai that he'd signed out from the office pool. They were expecting him, and the moment he pressed the intercom at the rear of the building, the steel doors slid back allowing him to drive into the parking garage. Martin Williams was waiting for them, this time in uniform. Shepherd parked and the two men climbed out. Shepherd had explained what needed doing and Williams had agreed to help, though it had been a bit of a squeeze to get him back into his uniform.

The sergeant walked over and shook Shepherd's hand. 'Thanks for this, Martin.'

'Happy to be of assistance,' said Williams.

'You met Sasha Zlatnar when he was taken into custody,' said Shepherd.

'Well, I knew him as Stretko Divak, obviously.' He smiled at Zlatnar. 'Welcome back, Mr Zlatnar, we'll do everything we can to keep you safe and well while you're here.'

'Thank you.'

'Now, Mr Zlatnar's details were entered into the system when he was originally taken into custody, and his DNA and fingerprints were taken at the time. All I've had to do was delete the fact that he left the custody suite in your charge.

Anyone who now looks at the computer will see that Mr Zlatnar never left and has been here the whole time.'

'Did you do as I asked about the requests to speak to a solicitor?'

Williams nodded. 'It's all in there now. Requests every day.'

'Nice one,' said Shepherd.

Williams nodded at Zlatnar. 'Right, Mr Zlatnar, I'm going to have to handcuff you before we take you into the building. No offence, it's procedure. And if anyone was to see you without the handcuffs on, they'd know that something was wrong.'

'Not a problem,' said Zlatnar, holding out his hands. Williams took a pair of rigid handcuffs from a pouch on his belt and attached them to Zlatnar's wrists. 'We'll have you in a cell at the end of the corridor closest to the processing area, and Donnelly is at the far end of the corridor. The doors and hatches are closed pretty much all the time so there's nothing unusual about the fact that he hasn't seen you. I've arranged to be on duty in the custody suite for the next twelve hours or so, so I'll be there to keep an eye on you. When I'm not there, another counter-terrorism officer will take my place.' He flashed Zlatnar an encouraging smile. 'There'll always be someone there for you, so you needn't worry.'

Zlatnar shrugged but didn't say anything.

'How do we make sure that Donnelly knows that Mr Zlatnar is in the cells?' asked Shepherd.

'We'll turn the water off in Donnelly's cell in the morning,' said Williams. 'At some point he'll ring the bell to complain and we'll listen to what he has to say and then move him to another cell. When that happens, we'll arrange to have Mr Zlatnar walked through the corridor to an interview room. Donnelly will see him but won't have the chance to speak to him.'

'Excellent. And next time Donnelly asks to see his solicitor you allow it, but reluctantly. If all goes to plan, the same solicitor will demand to see Mr Zlatnar and we're off and running.'

'Sounds like a plan,' said Williams.

Shepherd pulled a manila envelope from his jacket pocket. 'This is his phone, wallet, watch and keys,' he said.

Williams took the envelope. 'I'll take his jacket, belt and shoelaces off him once he's in the cell.'

Zlatnar frowned. 'Shoelaces?'

'Shoelaces can be used in suicide attempts,' said Williams. 'It's procedure. We have to do everything that would have been done if you were processed with Donnelly.'

Zlatnar looked at Shepherd. 'What if I need to talk to you?'

'You tell Sergeant Williams here. Or his replacement. You don't talk to anyone else. Just them. And they'll get word to me. I can't be seen inside the building, obviously. Once you're out you'll have the phone so you can contact me whenever you want.' He put his hand on the Serb's shoulder. 'I know this is going to be stressful, Sasha, but we'll be watching your back.'

'I trust you,' said Zlatnar.

Shepherd nodded and took away his hand.

'Right,' said Williams. 'I'll take Mr Zlatnar inside.' He gripped him on the upper arm. 'I have to keep a hold of you, sorry.'

'Procedure?'

'Exactly.'

Shepherd watched as the detective took Zlatnar over to a metal door with a glass hatch in it. Williams tapped a PIN code into a keypad and swiped a card through a reader. He pushed the door open and took Zlatnar inside. Shepherd realised he had been holding his breath and sighed.

The Serb was taking one hell of a risk. If anyone within The Office decided that he was a threat, they'd kill him without a second thought. Shepherd was fairly sure that he had covered all bases and if Zlatnar's cover was blown they would be able to move quickly enough to pull him out before his life was in danger. But there was always a risk when working undercover that something unforeseen could throw a spanner in the works. It had happened to Shepherd several times but he'd always been able to pull himself back from the brink and live to fight another day. Shepherd just hoped that he wouldn't end up betraying the man's trust.

CHAPTER 32

'That's the house,' said the man in the front passenger seat of the Mercedes. His name was Micky O'Brien and he had more than a dozen contract killings to his name. He nodded at the driver. 'The one with the Jag out front.'

The driver eased his foot off the accelerator as he glanced to his left. Simon Howes was a few years older than O'Brien but had only recently moved into the contract killing business. This would be his third, and fourth. According to the intel they had received there were at least two men in the house, and they had contracts to take out two – Tango One and Tango Two. They didn't know the name of the men, or why they were to be killed. The intel had come in the form of a screenshot of the house taken from Google Earth, and two head and shoulder photographs.

O'Brien and Howes had never met before. It was a rush job, and both men knew that they hadn't been first choice for the contract but they had been in London and available at short notice. It had been such a rush that Howes hadn't had time to fix up a vehicle and so was driving his own Mercedes which he wasn't happy about. He hadn't had access to a gun either, but O'Brien had come through on that front, supplying two Glock 17s that he swore had never been fired in anger and which were untraceable.

Howes had picked O'Brien up on the Hammersmith Road and there had been so little traffic on the M4 that they had arrived in Reading in less than an hour. Both men were wearing dark clothes, comfortable boots, leather gloves, and had their own ski masks. They had each been paid a deposit of twenty-five thousand pounds, with a further fifty thousand promised on completion. Howes had been paid in Bitcoin but O'Brien was a traditionalist and the money had gone into his Cayman Islands account.

They drove slowly by the house, then Howes took the next left and pulled up at the side of the kerb. He switched off the engine. They both checked their phones, but there was no additional intel.

'I hate rush jobs,' said O'Brien.

'Yeah. But if they'd had plenty of time, they might have offered the contract to someone else. Every cloud . . .'

'According to the intel, Tango Two is a cop and is probably armed,' said O'Brien. 'Tango One is hopefully unarmed but we'll assume the worst.'

He used his smartphone to access Google Earth and used the app to take a good look at the house and its surroundings. He held out the screen. 'I think we just go in the front way, around the house and in through the back. I didn't see any CCTV and the house is in darkness.'

Howes nodded. 'I could ring the front doorbell, cause a distraction while you go in the back.'

'This time of night, they'll know something's up,' said O'Brien. 'Looks like they're asleep so let's just go in softly, softly.' He nodded. 'Let's get this done.'

The two men climbed out and looked around. The street was deserted. O'Brien's gun was in an underarm holster and

Howes had tucked his into his belt. They walked towards the house, heads swivelling, looking for any signs that they were being watched. There were plenty of parked cars but all were empty and in darkness.

As they turned into the driveway, they pulled on their black ski masks and pulled out their guns. O'Brien had also provided bulbous suppressors and they screwed them in as they walked around the side of the house. A dog barked off in the distance, then fell silent.

They reached the rear of the house. The kitchen was in darkness but there was a soft light bleeding in from the hallway. Howes tried the kitchen door but it was locked. He bent down and picked up a small rock and drew back his hand. O'Brien grabbed his arm. 'What the fuck are you doing?'

'I'll smash one of the glass panels and reach in and unlock it.'

'Are you crazy?' O'Brien placed his gun on the green plastic recycling bin and reached inside his jacket. His hand re-appeared with a small leather case which he unzipped to reveal a selection of lock picks. He selected two and went to work on the lock. He had it open in just under three minutes and Howes patted him on the back.

'How long did it take to learn to do that?' he whispered.

'You don't want to know,' he said. 'And they keep changing locks all the time. Luckily this is a bog-standard Yale.'

He put the picks away, grabbed his gun, and eased the door open. The two men padded across the kitchen lino, their breath caught in their throats. O'Brien gestured at the stairs and Howes nodded.

The sitting room was to their right. The door was ajar and both men stopped when they heard a soft snort. There was someone in the room.

O'Brien pointed at Howes, then pointed at the stairs. Then he pointed at his own chest, and at the sitting room. Divide and conquer.

Howes nodded and moved silently up the stairs, keeping close to the wall. O'Brien tiptoed into the sitting room. There was someone lying on the sofa, covered in a blanket. O'Brien pointed his gun at the centre of the lump and pulled the trigger twice. The gun kicked in his hand and there was a double burst of feathers from whatever was under the blanket.

'Surprise,' said a gruff Scottish voice behind him and as O'Brien turned there was a loud bang and something punched him hard in the back. He fell to the floor, gasping for breath but it felt as if his lungs had emptied.

Howes froze on the stairs. He swung his gun around as a figure appeared in the sitting room doorway. His eyes narrowed as he realised it was a man in his late fifties with slicked back hair, holding a gun. His heart pounded. It was Tango Two. The cop. He tried to aim his Glock at the man but was too slow and the man fired once and the round smacked into his chest, a couple of inches below his throat. Howes fell back against the wall, his mouth working soundlessly, then the strength drained from his legs and he slumped down onto the stairs as everything went black.

CHAPTER 33

Shepherd's phone burst into life and woke him from a dreamless sleep. He was in his flat and he blinked his eyes as he focused on the screen. It was Jimmy Sharpe. Shepherd sat up and took the call. It could only be bad news. 'What's up, Razor?'

'We've had visitors,' growled Sharpe.

'Is Lewis okay?'

'We're both okay, thanks for asking,' said Sharpe. 'The visitors, not so much. I need a clean-up crew or whatever you're calling it these days.'

'What exactly needs cleaning up?'

'Two bodies. I've checked for ID and they're clean. One of them has car keys on him so there's probably a car parked nearby.'

'Neighbours?'

'All's quiet outside. I think everyone's asleep.'

'I'll be there within the hour, Razor.'

'I'll put the kettle on.'

Shepherd ended the call and rolled out of bed. He phoned Giles Pritchard as he padded over to his wardrobe. If Pritchard was annoyed at the early morning call, he managed to hide it. 'Hi, Dan,' he said.

'Really sorry about this but Razor has had visitors. Lewis

is okay but there are two fatalities and we'll have to move them. I'm heading to Reading.'

'I'll have a new option for you by the time you arrive,' said Pritchard.

'And we'll need a Code Black Clean-Up team. Apparently there's a mess.'

'Not a problem.'

'And in view of what's happened, I think we need to assign a couple of CTSFOs.'

'I think you're right. Okay, Dan, I'll get wheels turning, we'll talk later.'

Pritchard ended the call. As always, he was behaving like a true professional, but at some point he was going to want to know what had gone wrong. Safe houses were supposed to be safe, and the one in Reading was anything but that.

He dressed quickly, pulling on a sweater and jeans, then headed down into the underground car park to collect his BMW X5.

He was driving on the M4 through Slough when his phone rang. It was Harper. Shepherd took the call on hands-free. 'How's it going, Lex?'

'Yeah, all good. I have a name. A private eye in Barcelona, Kurt Kristiansen. He's the middle man that the Colombians used to take out the hit on Ricky Lewis.'

'Yeah, about that. Ricky had two visitors. He's okay but we're going to have to move him and review his security.'

'So, they know he was cooperating with you?'

'Seems it.'

'That's not good.'

'No, it's not. Look, what are you planning to do with this Kristiansen?'

'Yeah, about that. We might have to get heavy with him. The Colombians gave him up without too much trouble, but they were only betraying a middle man. We'll be wanting Kristiansen to betray The Office so we might need to be more persuasive.'

'I'll fly over once I've dealt with the Ricky situation.'

'I'd advise against that, Spider. Seriously. Plausible Deniability. You need to keep your distance.'

'What are you planning, Lex?'

'Best you don't know. I'll get you the intel you need, let's leave it at that.'

'You're sure?'

'Dead sure. You look after Ricky, I'll handle things over here.'

Harper ended the call.

Shepherd was passing Maidenhead when his phone rang again. This time it was Giles Pritchard. 'There's a plain-clothes CTSFO unit heading for the safe house now. They should be there within twenty minutes. I've ordered a Clean-Up Team and I'm assured they'll be there within the hour. And there's a new safe house ready for you in Chelsea Harbour. It's a flat in a secure building with CCTV, I figure they'll be safer there than in a house in the sticks. The flat can be accessed from a lift via the car park, and everything is keycard controlled. Your man should be safe enough there.'

'Thank you,' said Shepherd.

'At some point we need to have a conversation about what happened,' said Pritchard.

'I'll call you once I've had a chance to talk to Razor.'

'Pop into the office if you get the chance.'

'Will do,' said Shepherd. Pritchard had made it sound like a request, but it was clearly a summons.

Pritchard ended the call and a few seconds later the phone

buzzed to let Shepherd know he had received a message. It was an address, and a photograph of an apartment block.

He arrived in Reading almost an hour after he had left Battersea and sent Sharpe a text message. 'Arriving now.' He didn't want any nasty surprises when he rang the doorbell.

He parked in the road. As Shepherd walked up the driveway, Sharpe opened the front door. He looked tired, his hair was unkempt and there were dark patches under his eyes. Sharpe looked around and waved Shepherd inside before pushing the door closed. He took Shepherd down the hall and gestured at the sitting room. Shepherd went in and stopped when he saw the two bodies on the carpet. Both men were wearing dark clothing, boots and ski masks. There were two Glocks on the coffee table. There were three pillows on the sofa, one of which had been ripped apart by bullets, and a duvet.

'What happened, Razor?'

'They came in through the back. Picked the lock, then came down the hall. I was in here. They thought I was lying on the sofa and one of them put two rounds in what he thought was the body. I didn't have time to do anything fancy, I just took them down.' He pointed at the body closest to the door. 'He was on the stairs. I dragged him in here.'

Shepherd gestured with his chin at the nearest body. 'Looks as if this one was shot in the back.'

'He had a gun in his hand and he was turning towards me. I was hardly going to wait until he was facing me, was I?'

'Did you identify yourself as a police officer?'

Sharpe frowned. 'Are you serious? They knew who I was, they'd just tried to put two bullets in me on their way to killing Ricky.'

Shepherd looked around the room. There was a half-eaten sandwich on a plate next to the armchair by the fireplace. 'You were sitting there?'

'I was.'

'Waiting for them?'

'I wasn't going to sleep, was I? Not after Ricky had pulled his "Great Escape" act.'

'I get that. But the pillows and the blanket, that was a set-up, right?'

'Spider, if the two low-lifes decide to announce themselves by pumping rounds into a pillow, that's not my fault is it?'

'I'm just asking the questions that are going to be asked down the line, Razor.'

'By who? The Directorate of Professional Standards?'

'If it was to be investigated as a police shooting it would be the Independent Office for Police Conduct who would be asking the questions, but it won't come to that. There's a clean-up squad on the way, so in a few hours it'll be as if it never happened. But I need to be honest with Giles Pritchard.'

'They broke into the house to kill me and Ricky and they ended up dead. That's the be-all and end-all.'

'I'm on your side here, Razor. Where is Ricky?'

'I told him to stay upstairs and keep his door locked.'

'He must have heard the shots.'

'He came down and I told him to get back into the bedroom.'

'But he knows what happened?'

Sharpe shrugged. 'Like you said, he heard the shots.'

'He might be a problem, down the line.'

'I saved his life.'

'True. But now he has something on you, doesn't he? That's not ideal.'

'Are you suggesting that I go upstairs and put a bullet in his head?'

'Yes, Razor, that's exactly what I'm suggesting.' Shepherd shook his head scornfully. 'I'm just making sure that there's no pushback,' he said. 'If you were MI5 it'd be easier to sweep it under the carpet but you're with the National Crime Agency so in theory the Police and Criminal Evidence Act applies.'

'Under PACE I have the right to use "reasonable force" when necessary.'

'You do, yes.'

'And my memory might not be as good as yours, but I do remember that the Police Conduct Regulations 2020 state that officers can discharge their firearms to prevent a real and immediate threat to life.'

'That's exactly what it says. And the guidance is to aim for the torso of the target when possible, which you did. So that's good. Anyway, as I said, it's irrelevant, the fact that Pritchard is sending a clean-up squad means that there won't be an official investigation. Once they've done their thing there won't be any evidence.'

Shepherd's phone beeped. It was a text message from a number that his phone didn't recognise. 'Pulling up outside now.'

'That's the CTSFOs,' said Shepherd. 'Do you want to go upstairs and get Ricky prepped? Best if the two of you aren't here when the clean-up team arrives.'

'Where are we going?'

'A secure apartment in Chelsea Harbour.'

'For how long?'

'How long is a piece of string, Razor?'

'Are we any closer to nailing The Office?'

'We're getting there.'

'Ricky wants to go home. He's says he's had enough of being cooped up like this.'

'Yeah? Well explain to him how close he came to dying tonight. That might change his mind. Bloody idiot.'

Shepherd walked to the front door as Sharpe headed upstairs. When Shepherd opened the door the three CTSFOs were standing by a white Toyota Land Cruiser, looking around to get the lay of the land. They were typical CTSFOs, short and stocky with shaved heads, they wouldn't have looked out of place robbing an East End bank with sawn-off shotguns. They were wearing bomber jackets, tight jeans and sturdy boots, as if they had been outfitted by central casting. Shepherd would have happily bet money that they were all carrying Glocks, either the 17 or the 19.

The men moved down the path with the confident swagger that came from carrying a concealed loaded weapon. 'You Dan?' asked one. He was wearing a chunky Breitling watch and his boots were Altberg, the brand favoured by the SAS.

'I am,' said Shepherd.

The man held out his hand. He had short fingers with squarish nails and it reminded Shepherd of an entrenching tool, designed for digging in hard soil. He had a powerful grip but Shepherd could tell he wasn't using anywhere near his full strength. 'Ronnie,' he said, his smile revealing a wall of gleaming white slab-like teeth.

He introduced his two companions – Beefy and Harry – and they took it in turns to shake Shepherd's hand. He took them into the hall and pushed the door closed. 'There are two principals,' said Shepherd. 'Jimmy Sharpe is with the NCA, he's been looking after Ricky Lewis, drug dealer and all-round bad guy. There's a contract out on Ricky's life and two guys tried to collect earlier this morning.'

'Where are they now?' asked Ronnie.

'Ricky and Jimmy? Upstairs.'

'I meant the bad guys.'

Shepherd gestured at the sitting room. 'In there.' The three men filed in. 'Who did this?' asked Ronnie, looking down at the two bodies.

'Jimmy.'

'I thought the NCA weren't armed.'

'They're not. Jimmy is a special case.'

'That guy seems to have been shot in the back,' said Beefy, pointing at the body by the sofa.

'He was turning and carrying a loaded weapon,' said Shepherd.

Beefy grinned. 'That's all right, then.'

'Presumably the principals are being relocated,' said Ronnie.

'To Chelsea Harbour in London,' said Shepherd. 'I'll give you the address. The Jaguar outside is Jimmy's so it's obviously been compromised. I'll wait to supervise the clean-up so maybe you could take them in your vehicle and I'll meet up with you later.'

Ronnie nodded. 'Sounds like a plan,' he said. 'What sort of threat are we facing?'

'Professionals,' said Shepherd. 'There's a six-figure contract out on Ricky that we know about, and I'm sure that Jimmy is also in the firing line. The contract is through an agency that deals with all sorts of freelancers so there's no way of knowing who might come at you. You'll have to treat everyone as a possible threat. The good news is that the flat is in a secure building with CCTV everywhere so once you're inside you should be good.'

'We'll take good care of them,' said Ronnie.

CHAPTER 34

After the CTSFOs had driven off with Sharpe and Lewis, Shepherd did a pat down of the two bodies in the sitting room. There was nothing that could identify them, which marked them down as professionals. No wallets, no driving licences, and no credit cards. They both had smartphones and wads of cash, and the older one was carrying a lock-picking kit that they had obviously used to gain access. The younger man had a Mercedes key fob in his pocket. Shepherd pulled off the ski masks and used his own phone to take photographs of their faces.

It was still dark outside and there was no one around as he walked down the road. He found a Mercedes parked on a side road and its hazard lights flashed when he pressed the fob. He used his phone to take a picture of the registration plate, then opened the driver's side door and climbed in. A quick search of the car showed that it was as depersonalised as the two bodies.

He locked up the car and went back to the house. He switched on the kettle and sent the photographs of the men and the number plate to Giles Pritchard. He was pouring milk into a mug of coffee when his phone beeped. The message was from the clean-up crew, letting him know that they were five minutes away. Jimmy Sharpe had left him the keys to the

Jaguar so Shepherd went outside and parked it in the road, figuring the clean-up crew would want to get their vehicle as close to the house as possible.

He had the door open when their white Renault van arrived. It had the name of a furniture restoration company on the sides. The driver reversed in and switched off the engine. The rear doors opened and two men climbed out dressed in grey overalls and blue shoe covers. They were carrying large black plastic toolboxes. They hurried over to the front door and into the hall. 'Kettle's just boiled if you want a tea or a coffee,' said Shepherd. The two men grunted and headed for the kitchen.

The driver was wearing a denim jacket, black jeans and scuffed cowboy boots. He climbed out of the cab and pointed at the garage door, just a few feet from the rear of the van. 'Will that open?'

'I haven't tried, but I assume so.'

'The van won't go in but the closer we can get, the better.' He held out his hand. 'I'm Johnnie, I'll be supervising this morning's shindig, but I'm told it's a pretty straightforward disposal.'

Shepherd shook his hand, took him inside and closed the door. 'Two bodies, each with a single gunshot wound. One of the bodies had been moved from the stairs so there's a blood trail.'

Johnnie looked at the flight of stairs. 'Polished wood so that's easy to take care of.' He pointed at the sitting-room door. 'Bodies in there?'

Shepherd nodded and took him through. Johnnie looked at the two bodies, then surveyed the room. 'Easy-peasy, lemon squeezy,' he said. 'We'll roll the bodies up in plastic, then give the floors a quick clean. An hour should do it.' He frowned when he saw that one of the men had been shot in the back but didn't say anything.

'We don't have any ID, are you able to take DNA and fingerprints?'

Johnnie nodded. 'We do that as a matter of course, before disposal.'

'You don't store the bodies?'

'We do sometimes but the instructions for this say we go straight to disposal. My guys are in the kitchen?'

'Yeah, the kettle just boiled.'

'I'll get a brew on, then,' said Johnnie. 'If you could open the garage door that would be great.' He pointed at a door to their left. 'That's the access to the garage?'

Shepherd nodded. He grabbed the handle and opened it. On the other side was the garage, empty other than for a few cardboard boxes and a vacuum cleaner.

Johnnie peered inside and nodded. 'Perfect,' he said. 'Right, I'll grab a coffee and we'll get started.'

CHAPTER 35

'That's him,' said Harper. He was sitting in the back of the Mercedes, with Wallace in front of him and Marsden in the driving seat. They were in an upmarket area of Barcelona so the luxury sedan didn't stick out, in fact many of the vehicles parked around them were far more expensive. Like the Mercedes, most had tinted windows, and drivers waiting for their clients was the norm. The three men had been parked up for the best part of an hour and nobody had paid them any attention.

Kurt Kristiansen was walking quickly down the pavement, a mobile phone clamped to his ear and a briefcase in his left hand. He was portly and his trench coat billowed behind him like a sail as he headed for the building where he worked. Harper was holding a printout of a photograph he'd taken from the detective agency's website. The man in the photograph was thinner and had more hair, but it was definitely him, jowly and red-faced with thighs that seemed to be brushing together as he walked.

'Be easy enough to scoop him up now,' said Wallace.

'Too many prying eyes around, and CCTV,' said Harper. 'And we can't get to him while he's in the office.'

'Softy, softly, catchee monkey,' said Marsden.

'Yeah, but we're on a deadline,' said Harper. 'We don't have time for softly, softly.'

'So what's the plan?' asked Wallace.

Harper grinned and tapped his forehead. 'My thinking cap is on,' he said.

CHAPTER 36

The clean-up team were in the house for less than an hour, and when they left it was as if there had never been two dead men in the house. One of the crew followed the van in the Mercedes. When they had gone, Shepherd climbed into his BMW and drove the forty or so miles back to his flat. The traffic was bad and it took him the best part of an hour and a half. He parked in the underground car park and showered, shaved and changed into a suit before taking an Uber to Thornery House, walking around to Thames House. He went straight up to Giles Pritchard's office and Amy Miller flashed him a smile and told him to go through.

Pritchard waved him to a chair. Shepherd sat and waited while Pritchard continued to alternate his attention between his twin screens. It didn't appear to be a power play, Pritchard was peering through his spectacles and his brow was furrowed. Occasionally he made a clicking sound with his tongue. Eventually he sat back in his high-backed chair.

'It's going from bad to worse,' he sighed. 'The FBI have uncovered a plot to kill President Trump and it's looking as if it's the Iranians that are behind it. They've arrested a man who has been throwing cash around in Chicago, trying to put together a team to assassinate the President. According to the FBI, the guy they're looking at has links to the Quds Force and they're asking the various intelligence agencies across Europe what up-to-date intel they have on Quds operatives, so I either have to tell them what we're up to or find a bloody good reason for not telling them.'

Shepherd nodded. The Quds Force was a unit of Iran's Revolutionary Guard, formed after the country's 1979 revolution. The Quds Force was set up to carry out operations to advance the Islamic Revolution outside Iran. Over the years, they formed ties with armed groups across the Middle East, including Afghanistan, Iraq, Lebanon, Syria and the Palestinian territories. Their agents bombed the US Embassy and a Marine Corp Barracks in Beirut in 1983, collectively killing more than three hundred American and French soldiers and diplomats, and were renowned for using roadside bombs to kill US troops in Iraq. Iran also used the Quds Force to take on the Islamic State militant group in Syria and Iraq. Pritchard had been working on the theory that it was the Quds Force who were ultimately responsible for the killings of Iranian dissidents in the UK, though there was still no hard evidence to back it up.

'Do they have something definite?'

'It seems so. The FBI Special Agent in Charge says the focus of their investigation is one Ahmad Qalibaf who has been in the US for more than fifteen years. He came through Syria, was granted American citizenship ten years ago, and has spent most of the last five years in and out of several correctional facilities, usually on assault charges. With the benefit of hindsight, the FBI thinks he deliberately had himself sent to prison to make contact with potential assassins. He's been out for the past six months and has been acquiring weapons and phones and has been handing out cash like there's no tomorrow.'

'But how did they make the Quds connection?'

'Qalibaf was careless with his WhatsApp messages, apparently. But the FBI are keeping their cards close to their chest so I don't have specifics.'

'So, they want intel from you and are offering nothing in return?'

Pritchard smiled thinly. 'Our American cousins have always regarded intelligence sharing as a one-way street,' he said.

'Would they tell you if Qalibaf has a contact in Tehran?'

'That's one of the questions I'd like to put to them, but I don't see that I'd get an answer.' He clicked his tongue. 'The thing is, we don't have an Iranian connection yet. I mean, we know that Iranian dissidents are being targeted in the UK, and we know that The Office has carried out some of the contracts, but we don't have what the FBI appear to have, which is a link to Tehran.'

'Does their investigation overlap with ours at all?'

'Not that I can see, no. But if we knew who their Tehran connection was, we could look at any links from him to The Office.' He shrugged. 'But I don't see that happening.'

'Well, assuming we get an in with The Office, we'll be able to work back to their Iranian contacts. That's still the plan, right?'

'That's the theory,' said Pritchard. 'How are we on that front?'

'Still pursuing the Spanish connection.'

'Progress?'

'We've identified a middleman in Barcelona who has been passing contracts to The Office.'

'Lex Harper's work?'

Shepherd flashed him a tight smile. 'He gets the job done.'

'It's the collateral damage that I worry about.'

'I've told him to be on his best behaviour.'

Pritchard sighed and removed his glasses. 'Speaking of best behaviour, what went on in Reading?'

Shepherd grimaced uncomfortably. 'Ricky Lewis went AWOL. He snuck out to see a girlfriend while Jimmy was asleep. He used Jimmy's phone to call an Uber.'

Pritchard frowned. 'How did that lead the bad guys to Lewis?'

'Jimmy doesn't use Uber so Ricky downloaded the app and then used his own account.'

'Bloody idiot.'

'He didn't think,' said Shepherd.

'You can say that again.'

'Jimmy knew that there was a chance that they'd been exposed so he stayed awake. Two guys broke in and Jimmy took care of them.'

'Why wasn't Lewis relocated immediately?'

'It was the early hours of the morning. I didn't want to start waking people up on the off chance there was a problem.'

'I'd rather be woken up than have to send in a Code Black Clean-Up team.'

'That was my error,' said Shepherd. 'I had no idea that the bad guys would be able to run a trace that quickly.'

'The one positive is that we've identified the two men that Sharpe took care of, as you called it. Two single shots, I was told.'

'It was all over very quickly,' said Shepherd. If Pritchard knew that Sharpe had shot one of the men in the back, he wasn't letting on.

Pritchard put his glasses back on and peered at one of his screens. 'Both men are in the system,' he said. 'Micky O'Brien and Simon Howes. O'Brien is former military, Royal Marines, but he left under a cloud after an incident in Afghanistan that left two Afghan interpreters dead. Worked for a few private contractors in Iraq, then went under the radar. Now we know why. We're in the process of searching his house and putting his phones and finances under the microscope.

'Simon Howes has form for stealing high end cars but again has been under the radar for the past two years. He was using his own vehicle, which wasn't smart. It was probably a rush job. We've already had a quick look at their phones and just before they went into the house they received pictures of the house from Google Earth, the registration number of Sharpe's car, and photographs taken from Sharpe and Lewis's driving licences.'

'How would they have identified Jimmy?' asked Shepherd. 'They wouldn't have known about the Jag until they got to the house.' Realisation dawned and he grimaced. 'They would have ID'd him from the phone. Ricky calls an Uber, they spotted the order and the phone the order was placed on. They ID'd Jimmy from the phone and that would have led them to his driving licence and to his car.' He raised his eyebrows. 'These guys are good. I don't think we could work that quickly.'

'Because we have procedures that have to be followed,' said Pritchard.

'So they clearly have someone with the DVLA?'

'It's starting to look as if they have people everywhere,' said Pritchard.

'It's the speed of that you've got to admire,' said Shepherd. 'They must have been watching Uber, and spotted him the moment he opened his account. But what if he had used another of the ride-sharing apps? Were they all being monitored? And they traced Jimmy's phone. That must mean they have access to all the networks, they can't just have been lucky, surely?'

Pritchard nodded. 'I don't think there was any luck involved. Whoever got the intel was utilising very sophisticated hacking capabilities. And the Iranians certainly have that. GCHQ deals with dozens of Tehran-based cyberattacks every year.'

'Is it likely to be the Iranians though?' asked Shepherd. 'Isn't it more likely that it's The Office trying to clear up its mess? They wouldn't want the Iranians to know how close they'd come to being infiltrated. It would mean admitting failure. And possibly pissing off the Iranians.'

Pritchard nodded slowly. 'You're probably right, yes.'

'The Office must have its own hackers. Or access to them. I'll have to talk to Jimmy.'

'Well, the good news is that both the car and his driving licence are registered through cut-off addresses, so they won't be able to get to him that way. The fact that they have his photograph is obviously a worry.' Pritchard sighed. 'We really need to kick this investigation into gear. The sooner we shut down The Office, the better.'

CHAPTER 37

'Okay,' said Harper, patting Wallace on the shoulder. 'Let's get this done.'

Wallace had his mobile phone out and he called the number of Kristiansen's office. Wallace spoke almost perfect Spanish, and he identified himself as an inspector with the Guàrdia Urbana de Barcelona, the city's municipal police force. He asked to speak to Kristiansen and the receptionist put him through immediately. As soon as Kristiansen answered, Wallace began speaking in rapid Spanish until Kristiansen interrupted him and Wallace switched to English, speaking haltingly as if he was uncomfortable with the language.

'Mr Kristiansen, my name is Inspector Juan Lorenzo with the Guàrdia Urbana, I am afraid I have to tell you that there has been a break-in at your home. Two men were seen leaving with a number of items. We need you to come to your home now so that you can tell us what has been stolen.'

'Did they open my safe?'

'I do not know the details, Señor Kristiansen. I am in my office and the break-in is being investigated by two of my detectives. Can you get to your home now?'

'Yes,' said Kristansen. 'It'll take me about twenty minutes.'

'The officer heading the investigation is Sergeant Mark Morata. He will meet you there.'

Kristiansen thanked him in Spanish and ended the call. Harper laughed. 'You sounded like Manuel from *Fawlty Towers* there,' he said.

Wallace grinned. '"I know nothing,"' he said.

'Do you think he bought it?' asked Marsden.

'Hook, line and sinker,' said Wallace. 'It's a bit awkward that we don't know if he lives in an apartment or a house, but home covers both and he didn't seem bothered.'

'We'll know soon enough,' said Harper.

Kristiansen hurried out of the building less than five minutes later. He wasn't carrying his briefcase this time and hadn't bothered with his coat. He was walking briskly and his brow was furrowed.

'He's not a happy bunny,' said Marsden. He put the car in gear and drove slowly after the man.

Harper looked around, scanning the area for anything that might give them a problem, but the only pedestrians were office workers or tourists and there were no police vehicles to be seen.

'Let's do it,' he said.

Marsden accelerated to draw level with their target, then braked sharply. Wallace climbed out and hurried towards Kristiansen, calling out his name. Kristiansen stopped and turned. Wallace took out his wallet and flashed it, presumably showing his driving licence, keeping it moving so that Kristiansen had no time to focus on it. 'Mr Kristiansen, I am Sergeant Mark Morata, we have a car to take you to your home.' He spoke with a Spanish accent, less like Manuel this time. He waved at the car. 'We thought it would save time.'

'Do you know what they've taken?' asked Kristiansen.

'We hope you can tell us that,' said Wallace. He waved at the car again. '*Por favor.*'

'This is a fucking nightmare,' Kristiansen growled. 'I'm up to my eyes in work and this is the last thing I need.'

'*Lo siento,*' said Wallace. 'We won't keep you long.'

Kristiansen reached the car and started to ease himself into the back seat. Harper produced a taser, jammed the prongs against the man's fleshy neck and pulled the trigger. Kristiansen went into a spasm and then collapsed. Harper pulled him across the seat, Wallace climbed in and slammed the door shut, and Marsden accelerated away from the kerb. Harper looked around but no one had seen what had happened. 'Nice one,' he said.

'I think he's pissed himself,' said Wallace.

'Yeah, that tends to happen when you get tasered,' said Harper.

Marsden opened his window. 'We're never going to get rid of the smell,' he said. 'It'll soak into the leather.'

'It's not like it's your car, mate,' said Harper. 'And we're going to torch it when this is over anyway,' he said.

'Fair point,' said Marsden.

CHAPTER 38

Shepherd walked around from Thames House before calling for an Uber. It was a twenty-minute drive to Chelsea Harbour. Shepherd had the driver drop him in front of the adjacent building to where Sharpe was holed up, and he waited until the car had driven off before walking the vicinity to convince himself that the area was clear.

Glass doors led into a double height atrium. The lifts were to the right, shielded by glass security doors, and there was a reception desk with a uniformed doorman to the left. The desk, the front entrance, and the doors to the lift were all covered by CCTV cameras. The doorman was looking expectantly at Shepherd, and Shepherd nodded in his direction, then walked over to the CTSFO who was sitting on one of the overstuffed sofas that were dotted around reception. It was one of the guys he'd met at Reading. Beefy.

'Is everything good, Beefy?'

'No one followed us and there's been no one in who isn't a resident since I sat down, other than deliveries of course. Your man is on the twelfth floor, flat 1203.'

Shepherd thanked him and went over to the doorman. He told the man the flat he wanted to visit, and the doorman picked up a phone and spoke to someone upstairs before handing Shepherd a keycard and nodding at the lifts. 'Twelfth floor,' said the doorman. 'You'll need the keycard to access the foyer and to press the floor button. Ditto on the way down.'

'Do you allow delivery drivers to go up to the flats?'

The doorman shook his head. 'Everything has to be left here and collected,' he said. He grinned. 'If the tenant is a good tipper I'll go up myself. But we try to keep stranger traffic to a minimum.'

'Good to know,' said Shepherd.

He used the card to open the door to the lift foyer. One of the lifts was waiting with its door open. There was a keypad above the floor buttons and Shepherd pressed his card against it before pressing the button for the twelfth floor. The door glided shut and the lift rose smoothly. There was a CCTV camera looking down at him. Security seemed faultless, but Shepherd knew from experience that every system could be overridden or bypassed.

He arrived at the twelfth floor and the door slid open with barely any sound. There were four apartments on each floor and 1203 was to the left. Another CTSFO was sitting outside. It was Harry. He stood up as Shepherd stepped out of the lift, his hand moving inside his jacket, but he smiled when he recognised Shepherd. He pressed the doorbell and almost immediately Ronnie opened the door.

Ronnie's eyes darted left and right, his hand inside his jacket, but he too relaxed when he saw it was Shepherd. 'Welcome to our humble abode,' he said. 'I've never seen a safe house like this before.' He ushered Shepherd inside before closing and locking the door. 'It has, as the estate agents like to say, views to die for.' He took Shepherd along a corridor to a huge kitchen with floor-to-ceiling glass windows that overlooked the harbour, the river, and south London beyond. In the distance,

Shepherd could see his own block in Battersea. 'This place cost eight million quid,' said Ronnie.

'Sounds about right.' Shepherd knew the background to the apartment. It had been taken from an Irish drugs baron currently serving a twelve-year sentence in Belmarsh Prison. The flat, and three others, had been seized under the 2002 Proceeds of Crime Act, along with several million pounds and euros that the drugs baron had wrongly thought had been well hidden in overseas bank accounts.

'Oh, it's definitely right, I googled it. I guess Mr Lewis is some sort of VIP to warrant the five-star treatment?'

'I think the house in Reading is more his level, to be honest,' said Shepherd. 'But because of what happened there, security has become an issue, and this place is as secure as they come.'

Ronnie gestured at a large gleaming stainless steel coffee machine. 'Fancy a coffee? I think the beans are the ones that have been through a beaver or an otter or whatever.'

'Yeah, go on,' said Shepherd. He sat on one of six stools around a marble-topped island. Eight million pounds seemed about right, all the appliances were top of the range brands, and the countertops were made from the same marble as the kitchen island, probably Italian and definitely expensive.

Ronnie busied himself at the coffee maker. It hissed steam as a strong aroma of roasted beans assailed Shepherd's nostrils. 'Googled this too, and it turns out it's a Synesso Cyncra, made in America and retailing for twelve and a half thousand dollars. Milk?'

'Just a splash, and no sugar,' said Shepherd.

The CTSFO carried two mugs of steaming coffee over to the island. Shepherd took a sip and nodded his approval. 'Nice,' he said.

'Right, we're here until this evening and then two other CTSFOs will take over. Mitch Flynn and Marc Robinson. I gather you've already met them.'

Shepherd nodded. 'Perfect.'

Ronnie took another sip of coffee. 'Seems there was a bit of a shootout when they tried to get another of your charges to a safe house in Stanmore.'

'They told you about that, did they?'

Ronnie frowned and put down his mug. 'Was it need-to-know?'

Shepherd shrugged. 'I suppose not.'

'They said it got a bit hairy.'

'That's certainly true. The principal died.'

'Who is it exactly we're up against, Dan?'

'That really is need to know, Ronnie. Sorry. But I can tell you that they have access to a roster of hired guns. Some former military, some gang bangers, probably a lot we don't know about. And they seem to have access to various government databases, the likes of DVLA.'

'That's not good,' said Ronnie.

'It's not,' said Shepherd. 'They were on Ricky Lewis within hours of him using an Uber which is why we've had to move him here.'

'Your man does like to complain, doesn't he?'

'He is a bit of a moaner, yes.'

'We're just keeping away from him and letting Jimmy handle him.'

'Probably best. Where are they?'

'Out on the terrace. Zero risk of snipers but we've told them to come inside whenever a helicopter comes within range.' said Ronnie.

Shepherd finished his coffee and went back down the hall to the sitting room, which was in the corner of the building, giving it panoramic views south and east. One of the biggest TV screens he'd ever seen was on one wall, flanked by six-foot-high aluminium speakers. Sliding doors opened onto a large terrace where Sharpe and Lewis were sitting on two sofas placed at an angle to look out over the river. They both had their feet up on a chrome and glass coffee table and were holding bottles of beer. Lewis was puffing on a large cigar. They both twisted around to look at him as he walked onto the terrace. Sharpe raised his bottle in salute. 'Fancy a beer?'

'Nah, I'm good,' said Shepherd. He smiled over at Lewis. 'This is a bit more salubrious, right, Ricky?'

'It's still a bloody prison,' said Lewis. 'But if I was in prison, at least I'd be allowed to make phone calls. Jimmy won't let me have a mobile.'

'The guys who are after you are tech savvy, Ricky. We can't take the risk of them tracking you again.'

'And Jimmy says I can't go out. Is that right?'

'Ricky, mate, it's your call. We've resolved the Spanish situation for you, the Colombians will leave you alone for now.'

'Seriously?'

'Yeah, they've been warned off and they took it to heart.'

'So I can go?'

'As I said, it's your call. The Colombians won't be paying to have you killed, but The Office might well take your betrayal to heart. They almost killed you this morning. If Jimmy hadn't been on his toes, they could well have done what they set out to do and we wouldn't be having this conversation.'

'They were amateurs,' said Lewis. 'Great at shooting pillows, but people, not so much.'

'As I said, if it hadn't been for Jimmy it would have ended very differently.'

'The fact that two of their guys were killed means they're less likely to try again, right?'

'I don't know, Ricky. You can think about it and let Razor know what you decide. If you want protection, it'll be available until we shut down The Office. If you want to make your own arrangements, that's up to you.' He nodded at Sharpe. 'Can I have a word?'

'Sure,' said Sharpe. He stood up, put his bottle of beer on the coffee table, and followed Shepherd inside. Shepherd slid the glass door closed before speaking. 'There's a problem, Razor. They know who you are. They had the picture from your driving licence and the registration number of your Jag.'

'How the hell did they do that?'

'Almost certainly through your phone. Ricky installed the app, they tracked him through the Uber bookings, that gave them your phone number.'

'There's a hell of a jump from a phone number to DVLA information.'

Shepherd nodded. 'They've either got very sophisticated hackers or people on the inside. Either way, they know who you are.'

Sharpe shrugged. 'It's not that serious,' he said. 'My driving licence doesn't have my home address and the Jag is registered through an NCA address. I've disabled my phone so even if they had access to the GPS it's no good to them now.'

'Sure, but we don't know how much access they had. That's the problem. What if they could access previous GPS locations? Would that ID your home? What if they can access previous text messages and calls, would that lead them to friends and family?'

'I think you're jumping at shadows now.'

'I hope so. But in no time at all they went from an Uber booking to putting two rounds into what they thought was you sleeping on the sofa. And make no mistake about it, Razor, it wasn't just Ricky they were after. They had your photograph. There's a contract out on you.'

'It wouldn't be the first time. And I change my phone with every job. All the calls and texts are job related on that phone.'

'Just be careful, okay?'

'I always am. You didn't work undercover for twenty-five years without picking up a few pointers.'

'I'm not trying to teach my grandmother to suck eggs. I just don't want anything happening to you while you're in my care. What I'm saying is that you and Ricky need to stay here for the duration. It's as safe as Fort Knox.'

'Don't go jinxing it, Spider. They always claimed that the Titanic was unsinkable until the moment it bumped into that iceberg.' He grinned. 'I hear what you're saying and yes, we'll stay put. We can order anything we want from Deliveroo?'

'Within reason. I'll get some burner phones sent around.'

'And booze?'

'Sure, again within reason.'

'Well that and my NCA overtime payments will keep a smile on my face. How's the investigation going?'

'We've spoken to the guys who took out the contract on Ricky. Don't tell him that, though. They've given up their contact in Barcelona and we're hoping he'll roll over on The Office.'

'Are the Spanish cops involved?'

'Definitely not.'

'Probably best.'

'Yeah, that's my view, too. We're on the case, Razor, I'm hoping we can shut down The Office sooner rather than later.'

'Hey, so long as the overtime payments keep coming, I'm happy. I've been wanting to upgrade the Jag for a while.'

CHAPTER 39

'This looks as good a spot as any,' said Harper. They were in the Montseny Nature Reserve, an hour's drive from Barcelona. The reserve included three mountains, lush woodlands including cork oak woods and pine and fir forests. Marsden had driven the Mercedes into one of the pine forests, initially on a decent tarmac road, but for the last two minutes they had been driving on a single rutted track. Marsden nodded and came to a halt. He switched off the engine and they wound their windows down. There was nothing to hear other than the wind rustling through the pines and the occasional call of a bird.

'Where are we?' asked Kristiansen, his voice muffled by the linen bag they'd pulled over his head. Harper had used the taser to keep him quiet as they drove through Barcelona but there was no way they could keep doing that for a full hour so they had put the hood over his head and told him that if he didn't speak, they wouldn't hurt him. While he was unconscious, Harper had taken the man's mobile phone – a new model iPhone – from his pocket.

'Your destination,' said Harper. He opened the door, climbed out, and then dragged Kristiansen after him.

Wallace and Marsden got out and joined Harper. They bundled Kristiansen through the trees. Kristiansen kept stumbling and he was having trouble breathing. His foot caught on a root and he yelped as he hit the ground. Wallace and Marsden pulled him to his feet. Kristiansen's chest was heaving and his legs seemed to have gone numb. Harper reached over and pulled off the hood. Kristiansen looked around, his eyes wide and fearful.

'Calm down, mate,' said Harper. 'Just breathe slowly, get your heart rate down.'

Kristiansen took a couple of deep breaths. 'That's it,' said Harper. 'Now start walking.'

'Why? We can talk here, can't we? What do you want?'

Harper produced the taser again and pulled the trigger. Kristiansen flinched as the prongs crackled. 'Walk, don't talk. Okay?'

Tears welled up in Kristiansen's eyes but he nodded and started walking. Wallace and Marsden walked either side and Harper followed. The only sound came from their shoes crunching on the pine needles that littered the ground.

They walked for the best part of ten minutes then Harper told Kristiansen to stop. He did as he was told and turned to look at Harper. Tears were running down his face. 'Please don't do this,' he said.

Harper waved the taser in front of him. 'Take off your clothes,' he said.

'You don't have to do this,' he said. Harper reached out with the taser, his finger tightening on the trigger. 'Okay, okay,' said Kristiansen quickly. 'I'll do it.'

He took off his suit jacket, looked around as if expecting to see a hook to hang it on, then dropped it onto the ground. He took off his tie, his shirt, then a string vest. He dropped them onto the suit jacket, then kicked off his shoes. He looked at Harper fearfully. 'Everything?'

Harper nodded. 'Everything.'

Kristiansen bent down and pulled off his socks, then undid his belt and let his trousers fall down to his ankles. He stepped out of his trousers, bent down and picked them up, then dropped them on the rest of his clothes. Now he was only wearing underpants, soiled at the front where he'd wet himself. Harper gestured at them with his chin and Kristiansen took them off. He shuddered as he dropped the underpants onto the pile of clothes, then cupped his hands together over his privates, which had shrunk to almost nothing, either through fear or the cold.

'You don't have to do this,' he said.

Harper grimaced. 'Yeah, we do.'

'I've got money. I can pay.'

Wallace pulled a Glock from his jacket. Then he took a bulbous suppressor from his pocket and screwed it into the barrel. 'Better safe than sorry,' he said.

Kristiansen stared at the gun in horror. 'Whatever they're paying you, I'll double that,' he said, his voice trembling.

'What do you think, guys? Should we take his money?'

'How much does he have?' asked Marsden.

'That's a good question,' said Harper. He looked at Kristiansen. 'How much have you got?'

'Probably four hundred thousand euros in my safe at home. Maybe half a million. Plus, some US dollars. Two hundred thousand dollars. And my watches, I have a Patek—'

Harper silenced him with a wave of the hand. 'There's no way we're going back to your home.' He waved at Marsden. 'Do it.'

'No!' said Kristiansen, throwing up his hands. 'Please don't. I can do a bank transfer.'

'How are you going to do that when you're stark bollock naked in the middle of a forest?'

'My phone,' he said. 'I can use an app to make a transfer. You give me your account number and I'll make the transfer.'

Harper reached into his jacket pocket and took out the phone. 'How much can you transfer?'

'I've got a fifty thousand euro limit but I have three accounts so I can transfer one hundred and fifty thousand.'

Harper handed over the phone. 'Do it,' he said.

Kristiansen tapped at the screen with a trembling hand. After a few seconds he looked up. 'What's the account number?'

Harper gave him the sort code and account number of a bank in Gibraltar. Kristiansen frowned and tapped away at the screen for almost a minute. Eventually he looked up. 'Okay, it's done,' he said. 'A hundred and fifty thousand euros are now in your account.'

Harper took the phone from him and looked at the screen. The transaction had gone through.

'So, are we good?' asked Kristiansen. 'Can I go now?'

'Mate, you have to know that this was never about money.'

Kristiansen frowned. 'What do you mean?'

'You know what I mean. The people you've betrayed don't care about cold, hard cash. They care about trust. Their business is based on trust. And when you betray that trust . . .' Harper shrugged. 'Well, that's when you end up naked in a forest with three men you don't know.'

'I haven't betrayed anyone.'

'That's not what we've been told. Now, why don't you get down on your knees so that you don't have so far to fall.'

Kristiansen held up his hands. They were shaking. 'You have

to listen to me. I haven't betrayed anyone. You're talking about
The Office, right? About Nev?'

'I'm talking about betrayal, pal. Now get down on your knees.'

'No, no, no, listen to me. Let me speak to Nev. Neville
Kingsley. I've got his direct line. Let me call him, I'll get this
sorted out.'

Harper opened the phone's address book and scrolled
through it. 'There's no Neville Kingsley here.'

'I don't use his name. It's coded. He's listed as Pizza.'

'Pizza?'

'No one's going to think twice about a listing for pizza on
a phone, are they? Come on, give me the phone and let me
call him.'

Harper smiled. 'That's not going to happen.' He put the
phone back in his pocket. 'Do you want to die?'

'Of course not.' Kristiansen's hands were back covering his
privates.

Harper gestured at Wallace, who was filming on his phone.
'Well, if Neville Kingsley ever finds out that you gave us his
direct line, that's what's going to happen to you.'

Kristiansen shook his head in confusion. 'I don't understand.'

'Yes, you do,' said Harper. 'You've just betrayed Kingsley
and The Office, and we both know what he does to people
who betray him.'

'You're not going to kill me?'

'Well that wouldn't be fair, would it? Not after you gave us
a hundred and fifty thousand euros.'

'I'm free?'

Harper shrugged. 'Our business is done here, but if you
ever tell anyone, I've no doubt that The Office will send
someone else to finish what we started. So, mum's the word?'

Kristiansen frowned. "'Mum's the word"?'

'It means you keep quiet. You don't tell anyone. And I mean *anyone*. Do you understand that? You tell anyone, anyone at all, and if Kingsley doesn't kill you, I will.'

'I understand.'

'This Kingsley. What does he look like?'

'I don't know. I've never met him.'

'But you do business with him?'

'On the phone. Sometimes we talk, but usually we use Signal.'

'What do you know about him?' asked Harper.

'Just his name. And that he runs The Office.'

'But how did you first get in touch with him?'

'A friend of a friend gave me an email address. That's how I made contact. I had a client who wanted someone taking out in London. It went well, I paid the fee and the job was done. I've used him half a dozen times over the past couple of years. Word gets around, you know?'

'I know. Now you're the go-to guy for getting people killed, no questions asked. You might want to think about shutting down that line of business.'

Kristiansen nodded furiously. 'Yes, sure, I will.' He bent down and picked up his underwear.

Harper turned to go.

'Wait!' said Kristiansen. 'You're not taking me back to the city?'

'Yeah, that's not going to happen.' He nodded at Wallace and Marsden 'Let's go.'

'How am I supposed to get home?' said Kristiansen.

'That's your problem,' said Harper. 'Just be grateful you're not six feet under.'

CHAPTER 40

S hepherd spent the rest of the day in Thames House. He spent several hours with Donna Walsh running through the surveillance options for when Zlatnar was released. He had spoken to Martin Williams who confirmed that both Donnelly and Zlatnar had met with a solicitor and that the solicitor had made an application for bail. The GPS tracker in Zlatnar's phone was working, even though it was switched off. Shepherd spent the rest of the time on the office computer working his way through unsolved killings over the past ten years, trying to find more examples of The Office's work, and researching Iranian dissidents in the UK, looking for potential targets. The last census had shown that there were more than a hundred thousand Iranians living in the UK, half of them in London, many of whom had fled the Islamic regime. But there were supporters of the Islamic Republic also living in the UK, and there were frequent clashes between the two groups.

Counter-terrorism police regularly thwarted plots by Iran to kidnap or kill British or UK-based individuals it considered enemies of the regime, but it was only in the past two years that Iran had started paying for the assassination of its opponents, which is when MI5 had stepped in.

The most popular areas for Iranians to live were Regent's

Park, Acton, Finchley and Kensington. Most of the Iranians who had fled their country were happy enough to start new lives in the UK, but many were committed to bringing down the Islamic regime. There were London-based news agencies and TV stations dedicated to reporting the type of stories that were censored in Iran, and there were individuals who used social media to criticise and even make fun of the Islamic regime. All were now in the firing line, and there were so many that it would be impossible to provide protection for them all. Over the course of two hours, Shepherd had come up with more than a hundred potential targets.

While he was researching targets, Layla Latifi's name kept coming up. She'd had a website that received a lot of traffic, several thousand visitors a day, detailing life in Iran under the Islamic regime. Shepherd tried to go to the website but the site had gone. There was no sign of it.

Shepherd went down a floor and along to the Middle East and North Africa desk. In fact, there were half a dozen desks in two groups of three, and there were four analysts peering at computer screens. One of them was wearing large over-ear headphones and her lips were moving in sync with whatever she was listening to. In charge of the desk was Manoj Kamath, a middle-aged Asian with spiky black gelled hair and black-framed spectacles. He was in an adjoining office with three screens lined up across his desk. Shepherd tapped on Kamath's door.

'Can I pick your brains, Manoj?' Kamath was a Canadian who had spent eight years working for the Canadian Security Intelligence Service in Toronto before transferring to MI5 for what was supposed to have been a six-month secondment. He had enjoyed London so much that he had never left.

Kamath pushed his chair away from his desk. He was wearing a purple silk shirt with a Mandarin collar. 'Pick away, Dan.'

'You heard about the Iranian dissident who was killed in Richmond Park?'

'Ah, yes, Layla Latifi. That was terrible. Any joy finding the killer?'

'Not so far, no. It was clearly a professional hit.'

'Yeah, there's been too many of those lately.'

'She has a website, right? Reporting on events back in Iran?'

'She does, and there's a blog linked to the website. The blog is ostensibly written by a girl called Jasmine who is living in Tehran. But the writing style is the same as the articles on the website so we always assumed that Layla was Jasmine.'

'Did you ever meet her?'

'No, but we regularly checked her website. There was never anything groundbreaking on her site, mainly she just copied things she saw on TikTok and YouTube, along with her own comments. Her big thing was girls being beaten for not wearing the hijab, stuff like that.'

'The website seems to be down.'

'Strange,' said Kamath. He scooted his chair closer to his desk and tapped on his keyboard. He frowned. 'You're right. And the blog's gone, too. I can't imagine that's a coincidence.'

'Would you have backups?'

'Not personally, no. But you can never totally remove anything from the internet. Everything is out there somewhere. It's just a matter of digging until you find it.'

'Do you have someone who can dig?'

'I do. One of my guys is an internet wizard, I'll get him on it.'

'As a matter of urgency?'

Kamath grinned. 'Of course.'

Shepherd thanked him. Darkness had fallen outside and he decided to head home. It was a forty-minute walk but Shepherd took more than an hour to stroll along the Embankment, cross Chelsea Bridge and walk through Battersea Park. His mind was on the case, but he was also carrying out counter-surveillance.

Eventually he reached the main entrance of his apartment block and put out his hand to tap in the PIN code to open the door. He sensed something behind him and started to turn but froze when something hard pressed against the back of his head.

'Bang, bang, you're dead,' hissed a voice.

'How old are you, Lex?' said Shepherd.

'Just testing your defences,' said Harper. 'And you failed.'

Shepherd didn't turn around. 'You're wearing jeans that are a bit too tight for you, last year's Nikes and a brown leather bomber jacket over a denim shirt.' He turned around and grinned when he saw that he was a hundred per cent correct. It was Harper, making a gun with his right hand.

'You saw my reflection,' said Harper.

'No, mate, I saw you when I did a walk by on the other side of the road five minutes ago. I just wanted you to have your fun.' The two men hugged. 'Welcome back. All good?'

'Everything went as planned, so, yes.'

Shepherd opened the door and walked with Harper to the lifts. 'Nothing I need to be worried about?' Shepherd asked as they stepped into the lift.

'No bodies, if that's what you're worried about.'

'Excellent,' said Shepherd.

They rode up in the lift to Shepherd's floor in silence. They didn't speak again until they were inside Shepherd's flat. 'Beer?' Shepherd asked.

'What have you got?'

'Heineken. Peroni. And some cans of Guinness.'

'Oh yes, the black stuff will be fine.'

Harper dropped down on the sofa while Shepherd fetched two cans of Guinness from the fridge and two glasses from an overhead cupboard. He put the cans and glasses on the table and flopped down onto an armchair. Harper took a phone from his pocket and handed it to Shepherd.

'This belonged to the Danish private eye I mentioned, Kurt Kristiansen. The Spanish guys placed their contract through him. The password has been disabled, so feel free.' He popped the tab on one of the cans and carefully poured his Guinness into a glass.

'He gave this to you, did he?'

'He was naked in the middle of a forest with guys with guns,' said Harper. 'He'd probably have given me a blow job if I'd asked him.'

'But he's okay?'

'We let him go. He knows that his life will be worth nothing if The Office find out, so he's not going to be telling anybody what happened.' He gestured at the phone. 'Your man Kingsley is listed under Pizza.'

'Pizza?'

'No one looks twice at a listing for pizza,' said Harper.

'Have you had a look through it?'

Harper shook his head. 'Not my business,' he said. 'What happens now?'

'I'll get the technical boys to go through the phone and take a look at deleted messages and so on, and we'll take a good look at Kingsley's phone activity.' Shepherd put the phone on the coffee table and poured himself a Guinness.

'How much do you know about him, this Kingsley?' asked Harper.

'Nothing, other than a name. He's cagey.'

'And he does it for what? The money?'

'It seems like a professional set-up,' said Shepherd. 'But a lot of their recent contracts are political. The Iranians are getting rid of dissidents who are critical of the regime. I guess the guys carrying out the contracts don't care, right?'

'That would depend on the guy,' said Harper. He sipped his drink. 'Horses for courses. Some hired guns only care about the money. Women, children, old folk, they'll do whatever needs to be done to collect the fee. Others, well they need to know a bit more.'

'What about you, Lex?'

Harper held up a hand. 'Woah, Spider. Are you making this personal?'

'Sorry, mate. It's just you've never made a secret of the fact that you worked for The Pool, and The Pool does more than its fair share of dirty jobs.'

'It does. But when The Pool gets a contract, it's because someone's been naughty. You know that when you do a job for The Pool, you're on the side of the angels.'

'What about women and children?'

Harper shook his head. 'I wouldn't. But I'd never be put in that position. Charlie knows me, she knows I've got lines that I won't cross.'

'But she has others she can call on?'

Harper chuckled. 'The Pool has plenty of psychopaths on its books, that's true. Several of them from your old mob.'

Shepherd nodded. He had come across a fair number of psychopaths during his time with the Regiment. Selection tended to weed them out, along with the wannabes and fantasists, but some did get through and only revealed their true colours once they had won the right to wear the coveted sand-coloured beret. Killing was part of the job. Soldiers were warriors and part of being a warrior meant killing the enemy.

Shepherd had killed, but he had never taken pleasure from the act. Killing was a necessary evil, and taking a life was never a good thing, even when it was done for the right reasons. Even without his near-perfect photographic memory he would never forget any of the lives he had taken. Sometimes at night the memories would play back as he lay on his bed and stared up at the ceiling, visions of rounds smacking into bodies, of men taking their last breaths, their faces confused and saddened as their lives ebbed away.

The worst memories were from the days when Shepherd had been a sniper. He had come to hate those days with a vengeance. At the time, he had taken pride in his sniping skills, and the enemy in his sights was always an enemy that would happily have killed Shepherd if given the chance. He had pulled the trigger and waited seconds for the round to reach its target, then feel a warm feeling of satisfaction as the target had fallen and died. But over the years since, he had come to regret the lives he had taken at a distance, and the regret had solidified the day that he had taken a sniper's bullet in the shoulder in the badlands of Afghanistan. The man who had almost taken Shepherd's life didn't know anything about him, who he was, or what he was doing in his country, he had just aimed and pulled the trigger. A few inches to the side and Shepherd would have been dead. As it was, it was only a prompt medevac helicopter that had saved his life.

Shepherd had come to believe that if you were going to kill someone, they deserved to see the face of the man who was pulling the trigger. But even then, up close and personal, he never felt pleasure in taking a life. Satisfaction from doing a job well, perhaps, but not pleasure. Anyone who enjoyed taking lives was a psychopath, even if they were killing in the name of King and country.

Harper was right. The SAS had counted psychopaths in its ranks over the years, but they always revealed themselves eventually. When they were weeded out, they often ended up in the private sector, or living rough, or taking their own lives. Those that did end up working as assassins usually had no reservations about their targets.

'Do you know any that fit the bill?' asked Shepherd.

'Contract killers tend not to socialise together,' said Harper. 'They're not great ones for small talk. You'd need to ask Charlie Button who she has on her books.' He grinned. 'Not that she's likely to tell you.'

'I think she's already been asked at a level above my pay grade,' said Shepherd.'

'And they believe what she tells them?'

'She depends on the good grace of the government,' said Shepherd. 'They could shut her down in a heartbeat if they wanted to.'

'That's never going to happen. Who else would they get to do their dirty work?'

Shepherd sipped his Guinness. 'I take your point, but I don't think she'd lie. Not on the record, anyway.'

'Why don't you ask her?' said Harper. He grinned. 'Pillow talk.'

Shepherd shook his head. 'Never happened,' he said.

'Come on, there was always a spark between you, wasn't there?'

'You're a bad man, Lex.'

'You know I'm right, Spider. I tell you, I've always fancied her. Nice bit of posh, I always figured she'd be something special in the sack.'

Shepherd sighed. 'She used to be my boss, Lex.'

'Sleeping with your boss isn't illegal.'

'It's not encouraged, either,' said Shepherd. 'But it was never an issue.' He drank his Guinness. 'Anyway, back to the real world. I need you to shadow me for the next couple of days. Just be my wingman.'

'You really think they're after you?'

'They know that I was trying to infiltrate their organisation, they might want to take me out as a warning to others.'

'But do they know who you are? Presumably you used a decent legend?'

Shepherd nodded. 'Darren Griffiths. There's a flat in Wapping in that name, and a Range Rover parked under the building. The flat and the car are being watched.'

'MI5 legends are watertight,' said Harper.

'They are, yes. But these guys are a whole different level, Lex. They found one of our safe houses and got a team there within hours. That shouldn't have happened. They have government-level intel, so I need to assume the worst.'

'So, who's helping them? Or do you think they have sleeper agents in place? Criminal gangs have been doing it for years, getting their own people in the cops so that they can access the PNC and the like. And you know that even your own mob has been penetrated by Islamic fundamentalists.'

Shepherd narrowed his eyes. 'How do you know that?'

Harper chuckled. 'Mate, everyone knows. They're in Five, Six, the cops, the ports, the airports, hell, they're even in Border Force. Everyone has gone so crazy about increasing diversity that they've let their guard down. It's all part of the long game.'

'I can't believe you're still plugging away with those conspiracy theories, Lex.'

Harper shrugged. 'Tell me that Five hasn't had to sack people because they realised that their hearts weren't in the right place?'

'A few bad apples don't count,' said Shepherd.

'Oh, they do when one bad apple can bring the whole system crashing down. Anyway, conspiracy theories aside, I'm just making the point that these guys might well have their own people in place, and if they're in Thames House, you have serious problems.'

'They also seem to be able to track phones, almost in real time.'

'Sleeper agents in the phone companies? That's easily done.'

'But it's so well organised. Someone has to pull all this together.'

'Which brings us back to the fragrant Charlie Button.'

'There's no way she'd put me at risk. We've got too much history.'

'Who then?'

Shepherd grimaced. 'The Russians, maybe? The Chinese?'

Harper snorted. 'And you give me grief for conspiracy theories.'

'Hear me out,' said Shepherd. 'It's definitely the Iranian government who are placing the contracts, using The Office to do their dirty work. It keeps them twice removed from the assassinations, they pay The Office and The Office hires local talent. The guys doing the actual hit have no idea who the ultimate client is, so even if they get caught, the Iranians are safe.'

'Plausible deniability,' said Harper.

'Exactly. But I don't see how this Neville Kingsley character could have access to all these intel sources. That'd make him like some James Bond villain, pulling strings around the world.'

'Wouldn't that make you James Bond?'

'James Bond is MI6, Lex.'

'And a fictional character, let's not forget.' Harper sipped his Guinness. 'So what you're saying, if you don't mind me cutting to the chase, is that far from being a criminal master-mind, someone is running *him*? Pulling *his* strings?'

'That would make more sense. And that brings me back to the Chinese and the Russians. Both have been running all sorts of dirty tricks operations in the UK for years. Cyberattacks, messing with our supply lines, election interference, civil unrest, exploitation, social media disinformation. This is all proven, Lex. After those kids were killed in Southport, it was the Russians who were spreading the rumour that the attacker was an illegal immigrant leading to riots in the streets. And the Chinese have been accumulating intelligence sources across the country. They even got their claws into Prince Andrew. It would make perfect sense for either the Chinese or the Russians to be running Kingsley.'

'Would the Iranians know?'

'Possibly. The Russians have been helping Iran for years, with weapons sales, training, and intelligence sharing, and the Russians gave the Iranians a head start with their drone programme. And they worked together to support the Assad regime in Syria. Birds of a feather.'

'And China?'

'China's support for Iran has always been more economic than military. China is Iran's largest trading partner, and has helped Iran bypass US-led sanctions for years. And China has invested heavily in Iranian ports, railways, and energy facilities. But China wouldn't be doing this to help Iran, it'd be about screwing with the UK.'

'And let's not start on Covid,' said Harper, raising his glass in the air. 'How they got away with that, I'll never know. Started an epidemic that crippled the West, then sold us the equipment to deal with it.'

'We're back onto conspiracy theories, are we?'

'Did you allow them to inject the so-called vaccine into you?' asked Harper.

'I did, yes. Three times.'

'And how is that working out for you?'

Shepherd grinned. 'So far, so good.'

CHAPTER 41

Shepherd woke up to the smell of bacon frying. He grabbed a dressing gown and padded to the kitchen. 'Ah, the early bird,' said Harper, waving a spatula over a frying pan. 'Bacon butty?'

'Hell yeah,' said Shepherd. 'I'll make coffee.' He switched on the kettle.

'Now the big question is, of course, red sauce or brown?' said Harper.

Shepherd gestured at one of the overhead cupboards. 'The HP sauce is in there,' he said.

'Good call.'

Shepherd made two mugs of coffee while Harper made the sandwiches. They took the food over to the sofa and Shepherd used the remote to turn the TV to Sky News.

'What's the plan today?' asked Harper.

'I'll take the private eye's phone into the office and let Amar Singh work his magic.'

'You think that will lead to this Neville Kingsley character?'

'That's the plan.'

'And obviously you've run the name through all the data-bases?'

'Yeah. We're fairly sure it's not his real name. Paul Dutch, the guy who got killed, met him once and we have a physical description. I spoke to him on the phone once and he definitely has a Black Country accent, but that's all we have.'

'And it's all about money?'

Shepherd frowned. 'What do you mean?'

'I mean, is that all it is? This Neville makes his living from organising contracts. It's not huge money, is it? He takes a percentage of the contract, he can't be making more than a few million at most.'

'That's big money, Lex.'

'There's more money in drugs.' He chuckled. 'There's more money to be made on OnlyFans.'

'Yeah, well I don't think he'd get much flashing his tits on video.'

'You'd be surprised what sells out there,' said Harper. 'No, what I mean is that this dissident thing puts a different spin on it. I get that the Iranians are devious buggers and always try to get others to fight their battles, but it just feels that there's something else going on here. Like somebody's screwing with the British government.'

'Who would that be?'

Harper shrugged. 'Probably the French.'

Shepherd laughed. 'Seriously?'

'They've always hated us, the French.'

They finished their sandwiches and Shepherd went to shave, shower, and change into a suit and tie. When he got back, Harper had cleaned the plates, mugs, and frying pan, and wiped down the kitchen. 'Bloody hell, you're house trained,' said Shepherd.

'You have to be when you live alone.'

'I thought you'd have a team of maids in Thailand.'

'Never let strangers in your house,' said Harper. 'First rule of not getting caught.'

'Getting caught doing what?'

Harper grinned. 'Doing anything. How are you planning to get to the office?'

'I was going to cab it.'

'I'll drive. I'm here to protect you, right? Best way is if I start driving you. That way I'll be close by.'

'Okay,' said Shepherd. He tossed the key fob to Harper and they took the lift down to the underground car park.

Harper drove Shepherd to Thames House, but dropped him around the corner and parked up. 'Sure you don't want me to come inside?' Harper asked.

'I'm not sure that I can get you authorisation,' said Shepherd.

'I'm hardly an enemy of the state.'

Shepherd grinned. 'Not sure that everyone shares that view. Anyway, I won't be long.'

Shepherd climbed out and went to the main entrance on Millbank. He went straight up to Amar Singh's office. Singh was working on a circuit board with a soldering iron and he waved Shepherd over to a stool, his face covered by a protective mask. 'Won't be long,' he said.

Shepherd sat down while Singh worked away. After a couple of minutes, Singh sat back and flipped up his mask. 'All done,' he said. 'Sorry about that, it's a rush job.'

'No problem,' said Shepherd. He handed Kristiansen's phone over. 'Another rush job, I'm afraid. We need a full breakdown of all calls and messages made from this, with emphasis on anything to do with the number marked Pizza.' Singh grinned but Shepherd gestured with his chin. 'Pizza is Neville Kingsley, we think. The guy that runs The Office.'

'Got you,' said Singh.

'And we need anything we can get on the Pizza number.'

'Who's the provider?'

'I'm not sure.'

'What's the number?'

Shepherd gave it to him and Singh tapped on one of his keyboards. 'Vodafone,' he said. 'That might take time. They're always backed up.'

'Anything we can do to fast-track it?'

'Everyone fast-tracks their requests,' said Singh. 'The phone companies only have small teams dedicated to police data inquiries. It's a funding issue. They don't see why they should be paying for information retrieval when it's on the scale that it is now. When the cops first realised that they could use GPS data and call and text records to track criminals, there were only a few requests each day. Now there are hundreds, sometimes thousands. Criminal investigation 101 is now to check every phone they can and the phone companies are struggling to cope. Sure, I can mark it urgent but that's what everybody does. No one puts in a request and says there's no rush, do it when you can.'

'Is there any way of bypassing the phone companies?'

'If we have the phone, sure. I can do a data dump myself, and if the GPS was on I can follow the phone wherever it went. But if all we have is the number then we've got no choice other than to use the phone companies. I have contacts I can use in some of the companies, but Vodafone isn't one of them unfortunately. We've been trying to persuade the phone companies to give us direct access to their mainframes but they're resisting.'

'Presumably there are data protection considerations?'

'That's their line, yes.' He grinned. 'No pun intended.'

'Answer me this, The Office seemed to be able to track

phones in real time. Within hours rather than days. How are they able to do that?'

'Well, to be fair, we can do that if we have the cooperation of the phone companies. It's not difficult. We just need access to their GPS data, or if the GPS is off, we need to be able to look at their cell tower data to see where the phone is pinging off. Now the bad guys clearly aren't going to have the official cooperation of the phone companies, but they could easily have someone on the inside. Same as I do, I have personal contacts who'll do me a favour because they know I'm with Five. I did have a girl at Vodafone who would help, but she's on maternity leave. Anyway, I'm sure there are other employees who'll do the same thing for a brown envelope filled with cash.'

'But they'd need someone in every company and there must be dozens of mobile phone companies, surely?'

'It's not as complicated as that because there are basically only four mobile networks in the UK,' said Singh. 'Vodafone, EE, O2, and Three. There are lots of mobile providers, sure, but they're actually Mobile Virtual Network Operators and they all have to offer their services through one of the big four networks. So, in theory, you'd only need four bent employees to cover the whole country. They'd have to have access to the main computer, obviously. I mean your average sales assistant in a network shop wouldn't be any use, but there are thousands of head office workers who'd have access.'

Singh plugged a lead into the bottom of the phone, then bent over his keyboard. He tapped away for a couple of minutes and then sat back, grinning. 'Well that was easy,' he said. 'Is this a burner?'

'I guess so,' said Shepherd.

'Most of his communication has been through Signal and

WhatsApp, which are both encrypted at either end. Once deleted they're gone for good, but the last half a dozen texts to Pizza are still there. And the phone records show that he called that number several times two weeks ago.'

'That'll be him arranging the contract,' said Shepherd.

'He's had the GPS turned off, which means we'll need to talk to the Spanish service provider. There are four in Spain – Movistar, Vodafone, Orange, and Yoigo – and your guy is with Movistar. They'll be able to tell us which towers the phone pinged off, but I'll be honest, it'll take weeks rather than days. Since Brexit the Spanish seem to take pleasure in making life difficult for us.'

'No, there's no need,' said Shepherd. 'It belongs to a middleman, we're more interested in the Pizza number.'

'Okay, I hear you,' said Singh. 'I'll see what I can do. There's more than one way to skin a cat, as my old grandad used to say.'

'He wasn't speaking from experience, I hope.'

Singh laughed. 'Nah, he just loved using English expressions, the weirder the better. Especially any that were animal-related. Not enough room to swing a cat. Cat got your tongue. Let the cat out of the bag. Take the bull by the horns. Flogging a dead horse.'

'Sounds like a fun guy.'

'Oh, he was. Passed away more than ten years ago but I think about him every day, pretty much.'

'Sorry,' said Shepherd.

'Nothing to be sorry about,' said Singh. 'He had one hell of a life and left behind three sons, two daughters, twelve grandkids and almost as many great-grandkids.' His landline rang and he picked it up. He winked at Shepherd. 'No rest for the wicked.'

Shepherd took the stairs down to the Middle East and North Africa desk. Manoj Kamath was wearing another silk shirt with a Mandarin collar, this one a bright peach colour. 'Any joy with the website?' Shepherd asked.

'Still working on the website, but we've found the blog. The last year's worth, anyway.'

'Can I have a look?'

'Sure.' He tapped on his keyboard and sat back. 'Pull up a chair.'

Shepherd grabbed a chair and sat down next to Kamath. He caught a whiff of sandalwood and orange. 'You smell good, Manoj.'

Kamath laughed. 'Birthday gift from my wife.'

The header at the top of the blog featured the back view of a black-haired girl looking at the Azadi Tower, one of the most famous buildings in Tehran, forty-five metres tall and clad in cut marble. It looked like a futuristic fortress with two sweeping legs either side of an arch and above it a severe block with a line of windows marking the observation deck. If an Iranian girl was seen standing in front of the landmark with her head uncovered, retribution would be quick and severe.

The blog was called 'Surviving Iran: Jasmine's Guide to Navigating Chaos and Corruption'.

The last entry was the day before Layla Latifi was killed. It was a story about how easy it was to buy sexy underwear in Tehran, but that men weren't allowed into the shops so they couldn't buy items for their wives. It was a funny piece and Shepherd smiled as he read it. 'So, you think that Layla wrote this?'

'I think she has sources who tell her stuff and send her

photographs, but as I said, pretty much all the writing is in her style.'

The previous piece was more serious, about Iran's morality police beating a girl unconscious on a Tehran train for not wearing a hijab. There was graphic detail of the girl's injuries and a photograph of her in a hospital bed, heavily bandaged.

The blog was a mix of funny, sad, and disturbing, but as Kamath had pointed out, they were all written in the same style.

The fifth story was brief, just one paragraph and two photographs, that looked as if they had been taken on a phone in a bar. The photographs were of an Asian man, in his sixties with a grey straggly beard and circular thick-lensed spectacles. There were two girls sitting with him, a striking blonde to his left, a short-haired brunette with impressive cleavage to his right. In one of the photographs the man was clearly staring at the brunette's cleavage, in another he was drinking what looked like champagne. The caption read: 'This man enjoying himself in a five-star Dubai hotel with two lovely ladies of the night and a bottle of Dom Perignon claims to work for the Iranian government in Tehran. Does anyone know who he is? I would love to know.'

'That's a strange one,' said Shepherd.

'No, she does that a lot,' said Kamath. 'She loves to publish pictures of Iranian government officials in embarrassing situations. People know that and send her stuff all the time. This was obviously someone in Dubai.'

'Any idea who the guy is?'

Kamath peered at the screen. He smiled. '"OMG, I think that's Jafar Hosseini."' His fingers played across the keyboard and two photographs appeared on his left-hand screen, one of a man getting out of the back of a Mercedes, the other a head and shoulder shot that seemed be an official photograph. He was in his sixties with a hooked nose that gave him the look of a bird of prey. Kamath sat back and nodded at the screen. 'Yup, that's him. Jafar Hosseini. He's a moneyman for the Islamic Republic mullahs, one of the conduits they use to finance terrorism around the world. His name came up as one of the financiers of the 2023 Hamas attacks on Israel. Hosseini was responsible for paying for much of the ordnance used in the attacks, and he paid for a number of training exercises, including the use of paragliders.'

'Do you know where he is? I mean, Layla says those pictures were in Dubai. Is that where he's based?'

'I think we've always assumed he was in Tehran,' said Kamath. 'But he could be in Dubai. That's perfectly possible. Hamas and Hezbollah both have people across the Emirates and it would be an easy place to hand over large amounts of cash.'

Shepherd nodded. Dubai was a vibrant financial centre but tended not to look too carefully at who was living there and where their money came from. Various terrorist organisations – including Hamas, Hezbollah, ISIS, al-Qaeda and the Houthis – funnelled money through bank accounts and property in the city state. 'Is he connected to the Quds Force?' asked Shepherd.

Kamath pushed his glasses up on the top of his head. 'We think so, yes. Why do you ask?'

'The FBI have just foiled an Iranian plot to kill Donald Trump and the main suspect – Ahmad Qalibaf – was involved with the Quds Force.'

Kamath nodded. 'Yes, we are aware of Qalibaf. And yes,

Hosseini is indeed involved with them. Everything that Hosseini has been doing is with the blessing of the mullahs.'

Shepherd's phone rang. He pulled it from his pocket and checked the screen. It was Martin Williams. He mouthed a 'Thanks' to Kamath and went out into the corridor.

'Yes, Martin?'

'Just to let you know that Terry Edkins has been released. Obviously there was nothing we could do to keep him. It was explained to him that there was a contract out on him but he couldn't care less. Two guys in a black BMW picked him up.'

'Did you get the number?'

'Of course. I'll text it over to you. The owner is another Scouse drug dealer.'

'Do you have an address?'

'I do. I'll send that, too.'

'Does he know about Donnelly and Zlatnar?'

'He hasn't spoken to anyone here. In fact, he only made one call and that was to the guy who picked him up.'

'And what about Donnelly? Which lawyer did he see? The duty solicitor, or did he have a name?'

'A London firm that specialises in criminal law. Bonwick, Kilgallon, and Khan. Louis Bonwick himself came in and is handling the bail application for Donnelly and Zlatnar himself. I'll keep you posted.'

Shepherd thanked him and ended the call. He sent Harper a text message, asking him to pick him up outside Thames House. He got a text back within seconds. 'I hear and obey.'

Shepherd took the lift down to the ground floor and climbed into the BMW. 'Home, James,' he said.

Harper pulled away from the kerb. 'All good?'

'Terry Edkins is out. But there's still a contract out on him.'

His phone vibrated and he looked at the screen. It was the message from Williams.

'Terry'll be fine.'

'He wasn't that fine when they had him tied up like a kipper in a warehouse.'

'Yeah, but I'm sure they caught him by surprise. Now he'll be wary.'

'Do you know him?'

'Yeah, I crossed paths with him a few times, back in the day. When I was in the Paras he was getting started selling weed in Liverpool, but then he moved into cocaine and ended up doing a three stretch. He came out at about the time I left the Paras and we did a few deals together. Nothing major, but by pooling resources we could get a better deal. He never tried to rip me off, didn't hurt anybody who didn't need hurting.'

'So why would The Office have a contract on him?'

Harper shrugged. 'No idea. Do you want me to ask him?'

'Could you?'

'It'd have to be face-to-face, he's hardly likely to spill his guts over the phone.'

Shepherd wrinkled his nose. 'The thing is, I'm not sure that knowing who has it in for him helps us.'

'It might help him.'

Shepherd checked the message that Williams had sent. The owner of the car that had picked up Edkins was Tommy McMullen, his address was in Clapham, close to the common. 'Okay, we can give it a try.'

CHAPTER 42

Tommy McMullen lived in a terraced house to the south of the common, two storeys topped by a steeply sloping tiled roof. McMullen's BMW was parked some way down the road.

'How do you want to play this?' asked Harper, as he reversed into a gap between two cars.

'You need to do most of the talking, obviously,' said Shepherd. 'The last time he saw me he was tied to a chair and I had a loaded gun in my hand. I just hope he remembers that if it wasn't for me, he'd be dead now.'

'He should be grateful, right?'

'I can never tell if you're being sarcastic or not.'

Harper grinned. 'Bit of both, I suppose. Does he know you're a secret squirrel?'

'I can't see how he would. You can tell him I'm a cop, undercover.'

'And how do I know you?'

'We're mates. From way back. And I'm just there to warn him to watch his back.'

Harper grinned. 'Sounds like a plan,' he said, as he finished parking.

They climbed out, crossed the road and walked along the pavement to McMullen's house. Harper rang the bell. The door was opened by a stocky man with a crew cut wearing a leather jacket over a tight-fitting grey T-shirt. 'What?' he scowled.

'I'm hoping Terry's here,' said Harper.

'Who the fuck are you?' said the man, squaring his shoulders as if he was about to throw a punch. He had a strong Liverpudlian accent.

'Just tell him Lex Harper is here.'

The man tilted his head on one side. 'Lex fucking Harper?'

Harper grinned. 'Yeah, but the "fucking" is silent.'

'*The* Lex Harper?'

'I think there's only the one of me, yeah.'

The man held out his hand. 'Tommy McMullen, mate. Terry talks about you all the time. Says the sun shines out of your arse.'

'That's probably a bit of an exaggeration,' said Harper.

McMullen twisted his head around and shouted down the hall. 'Hey, Terry, you'll never guess who's here.' He patted Harper on the shoulder. 'Come on in, mate.' He ushered Harper into the hall, then looked at Shepherd.

'This is my pal – Roger,' said Harper.

'Any friend of Lex's is, you know . . .' said McMullen, patting Shepherd on the shoulder. Shepherd followed Harper down the hall as McMullen closed the front door.

Edkins came out of the kitchen, arms outstretched. 'Lex fucking Harper, you're a sight for sore eyes,' he said, and hugged Harper. As he patted him on the back, he noticed Shepherd. 'What the fuck?' he said. He pushed Harper away and pointed at Shepherd. 'That's one of the fuckers that was planning to kill me!'

McMullen shoved Shepherd in the back, pushing him against the wall. He grabbed Shepherd's right arm and twisted it up between his shoulder blades. 'Hey, easy, easy,' Shepherd protested.

'Terry, mate, it's okay, he's one of the good guys,' said Harper.

'He shot at me, Lex.'

'I fired to miss,' said Shepherd calmly. 'I was the one who called the cops.'

'He's with me, Terry. He's a good guy.' He looked over at McMullen. 'Tommy, he's former SAS, if you keep annoying him like that he'll likely have your guts for garters.'

McMullen released his grip on Shepherd's arm and stood back. 'Who is he?' he growled.

'He's with me, that's all you need to be worried about.'

Shepherd massaged his arm. 'I was trying to penetrate the organisation that had taken out a contract on you,' he said to Edkins. 'They were using you as a test, to see whether I'd be prepared to kill you or not.'

'You pulled the trigger,' said Edkins.

'Mate, if I'd wanted to kill you, you'd be dead.'

'It's true, Terry. You were lucky he was there, if it had been anyone else you wouldn't be here now.'

Edkins nodded slowly. 'Okay. Yeah. Okay.' He held out his hand. 'I guess I owe you one,' he said. 'And you did beat the crap out of those other guys.'

'I did,' said Shepherd. They shook hands.

'You want a cuppa, Lex?' asked Edkins. 'I've just made a pot.'

'Yeah, go on,' said Harper. They followed Edkins into the kitchen. Edkins took two mugs from an overhead cupboard and added them to two that were already standing by a large red earthenware teapot. 'I never use teabags,' said Edkins. 'Can't beat a proper brew.'

'You're preaching to the converted,' said Harper. He sat

down at a table overlooking the rear garden. Shepherd joined him.

McMullen stood by the door, his arms folded. Edkins looked over at him. 'Relax, Tommy. If Lex vouches for . . . what did you say your name was?'

'Roger,' said Shepherd. 'Rog.'

'Roger the Dodger,' said Harper.

'If Lex vouches for Rog, that's good enough for me.' He took a bottle of milk from the fridge and poured a splash into each of the four mugs, then added tea. He put the mugs down on the table, then put down a bowl of sugar lumps and four teaspoons. 'Help yourself to white death,' he said. He sat down next to Harper. 'So, I'm guessing this isn't a social visit,' he said, and sipped his tea.

'Did the cops tell you that you were at risk?' asked Shepherd.

Edkins laughed. 'You know what I do for a living, right? Everything I do is a risk.'

'There's a contract out on you, Terry. And from my experience, the guys with the contract don't give up.'

'They won't be the first to try to take me out,' said Edkins, 'and they probably won't be the last. So, you're a cop?'

'Sort of,' said Shepherd.

'He was undercover,' said Harper. 'His operation was blown because he couldn't shoot you, and now we're here to tell you to be careful. The contract is still open.'

'I'm always careful, Lex.'

'If that's true, why were you duct-taped to a chair in a warehouse?' asked Shepherd.

'They jumped me when I was parking my car,' said Edkins. 'It won't happen again.'

'We can offer you protection, until this is over. Armed guards.'

'Plod with guns?' Edkins snorted derisively. 'How would that look?' he said. 'Everyone would assume that I'm a grass.' He shook his head. 'Nah, now I know there's a threat, I'll take precautions.'

'Where are you based these days?' asked Harper.

'London. But I'll hole up in Liverpool till this blows over.'

'Do you have any idea who might want you dead?'

'I can think of a few guys. I've had a few run-ins down here. But I would have thought they would come after me themselves. I mean, who uses a hitman to do their dirty work?'

'It happens,' said Shepherd. 'More than you'd think. A hitman is a pro, so a lot less likely to get caught. And whoever pays for the hit can set up an airtight alibi.'

'How much would it cost?'

'Probably six figures.'

Edkins snorted. 'Bloody hell, you can get someone knocked off for a couple of grand in Liverpool.'

'Yeah, but you'll be using some druggie earning his next fix, and more than likely he'll get caught in the act and roll over on the client first chance he gets,' said Shepherd. 'These guys are pros. And in the unlikely event that they do get caught, they don't know who took out the contract. The buck stops at The Office – the middleman.'

Edkins sipped his tea again. 'I'm almost flattered that someone thinks it's worth a hundred grand to knock me off.' His mouth opened and his eyes widened. 'Oh shit. I think I know who it might be. The husband of this girl I met in The May Fair. She was desperate for some blow and I gave her some and then I gave her one in the toilets.' He saw the look of disgust on Shepherd's face. 'It was consensual. In fact, I met her a few times afterwards, she loved screwing on coke, loved it. But then last month she broke it off, said her husband suspected something was going on and that he'd hired a private dick to follow her. Haven't seen her since.'

'And who was the husband?'

'Some hedge fund guy in the City. Thirty years older than her and richer than God. He has this huge flat in One Hyde Park. She took me back there one afternoon and had me screw her in every room.' He grinned. 'Took forever.'

'What's his name?'

Edkins shrugged. 'Fucked if I know. I only knew her as Celia, never knew her surname. Anyway, water under the bridge.'

'Yeah, but the husband might not see it that way,' said Shepherd. 'And the contract is still live, so you need to be careful.'

'What sort of killers do they use?' asked Edkins. 'Do I have to worry about snipers and car bombs?'

'Usually it's two guys on a motorbike,' said Shepherd. 'Though there was a lone shooter in Richmond Park recently. But we don't know for sure, a lot of the killings are below the radar, people just disappear. What we do know is that they're able to track people through their phones, so you need to be careful.'

'We always use burners,' said Edkins.

'That's good, but burn them often,' said Shepherd.

Edkins nodded and looked over at Harper. 'So how are you involved in this, Lex? You're not Five-O now, are you?'

'That'll be the day. No, I'm watching his back until it's over.'

Edkins looked back at Shepherd. 'They're after you, too?'

'I'm afraid so.'

'Bugger.'

'Yeah.'

CHAPTER 43

Harper drove Shepherd back to Battersea, taking the long way around as he ran counter-surveillance measures before driving into the underground car park. They took the lift up to Shepherd's floor, and as soon as they were inside his flat Shepherd grabbed two bottles of lager from the fridge. 'Do you think Terry'll be all right?' asked Shepherd as he dropped onto the sofa.

'He's a big boy, he can take care of himself.'

'I hope so, Lex.'

'You warned him, it's down to him if he doesn't follow your advice.' He sipped his lager. 'What's the plan tomorrow?'

'Hopefully Amar will have intel from Kingsley's phone. Ideally a location.'

'If he was using a burner, it could be gone by now.'

'That's possible. But if he trusted Kristiansen it might have been a long-term phone. He might have individual phones for individual contacts.'

'That sounds like the voice of experience.'

Shepherd nodded. 'Yeah, I tend to do that when I'm under-cover. That way when the phone rings, even if they're withholding their number I know who it is. Sometimes I might have half a dozen burners on the go. Kingsley might be doing the same.'

'And if you do find him, what then?'

'He'll be arrested and charged.'

'Conspiracy to murder?'

Shepherd nodded. 'A life sentence. And if we're lucky we'll arrest his contractors. His whole operation will be shut down.'

'Yeah, but it's like drug dealers, isn't it? You shut down one and two others will spring up to take their place. You take Kingsley down and someone else will step up.'

'What, you think we should do nothing?'

'I'm just pointing out that you're in a never-ending war that you can never win.'

'I'm happy enough to fight one battle at a time,' said Shepherd.

'And what about the Iranians?'

'What about the Iranians?'

'Well presumably Five isn't on the case because a few drugs dealers have been getting their just deserts. You're involved because the Iranians are killing off their dissidents.'

'True.'

'So, target the Iranians. Expel their ambassador. Start trade sanctions.'

'That's not going to happen until we've got evidence.'

'Don't the dead dissidents count?'

'Of course they count. But the government isn't going to do anything without proof.'

Harper gulped down some lager and wiped his mouth with the back of his hand. 'Don't you get frustrated, doing what you do?'

'Putting away bad guys, you mean?'

'I mean that no matter what you do, no matter how hard

you work, nothing really changes, does it? The world is still going to hell in a handbasket.'

Shepherd grinned. 'That's an expression I've not heard in a long time. Do you know where it came from?'

'No, but I'm sure you do.'

'Back in the 1840s, in the California gold rush, miners were lowered by hand in baskets to set explosives, and it wasn't unusual for things to go badly wrong.'

'But you take my point? Nothing you do really changes anything.'

'You're wrong, Lex. We tend not to trumpet our successes but barely a month goes by without MI5 stopping a terrorist incident. We save lives. A *lot* of lives.'

'But still they keep on coming. They keep allowing people in who don't have the best interests of the country at heart. And then you guys have to run around trying to stop things from kicking off. You're like hamsters on a wheel, running flat out and never getting anywhere.'

'Nice analogy,' said Shepherd. 'Are you hungry?'

'Are you trying to change the subject?'

'Damn right, you're starting to depress me. I was thinking about making cheesy scrambled eggs on toast. It was always my boy's favourite breakfast and I got a taste for it.'

'How is Liam?'

'He's fine. He's with the Joint Special Forces Aviation Wing these days, based in Hampshire, so I get to see him quite often. In fact, he's due up later this week.'

'What does he fly?'

'Mainly the Chinook, but he's rated for the AgustaWestland Wildcat.'

'Rather him than me,' said Harper. 'Noisy and unstable at the best of times.'

Shepherd grinned. 'Bit like you, then.' He stood up. 'So cheesy scrambled eggs?'

'Yeah. And heavy on the cheese.'

CHAPTER 44

S hepherd pointed at one of the six screens in front of him. 'There they are,' he said. 'That's Donnelly on the left and Zlatnar on the right.'

He was sitting on a plastic stool in the back of an Openreach van parked on a side street overlooking the featureless brick and concrete building that housed Bromley Magistrates' Court. The van was one of more than a dozen operated by MI5's surveillance division and there were cameras secreted all around the vehicle, and microphones capable of picking up conversations more than fifty feet away.

Sitting next to him on another plastic stool was Janet Rayner, a thirty-something brunette, her hair tied back with a Barbie-pink scrunchie. Rayner had spent a year with the Metropolitan Police's surveillance team before joining MI5, and was one of the best followers in the business.

The third member of the team in the back of the van was Matty Clayton, who had recently turned fifty and who had spent almost half his life running surveillance operations for MI5. He peered over Shepherd's shoulder. He was wearing a lightweight headset.

Along with the monitors showing the camera feeds, there was a larger screen with a GPS plan of the area and a laptop running the Met's automatic number plate recognition software. The GPS screen showed a small red dot, indicating the position of Zlatnar's mobile phone.

Shepherd had stuck photographs of Donnelly and Zlatnar on the wall of the van, either side of the monitors.

'Looks like they have a car waiting for them,' said Shepherd.

A blue Audi SUV was parked in front of the courthouse. A man climbed out of the front passenger seat and opened the offside rear passenger door. He was big, well over six feet tall, wearing a black leather jacket that strained across his shoulders. He was facing away from the van's cameras so they couldn't get a look at his face.

Donnelly and Zlatnar were wearing the same clothes that they had been wearing when they had picked up Shepherd at his flat. Between them was the solicitor who had represented them in court, Louis Bonwick, tall and well groomed, wearing a Savile Row suit and carrying a Prada briefcase. Behind them were two of Bonwick's assistants, a young Asian girl pulling a wheeled carry-on case and a tall, thin black man in a long raincoat who was carrying two large holdalls.

They walked towards the Audi, then stopped. Bonwick shook hands with the two men, and they climbed into the back of the vehicle. Bonwick and his two assistants walked away.

'Tango One and Tango Two are getting into a blue Audi Q7 SUV, hereon in designated as Victor One,' Clayton murmured into his microphone. 'Victor One is on the Bromley Road, pointing west. All units confirm you have eyeball.' He read out the Audi's registration number and Rayner turned to the side and tapped it into the laptop.

'Mike One has eyeball,' said a man over the radio. It was Roger Hunter, who was sitting on a Deliveroo moped. He was another surveillance veteran, he had been following people for a living for almost twenty years.

'Mike Two has eyeball.' Mike Two was a black cab being driven by Carl Baron. Baron had been a genuine black cab driver for more than two decades before moving to MI5, though he still worked as a regular driver on his days off, usually dressed in knee-length shorts and sandals.

'Mike Three has eyeball.' Mike Three was B.A. Parker, who was sitting astride a powerful Honda motorbike. No one knew Parker's first names, he was B.A. to everyone. He was a keen biker and owned two classic Triumphs, a Bonneville and a Thruxton, though sadly neither were suitable for surveillance operations.

'Just to confirm, we have a tracker on Tango One so there's no need to get too close,' Clayton murmured. 'We can give them plenty of room.'

'Roger that,' said Mike Two.

The man in the leather jacket slammed the Audi rear door shut and walked around to the front passenger door. For the first time, Shepherd got a good look at him and his photographic memory kicked in. 'I know him,' he said. 'Ian McAdam. He was doing a three stretch in Bradford Prison when I was there.'

'What were you doing in prison, Spider?' asked Rayner. 'Been a naughty boy?'

'I was undercover as a prison officer, Janet, thanks for asking.'

'That's right, it all kicked off in there, didn't it?'

'Yeah. It was pretty hairy for a while. But McAdam wasn't involved. He was in for GBH. Had less than three months to go so he was keeping his nose clean.' Shepherd let the man's details flow through his memory. He'd familiarised himself with the records of everyone at the prison – inmates and staff – in case he'd crossed paths with them before. McAdam was in his late forties, and his most recent sentence had been for breaking the arms of a gambler who had owed money to a Birmingham bookie. There was nothing in his file that suggested any connection with London, or The Office. Nor could Shepherd remember anything that connected McAdam with Billy Donnelly.

'He's not likely to be carrying, is he, Spider?' asked Clayton.

'Nah, he uses his fists,' said Shepherd. 'He was a kickboxing champion in his youth.'

'The car is leased from a company in Birmingham,' said Rayner, reading off the screen. 'Off the shelf company by the look of it.'

'Just so you all know, the Audi is Birmingham based so they might be heading up to the Midlands,' Clayton murmured into his mic.

'Goody, goody,' said Mike Two. He was using his own cab and was paid a very healthy mileage allowance on top of his MI5 salary. A run up to Birmingham and back could well add several hundred pounds to his earnings.

The Audi moved away from the kerb and edged into traffic.

'Victor One is on the move, heading west, west, west,' said Clayton. 'Give them plenty of room, the GPS is functioning perfectly.'

The red dot began to edge across the GPS screen. Blue dots marked the positions of the surveillance vehicles and a single green dot showed where the Openreach van was.

'Mike Three has eyeball.' The blue dot representing the Honda motorcycle moved after the red dot.

'If they are heading to Birmingham then there are three main routes,' said Rayner. 'The M11 and the A14, the M25 followed by the M1, or the M25 followed by the M40. The fact that they're heading west suggests that it's the M40, but obviously I'm not one for assumptions.' She grinned at Shepherd. 'I hope you went before you got here because it's a three-hour drive to Brum.'

'I've got Ziploc bags if he needs to go,' said Clayton.

'I'll be fine, guys, thank you for your concern,' said Shepherd.

Clayton grinned and passed him a bottle of water. 'Don't forget to stay hydrated,' he said.

'I'll pass, Matty.'

CHAPTER 45

Rayner was right, the Audi took the M40 North. The Openreach van stayed more than a mile behind. The Deliveroo moped, Mike One, had dropped out when the Audi left the M25. There was no real reason for a Deliveroo bike to be using the motorway so it would have stuck out. Rayner had sent Mike One on his way and had arranged for a surveillance bike from Birmingham to join the surveillance operation once they reached the city.

Mike Three had stayed ahead of the Audi. Getting ahead of a target vehicle was always the best way of tracking it, most people only checked their mirrors for surveillance. The only downside was that the bike would be blindsided if the Audi turned off the motorway, but there was no sign of that happening.

Mike Two, the black cab, stayed between the Audi and the Openreach van, sticking to the inside lane unless overtaking.

The Audi kept to just above the speed limit and the driver indicated whenever he changed lanes.

Twenty miles outside London, Clayton took a Marks & Spencer chicken salad sandwich from his backpack. He offered half to Shepherd. Shepherd took it, but turned down the offer of a coffee from Clayton's Thermos. Shepherd chewed on the sandwich as he considered his options. Was Neville Kingsley based in Birmingham? Nothing so far during the investigation had suggested that The Office wasn't London based, and as that was where most of the killings had taken place, it had seemed a safe assumption.

He took out his mobile and called Amar Singh. Singh answered almost immediately. 'I was just going to call you,' said Singh. 'Giles Pritchard has given the phone company a nudge and we're right at the top of their to-do list.'

'That's good to hear, Amar,' said Shepherd. 'Any idea how long?'

'I'm told later today.'

'Excellent. And when you get the data, can you keep an eye out for anything Birmingham related. Calls or GPS data.'

'No problem.'

'Thanks. And thanks for the rigged phone. It's working like a dream.'

'Happy to be of service.'

Shepherd ended the call and looked at the screen. The Audi was heading north, the black cab several hundred yards behind it and Mike Three about the same distance ahead of it. The Audi was level with Bicester Village, the Oxfordshire designer outlet shopping centre. One of the millions of facts filed away in Shepherd's trick memory was that the centre was the second most visited location in the United Kingdom by Chinese tourists, after Buckingham Palace.

'Mike Three, Victor One is under attack.'

'Say again, Mike Three,' said Clayton, no trace of anxiety in his voice.

'Victor One is under fire,' said Mike Three. 'Two guys on a bike. Oh hell, Victor One is off the road, I repeat, Victor One is off the road.'

'Mike Two, do you have eyeball?'

'Negative,' said Mike Two.

The blue dot representing the black cab started to accelerate, closing the distance between itself and the Audi.

'Mike Three, Victor One is off the road. I see the bike, heading this way. What do you want me to do?'

Clayton looked at Shepherd. Shepherd nodded. He knew what Clayton was asking. 'Mike Three, keep eyeball on the bike, hereon designated as Victor Two.'

'Roger that.'

The blue dot representing the bike slowed, obviously allowing the other bike to catch up with it.

'Mike Two, I have eyeball on Victor One. Victor One is off the road and upside down. It's a shit show.'

'Mike Three, I have eyeball on Victor Two. I am in pursuit.' The blue dot representing Mike Three's bike picked up speed.

'Mike Two, can you call in emergency services to your location?' said Clayton.

'Roger that,' said Mike Two.

'How the hell does this happen, Spider?' asked Clayton.

'I wish I knew,' said Shepherd.

'Who else knew that they were driving up to Birmingham? Who knew they'd be on the M40? We didn't know until half an hour ago.'

Shepherd grimaced. It was a good question, and one he couldn't answer.

CHAPTER 46

'I see them,' said the driver of the Openreach van. 'It doesn't look good.' Their green dot was rapidly approaching the red dot on the screen.

'Any sign of emergency vehicles?' asked Shepherd, though he already knew the answer. Any ambulance or police vehicles would have had to have passed them.

'Negative,' said the driver. 'But Carl is out of his cab.'

The Openreach van slowed, and Shepherd heard the indicator clicking. The van moved over to the left and came to a halt. Shepherd threw the rear door open and stepped out. The van had stopped behind the black cab, its indicator lights flashing. Carl Baron was standing by the twisted remains of the crash barrier, a mobile phone to his ear. Shepherd joined him. One look at the wreckage of the Audi explained why Baron hadn't gone down to help. Both offside tyres had blown, which is presumably what had made it spin off the motorway. All the windows were shattered and there were dozens of bullet holes in the doors. All the occupants were clearly dead, blown apart in a hail of gunfire.

'Overkill,' said Baron, putting his phone away. 'Literally.'

'Looks like a machine pistol,' said Shepherd. 'Set to automatic.'

'The ambulance is on the way but . . .' Baron shrugged.

'Yeah,' said Shepherd. 'Not much they can do other than to take away the bodies.'

Shepherd went carefully down the incline towards the Audi. The engine was hissing and there was steam oozing from under the ruptured bonnet.

There seemed to be two lines of shots across the doors, both running from left to right. And there had probably been a third that had shattered the windows. Shepherd did a quick count of the middle row of holes. Eight, pretty much split four and four across the two doors. The rounds would have gone straight through the doors which were of thin steel and offered as much protection as a few sheets of cardboard. The holes were the result of .45 ACP rounds rather than 9mm. An Uzi magazine usually held twenty-two .45 rounds and a MAC-10 generally had thirty. More than enough to stop a car and kill everyone in it, but a pro would have been carrying spare magazines, just in case more were needed.

There were just three holes at the bottom of the doors. Shepherd figured the rest had ripped the tyres apart. They had probably sprayed the windows first, killing or at least maiming the occupants. Then a second spray through the doors. And a final rake across the tyres, sending the vehicle spinning off the motorway.

He bent down and peered inside the car. Donnelly and Zlatnar had taken most of the hits. They had both been shot in the face and the top of Zlatnar's skull had been blown away. Zlatnar had also been hit in the chest and Donnelly had wounds in his shoulder and throat.

'I'm sorry, Sasha,' Shepherd whispered. 'I let you down.'

Like Paul Dutch, Sasha Zlatnar had put his faith in Shepherd and had died as a result. What Shepherd had said to Pritchard echoed in his mind – live by the sword, die by the sword. Zlatnar had killed more than his fair share of people over the years, but that didn't make it any easier for Shepherd to accept what had happened. At least the end had come quickly, but that didn't provide any comfort for Shepherd.

'I'll take care of your family, Sasha,' Shepherd whispered. 'I promise.'

Shepherd moved nearer to the front. Both airbags had gone off, but by then the two men in the front had almost certainly breathed their last. The airbags were smeared with glistening blood.

As Shepherd climbed back up to the motorway, he heard the sound of a police siren off in the distance. 'Probably best if the van isn't here when they arrive,' Shepherd said to Baron. 'Are you okay to handle the cops?'

'Sure,' said Baron. 'Not much to say. I didn't see it happen, it was all over by the time I got here.'

Shepherd patted him on the shoulder, then jogged back to the van. He climbed in the back and pulled the door shut. As he sat down on his plastic stool, the van accelerated away.

'Is it bad?' asked Rayner.

'As bad as it gets,' said Shepherd. He looked over at Clayton. 'How's B.A. getting on?'

'He's tailing the bike but he can't get too close, obviously. They left the M40 at Baynards Green and are now on the A43.'

Shepherd looked at the GPS screen. The blue dot representing Mike Three was several miles away, heading north east. 'Where could they be going?' he asked.

'Brackley's a good bet,' said Rayner. 'There's a Tesco

superstore there and an industrial estate. Easy enough for them to switch vehicles there.'

'Matty, can we get watchers to Brackley?'

Clayton shook his head. 'It's an hour and a half away by car. Even a bike flat out is going to take thirty minutes and they'll have been and gone by then.'

'And a helicopter's out of the question?'

'If we were in London the Met might be able to help but this might be Thames Valley or Northamptonshire Police, I wouldn't even know who to call.'

'Can I talk to B.A.?' Shepherd asked, holding out his hand.

'Sure,' said Clayton, pulling off the headset and handing it to Shepherd.

Shepherd put the headset on and pushed the mic closer to his lips. 'B.A., this is Dan, are you okay?'

'All good, Dan. I'm about three hundred yards behind the bike. They're two up so I can easily catch them up if I have to.'

'Make sure you don't put yourself in any danger,' said Shepherd. 'These guys are stone cold killers.'

'Roger that,' replied Parker.

'It looks as if they might be planning a vehicle switch at Brackley. Ideally we want eyes on the transfer but I don't want you taking any risks.'

'I hear you, Dan.'

'There's a Tesco there with a big car park and an industrial estate. If they do a switch, don't show out. They'll kill you without a second thought. Did you see them take out Victor One?'

'Only in my mirror. It was over in seconds. They pulled up alongside and sprayed it with bullets, the Audi spun off the motorway, and that was that. I let them overtake me and I've been on their tail since. What about the people in the car?'

'All dead. They didn't stand a chance. Did you get a look at the gun?'

'The passenger had something under his jacket, but it was hidden.'

'Give me a description of the bike and the shooters, will you?'

'Sure. The bike is a Honda NX500, grey and black.' Parker gave him the registration number. 'The driver is wearing full leathers, black with a lime green stripe down the arms and legs, boots with straps on them, and a white full-face helmet with a tinted visor. The pillion passenger has a Belstaff waxed jacket on, with jeans and what look like Timberland boots. I'm assuming it's a guy, but they're wearing full-face helmets and visors so I couldn't be sure.'

It made sense that the pillion passenger wasn't wearing full leathers, it would be impossible to hide a gun, least of all a submachine pistol, in the skin-tight protective gear.

'All right, B.A., thanks for that,' said Shepherd. 'Just stay well back, don't give them a reason to pick a fight with you.'

'Don't worry, Dan, I've seen what these guys are capable of. I'll be careful.'

Shepherd took the headset off and gave it back to Clayton. They watched as the blue dot continued towards Brackley.

'How do you think we play this?' asked Rayner.

'I'm open to suggestions,' said Shepherd. 'We're not armed and they clearly have no qualms about shooting.'

'We could call in ARVs,' said Clayton.

'We could, but we might be inviting them to a bloodbath,' said Shepherd. 'They'll see ARVs coming a mile off and they'll almost certainly open fire first. Plain-clothes CTSFOs would probably be the way to go but it'd be an hour or so at the earliest to get them here. And even with CTSFOs there's a good chance it'd end in a firefight.' He reached for a bottle of water and took a swig. 'As crazy as it sounds, unless we approach them, they're not a danger to anybody. They've carried out their hit and now they're on their way home. So far as nothing gets in their way, there's no reason for them to pull the trigger again.'

Clayton flipped a switch to run the headset feed through a wall-mounted speaker. It was Carl Baron checking in. 'Cops didn't want to detain me,' he said. 'In fact, they wanted me to leave. They've taped off the area and there's a forensics team on the way.'

'They ran you through the Police National Computer?' asked Clayton.

'They did and it was all good. I told them I didn't actually see it happen, I just saw that a car had left the road and stopped to see if I could help. They checked me on the PNC and took my phone number. From what they were saying, they figure it was gang related.'

Shepherd looked at the GPS screen. The cab was about ten miles behind them, moving quickly.

'We think the shooters are going to ditch their bike at Brackley, so get there as soon as you can,' said Clayton.

'Roger that,' said Baron.

CHAPTER 47

'They're turning off the main road, heading into Brackley,' said Mike Three. Shepherd looked at the GPS screen. B.A. Parker was on the A43, opposite the Buckingham Road Industrial Estate.

'Give them plenty of room, B.A.,' said Clayton. 'We need to know what vehicle they're changing to, but don't put yourself at risk.'

'Roger that,' said Parker.

The blue dot representing Baron's black cab was still catching up with the van and was now about a mile away.

'What's the plan guys, do we also drive onto the industrial estate?' asked Rayner.

'I think so,' said Clayton. 'They won't have seen us, we've always hung well back.' He looked over at Shepherd who nodded in agreement.

'I'll just point out that the sides of the van are most definitely not bulletproof,' said Rayner, 'and that no one in here is carrying a gun.' She smiled at Shepherd. 'Unless you're ignoring regulations.'

'No, I'm not carrying,' said Shepherd.

'Then I suggest we continue to keep our distance,' said Rayner. 'These guys clearly mean business.'

'I hear you,' said Clayton. He relayed instructions to the

driver, asking him to follow B.A. but to hang back. After a couple of minutes, they heard the indicator kick in and the van moved to the left.

'The bike is slowing,' said Parker over the radio. 'They're pulling up outside one of the units. Fairview Engineering. Looks like it's closed but there are a couple of cars parked outside.'

'Don't get too close, B.A.,' said Clayton.

'They've stopped,' said Parker. 'I'm at the front of the unit, they're at the side and I can't see what car they're getting in to from here.'

'Stay back, B.A.,' said Clayton. 'You'll see them when they drive away.'

'Roger that,' said Parker. 'But at the moment I do not have eyeball.'

'That's not a problem,' said Clayton. 'We've just turned on to the industrial estate, we'll be with you in a couple of minutes.'

Shepherd looked at the GPS screen. The green light representing their van was on the edge of the estate, Parker's bike was outside one of the units close to the centre. Baron's black cab was half a mile away now. Between the three of them they stood a good chance of carrying out surveillance on whatever vehicle the killers switched to.

'They've just torched the bike,' said Parker over the radio. 'I can see the smoke from here.'

'Any sign of their new vehicle yet?' asked Clayton.

'Negative, I do not have eyeball.'

'We're a hundred metres away from you,' said Clayton.

'Vehicle is leaving the car park,' said Parker. 'Oh shit . . .' They heard a series of dull popping sounds over the radio and a gasp followed by a crashing sound.

'B.A., are you okay?' asked Clayton.

Parker groaned. 'I've been hit.'

Clayton shouted at the driver to speed up and the van lurched forward, almost throwing Shepherd off his plastic stool. The van's tyres screeched on the tarmac as it sped towards Parker.

'Carl, B.A. has been shot,' said Clayton. 'Step on it.'

'Is he okay?'

'We don't know.'

The van came to a stop and Shepherd threw open the rear door. He saw Parker's bike immediately, but there was no sign of the car containing the killers. Parker was lying on his back, arms outstretched. Shepherd ran over to him. There were two holes in Parker's leather motorcycle jacket, one in his shoulder, one in the chest. Shepherd flipped up the visor of Parker's helmet. 'B.A., can you hear me?'

Parker's eyes were closed but they flickered open at the sound of Shepherd's voice. 'I'm hit.'

'Yes, I know. I'm going to remove your helmet, shout if there's any pain.' Shepherd undid the strap under Parker's chin and slid the helmet off.

'It was a grey Vauxhall Corsa, I only saw it side on so I didn't get the reg,' gasped Parker.

'Save your breath, I'm guessing your right lung has collapsed.'

'That's not good,' Parker wheezed.

Rayner ran across from the van, carrying a first-aid holdall. 'Health and Safety finally comes good,' she said, kneeling down next to Shepherd and unzipping the bag.

'Looks like there are two wounds, one in the shoulder and one in the chest,' said Shepherd. 'B.A., mate, sorry about this but I'm going to have to roll you onto your side to look for exit wounds. It's going to hurt, so scream if you have to.'

'Screaming helps?' Parker gasped.

'Whatever gets you through it. Okay, one, two, three . . .'

On three, Shepherd rolled Parker onto his left side. There were no exit wounds, so good news, bad news. The good news was that there were only two bullet holes to worry about, the bad news that there were two bullets still inside him. He gently lowered the injured man on to his back. 'No exit wounds, so that'll reduce the blood loss. You're going to be okay, just hang on in there.'

'I'm feeling numb, Spider.' His voice was a raspy whisper. There were flecks of blood on his lips.

'That's the endorphins kicking in, B.A., just stay awake. Trust me, you're going to be fine. You're listening to the voice of experience here.'

Shepherd unzipped Parker's motorcycle jacket and opened it. His Triumph sweatshirt was soaked in blood. Rayner grimaced and looked anxiously at Shepherd. Shepherd flashed her what he hoped was an encouraging smile. Parker was in a bad way, but if they were lucky, he'd get through this. The key was getting him to an accident and emergency department, and quickly.

Shepherd took a pair of scissors from the first-aid holdall and cut up the centre of the bloody sweatshirt. 'Get me a large wound dressing,' he said to Rayner.

Rayner pulled a dressing pack from the holdall and ripped it open.

Shepherd heard a screech of brakes and looked over his shoulder. It was Baron in the black cab. Baron threw open the driver's door and ran over, his face ashen. 'Is he okay?'

'He will be,' said Shepherd. He took the dressing from Rayner and placed it over the chest wound. 'Janet, keep pressure on the pad. Medium pressure, just enough to stop the bleeding.' Rayner nodded anxiously and placed her hands on the pad.

'Carl, we need to get him to hospital ASAP. The nearest A&E is—' He was interrupted by Parker going into spasm, his whole body jerking up and down. 'B.A., stay with me!' Shepherd shouted.

Bloody froth was spilling between Parker's teeth and his eyes were wide with panic. His boots drummed against the ground and then his back arched for a couple of seconds and he went still, the life fading from his eyes.

Shepherd sat back on his heels, gritting his teeth.

'CPR,' said Rayner. 'We need to start CPR.'

'He's gone,' said Shepherd. 'I'm sorry.'

'No, there must be something we can do,' said Rayner. She was still applying pressure to the dressing.

'I'm sorry, Janet.'

'Bastards,' said Baron. He stamped his foot in frustration. 'Fucking bastards.'

Shepherd stood up. Rayner looked up at him as if she was trying to make him change his mind from the force of her will. 'He bled out internally, Janet. There's nothing we could do . . .' He shrugged.

Tears were running down her face. 'He was talking to us.'

'I know. But he's gone.'

Rayner stared down at her bloody hands as if she was seeing them for the first time. 'This is so unfair,' she whispered.

Shepherd's first thought was to say that life wasn't fair, but that wasn't what she needed to hear. He bent down and placed a comforting hand on her shoulder. 'We did everything we could, Janet. Sometimes it's just not enough.' He helped her to her feet and put his arm around her.

'Are we going after them?' asked Baron.

'They're long gone,' said Shepherd. 'B.A. gave us the make and colour but he didn't see the registration number. I'll get the CCTV checked.'

'We should have had an armed unit with us,' said Baron.

Shepherd didn't reply. Twenty-twenty hindsight was a wonderful thing, but they had no way of knowing that Zlatnar and Donnelly had been moved to The Office's hit list.

Matty Clayton climbed out of the back of the van and walked over to them.

'B.A.'s dead,' said Rayner.

'Ambulance is on the way,' said Clayton. 'Armed cops, too.'

'Yeah, well that horse has well and truly bolted,' said Baron, his voice loaded with bitterness.

'The car they switched to is a grey Vauxhall Corsa, but that's not much help,' said Shepherd. He looked around. 'There's no CCTV here either, which is probably why they chose it. But there are cameras at the entrance to the industrial estate, can you get access to their feeds?'

'I'm on it,' said Clayton. He headed back to the van.

'So that's it?' said Baron. 'B.A.'s not even cold and all we're doing is checking CCTV?'

'Carl, they had this planned right from the start. The hit, the vehicle switch and their escape route, it's all been well thought out. We'll catch them, you have my word on that, but we won't catch them by running around like blue-arsed flies. We have the type of car they're using and they won't know that we have that information. At some point we'll pick them up on CCTV and once we have its registration number we can use ANPR and hopefully that'll lead us to them.'

Baron sighed and nodded. 'You're right. Sorry.'

'No need to apologise, this is a shit show and I'm as upset as you are. But the best thing you can do now is to head back to London. Matty and I will deal with the cops. And you might as well take Janet with you.'

'No!' said Rayner. 'I'm staying with B.A. until the ambulance gets here.' She knelt down and took Parker's gloved right hand in her own.

Baron nodded and headed back to his cab. In the distance, Shepherd could hear the siren of an ambulance. He took out his mobile and walked away from Rayner. Giles Pritchard needed to hear the bad news right away and he wasn't going to be happy.

CHAPTER 48

S hepherd saw Pritchard walk into the park from the south. It was a twenty-minute walk from Thames House to Green Park, and Shepherd had been sure that he would come by foot and not use an office car. He'd have to have walked by Buckingham Palace and then through the Canada Gate. A cold wind was blowing through the park from the north and Shepherd was wearing a black fleece over a heavy polo neck sweater. Pritchard wore a long black overcoat with a Burberry scarf wrapped around his neck. He had his hands thrust deep into his pockets and his head down as if he was deep in thought.

Shepherd watched Pritchard for several minutes to be sure that he wasn't being followed before stepping from behind the tree that he'd been using as cover and walked towards him. Pritchard didn't lift his head until Shepherd was just a few metres away, but Shepherd sensed that the man had seen him coming. 'This is all very John le Carré,' said Pritchard.

'Yeah. Moscow Rules.'

'I guess you have them committed to memory? All ten of them?'

'I never commit anything to memory, it just happens,' said Shepherd. 'But yeah. Moscow Rule number one: assume nothing. Two, never go against your gut. Three, everyone is potentially under opposition control. Four, do not look back;

you are never completely alone. Five, go with the flow, blend in. Six, vary your pattern and stay within your cover. Seven, lull them into a sense of complacency. Eight, do not harass the opposition. Nine, pick the time and place for action. Ten, keep your options open.'

'And eleven, when the shit hits the fan, stay away from the office?'

'I just thought, after what happened, better we meet outside. If it is open season on me, they might be watching Thames House. Here at least I'll be able to see them coming.'

'And you have Lex Harper as protection.'

'You spotted him?' Harper was fifty yards away, tucked in behind a spreading oak tree.

'Dan, I wasn't born behind a desk. I've done more than my fair share of field work.'

Pritchard started walking and Shepherd kept pace with him. 'Sorry about B.A.,' said Pritchard.

'You and me both.'

'We'll get them, Dan. I'll move heaven and earth.'

'I know,' said Shepherd. 'Any joy with the car?'

'Without the reg number, we're restricted to manually checking CCTV feeds in the area. We're on it, but it'll take time. And if we do see a grey Vauxhall Corsa, that doesn't mean it's the killers that are in it. It's a popular car. There are more than a million of them in the UK, and grey is the most popular colour. It's a good lead, and once we do have a registration number we'll know where they went, but these guys are pros, there's every chance they'll have burned it by now.'

'It has to be The Office that did this,' said Shepherd. 'It could only have been someone who knew what route they'd be taking, and even we didn't know that, not until they turned onto the M40.'

'The killers could have followed them from the magistrate's court, same as you did.'

Shepherd shook his head. 'No. If they had been in the vicinity of the court, I would have seen them. And they definitely weren't on the motorway when the Audi headed out of London.'

'Your trick memory?'

'Exactly. They appeared from nowhere when the Audi was close to Bicester. So the killers probably joined the M40 at the A41 intersection. But they could only have done that if they knew in advance which route they were taking.'

'They could have been in radio contact with someone else following the Audi.'

'I would have seen them,' said Shepherd. 'And the killers would have to have been in Bicester before the Audi left the court. At that point we had no idea where they were going. They could have planned to just drive a few miles in London for all we knew. But whoever killed them, they knew where the Audi was headed.'

'Maybe the driver of the Audi was in on it. He presumably knew the route they would be taking. Do we know who he was?'

'Harry Goodman, from Birmingham. No convictions, just speeding and parking tickets. We have an address but nothing else. No connections to Donnelly or Zlatnar that we can see. The vehicle is owned by a shelf company. The guy in the front passenger seat was Ian McAdam. He was in Bradford Prison when I was undercover there, but our paths never crossed. He was in for GBH and is something of an enforcer – was, I should say. Again, no obvious connections between McAdam and Donnelly and Zlatnar. Which means I don't think they arranged the ride, I think it was sorted for them.'

'By The Office?'

'I don't see who else would possibly want them dead.'

'But why would they decide to kill them straight away, wouldn't it have made sense to have talked to them first?'

'Not if they already knew that we were following them.'

Pritchard frowned. 'So you think they knew that we'd turned Zlatnar and that we were using him to get to Kingsley?'

'That would be the only reason to kill them en route.'

Pritchard's frown deepened. 'I don't like the implications of this, Dan, not one bit. Who knew that Zlatnar had turned?'

'You. Me. Amar Singh. Matty Clayton and the surveillance team. A sergeant from SO15, Martin Williams. He was looking after Zlatnar at Lewisham nick.'

'Could this Williams be the weakest link?'

'To be honest, the only person I can vouch for with any certainty is myself.'

Pritchard looked pained. 'Well I'll try not to take that personally.'

'You know what I mean. Of course, I trust you. After everything we've been through, how could I not? But with something as big as this, who can tell? It's not just about money, is it? These people can apply pressure in lots of different ways. Nobody really knows what's going on behind the scenes, do they?'

'You're saying we can't trust anybody?'

'The way they're able to track people in almost real time shows how powerful they are. They must have people on the inside.'

'Is it possible that this sergeant has been compromised?'

'It's possible. Or someone else at Lewisham nick could have realised what was happening. Williams had to let Donnelly know that Zlatnar was being held at Lewisham, so he orchestrated a walk-by. That would have involved several people, any one of whom could be on The Office's payroll.'

'Do we put the staff under the microscope?'

'We could do, but that doesn't get us any nearer taking down The Office, does it?'

'If we find a mole we could turn him, if he's already bent.'

'We could try, but our track record for protecting sources isn't great, is it?'

'So how do you want to play it?'

'Donnelly and Zlatnar were represented by a high-powered solicitor, Louis Bonwick of Bonwick, Kilgallon, and Khan. Bonwick went in to see Donnelly and Donnelly informed him that Zlatnar was also being held there, so Bonwick reached out to him and represented them both at the bail hearing. I can't see a low-life like Donnelly would have Bonwick's number, it's much more likely that he is being paid by The Office.'

'Bonwick isn't going to say anything, is he? Client confidentiality.'

'He's not going to talk to us, of course. But his phone records might be helpful.'

'Again, client confidentiality.'

'That would depend on The Office being a client, wouldn't it? Yes, Donnelly and Zlatnar were clients, no question. But would Bonwick have signed a client agreement with Kingsley? I doubt it.'

'It's a grey area.'

'We wouldn't be looking to listen to calls or read messages, all we'd need is the phone records.'

'Looking for what, specifically?'

'Probably calls to and from a Birmingham number,' said Shepherd. 'That's where the Audi came from. And then we could look for any matches with numbers on Kristiansen's phone.' Shepherd saw the narrowing of Pritchard's eyes. 'The private eye in Barcelona, the one who placed the contract on Ricky Lewis,' he added. 'It's a long shot because if Kingsley is smart he'll be using individual burner phones, but it's worth a try.'

Pritchard nodded. 'Okay, leave that with me.' He sighed. 'As one door shuts, another one gets slammed in our faces. We're no closer to getting to Kingsley than when we started, are we?'

'Not really, no. We don't even know if this Kingsley actually exists. All right, Paul Dutch met him once and we have his description – in his sixties, balding with a Black Country accent – but there's no proof that the man he met was actually Kingsley. Or if Kingsley is his real name.'

'You spoke to him, right? In the warehouse when they wanted you to shoot the guy.'

'I did, and he sounded in his sixties and he definitely had a Black Country accent, but that's still no guarantee that it was him. It could all be dressing. A subterfuge. Which means we're chasing a ghost.'

'There has to be somebody running things,' said Pritchard. 'Someone is pulling the strings. We just happen to have the name Neville Kingsley.'

'A rose by any other name?'

'The name is irrelevant, frankly. It's the man we want.'

'But is it?' said Shepherd. 'Is it really? It's like Lex said, if we take Kingsley, whoever he is, out of the game, somebody else will take his place. And if we shut down The Office completely, something like it will take its place and the Iranians will use them to do their dirty work instead.'

'There are two issues. Kingsley needs to be caught and punished for the killings he has carried out. But we need proof – *definitive* proof – that the Iranian government has been ordering the assassination of its opponents. Once we have that, our government can act. Ordering an assassination is a violation of international law and human rights and is considered a war crime in both times of peace and war. The Iranian leaders can be hauled in front of the International Criminal Court in The Hague.'

'If they leave Iran, which they tend not to.'

'True, but a conviction in the ICC can be followed by severe sanctions, and that's when they'll feel the pain. Hopefully enough pain for them to stop doing what they're doing. Anyway, no point in crossing bridges before we get anywhere near them. The job now is to round up The Office, so let's put our thinking caps on as to how we can move forward.' He looked at his watch. 'I've got a call booked with the US; I need to get back to Thames House. And I'm taking on board what you've said about The Office having access to our plans for Zlatnar. I'll get someone on it.'

'About Zlatnar. He's got a family back in Belgrade. A wife and three kids. The Office clearly bear grudges so they'll be in the firing line.'

'Zlatnar didn't actually do anything for us.'

'Seriously? He died for us. They shot him because he was working with us.'

'We don't know that for sure. They shot Donnelly as well. And the two other guys in the car.'

'It was Zlatnar they were after.'

'Maybe, maybe not. They might just have decided to clean house. Donnelly and Zlatnar were caught, and while they might have got bail, they'd still have to appear in court. Maybe they took the view that taking them out was the best option. If that's the case, Zlatnar's family are free and clear.'

'That's a gamble.'

'Life is a gamble, Dan.'

'This isn't funny,' snapped Shepherd. 'I had a deal with Zlatnar. He agreed to help us nail The Office and in return we said we would get his wife and children to London. He did help us and now he's dead. A deal is a deal.'

'Do you have that in writing?' Pritchard asked, but he took his hands out of his pockets when he saw the look of anger flash across Shepherd's face. He held his hands up, fingers splayed. 'That was uncalled for, I'm sorry. I know what you said to Zlatnar, but we don't know for sure that he was blown, and if he wasn't blown then his family aren't at risk.'

'Either way, we have a debt to them. Look, you know the way the world is at the moment. If they can get to Calais and get onto a rubber boat to Dover, we'll give them a phone, a room in a five-star hotel, and citizenship in five years. Same as we give to pretty much every man of fighting age who makes it across the English Channel, no matter where they're from. At least Mrs Zlatnar and her children won't be planning any terrorist atrocities here any time soon.'

'That's a very jaundiced view of the UK's asylum policy, Dan.'

'It is what it is,' he said. 'We're allowing tens of thousands in every year, I don't see that four more will make any odds. And as I said, Zlatnar and I had a deal. I gave my word.'

Pritchard slid his hands back into his coat pockets. 'It'll be done.'

'They'll need to be pulled out ASAP,' said Shepherd.

'It's the first thing I'll do when I'm back in the office, I promise.'

Shepherd forced a smile. 'No need to promise, Giles. I trust you.' He nodded and walked away, towards the tree that Harper was still hiding behind.

'How did it go?' asked Harper as he watched Pritchard walk back to Canada Gate.

'About as well as expected. He's going to be looking for whoever has been passing intel to The Office, but I won't be holding my breath.'

'My money is on someone at Lewisham nick.'

'Yeah, well you've never really been a fan of the boys in blue, Lex.'

'For good reason.'

'The thing is, The Office managed to assassinate Paul Dutch on the way to a safe house in Stanmore. Lewisham had zero involvement in that. They had four guys on two bikes and they knew exactly where he was. And The Office sent two guys to kill Ricky Lewis at another safe house. If Jimmy Sharpe hadn't been waiting for them then they might well have succeeded. And there was no Lewisham involvement in that, either.'

'They've probably got more than one bad apple on their books,' said Harper. 'You need to be careful, Spider. These are serious people after you. I told you I should have been with you when you were following that Serb.'

'That Serb had a name, Lex. Zlatnar. Sasha Zlatnar.'

'Of course he did. But I still should have been there with you.'

'There wasn't room in the van.'

'That's neither here nor there. These bastards are dangerous, Spider, and I'm not letting you out of my sight until this is over.' He patted Shepherd on the back. 'Think of me as your guardian angel.'

'I do,' said Shepherd. 'I really do.'

CHAPTER 49

S hepherd and Harper walked out of the north gate of Green Park and turned right on Piccadilly. They were fairly sure they weren't being followed but flagged down a black cab and had it take them the few minutes to Leicester Square tube station. Harper paid off the driver and they hurried down to the southbound Northern Line platform. They only had to wait thirty seconds before a train arrived and they could be sure they weren't being tailed. They got off the train at Battersea Power Station and spent five minutes running through basic counter-surveillance measures to make sure that they were still tail-free before heading to Shepherd's apartment building.

'How secure is your flat?' asked Harper.

'As safe as anywhere, pretty much. Keypad to get in the building, keypad to get to the lifts. But you know how easy it is to get into blocks like this, you just follow someone in. Or ring any flat and say it's a food delivery. More often than not you'll get buzzed in.'

'So not secure at all, then. How easy would it be for bad guys to know about the flat?'

'They'd have to know who I was, and the legends I use are always watertight.'

'Could The Office know who you are? Your real name?'

'I don't see how. The Darren Griffiths legend I used held

up. I mean, sure, they know now that Griffiths didn't really exist and that I was undercover, but I don't see how they'd get from Darren Griffiths to me.'

'Lewisham nick,' said Harper.

'You really don't trust the cops, do you?'

'They dropped their standards years ago to meet their diversity standards, they started letting people in just because they ticked the right boxes. All sorts of criminal organisations have managed to get their own people on the job. And the prisons are even worse. How do you think so many phones and drugs get into prisons? They'll tell you it's drones or visitors smuggling stuff in but anyone who knows what's really going on knows that it's corrupt prison officers that are the problem. And most of them joined because they wanted to embrace corruption. Drugs increase in value ten-fold if you can get them into prison.' He saw Shepherd about to respond and he raised his hand. 'I know, I know, you're going to say it's all conspiracy theory nonsense, but you've got to assume the worst, these guys killed five people today without a second thought and if they do find out who you are, they'll add you to the list.'

'I hear you, Lex.'

'So, who did you talk to at Lewisham?'

'I dealt with a counter-terrorism sergeant by the name of Martin Williams.'

'You trust him?'

'I've known him for a few years, and yes, I trust him. Though, as I said to Giles Pritchard, the only person I can vouch for with any certainty is myself.'

'And your good mate Lex Harper.'

Shepherd grinned. 'Yeah, and my good mate Lex Harper.'

They reached the entrance to the building and Shepherd had a quick look around before tapping in the four-digit PIN. He held the door open for Harper and followed him inside.

'Who else did you speak to at Lewisham?' asked Harper as they walked to the lifts.

'No one, really. The first time Martin signed me in, but he wouldn't have used my name. There was a uniform standing outside Zlatnar's room, but he wouldn't have known my name. No one else. Martin took Zlatnar from Lewisham to a safe house in Maida Vale. He did that on his own. I took Zlatnar back to Lewisham and Martin took him inside.'

Shepherd pressed the keypad to access the lift lobby.

'What about this Zlatnar? Could he have said something to the lawyer and the lawyer could have tipped off The Office?'

'He's got a wife and kids.'

'Doesn't mean he wouldn't put himself first.'

'No, he wasn't faking his concern for his family. He'd do anything to protect them.'

They went up in the lift to Shepherd's floor.

'He'd have known that even if he told them what was going on, they'd be unlikely to let him live. His only chance was to help us, that was his ticket to a new life for him and his family.'

The lift doors opened and Harper stepped out. There was a man standing to the side of the lift doors. Harper moved quickly, grabbing the man by the throat with his left hand and pushing him against the wall, bringing his right hand up and bunching it into a fist.

'It's Liam, it's Liam!' shouted Shepherd.

Harper immediately released his grip on Liam's throat and stepped back, raising his hands in the air. 'Sorry,' he said. 'My bad.'

'Bloody hell, Dad, what's going on?' gasped Liam, massaging his throat. He was wearing a black pea coat over a green pullover and olive cargo pants. His hair was shorter than last time Shepherd had seen him, though the sideburns were longer.

'Sorry, you caught us by surprise,' said Shepherd. 'What were you doing loitering in the corridor?'

'I wasn't loitering, I forgot my key. I called but it went straight through to voicemail.'

Harper stuck out his hand. 'I'm Lex, friend of your dad's.'

'You're not going to hit me again, are you?'

'No, I'm done.'

'That's a relief,' said Liam. He stuck out his hand and they shook.

'Sorry I'm late, we had a meeting outside,' said Shepherd.

'And I was early,' said Liam. 'A pal gave me a lift and dropped me off here.' He picked up his holdall.

'Still staying for the weekend?'

'Is that okay?'

'Of course it's okay,' said Shepherd. He unlocked the front door and opened it. 'Lex is in the spare bedroom, are you okay on the sofa?'

'Sofa's fine,' said Liam.

Shepherd led them into the flat. 'Beer?' he asked.

'Sure,' said Liam. He dropped his holdall by the side of the sofa and sat down.

Shepherd went over to his fridge, took three bottles of lager out and uncapped them. He handed them out and then flopped down on the sofa next to Liam. 'Good to see you,' he said. He leaned over and clinked his bottle against Liam's. 'Tell us what you've been up to.'

CHAPTER 50

They had drunk three beers each by the time the sun had gone down and Liam had brought them up to speed on his work with the Joint Special Forces Aviation Wing. Shepherd couldn't help smiling with pride at the way his son had turned out. He was confident but not boastful, proud of his achievements but also modest, and he had a sense of humour that had Shepherd and Harper laughing out loud.

'Must be tough flying those Chinooks,' said Harper. 'Like flying two choppers at the same time.'

'Nah, the technology does most of the hard work,' said Liam. 'You just have to learn to trust the Automatic Flight Control System. Once you realise it's not trying to kill you, you can relax. A single rotor bird requires a lot more control.'

'And what's it like dealing with your dad's old mob?'

'Yeah, that's kinda cool, I get to see the sort of things he must have done, back in the day.'

'He had a few scrapes, that's true,' said Harper.

'You served with dad?'

'Not in the Regiment. I was a Para for my sins, but for a while I was attached to the Regiment and went on a few operations with him in Afghanistan.'

'Dad never talks about it.'

'We're not allowed to talk about it,' said Shepherd. 'You know that.'

'Of course, sure,' said Liam. 'That's why it's cool to see what they do. Every time the guys do a free fall from the rear ramp I imagine you doing it.'

Shepherd laughed. 'You hadn't been born back when I was jumping out of helicopters,' he said. 'It was a lifetime ago.'

'But you did it, right? Jumped from a Chinook?'

Shepherd raised his bottle. 'Many times. And abseiled down.'

Liam grinned. 'Yeah, that's when you need your wits about you, keeping it in a hover while the guys slide down the ropes. That does need some concentration.'

'You knew your dad was in the SAS when you were a kid?'

'Not really,' said Liam. 'Dad had left the Regiment not long after I was born so when I was growing up he was with the cops. But even then he never talked about it. Kids at school would ask what he did and I'd say he was a policeman but when they asked for details I didn't have any.'

'Most of my work was undercover back then,' said Shepherd. 'I was with an undercover unit that covered most of the country.'

'Which is why I hardly ever saw you,' said Liam.

'I know, it was crazy,' said Shepherd. 'I left the Regiment to spend more time with you and I ended up seeing even less of you.' He smiled ruefully. 'I'm sorry I was such a crap dad.'

'You weren't a crap dad, don't say that. You were always great when you were there.' He shrugged. 'You were just away a lot, that's all. But I always understood that you were busy. And I get it even more now because flying for the wing means that I'm sometimes away for weeks at a time and usually leaving with little or no notice.' He sipped his beer. 'What about you, Lex? Why did you leave the Army?'

'I got fed up with following orders,' he said. 'I thought of trying for the SAS but when I realised what a commitment it was I decided to just leave.'

'And what do you do now? Other than assaulting people in corridors?'

'I have a few business interests that keep the wolf from the door, but I'm semi-retired these days. I spend most of the time in Thailand.'

'The Land of Smiles?'

'Oh yes, there's plenty of happy people out there. Brits always look so unhappy, don't they? I guess the weather has a lot to do with it. Thailand has blue skies every day and you never need a jacket, never mind a coat.' He looked at his watch. 'Guys I'm hungry, do you fancy a curry?'

Liam grinned. 'I never say no to a curry.'

'There's a place not far from here,' said Shepherd. 'Tandoori Nights.'

Harper drained his bottle. 'Let's go, then.'

Shepherd and Liam finished their beers and they went down in the lift and out of the front door. Harper switched into protective mode, walking out onto the street first and looking around. Shepherd also scanned the area as he left the building. A middle-aged couple were walking hand in hand on the other side of the road. A white Prius was parked up, its hazard lights flashing, probably an Uber. A black cab went by, its yellow light off, two women in the back. 'Which way?' asked Harper.

Shepherd gestured with his chin to the left. 'That way, about a hundred yards, then off to the right.'

Harper waited for them and then the three of them walked along the pavement, with Liam in the middle.

'Is there something wrong?' asked Liam.

'What do you mean?' said Shepherd.

'You're on edge, both of you, and your heads are on swivels.'

'It's London,' said Harper. 'Stab city. You have to keep your wits about you.'

Shepherd and Harper both heard the growl of a motorbike engine and they both turned to look towards the source of the noise. 'See, look at you guys,' said Liam. 'You really need to relax.'

Shepherd's eyes locked onto the bike and the two men on it. The fact that there were two men on the bike was a red flag straight away. Most bikes had single riders, if there was a pillion passenger, more often than not, it was a wife or girlfriend. But it was the clothing that set Shepherd's pulse racing – the driver was wearing black leathers and the passenger a black Belstaff jacket. The passenger had flipped up the visor of his helmet.

'Hostiles incoming!' shouted Shepherd, but Harper had already seen the passenger pulling a gun out. Liam still hadn't turned, but his jaw had dropped when Shepherd had shouted.

The bike sped towards them, the tyres squealing on the tarmac. The weapon was a machine pistol with a bulbous suppressor. The passenger had his gloved left hand on the suppressor to steady his aim. The bike turned to the right and the passenger swung the gun around as he pulled the trigger. Even with the suppressor the noise was loud, an angry roar, compressed into short, violent bursts.

A round passed by Shepherd's face, so close that he felt the heat and a rush of air, the window behind him exploded in a shower of glass, a second round grazed his shoulder and he felt the material of his jacket rip, then Liam grunted as a third round smacked into his shoulder. 'Down, down, down!' shouted Harper, but Shepherd had already put his arm around Liam and was dragging him behind a parked car. More rounds thudded into the building behind them, smashing glass and screeching off metal. Brass casings scattered from the gun and bounced on the tarmac.

Harper dropped into a crouch, reaching behind him with his right hand and pulling a pistol from the back of his jeans. He fired almost immediately but the recoil made the shot go high. He brought his left hand up and cupped it around his right hand as he fired again. This time the round hit its target, smacking into the chest of the man with the machine pistol. The man jerked back, letting go of the suppressor. His finger was still on the trigger and rounds spat into the air. Harper fired again. The shot ricocheted off the man's helmet, snapping his head back.

Shepherd looked down at Liam. Blood was staining his jacket around his right shoulder. 'I'm okay, I'm okay,' said Liam, though he obviously wasn't.

Harper fired a fourth shot which hit the driver in the chest. His left hand came off the handlebars and the bike began to fishtail. The next shot hit the passenger in the face and the machine pistol clattered to the ground, finally silent.

The driver's right hand released its grip and the bike tipped over, spilling the two men into the road.

'Stay down!' Harper barked at Shepherd as he began to move towards the two men.

Shepherd kept one hand on Liam as he peered over the car. Harper moved cautiously towards the bike. Its engine was still racing. The shooter was lying on his back, his face a bloody mess. The gun, an Ingram MAC-10, was inches from the man's gloved right hand and Harper kicked it away. It clattered across the tarmac and disappeared under a parked Toyota. Shepherd took out his mobile and called Pritchard. Pritchard answered almost immediately. 'We're under fire, two men on a bike. I think it's the guys who shot B.A.'

'Are you okay?' asked Pritchard.

'I'm okay but Liam has taken a bullet. I'm going to need you to clear it with the cops, Lex shot the guys.'

'What the hell is he doing with a gun?'

'I don't know. It caught me by surprise. But it was a good job he was able to return fire or I wouldn't be talking to you now.'

'He needs to get out of there, now.'

The driver was moving, his legs scraping against the tarmac. Blood glistened on the man's leathers and he groaned. Harper raised his gun and aimed at the man's chest.

'Lex, no!' shouted Shepherd.

Harper looked over at him, his finger still on the trigger. 'Are you serious?'

'He's not a threat.'

'He was trying to kill you. Fuck that – he was trying to kill us all.'

'And you stopped them. But you can't shoot an injured man. You know that. Does he have a weapon?'

Harper shook his head. 'No.'

'Then leave him be.'

Harper sighed. 'Your call,' he said.

'What's going on?' asked Pritchard.

'It's all good,' said Shepherd. 'But I have to go.'

'I'll reach out to the Met. Are they there yet?'

'They're on the way.'

Shepherd ended the call as Harper walked over. 'If it was down to me, I'd have double tapped him.'

Shepherd bent over Liam. Liam's eyes were closed but he was breathing slowly and evenly. Shepherd took a red Swiss Army knife out of his pocket and flipped out the blade. He used it to cut away the bloody jacket around Liam's injured shoulder.

'You didn't tell me you had a gun,' said Shepherd.

'I'd be a poor sort of bodyguard if I couldn't return fire,' said Harper.

'Where did you get a gun from?'

'Spider, mate, this is London. You can buy a gun in half the pubs in the East End.'

Shepherd finished cutting away the jacket. Liam's shirt was soaked in blood and Shepherd used the knife to cut it away.

'Cops will here in minutes, Lex. You need to go.'

'I'm not leaving you. Not after this.'

'You have to. They'll take you in and we'll both have a lot of questions to answer. Take the gun and I'll catch up with you later.'

'I thought you spooks had a get-out-of-jail-free card.'

'We do, sort of. But you don't. And you've just killed two guys.'

'One. The big one is still breathing.'

'Go, Lex.'

'He's right, Lex,' said Liam, opening his eyes. 'You need to go. And thanks.'

'Thanks for what? You getting shot in the shoulder?'

'It would have been a lot worse if you hadn't been here.' They heard a siren, off in the distance. 'That's your cue to get the hell out of Dodge.' He forced a smile. 'Go,' he said. 'Rain check on the curry.'

Harper bent down and patted Liam on the leg. 'Catch you

later,' he said. He straightened up, shoved the gun in the back of his jeans, and walked away, his head down.

Shepherd stripped away the shirt from around Liam's injured shoulder and was finally able to get a good look at the wound. The round had entered at the top of the back of Liam's shoulder and passed straight through, missing the bone by millimetres. It was a flesh wound, albeit a messy one. He used the knife to hack out a piece of Liam's jacket and pressed it against the torn flesh. 'You're going to be okay, Liam.'

'Will I still be able to play the piano?'

Shepherd chuckled. 'You've never been able to play the piano,' he said. 'But you'll be able to fly a Chinook, and that's what matters.'

'That was pretty impressive shooting for a guy who claims to be a semi-retired businessman,' said Liam.

'Yeah, Lex is a good guy to have in your corner when it kicks off,' said Shepherd.

'What do we tell the cops?'

The siren was louder now and heading in their direction. 'You've been shot, Liam, they're not going to be questioning you. They'll take you straight to hospital, so I'll do the talking.'

'I'll need to say something at some point.'

'Just say we were on the way for a curry when two guys on a bike started shooting. You got hit and you've no idea what happened after that.'

'What do I tell them about Lex?'

'Lex was just a guy in the street.'

'There's CCTV everywhere, they'll see that he came out of the building with us.'

'It'll take them time to check the CCTV and talk to any witnesses, and by then it'll all be squared away.'

'A street shooting can just be swept under the carpet?'

'If necessary, yes. How do you feel?'

'Like I've been shot.'

'You're doing fine.' A blue flashing light pulsed against the wall of the building behind them and the siren went dead. Shepherd looked over his shoulder. An ambulance had pulled up in the street. The front passenger door opened and a heavy-set man in green overalls climbed out. Shepherd waved at him. 'Over here!' he shouted.

The paramedic grabbed a large green and yellow holdall and jogged over. He knelt down besides Shepherd.

'Gunshot wound, right shoulder,' said Shepherd. 'It's not too deep and there doesn't appear to be any bone or nerve damage. His blood group is O negative.'

'You a doctor?'

Shepherd shook his head. 'No. Just his dad.'

A second paramedic appeared from the rear of the ambulance, pushing a gurney. He headed for Liam but stopped when he saw the two bodies lying by the motorcycle. He hurried over to the two men. One was obviously dead, his face behind the shattered visor a red pulpy mess, but the other man was still breathing, a red patch on his motorcycle leathers. The paramedic knelt down and started to examine the man.

'Do you need help to get him into the ambulance?' Shepherd said to the paramedic who was working on Liam.

'I should be able to manage, sir, just give me a minute.' He took a dressing pack from his holdall, ripped it open and slapped it on Liam's shoulder wound. 'Can you help me get him up into a sitting position?'

'Sure,' said Shepherd. Together they eased Liam up so that he was sitting with his back to the car wheel.

'Stan, I need you over here!' shouted the other paramedic.

'Sir, could you keep this pressed against the wound,' the paramedic said. 'I won't be a minute.'

'We need to get him to hospital,' said Shepherd.

The paramedic straightened up and Shepherd put his right hand on the dressing. 'We will do, sir, let me just check with my colleague,' said the paramedic, picking up his holdall.

'What's going on, dad?' asked Liam, as the paramedic jogged over to the bike.

'Apparently the paramedics think that the guy who tried to kill us is more deserving of first aid than you.'

Liam winced. 'That's funny.'

'It's the way of the world,' said Shepherd. 'He took a shot to the chest so he's in a worse condition than you.'

'That's good to know.'

'You'll probably end up in adjacent beds.'

'That wouldn't be good.'

'I was trying to be funny. I'll make sure that doesn't happen.'

A second ambulance arrived, with no siren or flashing lights. A paramedic climbed out and went to join the other two, who were stripping off the driver's leathers. 'I need help over here!' shouted Shepherd.

The newly arrived paramedic spoke to his colleagues and one of them pointed at Shepherd. The new arrival jogged over. She was a woman, her red hair tied back in a ponytail. She smiled. 'Hello, sir, I'm Jenny, I'll be your paramedic tonight.'

Shepherd couldn't help but smile back. 'I'm Dan, this is my son Liam. He's walking wounded, I think we can get him to the ambulance without a gurney.'

Jenny squatted down. 'Let me have a look.' Shepherd took his hand away and Jenny peeled the dressing back.

'He's O negative,' said Shepherd.

'Universal donor,' said Jenny. She smiled at Liam. 'Your blood is valuable. Best to spill as little of it as possible.'

'I'm doing my best,' said Liam.

Jenny put the dressing back in place and used some tape to keep it in place. 'Liam, do you think you can walk?'

Liam nodded. 'I think so.'

'If the pain gets too bad or you feel weak, just let me know.'

'I will.'

Jenny and Shepherd got Liam to his feet. Liam grunted but he seemed okay. 'Where will you take him?' Shepherd asked.

'St Thomas' Hospital is closest but I know they're backed up tonight so we'll cross the river to Chelsea and Westminster,' said the paramedic. 'Do you want to come with us?'

'I do, but I think the police will want to speak to me.' A BMW SUV roared down the road towards them, siren wailing and blue lights flashing. It had yellow circles in the corner of its windows, showing that it was an ARV – an armed response vehicle.

Shepherd and Jenny walked Liam across the road. The other two paramedics were still working on the injured driver. They had stripped the leathers away from his upper body and cut away his sweatshirt to reveal a jagged hole in his chest.

They got to the ambulance and Shepherd helped Jenny get Liam into the back and onto a gurney.

The BMW's siren turned off and the passenger side doors opened and two firearms officers climbed out, a young blonde woman and a bald man who was probably twice her weight. The woman was in the back and she handed a carbine to her male colleague and shouldered her own weapon as they walked towards the paramedics.

'I need to talk to these guys,' said Shepherd.

'No problem,' said Jenny. 'I'll get Liam comfortable and set up a drip.'

Shepherd turned to face the firearms officers. He kept his hands to the side, palms open. He didn't want there to be any misunderstanding. 'Two shooters, one dead, one injured,' said Shepherd. He addressed the woman, she was the one with the sergeant's stripes. 'They came at us on a bike.' He gestured with his chin. Pointing was never a good idea when faced with armed cops. 'My son took a bullet in the shoulder, but it's not life threatening. His name is Liam Shepherd. I'm Dan Shepherd. The shooter had an Ingram machine pistol. The gun is under the Toyota over there.'

The male officer bent down and peered under the car. 'I see it,' he said.

'You in the job, Mr Shepherd?' asked the sergeant.

'I used to be,' he said.

'And now?'

'I work for another agency,' said Shepherd. 'They should be in touch shortly. Until then, I'd like to go to the hospital with my son.' He gestured at the ambulance with his chin. 'He's bleeding quite heavily.'

'I'm afraid we'll need you to stay here until the detectives arrive,' said the sergeant.

Shepherd knew there was no point in arguing with her. They had procedures to follow and until they knew for sure what had happened, they had to consider him a potential threat. 'Not a problem,' he said.

'What happened here, Mr Shepherd? Who shot these two men?'

'I'll explain everything to the detectives when they get here.'

'You can explain to me. Now.'

Shepherd shook his head. 'No. You need to protect the crime scene for the SOCO team. And make the weapon safe.'

The sergeant slowly moved her carbine so that it was pointing at Shepherd's chest. Her finger was on the trigger. 'Are you going to give me a problem, Mr Shepherd?'

Shepherd slowly raised his hands, fingers splayed. 'Absolutely not,' he said. 'My son has been shot, we're the victims here.'

'So, I'll ask you again. If the two men shot your son, who shot them? Was it you?'

'I don't have a gun, sergeant. As you can see.'

'Are you carrying any weapons?'

'I have a Swiss Army knife in my left jacket pocket.'

'A knife? Why do you need a knife, Mr Shepherd?'

'It's a Swiss Army knife. The blade is three inches long and so is permitted under the 1988 Criminal Justice Act. I used it to cut away my son's jacket.'

The sergeant held her carbine with her right hand and used her left hand to fish out Shepherd's pocket knife. She looked at it, then slipped it into a pocket on her Kevlar vest. 'I'll look after that for you,' she said.

Shepherd knew that he had every right to carry the knife, but he didn't argue. There was no point.

'Someone must have shot the men on the motorcycle, meaning there was someone else here. Who was that?' she asked.

'Sergeant, all you need to do is secure the crime scene.' Shepherd gestured over at the paramedics who were still working on the driver of the bike. 'And once he's in hospital, you need to make sure that he's handcuffed to his bed, and that he's kept under armed guard.'

'I doubt he's a threat to anyone at the moment.'

'He's a professional assassin, sergeant. And even with a bullet in his chest, he's still a danger. Plus, the organisation he works for is very much a threat. He failed in his mission which means his bosses might well decide that he's a liability that needs to be taken care of. So, he needs an armed guard until he's well enough to be taken into custody.'

'Who the hell are you, Mr Shepherd?' Her radio buzzed. 'Receiving,' she said. She walked away, obviously listening to someone through her earpiece. Her colleague kept his carbine aimed at Shepherd's chest. Shepherd had his hands in the air, palms open, an easy smile on his face. 'Nice night for it,' said Shepherd. He nodded at the ambulance. 'Can I take care of my son now?' he asked.

'You need to stay where you are until we know what's going on,' said the man.

Shepherd kept his hands in the air as he turned to look at the ambulance. 'Liam, are you okay in there?' he called.

'He's fine, Mr Shepherd,' said Jenny. 'He's hooked up to a drip and his blood pressure and heart rate are good. We'll be heading off shortly.'

The other two paramedics lifted the injured rider onto the gurney and raised it before pushing it over to the first ambulance. Shepherd smiled thinly. At least the man wouldn't be travelling with Liam.

The sergeant returned and flashed him a cold smile. 'Right, Mr Shepherd, I'm told that I'm to offer you every assistance.' She looked over at her colleague. 'Mr Shepherd apparently has friends in high places, Barry,' she said. 'Can you go with the rider in the ambulance and stay with him until we get a team to the hospital?'

'No problem, sarge.'

'It'll probably be Chelsea and Westminster,' said Shepherd. 'Can I attend to my son, please?'

'Of course,' said the sergeant.

'And I want to go to the hospital with him.'

'That's your call, Mr Shepherd. I'm told that whatever you want, you get.' Shepherd could tell from her tone that she wasn't happy about the situation, but there was too much going on for him to care about her hurt feelings.

'That's what I want, sergeant. If and when CID turn up, you can tell them I'll be at the hospital. Are we good?'

'I think we are, Mr Shepherd,' said the sergeant. 'Though I will be speaking to CID before they interview you. There are a number of questions that need answering.'

Shepherd lowered his hands slowly. 'And could I have my knife back?' he said. 'Please?'

The sergeant looked as if she wanted to refuse his request, but she reached into the pocket of her vest and took it out. She looked at it and he could tell that she was measuring it with her eyes, hoping that the blade was above the three-inch legal limit. It wasn't and she gave it back to him. He thanked her and walked over to the ambulance.

Jenny was checking Liam's IV bag. 'All right if I ride in with you?' he asked.

'Of course,' said Jenny. She nodded at the police. 'Are they all squared away?'

Shepherd smiled ruefully. 'For the moment.'

CHAPTER 51

Jenny and the ambulance driver wheeled Liam into the accident and emergency room on a gurney, even though he protested that he was perfectly able to walk. He was examined almost immediately by a young Asian doctor who confirmed that no nerves or bones had been damaged, and that the round had passed clean through the flesh. The doctor's place was taken by two nurses who efficiently cleaned the wound before applying antiseptic ointment, packing it with gauze and bandaging it. Jenny had given him painkillers and they seemed to have done the job.

After the nurses had finished, the doctor came back, inspected their work and nodded his approval. 'How do you feel now pain-wise, on a scale of one to ten where one is barely noticeable and ten would have you screaming in agony?'

'Two, or three maybe,' said Liam. 'A bit more if I move it.'

'Yes, you don't want to be moving it for a few days,' said the doctor. 'We'll put a sling on to restrict movement while the shoulder heals, but I'm reluctant to keep you in. To be honest, the longer you stay in hospital, the more likely you are to catch something unpleasant. I think you'd be better off at home.'

'I can take care of him,' said Shepherd. 'Can we leave?'

'I'm afraid we have to wait for the police,' said the doctor.

'They have to be informed of all gunshot wounds and then it's up to them.'

Shepherd nodded. He knew there was no point pushing his point, the medical staff had procedures that they had to follow. 'Sure,' he said. 'Do you know how long they'll be?'

'We made a call. Sometimes they're here in minutes, sometimes it can take hours. It depends on how busy they are.' He smiled and nodded at the entrance to the emergency room. 'Speak of the devil,' he said. Two men were standing there, talking to a nurse. One was tall and thin, wearing a dark brown raincoat, his brown hair flecked with grey. The other was a woman, her jet-black hair cut into a sharp bob that grazed her jawline. Her skin was pale, almost porcelain, but dotted with freckles along her nose and cheekbones. Both had the world-weary look of people who had been lied to for years. The nurse pointed in Shepherd's direction and they walked purposefully towards him.

'I'll leave you to it,' said the doctor, and he hurried away, his white coat flapping behind him.

The detectives both produced warrant cards, but it was the woman who spoke. 'Are you Mr Shepherd?' she asked.

'Dan Shepherd, yes. This is my son, Liam.'

'I'm Detective Sergeant Patricia Harris, this is my colleague, Detective Constable Philip Steele. We're investigating the shootings in Battersea this evening.' The detectives put their warrant cards away. 'For reasons best known to him, my boss has told me that I'm to put you under no pressure and that any assistance you might offer will be voluntarily. What can you tell me about what happened, Mr Shepherd?'

'My son and I were walking to an Indian restaurant when a guy on a motorcycle started shooting at us. Liam was hit, and we both fell behind a car. That's pretty much all I remember.'

The sergeant looked at Liam. 'And you, sir?'

'I really didn't see anything,' said Liam apologetically. 'I was shot from behind.'

'Why would anyone want to shoot you?' asked Steele.

'I have no idea,' said Liam. 'I assume it was a random nutter.'

'What do you do for a living?' Steele asked.

'I'm a helicopter pilot.' Liam smiled. 'A glorified chauffeur, really. Just moving people from one place to another.'

'And you Mr Shepherd?' said Harris. 'Are you able to tell me who you work for.'

'I'm a civil servant.'

The sergeant smiled thinly. 'Yes, I bet you are. And do you have any idea why someone might want to kill you?'

'You really should be asking the guy who was driving the motorcycle,' said Shepherd.

'Now of course I'm in an awkward position, aren't I, Mr Shepherd? My copper's instinct tells me that you know more than you're saying, but as I told you, I'm not supposed to put you under any pressure. I'm assuming you know why that is, and I have my suspicions, but we all have to deal with the world the way it is and not with the way we'd like it to be, so I shall just have to hold my peace.' She gave him a sarcastic smile to let him know that she was far from happy with the position she found herself in. 'Anyway, we've just been to see the motorcycle rider. He's in the ICU, in a life-threatening condition, they say.'

'Did he tell you anything?'

'He can't speak. He's unconscious and they're not sure if he'll recover or not.'

'Have you taken his prints and DNA?'

The sergeant shook her head. 'We're not geared up for that. We'll have to wait for a forensics team.'

'We're in a hospital, how difficult can it be?'

'Point taken,' said the sergeant.

'Did he have any ID on him?'

'Nothing.'

'Have you run the bike through DVLA?'

'It was stolen, two days ago.'

Shepherd grimaced. Of course it was. They were pros, and if things had gone to plan the bike would have gone up in flames and they would have made their escape in another vehicle. But Lex Harper had put paid to their plans. And saved Shepherd's life. Liam's too, probably. The shooter didn't seem to be worried about who his shots hit. Spray and pray, pretty much.

'And the other shooter, the one who shot the two men on the bike?' said the sergeant. 'What can you tell me about him?'

'Nothing, I'm afraid,' said Shepherd.

'Because you can't, or because you won't?' asked Steele.

Shepherd smiled but didn't answer the question.

'Whoever he was, he knew what how to handle a gun,' said Harris.

'I'd guess so.'

'And he was a regular good Samaritan by all accounts. Saved your bacon, from the sound of it.'

Sergeant Harris looked at Liam. 'What about you, sir? Can you remember anything about the man?'

'I was shot from behind and I hit the floor,' said Liam. 'I really don't remember anything after that.'

'No description? Of him or what he was wearing?'

Liam pulled a face. 'No, sorry.'

'That's a pity,' said the sergeant. She looked at Shepherd. 'Now is there anything else that you can tell us that might help our investigation? I'm under instructions not to press you, but I could do with some help here.'

'There was a shooting outside Bicester yesterday. That's Thames Valley so it might not have come across your desk. Four people were killed on the M40, shot with a .45 machine pistol. And another man was shot and killed on the industrial estate. The guys who shot at us were the guys responsible for those killings. So you need a ballistics report on the MAC-10 in Battersea. There's every chance that it's the same weapon.'

The sergeant's eyebrows shot skywards. 'That is helpful, thank you.'

'Thames Valley will have sent a forensics team out there so you should liaise with them. But I do think that at some point the investigation might well be taken off you.'

'For reasons of national security?'

Shepherd nodded. 'Yes.'

'So, I'm just going through the motions?'

'I wouldn't say that. We're working towards the same ends.'

'Can you tell me if this is terrorism-related, at least?'

Shepherd shrugged. 'I'm sorry.'

'It's not the first time, and I'm sure it won't be the last,' said Harris. 'I won't take up any more of your time.'

The two detectives headed out.

'So, we can go home now?' asked Liam.

'We need to get a sling on you,' said Shepherd. 'And we need to get you sorted with some clothes – your jacket and shirt were pretty much destroyed.'

Shepherd looked around for a free nurse but grinned when

he saw Harper walking into the emergency room, swinging an Adidas duffel. He had changed his clothes and was wearing black jeans, a grey sweatshirt and a shapeless beige linen jacket, topping the outfit off with a Liverpool baseball cap.

'What are you doing here?' Shepherd asked.

Harper held up the bag. 'Popped back to get a change of clothes for Liam, I figured what he had on is probably ruined.' He gestured at Liam's blue hospital robe. 'And those have never really been a good look.'

'Good man,' said Shepherd. 'Can you do me a favour and once he's changed see if you can get them to put a sling on.'

'Where are you going, Dad?' asked Liam.

'I'm going to check on the guy that shot you.'

'Seriously?'

'Seriously,' said Shepherd. 'I won't be long.' He left the emergency room and followed the signs for the ICU. The armed officer who had been at the Battersea scene was standing outside a door, cradling his carbine. 'Everything okay, Barry?' said Shepherd.

The officer frowned, then nodded as he recognised Shepherd. 'In a coma, apparently.'

'Did a couple of detectives visit him?'

'Yeah. In and out. He obviously can't say anything.'

'What about you? How long will you be here?'

'They're trying to get a replacement but they're short-handed today.'

'Sorry about that.'

'Nah, it's not a problem, I'm grateful for the overtime. But he's not going to be going anywhere soon.'

'It's not that, it's more that the people he works for have a habit of cutting their losses. Just keep your eyes open.'

'You think they'll try something at the hospital?'

'I think they wouldn't think twice about it.' He nodded at the door. 'Is it okay if I go in?'

'The sarge says you have friends in high places, so sure. Go ahead.'

Shepherd thanked him and pushed the door open. There was only the one bed in the room, flanked by beeping machines. The man was lying on his back, his face obscured by a breathing tube. Shepherd closed the door and went over to stand by the bed. The man was in his thirties with a square chin and a receding hairline. His eyes were closed. Shepherd's jaw clenched as he stared down at the man who only a few hours earlier had tried to end his life. The man who had come close to killing Liam. For money.

It took a particular sort of human being to kill for money. It was true that soldiers were paid to kill, but soldiers fought for a reason, to defend their country or to protect their government's interests. And when soldiers did fight, usually the enemy was fighting back. But assassins, hired killers, didn't have any moral right on their side, they had no justification for taking lives other than to improve their bank balance.

The man lying in the hospital bed had shown no qualms about firing a machine pistol in a public place and hadn't cared whether or not civilians got caught in the cross fire.

'You almost killed my son,' Shepherd said quietly. He held up his hand, first finger and thumb an inch apart, even though the man in the bed couldn't see him. 'You and your mate came this close to killing him. The doctors say you're in a coma so I don't know if you can hear me or not, but I want you to know that however this works out, your life is over. If you die, you die, I doubt anyone will shed a tear for you. If you pull through, you'll be questioned, and I'll be one of the men questioning you. By the time I'm finished, I'll know everything there is to know about you. The way our court system is at the moment, you'll probably only go to prison for a few years, ten at the most. But I'll be waiting for you when you do get out, and I won't be spraying bullets in a public street, I'll be in a room somewhere standing a few feet in front of you, probably with a Glock in my hand, and I'll be looking into your eyes as I double tap you in the face.' He forced a smile. 'Just so you know.'

CHAPTER 52

B ack in the emergency room, a pretty West Indian nurse was fitting a sling on Liam, who was now wearing one of Shepherd's polo shirts.

Harper walked over to Shepherd. 'All good?' he asked.

'He's in a coma.'

'Do you want me to . . .' Harper left the sentence unfinished.

'Lex, we're in a hospital.'

'Wouldn't be the first time,' said Harper, with a shrug.

'I'm sure, but no, we need to talk to him if he ever wakes up.' He grinned over at Liam. 'You okay?'

'The painkillers they gave me have kicked in nicely,' he said. 'I'm going to be off flying duties for a while so my CO isn't going to be happy.'

'I can get someone from the Regiment to talk to him.'

Liam laughed. 'I'm not a kid, Dad.'

Shepherd held up his hands. 'Sorry. Just trying to help.'

'I'm grateful, really, but I can handle it. I'm not due back for a couple of days and they'll be able to find me a desk role until I'm fit to fly again.'

'There you are, you're good to go,' said the nurse. 'And we'll see you tomorrow to change the dressing. Just tell the desk why you're here and we should be able to do it straight away, assuming we have the staff.' She smiled apologetically.

'Though that's a big assumption,' she said. She looked at her watch. 'Actually, you could probably leave it until the day after tomorrow. First thing is usually the quietest time, between five and seven. Definitely avoid late evening, it can be bedlam.'

'Thank you, Gemma,' said Liam. He flashed her a beaming smile and held the nurse's look for a couple of seconds before she blushed and looked away. 'I don't suppose I could have your phone number, just in case I have problems with the sling?'

She laughed. 'Maybe next time I see you.'

'Will you be here first thing the day after tomorrow?'

'I will,' she said.

Liam grinned. 'So it's a date.'

She laughed again and her soft brown eyes sparkled. 'No, it's not. It's an appointment.' She was still laughing as she walked away.

'Pretty girl,' said Shepherd.

'Smart, too,' said Liam. 'Did you know that all nurses have to go to university?'

'It's been that way since 2013,' said Shepherd.

'I don't think they could ever make the armed forces a degree-only profession,' said Liam. 'What about you, Lex. Did you go to university?'

'The University of Life,' said Harper with a grin. 'I graduated with honours.' He took a Wrangler denim jacket from the Adidas bag and draped it over Liam's shoulders. 'Right, I think we're good to go,' he said. He looked over at Shepherd. 'How do you want to play it? An Uber back to Battersea?'

'Let's stay on the safe side,' said Shepherd. 'We can flag down a black cab outside the hospital and switch cabs at Imperial Wharf station.'

'You think they might be following us?' asked Liam.

'Better safe than sorry,' said Shepherd. 'Until we find out for sure how they knew where I was, we need to be careful.'

'It'll be fine, Spider,' said Harper. 'Lightning doesn't strike twice. Besides, one's dead and the other's in ICU, I think they've learned their lesson. But sure, it always pays to be careful.'

Shepherd and Harper walked Liam outside. 'Are you okay?' asked Shepherd.

'You don't have to keep asking, Dad,' said Liam. 'I'm fine. And now we have matching scars. That's pretty cool, right?'

Shepherd chuckled. 'That's right.' Shepherd had taken a bullet in the shoulder in Afghanistan many years earlier, fired from an AK-74. 'Though mine wasn't a through and through, they had to dig the bullet out.'

'It's not a competition,' said Liam.

'You're right,' said Shepherd. He smiled. In fact, the AK-74 round had come very close to killing him. The round hit the bone and went downwards, missing an artery by half an inch. If there hadn't been a helicopter handy to medevac him to safety, he would have died in the desert. But he had no intention of telling that to Liam. 'But if it makes you feel any better, you got hit by the bigger round, so you'd win.'

'It doesn't,' said Liam. 'But yes, I guess I would.'

They reached the road and Harper flagged down a black cab. 'Walking wounded,' said the cabbie cheerily as he spotted the sling.

'Imperial Wharf,' said Harper. They climbed into the back of the cab. Shepherd and Harper looked around as the cab sped off. There were no obvious tails but they kept checking during the five minutes it took to drive to the station. Harper gave the driver a ten-pound note and told him to keep the change, then the three men hurried inside the station. They spent a couple of minutes reassuring themselves that they hadn't been followed before heading out again and taking a second black cab to Battersea. Again, Shepherd and Harper were constantly looking around to check that they didn't have a tail.

The cab pulled up outside the building and Harper handed over another ten-pound note. Harper got out of the cab and looked around before helping Liam out. Shepherd followed, slammed the door shut and waved at the cabbie.

'Do you see it?' asked Harper as the cab pulled away from the kerb.

'The black Lexus GX with the engine running?'

'Of course you saw it. What do you think?'

The Lexus was on the other side of the road, exhaust fumes feathering from the rear.

'I don't think hitmen tend to use sixty-five grand cars for their hits. And there are four people in the car, which would be overkill.'

'Car could be stolen, and after they fucked up last time, they might want to make sure.'

'You two never relax, do you?' said Liam.

'It's called heightened awareness,' said Shepherd. 'It's a survival skill.'

'Get your dad to talk to you about fire extinguishers some time,' said Harper. 'It's an eye-opener.'

'Fire extinguishers?' repeated Liam.

The rear passenger door of the Lexus opened. 'Here we go,' said Harper, moving to stand between Shepherd and Liam and the car. He handed the holdall to Shepherd. 'Move to the entrance, quickly,' he said, reaching behind him with his right hand.

'Are you still carrying, Lex?' asked Shepherd.

'Go,' said Harper. 'I'll take care of this.'

'Come on,' he said. Shepherd put his arm around Liam's shoulder and guided him to the entrance.

'Stand down,' called Harper, releasing his grip on whatever he had tucked into the back of his pants. 'False alarm.'

Shepherd turned to look at the Lexus, and he smiled when he recognised who had climbed out. It was Charlotte Button, his former boss at the long since disbanded Serious Organised Crime Agency who had gone on to work for MI5. She had also been his boss at MI5 before she had left under a cloud, the cloud being that she had used government resources – including the Pool – to take revenge on the Islamic terrorists responsible for the death of her husband. Her chestnut hair was slightly longer than the last time he had seen her, and the colour probably owed more to dye than to her genes these days, but other than that, she had barely changed. Her chin was up as she looked over at him and he caught a flicker of a smile.

'You know her?' asked Liam.

'My old boss,' said Shepherd.

'She doesn't look that old,' said Liam. 'In fact, I'd say she's fit.'

'Old as in former,' said Shepherd.

'Liam's right though, she is fit,' said Harper.

A man in a black suit climbed out of the back, broad shouldered with a shaved head and black Oakley sunglasses shielding his eyes. Another big man, this one in a blazer and black trousers, got out of the front. His sunglasses were perched on top of his head. Both men were looking around, hands free at their sides. Shepherd couldn't see any telltale bulges, but he would have bet good money that they were carrying.

Button's heels clicked on the tarmac as she walked across the road. She was wearing a Burberry raincoat and carrying a black Prada handbag. 'Dan, so good to see you,' she said. 'You've had an interesting few days, I gather.'

The two minders crossed the road, giving Button plenty of space but staying close enough to intervene if there was a problem.

'That's one way of describing it, yes.'

Button smiled at Liam. 'Sorry to hear what happened to you, Liam.' She nodded at the sling. 'Under the circumstances, I won't offer to shake hands, but it's very nice to meet you. My name is Charlie, I used to work with your dad.'

'And with me, let's not forget,' said Harper.

'How could I possibly forget, Lex?' she said. She smiled at Liam. 'How's the shoulder?'

'It's okay, the painkillers have kicked in and the doc says there won't be any permanent damage. It's a pity it didn't happen while I was on duty, I'd be up for a medal.'

'What are your plans for the next few days?'

'I'll stay with Dad until the arm's fixed. I have to go back every day to get the dressing changed.'

'I'm sure Dan will take good care of you,' she said. She turned her smile to Shepherd. 'Can I have a word, in private?'

'Sure, come upstairs. I'll make tea.'

She gestured at her car. 'More privacy there,' she said. 'It's swept for bugs first thing in the morning and last thing at night.'

'I'm sticking with Spider until this is over,' said Harper.

'That's good to hear, but my guys are perfectly capable of keeping him safe, Lex.'

'I could take them.'

Button chuckled. 'I'm sure you'd give it a go, but really, he'll be safe in my hands. Dan and I will sit in my car and have a chat, you can wait inside with Liam. We'll be fifteen minutes at most.'

Harper looked across at Shepherd and Shepherd nodded. 'It'll be fine.'

'Call me if you need me.'

'Of course.'

'Come on, Liam, let's leave the adults to talk,' said Harper.

'Nice meeting you, Charlie,' said Liam.

'And you, Liam.'

Harper took Liam inside the building. Charlotte nodded at the guy in the black suit and he walked over, taking a grey pouch from his pocket. 'I know this sounds paranoid, but can you pop your mobile in there for the duration,' said Button.

'Seriously?'

'I know, it's a brave new world, isn't it? But needs must.'

Shepherd took out two mobile phones and put them in the pouch. The minder sealed it and put it back in his pocket. Button walked with Shepherd across the road to her car. He opened the door for her and she smiled. 'Always the gentleman,' she said. 'Thank you.'

She got in and Shepherd closed the door. He walked around the rear of the car and climbed in the other side. Button spoke to the driver, 'George, if you could just leave us alone for a few minutes, that would be great,' she said.

'No problem, ma'am,' he said, and got out of the car to join the two bodyguards.

'Must be nice living so close to the park,' she said. 'Easy place to exercise in the fresh air.'

'It is,' he said.

'You know the story about the Duke of Wellington and the Earl of Winchilsea?' asked Button.

'I don't,' said Shepherd.

'Before our time, obviously,' she said. 'Way back in 1829, almost two hundred years ago. The park was known as Battersea Fields then, and it was a popular spot for duelling. Anyway, the Duke of Wellington and the Earl of Winchilsea met there to settle a matter of honour, I can't remember what it was, but they decided to settle it with pistols. So, they got set up, a pistol each, and they faced each other. The order to fire was given and the duke aimed wide and the earl fired his pistol into the air. End of duel.'

'Bit of a waste of time, then.'

'Well, I suppose that's one way to look at it,' said Button. 'Certainly, the world was a very different place back then. More chivalrous.'

'I'm sure that made up for the open sewers, air pollution, cholera, and the fact that most people died before reaching fifty.'

'Swings and roundabouts,' said Button, with a smile.

'I do remember that 1829 was the year that Sir Robert Peel set up the Metropolitan Police.'

'Indeed. And I wonder what he'd think of the state of the capital almost two centuries later? I mean, what happened to you and Liam almost defies comprehension. Who uses a machine pistol to carry out a targeted killing? And clearly you were the target, not Liam.'

'Clearly,' said Shepherd, wondering where the conversation was heading. Charlotte Button was not one for idle chit-chat.

'But they didn't care, did they? About the collateral damage?'

'We think it was the same team who took out a car outside Bicester,' said Shepherd. 'And I'm fairly sure they also killed another guy as we were moving him to a safe house.'

'Paul Dutch? The Dutchman?'

'You know about that?'

'You'd be surprised at what I know, Dan.'

'The MAC-10 made sense when they were firing at vehicles, but today was a bad call on their part. They would have had more success if the shooter had got off the bike and used a handgun.'

'I'm sure Lex would have handled it, either way.'

'Well, we heard the bike so Lex had time to get his gun out. If the shooter had been on foot and got closer . . .' He grimaced. 'They made a bad decision and we were lucky.'

'Liam was *very* lucky. A few inches to the left and . . .' She shrugged. 'Anyway, there's no point in thinking about what might have been, is there?'

'Usually not, no.'

'How do you feel about the men who attacked you?'

'How do I feel? What sort of question is that?'

'I'm told you went in to talk to the surviving member of the hit team.'

Shepherd's eyes narrowed. 'What big ears you have.'

'And I keep them close to the ground.'

'He didn't say anything,' said Shepherd. 'He's in a coma and not likely to pull through.'

'I'm sure the doctors will do everything they can, the NHS is a wonderful institution,' she said, and Shepherd couldn't tell if she was being serious or ironic. 'Look, Dan, I think I should get to the point.'

'That would simplify things, yes.'

'I've been asked to get involved in the investigation of The Office. The feeling is that my specialist knowledge might be useful.'

'Asked by whom?'

'Giles Pritchard, of course.'

'Then why are you and I having this conversation, Charlie? Why isn't Giles Pritchard telling me this?'

'Two words: plausible deniability,' said Button. 'This is not a conversation he can ever have with you. I'm acting as a buffer, giving you the information you need but without any connection to him. So if, down the line, he is asked about who said what, he can put his hand on his heart and say that he never discussed this with you. The Prime Minister has been similarly isolated.'

'So . . . this conversation never happened?'

'Oh, it happened, Dan. But it's well below the radar and will stay that way. We now know who is running The Office, and it isn't good news. A decision has been taken at the highest level to close down The Office.'

'Presumably not through the courts?'

'After what has happened over the past few days, any court case would result in a lot of dirty laundry being aired in public, and no one wants that.'

'You've been asked to take care of it? Another dirty job for The Pool?'

'I have been asked to get involved, yes.'

'Which is handy, as it will get rid of your competition.'

She shook her head. 'Oh, Dan, The Office isn't competition. The Pool is government-sanctioned, we couldn't possibly act without their protection. And those private sector jobs that we do carry out can never be in conflict with our government. We wouldn't be caught dead spraying bullets from a machine pistol in a crowded street. My people are professionals and they behave that way.'

'Even so, you can't deny that you're in the same business.'

'Only in the way that McDonalds and a Michelin star restaurant are both in the business of feeding people. The point is that the government wants this handled off the books, which is why I am now involved.'

'Which is great for you, but why am I here?'

'Giles wants one of his own people on board, and you have been on the case from the start. Plus, you have a personal involvement, of course. After what happened to Liam, I'd have thought that you'd relish the opportunity to get involved.'

'I'm not really one for revenge,' said Shepherd.

Button flashed him a tight smile. 'Come on, Dan, we both know that's not true.'

She looked into his eyes and he looked away first. Charlotte Button knew most of his secrets and, yes, he had taken revenge before. He had taken no pleasure in it, but there were times when wrongs needed righting and to do that he had taken matters into his own hands.

'We have identified the man who was calling himself Neville Kingsley, but he is just a frontman, a point of contact. That's not his real name, which I think you suspected. He is actually Maxwell Wheeler, who was a hitman himself in the eighties and nineties but switched over to the agency model. But two years ago, a couple of Russians muscled in, and now he really is just a frontman.'

'So, he works for them now?'

'From what I was told, they didn't give him a choice. Max

has five kids and several dozen nieces and nephews. There's a lot of leverage. And the Russians are nasty pieces of work who used to work for the FSB.'

'That's not good,' said Shepherd. The FSB – the Federal Security Service of the Russian Federation – was the successor to the Soviet Union's KGB, and was based in the KGB's former headquarters in Moscow's Lubyanka Square. The FSB's responsibilities included internal and border security, counter-intelligence and counter-terrorism, but some of its shadier units carried out assassinations for the Russian president, at home and abroad. 'How do we move forward?'

'The Russians are based in London, but most of their finances are offshore. We're following the money trail as we speak, looking for the Iranians responsible for placing the contracts with The Office.'

'How did you get all this intel?' asked Shepherd. 'We've been banging our heads against walls for months.'

'We have our sources, obviously. We pay well for intel, and people know that. People might tell you things out of duty or because you threaten them with legal action, but when you want intel, nothing works better than cold hard cash.' She grinned. 'Or these days, Bitcoin.'

'And Pritchard approached you?'

'He didn't have a choice,' said Button. 'Thames House has been leaking like a sieve, not that he'll ever admit to that. But what happened on the M40 was an absolute disgrace. And you lost a surveillance guy, too, didn't you?'

Shepherd nodded. 'B.A. Parker. It was the same guy who shot Liam.'

'We can't afford to have anything like that happening again,' she said. 'So far, the only people who know what's going to go down are you, me, Giles Pritchard, and the PM. There's nothing on the record, no notes, no diary records, just an informal chat at a cocktail party between Giles and the PM at Number Ten and a face-to-face with me. Giles made it clear that I shouldn't visit Thames House, and because of what's happening, Giles doesn't trust the phones. We had a very nice drink at The Rivoli Bar at The Ritz.' She smiled. 'It's always easy to tell if you're being followed at The Ritz. Any watchers tend to stand out. Anyway, he asked for my help and I agreed. But as of today, there are only four people who know what's being planned.'

'How did you get the names of the Russians?'

'We had surveillance outside Maxwell Wheeler's house. Reznikov paid him a visit two days ago. We got decent photographs of him and facial recognition did the rest. When we looked at his visa application, we got a cross reference with Vladimir Lazovsky and it was a simple matter to join the dots.'

'Nice work.'

'Why thank you. We do our best.'

'It's the sort of work that MI5 should be doing.'

'Well, you say that, but there's no way you would have got the original tip-off that Max Wheeler runs The Office.'

'I guess not,' Shepherd replied, 'but I have something that you don't. I might know who the Iranian contact is.'

'Oh, now that's interesting. I'm all ears.'

'He's a guy called Jafar Hosseini. He's thought to be one of the guys who helped the Islamic Republic finance the 2023 Hamas attacks in Israel. He might be in Dubai at the moment.'

'And how did you come up with his name, pray tell?'

'The girl who was shot in Richmond Park, Layla Latifi, the Iranian dissident, wrote about Hosseini on her blog a couple of weeks before she died.'

'Could be a coincidence?'

'Could be, yes. But after she died, her website and blog were taken down. My hunch is that she would have been on the Iranian hit list anyway, but the blog posting moved her to the top. Hosseini kills two birds with one stone, he gets rid of a dissident and a thorn in his side.'

'What was the blog post about?'

'Pictures of Hosseini drinking champagne with a couple of hookers in Dubai. Layla didn't name him but if anyone back in Iran had recognised him, he'd be in big trouble.'

'Does Giles know about this?'

'I haven't had the chance to run it by him. But even if he was aware of it, I'm not sure he'd be up for mounting a surveillance operation in Dubai. It'd mean asking Six for help and they're as stretched resources-wise as we are.'

'Well I can certainly start looking for Dubai connections to our two Russians,' said Button. 'I'll get right on it.'

'What are your next steps? Are you going to take out the Russians? If they're former FSB goons, your people will need to be careful.'

'I thought first we should approach Max. If the Russians are threatening him and his family, he might be prepared to help. Giles is amenable to us offering him a deal.'

'Us?'

'Well, Five, obviously.'

'Where is he?'

'Birmingham. We can go up tomorrow. We'll pick you up at five.'

'Five? Five in the morning?'

'Max never leaves his house before ten. His wife Rachel does the school run for their kids, morning and afternoon.

We'll catch him at home while she's out. Best we aim for the morning run, so we need to get to Birmingham about eight o'clock.'

Shepherd nodded. 'Okay, I'll be ready.'

They climbed out of the back of the car. The minder with the pouch gave it to Shepherd. Shepherd opened it and took out his phones.

'You might want to give some thought to changing your phones,' said Button.

'I was wondering that myself.'

'You were attacked here outside your building. And they were waiting for you. Either they got your address from somewhere, in which case you really do have a problem at Thames House, or they're able to track your phones.'

'I got rid of the phone I was using when I was undercover,' said Shepherd. 'These are my personal phones.' He frowned as he realised the implications of what she was saying. 'Shit.'

'I don't want to make you paranoid, but you need to think about how they were able to track you so easily. In a way, it'd be better if it was your phone they used, because if they know where you live then you're going to have to think about moving.'

'Yeah,' said Shepherd. 'I'm going to have to give this some thought.'

'In the meantime, we'll walk you back to your door. I'd hate for something to happen to you on my watch.'

CHAPTER 53

When Shepherd got back to the flat, Harper was frying bacon in the kitchen and Liam was on the sofa, a bottle of lager in his good hand. 'Beer and bacon butties,' said Harper, waving a spatula. 'The breakfast of champions.'

'Bit late for breakfast,' said Shepherd, helping himself to a bottle of lager from the fridge.

'It's never too late for breakfast,' said Harper.

Shepherd went over to Liam and sat down in the armchair opposite him. He raised his bottle in salute. 'Here's to narrow escapes,' he said.

'I'll drink to that,' said Liam. He leaned over and clinked his bottle against his dad's.

'I'm sorry you were put in that position,' said Shepherd.

Liam grinned. 'Shit happens,' he said. 'So, tell me about the fire extinguishers.'

'Yeah, Lex always teases me about that,' said Shepherd. 'It's basic tradecraft. Whenever you visit a new location, you check for fire extinguishers. You need to know how many and where they are.'

'Because?'

'Partly because fire extinguishers are usually kept close to fire exits, and you always need to know where your exits are and to be able to find them in the dark or when the place is full of smoke.'

'That makes sense,' said Liam.

'But fire extinguishers can also be used as weapons. You can pick one up and belt somebody with them, or if it's a CO_2 extinguisher you can activate it and spray someone in the face.'

'And then hit them with it?'

'Exactly,' said Shepherd.

'That's useful to know,' said Liam.

'Joking apart, it might save your life one day. Especially knowing where your exits are.'

Liam looked over at Harper. 'We didn't really do holidays when I was a kid, but when we did go away and stayed at a hotel, the first thing Dad would do was to show me all the fire exits. Without fail.'

Harper grinned. 'I do exactly the same,' he said. 'Your dad's right. One day it might save your life. It's like always checking under your car to make sure there isn't a bomb there.'

'You're joking, right?'

Harper's grinned widened. 'Maybe.'

Shepherd put his bottle down on the coffee table and went over to a sideboard. He knelt down, opened a drawer, and took out three boxes. He handed one to Liam. 'I need you to deactivate your phone and use this,' he said. It was a cheap Samsung smartphone.

'Oh, come on, Dad, you know I always use iPhones.'

'No one uses an iPhone as a burner phone.'

'That's what this is?' he asked, looking at the box. 'A burner phone?'

'Just until we get this sorted,' said Shepherd. 'These people could be tracking my phone and if they're tracking my phone, they could well be tracking yours and Lex's.'

'I only ever use burner phones,' said Harper, as he carried a large plate piled high with bacon sandwiches over to the coffee table. 'I'd say that breakfast is served but your dad is insisting that I call it dinner.'

'Best you change your phone, too,' Shepherd said to Harper.

'Will do.'

'I don't have to destroy my SIM card, do I?' asked Liam. 'I can't afford to lose all my numbers, I don't have your freak memory.'

'You don't have to destroy the card, you can use it again once this has all been resolved. But you can't use it in your burner phone. Best you write down any numbers you need and input them manually into your burner phone. And you need to remove the battery of your old phone.'

'I don't know how to do that,' said Liam. 'It's an iPhone and they're sealed, aren't they?'

'It's easy enough,' said Harper, picking up a bacon sandwich. 'I'll do it for you.'

Shepherd went back to the sideboard, opened another drawer and took out three SIM card packs. He gave one each to Harper and Liam, then sat down and took out his phone. He pulled off the back and removed the battery and SIM card. Then he unwrapped the new phone and in between bites of his sandwich he inserted the SIM card and powered the phone up.

'Lex, I need to go out,' said Shepherd.

'No problem, I'll ride shotgun.'

'Nah, you should stay here and look after Liam.'

'I don't need looking after, Dad,' protested Liam.

'I'm only popping out to see my boss,' said Shepherd.

'Charlie?' asked Harper.

'My other boss,' said Shepherd.

'I'll drive you to Thames House and wait for you,' said Harper.

'I won't be going to Thames House. I'll black cab it, and take the long way around. Any problems and I'll call you.'

'On my bright shiny new burner phone?'

Shepherd smiled. 'Exactly.'

CHAPTER 54

S hepherd took an hour to get to Giles Pritchard's house. It was a four-bedroomed detached house in Highgate, with a manicured garden in front and a single garage to the side. Shepherd knew that Pritchard never drove his own car to Thames House – an office car picked him up and drove him home at night. He usually left the office after six, but it wasn't unusual for him to be in Thames House much later, especially if there was a major operation on the go.

Shepherd had the black cab drive him a couple of hundred yards from the house. He was wearing a long black coat and a scarf and was carrying a dog lead. A dog lead provided the perfect cover for a single man out on his own, any passer-by would assume that he was looking for an errant pet.

Mrs Pritchard arrived home at just before six o'clock, with two teenage schoolchildren in the back seat of her Volvo. The garage door opened automatically and she drove in, the door closing behind her. After a minute or so, lights went on inside so Shepherd assumed they had used an internal door.

Darkness fell and the temperature dropped. Shepherd didn't want to wait in the garden in case Mrs Pritchard spotted him. The last thing he wanted to do was to explain to a couple of cops why he was hiding behind a tree. The house to the left of Pritchard's appeared to be empty, the lights stayed off and there was mail sticking out of the letter box. Shepherd waited until the pavements were clear before opening the gate to the house and slipping inside. It was also detached, but smaller than Pritchard's house and with a double garage. The border between the two gardens was marked with a privet hedge, about six feet tall.

Shepherd found a hiding place between the garage and the hedge. He leant against the wall and went into waiting mode, slowing his breathing and focusing on listening and watching. In the SAS he spent days, sometimes weeks, in outdoor hides, lying on a groundsheet and filling Ziploc bags with his waste, putting up with everything from the cold dampness of a Crossmaglen ditch to the blistering heat of the Afghan desert. Waiting for a few hours outside a Highgate house was a walk in the park by comparison.

Each time a car went by he would tense, but it was almost two hours after Mrs Pritchard had returned home that her husband arrived. The Prime Minister tended to be driven everywhere in an armoured Range Rover Sentinel and government ministers were generally afforded the protection of an armoured Audi A8, but the grey Tesla Model 3 that dropped Pritchard outside his house was a bog-standard car with no added protection.

Shepherd moved quietly alongside the hedge and as the Tesla drove away, he slipped through the gate and hurried after Pritchard. Pritchard heard his footsteps and turned, his hands coming up instinctively to protect himself. He breathed a sigh of relief when he realised it was Shepherd. 'Bloody hell, Dan. You almost gave me a heart attack.'

'Sorry, but I needed to talk to you.'

'You could have just come to Thames House.'

'I wasn't sure whether you'd want to see me or not. Plausible deniability and all.'

Pritchard smiled thinly. 'Ah, Charlotte has reached out to you.'

'She has.'

Pritchard looked around as if he feared that they were being watched. 'Look, Dan, I can't offer to take you inside and I don't want to stand in the driveway with you, are you okay to walk for a bit?'

'Sure.'

They walked back down the drive to the pavement. Pritchard headed left, which Shepherd realised was towards Highgate Cemetery. 'So you met with Charlotte. That's good. And you're okay with what she had to say?'

'I'm just confused. Is it an official operation or not?'

'It's off the books, and it's important that what happens is not linked to MI5 or to Number 10. If you've spoken to Charlotte, you'll know the reason why. Which is why I don't want to be put into a position where I am asked about conversations you and I might or might not have had on the matter. So please choose your words carefully.'

A car engine revved behind them and they both turned to look. It was an Openreach van. Shepherd smiled. 'It's not one of ours,' he said.

'How do you know?'

'The reg.'

Pritchard shook his head. 'That memory of yours really does come in useful, doesn't it.'

'It's a blessing and curse,' said Shepherd. He grinned. 'Joke. It's a blessing. You want me to choose my words carefully. Is that because you don't want to lie down the line?'

'I work for MI5, lying is our business. But I can't lie to a Commons committee, for instance. Or to a court. So I want to be able to put my hand on a stack of bibles and swear that I was not told what The Pool might or might not be doing. And as you'll be liaising with Charlotte, best we keep some distance between us. No offence.'

'None taken. So, The Pool is going to take care of the Russians?'

Pritchard winced. 'She knows what she has to do, let's leave it at that,' he said. 'I do know that the Prime Minister wants to bring this matter to a close as quickly as possible but without any adverse publicity. I'm sure he'd welcome the opportunity for outside agencies to resolve the matter for him, especially as so many of his colleagues – and former colleagues – have links to various oligarchs.'

'Okay, I hear you,' said Shepherd. 'There's another reason I wanted to steer clear of Thames House.'

'You're worried we might have a leak?'

'Aren't you? They know where I live. How did that happen? That flat is mine, sure, but it's owned through an offshore shelf company. There shouldn't be any way of linking it to me, but The Office managed it.'

'Couldn't they just have followed you?'

'My counter-surveillance hasn't let me down before.'

'But these guys are pros. They could have had a team on you.'

Shepherd wrinkled his nose. He wasn't happy at the idea that his tradecraft had let him down, but yes, it was a possibility. 'Maybe I should take a week's holiday?'

'I think that would be a marvellous idea,' said Pritchard.

'I might go somewhere hot and sunny.'

'Birmingham?'

Shepherd chuckled. 'I'll see you in a week.' They reached the stone wall that ran around the cemetery.

'Best not send me a postcard,' said Pritchard.

'There's something else you should know. I might have found the Iranian connection, a member of the Quds Force who is in Dubai. The girl who died in Richmond Park mentioned him in her blog not long before she was killed.'

'Who is he? The guy?'

'Jafar Hosseini. According to Manoj, he was one of the financiers of the October 7 attacks.'

'So he could also be financing The Office? That makes sense.'

'Charlie says she's going to see if there's a money trail, and she'll look at phone traffic. Speaking of which, I've changed my personal phone. I'll text you the new number. After everything that's happened it's also possible that they tracked my phone.'

'Your phone or your legend's phone?'

'That's the problem. I ditched the legend phone when Dutch was killed. It would have to be my office phone or my personal phone.'

'That's not good, Dan.'

'Tell me about it.'

'Are you going to move flats?'

'I don't want to, but I might not have a choice. Lex says I shouldn't worry, that lightning never strikes twice.'

'Unfortunately, it does. Often. In fact, that's the way lightning conductors work.'

'I'll tell him that.' Shepherd turned and walked away into the darkness.

CHAPTER 55

'Run this by me again,' said Harper, waving his lager bottle in the air. 'You can pop up to Birmingham and slot the bastard who has been causing all this mayhem and chaos, but Pritchard doesn't want to know about it?'

'Plausible deniability.'

'And if you'd started to talk about it, what would he have done? Stuck his fingers in his ears and started humming?'

'Probably.'

They were in Shepherd's sitting room, their feet up on the coffee table. The blinds were open and it was a cloudless night giving them a perfect view of a three-quarter moon. Liam had gone to bed. The painkillers were making him drowsy and he had almost nodded off on the sofa several times.

'And the Russians?'

'Same. He's leaving it up to Charlie and The Pool.'

'These Russians, are they acting with the authority of the Kremlin, or are they freelance chancers?'

'Charlie thinks that they've got the Kremlin's blessing. She's still looking at the finances but she's sure that The Office is funded at least partly through Russia.'

Harper sipped his beer. 'So, the plan is to use The Pool to shut down The Office? Am I the only one who thinks this is ironic?'

'Ironic in what way?'

'Well for a start, The Office is pretty much the same as The Pool, isn't it? A bunch of shady characters carrying out murder for hire.'

'That's a small part of what The Pool does, Lex.'

'It may be a small part, but it's still a part. And I speak from experience.'

'The Pool is government-sanctioned. It acts for the greater good.'

Harper laughed. 'I think you'll find that it acts in the best interests of the government,' he said. 'Charlie does the dirty jobs that they can't be seen to be doing themselves.'

'I'm not arguing with you, but The Pool doesn't go around assassinating dissidents and they sure as hell don't put civilians at risk. You're not comparing like with like.'

'Maybe not, but I still think it's ironic that The Pool is going to be paid to kill people who kill people for money.'

'Actually, I'm pretty sure that The Pool won't be getting paid.'

'Charlie's working pro bono?'

'I think the jobs that she does for the government are the price she pays for their protection. I'm fairly sure there isn't a money trail that can be followed.'

'Yeah, Sir Teflon wouldn't go for that. He's made a career from plausible deniability, hasn't he? From Jimmy Savile to the Rochdale grooming gangs.'

Shepherd wagged a finger at him. 'And there we are, back to conspiracy theories.'

Harper grinned and drank his beer. 'What do they want you to do? Head up to Birmingham and wreak havoc?'

'Initially just for a chat with the guy who runs The Office.'

'A chat with the man who sent assassins to mow you down in the street?'

'Yeah.'

'I'll come with you.'

'You need to talk to Charlie about that. It's her operation.'

Harper shook his head. 'I don't care what she says. I already told you, I'm your guardian angel until this is sorted. Where you go, I go.'

'Much as I appreciate that, Lex, I'd be happier if you were here with Liam. Charlie has bodyguards, but Liam would be here on his own, and I wouldn't be able to relax if I knew that he was at risk.'

Harper looked at him for several seconds before nodding. 'Yeah, okay, I hear you.'

CHAPTER 56

S hepherd had shaved and showered and was standing in front of his wardrobe wondering what he should wear when his phone rang. It was Button. 'We'll be downstairs in fifteen minutes,' she said. 'Can you dress like a CID officer?'

'Cheap suit and scuffed shoes?'

'Exactly. See you in fifteen minutes.'

Shepherd took a white shirt, navy tie and a grey suit from the wardrobe and put them on before heading for the sitting room. Liam was sitting on the sofa, watching Sky News. He chuckled when he saw what Shepherd was wearing. 'You look like a double-glazing salesman,' he said.

'That's not the look I'm going for.'

'Where are you going?'

'I've got to interview someone, I probably won't be long. Where's Lex?'

'Still sleeping, I think.'

'Okay, don't go out until I get back.'

'We need milk.'

'I'll bring some back with me.'

Shepherd headed downstairs. There were two cars parked up, engines running. There were three men in the black Lexus GX, but Button was sitting alone in a three-year-old grey Vauxhall Corsa. She waved him over and he jogged across the road. 'Where are we off to?' he asked as he climbed into the front passenger seat.

'Bournville,' she said. 'Famous for its chocolate and one of the posher bits of Birmingham.' She was wearing a blue suit that looked as if it had seen better days, and had swapped her usual Cartier watch for a cheap Casio.

'I didn't realise that Brum had any posh bits.'

'I'll have you know that Bournville has been voted as one of the nicest places to live in Britain,' said Button as she pulled away from the kerb. She drove by the Lexus, which then followed her down the road.

'That'll be about a two and a half hour drive?'

'I think so,' said Button. 'Traffic permitting.'

Shepherd settled back in his seat. 'What do we know about the guy?'

'Maxwell Wheeler seems to be his real name, we have a birth certificate and school record. Left school at eighteen, worked as a clerk for Birmingham City Council for a few years, then as a care home worker in various old folks' homes in and around Birmingham. His employment record stopped about twenty years ago, for six years he simply dropped off the radar. Then he resurfaced back in Birmingham, as a company director.'

'And the company does what?'

'Provides consulting services. Registered for VAT and he pays his corporation tax every year. He married a local girl, Rachel Jones, and has five children, aged from three to eleven. Interestingly, he also has French citizenship, though not through birth apparently, as both parents and all grandparents are British.'

Shepherd smiled. 'Ah, that explains it,' he said.

'Explains what?'

'The consulting services company is presumably a way of washing the money he earned back in the days when he was a contract killer.'

'That's my assumption.'

'So how does a care worker turn into a stone-cold killer?'

'I'm guessing you know the answer to your own question?'

Shepherd's smiled widened. 'The French Foreign Legion. Young Maxwell Wheeler obviously decided he wanted a more adventurous life, so signed up with the legion. You put in five years and you get citizenship, even a new name if that's what you want.'

Button grimaced. 'I missed that. It does explain a lot.'

'And what about The Office finances?'

'It looks as if some of the money goes through his company, but most is held offshore.'

'And what about the killings he carried out on his own?'

'All hearsay,' said Button. 'He had a reputation but he was careful. Never got caught, never charged, never appeared in court. Even the Birmingham cops have nothing on him intelwise. He was a ghost. But our contacts in the Brum criminal underground reckon that he was responsible for two dozen or so killings, usually crims, and more often than not the bodies were never recovered.'

'And the Russians?'

'They're here under their own names, ostensibly working for Mikhail Gagarin, an oligarch based in London. Gagarin claims to be related to the first man in space but there's no evidence of that. He got them visas as IT consultants, and there was no mention of their FSB service in their visa applications. That means they could be deported easily enough, but if we do that, they'll only be replaced.'

'Did you find this out, or did Five?'

She smiled. 'We did the digging. But we've shared the intel with Giles.'

'And he wants you to handle it because they're Russians?'

'He wants it handled off the books, yes. The worry is that if we go through official channels they'll just vanish and someone else will take their place. They're based in the UK, but most of their finances are offshore. We're following the money trail as we speak. But as of today, we're not much further on with Lazovsky and Reznikov, which is why we really need to talk to Wheeler.'

'So good cop, bad cop?'

Button smiled. 'Whatever works,' she said. She reached into her jacket pocket and took out a small black leather wallet with a Metropolitan Police crest on it. 'I'm not expecting to have to show ID, but just in case.'

Shepherd took the wallet and flicked it open to reveal a warrant card with his photograph and a scrawled signature. He smiled when he saw the name. DS Aiden Healy. 'Oh, that's funny,' he said.

'I wondered if you'd get it.'

'I probably watch too much TV,' he said. DS Aiden Healy was the sidekick of TV detective DCI Vera Stanhope. 'You realise that makes you Vera?'

'She's a very effective detective,' said Button. 'One of my favourites.'

CHAPTER 57

There were roadworks on the M40 so it took them almost three hours to drive to Birmingham. Button stuck to the speed limit and the Lexus followed them all the way. Madden lived in a huge detached house on a tree-lined road in Bournville, close to Rowheath Playing Fields. As they left the motorway, Button received a text message. She checked her phone. 'Mrs Wheeler has just left on the school run,' she said.

Wheeler's house was painted white with a steep slate roof and several chimney stacks. It was surrounded by a low stone wall with no gate, and a large circular gravelled drive in front of the house. There were two cars parked in front of a double garage, a black Bentley and a red Porsche Cayenne, both of them less than a year old.

'Mrs Wheeler usually uses a people carrier for the school run,' said Button. 'It usually takes her close to an hour, the kids go to two separate schools and one of them is to the north of Birmingham. So we've got about three quarters of an hour.' She made a call, hands-free. 'Gordon, if you could park some distance away, that would be great. If I need you I'll send you a text, but I'm not expecting trouble.' She smiled at Shepherd. 'Right, Aiden, let's do this,' she said.

'I'm with you all the way, Vera.'

Shepherd looked around. He didn't see any watchers outside

the house, but Button clearly had them in place. Whoever they were, they were good.

Button pulled in behind the Bentley and parked. They climbed out and walked to the front door. There was a doorbell and a large brass knocker in the shape of a lion's head. Shepherd pressed the doorbell, twice. After almost thirty seconds they heard a bolt rattle and the door opened a few inches. A man peered out. He was five ten or eleven, with greying hair tied back in a ponytail and wearing wire-framed spectacles. His eyes narrowed as he looked at Button. 'We'd like to come in and have a chat with you, Mr Wheeler,' she said. 'Before your wife returns.'

'What's this got to do with my wife?' Wheeler blinked as he looked at Button and then over her shoulder at the Vauxhall. His jaw tightened as he put two and two together and came up with cop. He saw Shepherd for the first time. 'You're Darren Griffiths.' he said. His face hardened. 'What are you doing here?'

'Your time is running out, Mr Wheeler,' said Button. 'We've tried to be nice about this by waiting until your wife leaves and ringing your doorbell, we could have broken down the door with the heavy mob.'

'I need to call my lawyer.'

'In which case we'll happily wait right here until Rachel comes back. Maybe we should talk to her anyway.'

'What's this about?' snapped Wheeler.

Button flashed him a cold smile. 'You know what it's about,' she said. 'And if you'd rather talk to us under caution at a police station, well, that can certainly be arranged.' Shepherd had to admire her poker face – there was nothing to even remotely suggest that she was lying. 'But I wonder how your

Russian partners would react if you were to be taken into police custody?'

The colour drained from Wheeler's face. 'They're not my partners.'

'Your bosses then,' said Button. 'Look, it doesn't matter what terms you use to define your relationship with them, the longer we stand here on your doorstep, the more likely it is they'll find out that you're talking to us.'

'They're not my bosses,' snapped Wheeler. 'Do you have a warrant?'

'Of course I don't have a warrant, Max. We're just here for a chat. And perhaps a cup of tea if you can run to one.' Wheeler's eyes narrowed as he stared at her. She smiled brightly. 'Now you're wondering how easy it would be to have me killed, but I'm here to tell you that it wouldn't be easy at all, Max.'

'Who the hell are you?'

'Well, if names are important, you can call me Samantha. Darren you already know, obviously.'

Shepherd was impressed at the casual way that Button used the name of his legend. She had obviously picked up on the fact that Wheeler didn't seem to know who Shepherd really was.

'Look, Max, you know you're neck-deep in shit and Samantha is the only person who is offering you a snorkel,' said Shepherd. 'In the last week you've had at least seven people killed that we know about, and your people came very close to killing me. One of your team is in a coma, God bless him, but the other is well dead, as you probably know. And we're fairly sure that it was same two who killed five people outside Bicester. Their fondness for the MAC-10 is a bit of a giveaway.'

'What do you want?' Wheeler growled, keeping a tight grip on his door.

'How many times do I have to tell you?' said Button. 'A chat.' She looked at her Casio watch. 'Your wife will be home in less than an hour, Max. Tick, tock. Tick tock.'

Wheeler gritted his teeth, then reluctantly opened the door. For the first time they could see what he was wearing: Versace jeans and a Ralph Lauren denim shirt. He had a thick gold chain on his right wrist and a diamond encrusted Patek Philippe watch on his left. 'In,' he said.

Button followed Shepherd into the hall. Wheeler closed the front door. He was barefoot, Shepherd realised, his toenails perfectly manicured. 'In there,' said Wheeler, pointing at a door down the hall. Button and Shepherd went in. It was a huge room with French windows overlooking a well-kept lawn and beyond it a large white wood gazebo covered in roses.

There were two overstuffed leather sofas either side of a chest-high Victorian fireplace and a dozen or so other pieces that wouldn't have looked out of place in a West End antiques store.

Button sat down but Shepherd went to stand by the French windows. Just outside was a tiled terrace with a large brick-built barbecue and a wooden table with a dozen chairs around it. Wheeler walked in and stood with his back to the fireplace. 'Well, you're here. Now talk.'

'No tea, then?' said Button.

'Just say what you've got to say, then you can get the hell out of my house.'

'You really don't seem to understand that we are here to help you, Max. It is okay if I call you Max?'

'You can call me whatever the hell you want. Just spit it out. Why are you here?'

'You must realise by now that we know who you are and what you've been doing, Max. You are responsible for dozens of assassinations – contract killings – through the organisation you run that is known as The Office. Prior to setting up The Office you had considerable success as a contract killer in your own right, but that's not why we're here.'

Wheeler frowned. 'What's your name? Samantha, you said? Samantha what?'

'My name is neither here nor there, Max. If this was official, a SWAT team would have kicked down your door and you'd be up against a wall with a gun pressing against the back of your head. Not that we have SWAT teams, of course. That's an Americanism. We have what they call Armed Response Units. ARUs. But SWAT is so much punchier, isn't it? Anyway, SWAT or ARU, we'd be taking you away in handcuffs and interviewing you under caution, but if we did that I don't think I'm exaggerating when I say that you'd be dead within days. You know exactly what I mean, Max. You had no qualms about ordering the killing of Paul Dutch, AKA The Dutchman, because he was helping us. And you sent a team to kill Ricky Lewis and his minder. And of course, you paid someone to kill Darren. Without much success, it has to be said.'

'Let's not forget Donnelly and Divak and the two other people in the car,' said Shepherd. 'Why did you have them killed, Max?'

Wheeler shrugged but didn't answer.

'It does seem to me that even talking to the police merits a death sentence in your organisation,' said Button.

'You can't prove that I had anything to do with those killings,' said Wheeler sullenly.

'Well, you might be wrong there,' said Button. 'We have

phone records and we're following the money trail, and once you're arrested we'll have access to all your computers and files. But more importantly, we'll have access to all the killers you've hired over the years. The one in hospital is recovering, I'm told. And it won't be long before we've identified other killers that you've used. It only takes one of them to turn and we'll have everything we need to put you away for ever.' She smiled brightly. 'But you're missing the point, Max. This isn't about putting you on trial. We have bigger fish to fry. Vladimir Lazovsky and Boris Reznikov. They're the ones we want. Now, you must know that the moment we charge you with anything, Lazovsky and Reznikov will put out a contract on you. And if you're not cooperating, you won't have our protection. In prison or out, they'll have no problem in getting to you.'

Wheeler shook his head. 'You don't know what you're doing.'

'Oh, I know exactly what I'm doing. I'm showing you what lies ahead of you if you don't start talking.'

'They'll kill my wife. And my kids. And worse.' He blinked away tears. 'You have no idea what they're capable of.'

'So why did you go into business with them?' said Shepherd. 'You must have checked them out, surely? Didn't you realise who they were and what they do?'

Wheeler glared at him. 'I didn't go into business with them, how stupid do you think I am?'

'The jury is still out on that, Max,' said Button. 'It's time you told us what's going on.'

Wheeler walked over to a sideboard, opened it and took out a bottle of brandy and a chunky crystal tumbler. He poured himself a large measure and then walked back to stand in front of the fireplace. 'Coming here today, you might have killed me and my entire family. Do you realise that?'

'Of course not,' said Button. 'Even if it were true, how could we possibly know that?'

Wheeler sighed and took a long drink of brandy. 'Two and a half years ago, thereabouts, these two Russians rang my doorbell, pretty much as you did today. They had a miniature pony with them, said it was a present for my youngest daughter. It was her birthday the following day. I didn't know them from Adam, but I invited them in. Rachel and the kids were out on the school run. I gave them a drink and they got to the point.'

'This was Lazovsky and Reznikov?' said Button.

Wheeler grimaced. 'It was, but they used different names back then. They wanted to invest in my business, they said. They knew what I did and they wanted to help me grow the business. Passive investors, is what they said. But their idea was to bring in more work so I explained to them that that wasn't passive, they wanted to be active investors and I wasn't interested. They seemed okay about it. They finished their drinks and left. I wanted them to take the pony with them but they insisted that it was for my daughter.' He gulped down more brandy. 'A few days after my daughter's birthday, Rachel found the pony in the garden, with its throat cut and its guts strewn across the grass.'

'They made you an offer you couldn't refuse,' said Shepherd.

'Yeah, I don't think they'd ever heard of *The Godfather*. I think they came up with it themselves.' He drank more brandy. 'A couple of days later they were outside the school my boys go to and they gave my wife a letter to give to me. They were just proving a point, of course. That they knew where we lived and where my children went to school.'

'And the letter?'

'Offering to buy a 50 per cent stake in my business.'

'For how much?' said Button.

'They didn't mention a figure. But it was never about money.' He walked over to the sideboard and refilled his glass. 'That's when I had them checked out. They'd given me a phone number and I got an address for a company they ran and eventually I got addresses for them both. Got their real names, too. They were clearly threatening me and my family so I felt justified in reacting.'

'You took out contracts on them?' said Shepherd.

'I sent two top guys after them. It was going to cost me close to a hundred grand but I figured it would be money well spent.' He sipped his drink and went back to the fireplace. 'Biggest mistake of my life. The next day I got a phone call. It was the two shooters, begging for their lives. Telling me that I had to do what the Russians wanted. That I had no choice, I had to do what they said. Then I heard both guys being killed. Throats cut, from the sound of it. Then one of the Russians came on the line. I don't know which one it was. He said they were through being nice and that if I didn't agree to what they wanted, they would kill my family. Then they would kill me. Then they would take The Office anyway.' He sighed and shook his head, then took another drink. 'The next day, Reznikov came to my house. He told me that I would never see the two of them together again, so that if I did ever try something on with one of them, the other would carry out their threat. And they've stuck to that. So it's not a partnership. I don't work with them. I just do what they say or I'm dead. And now you've turned up, the moment they find out that I've spoken to you, they'll kill me.' He drained his glass. 'And my family will die, too.'

'It doesn't have to be that way, Max,' said Button. 'It's the

Russians we're after. And their Iranian contact, too. Help us get them and we'll offer you protection. We can provide new identities and a new home.'

Wheeler frowned. 'Iranian contact? What Iranian contact?'

'You've handled a number of contracts for Iranian dissidents over the past year. Layla Latifi was the most recent.'

'That contract came from the Russians. And I never ask why a contract has been raised. I'm only ever interested in who and how much. Anything else is irrelevant.'

Shepherd kept his face impassive. So Wheeler didn't know that The Office was being used by the Iranian regime to kill its opponents. But the Russians obviously did.

'That's another point in your favour, Max,' said Button. 'You need to help us take down the Russians and in return, I'll guarantee safety for you and your family. But we need to move quickly. Every hour that passes makes it more likely that the Russians will realise that we are on to you.'

'How can I trust you?'

'Who else can you trust, Max?' said Button. 'Do you want to phone Lazovsky or Reznikov and ask for their protection? Ask them for a new life for you and your family. In Moscow, maybe? I'm told it's lovely this time of year.' Wheeler went back to the sideboard. 'And if I were you, I'd go easy on the booze,' she said. 'You'll need a clear head for what's coming next.'

Wheeler roared and threw the glass at her. It flew over her head and smashed against the bookcase behind her. Button didn't even flinch and Shepherd realised that Wheeler had deliberately thrown the glass high. It had been a show of anger rather than a deliberate attempt to cause her harm. 'Fuck you!' said Wheeler.

'Sadly, that can't be part of any deal that we make, but I do appreciate your attempt to negotiate,' said Button. 'The deal is that you help us get the Russians, and we protect you. So, as they say on that TV show, "Deal or No Deal"?'

'What do I have to do?' said Wheeler. He picked up the bottle of brandy, looked at it for several seconds, then put it back on the sideboard and turned to face her.

'We need all the intel you have on Lazovsky and Reznikov. We need to get them behind bars as quickly as possible. We will also need a full list of contracts fulfilled by The Office since its inception.' She saw the frown that flashed across Wheeler's face and she raised a hand. 'You will have immunity from prosecution, what we want is to nail down which killings occurred while the Russians were running the show. We need to move quickly, obviously.'

'You say behind bars. What do you mean?'

'They'll be arrested on terrorism charges. They won't get bail. In all likelihood they'll be sent away for life with a minimum of forty years.' A faint smile flickered across Wheeler's face. 'If you're thinking that you could have them killed when they're in prison, please don't,' said Button. 'As part of this deal you will need to forgo any future criminal acts.'

'Sure,' said Wheeler, though Shepherd could tell from his expression that he was already thinking about how easy it would be to have the Russians killed once they were behind bars.

'So, what can you give us in the way of intel?'

'What do you know about them?' asked Wheeler.

'We know their names, we know that they used to work for the Russian intelligence services and probably still do, and we have the details of the visas they were granted,' said Button.

'But we don't know where they are. And we would like any information on anything you have regarding their financial transactions.'

Wheeler nodded. 'I have their addresses. And I can give you bank details and the crypto wallets they use.'

'That's good news,' said Button. 'Can you do that now? We really would like to strike while the iron is hot.' She looked at her watch. 'And we'd like to be out of here before your wife gets back.'

Wheeler stared at her for several seconds, then went over to a framed photograph on the wall, a family photo with Wheeler in a double-breasted suit standing next to his wife and four children. Mrs Wheeler was in her thirties, with long blonde hair and porcelain white skin, and she had some pretty impressive jewellery around her neck and wrists. The children were all good looking and confident, chins up as they smiled at the camera, revealing perfect white teeth. Wheeler pulled at the side of the frame and it swung open to reveal a large wall safe.

Shepherd stood up and moved to the side to get a better look as Wheeler tapped on a keypad and then pressed his thumb against a reader. Wheeler opened the safe and Shepherd saw that it was filled with stacks of cash and red velvet boxes that presumably contained jewellery or watches. There was no sign of a weapon, and when Wheeler's hand reappeared from the safe it was holding two thumb drives. He closed the safe door, replaced the picture, and went over to Button. He gave her the drives. 'They're both password protected, enter the wrong password three times and the contents are wiped,' he said. 'The red thumb drive is my wife's first name followed by her date of birth, day, month and last two digits of the year.

The black one is my oldest son's name and date of birth. I'm assuming you have the dates.'

'We do,' said Button. She slipped the thumb drives into her jacket pocket.

'I have a question for you, Max,' said Shepherd. 'How did you know which direction your guys would be going in when they left Lewisham police station?'

'It was my car. I sent it for them. I told them I needed to see them in Birmingham.'

'So your plan was always to kill them?'

'It wasn't my plan,' said Wheeler. 'It was the Russians. They wanted it done. Insisted on it. Reznikov came round, said it was them or me. Brought a gun with him to prove his point. He said they knew too much.'

'That's all?' asked Shepherd. '"They knew too much"?'

Wheeler shrugged. 'I tried to talk him out of it but he wasn't having it. He ended up saying that it was them or my family so I did what he wanted.'

'And what about Paul Dutch? And Ricky Lewis? How did you know where they were?'

Wheeler grinned. 'Pretty impressive, yeah?'

'That's why I'm asking.'

'The Russians can do it. They were boasting about these hackers they use, out in Russia. Something called Sandworm.'

Shepherd nodded. Sandworm was a hacker group operated by Military Unit 74455, a cyberwarfare unit of the GRU, Russia's military intelligence service. Sandworm had been behind a cyberattack on the Ukraine power grid in 2015 and interference in the 2017 French Presidential election. Sandworm also mounted regular cyberattacks against the UK government and National Health Service and MI5 had issued a warning about Sandworm hackers trying to influence the 2016 Brexit vote. Sandworm would be more than capable of hacking the UK's mobile phone companies, and could probably access government databases like the DVLA.

'I could give them a mobile number and within minutes they would have details of the phone's location and any calls and messages made. It's quite something. Made our job a lot easier.'

'And just to confirm, you don't know who was placing the Iranian contracts?' said Button.

'I wouldn't know if they were Iranian or not,' said Wheeler. 'I never ask. The Russians just gave me a name, location, and photographs, and I would pass them on to whoever was carrying out the contract.'

Button stood up. 'Well, we'll say our goodbyes now, Max. But we'll be in touch in a day or two, hopefully to confirm that we have arrested Lazovsky and Reznikov. And to discuss what arrangements you will need.'

'If they're behind bars, we'll be fine,' said Wheeler. 'I can buy in as much protection as I need.' He gestured at the door, obviously keen for them to go. Button headed out. Shepherd motioned for Wheeler to follow her, Wheeler didn't have a weapon but Shepherd wasn't comfortable walking ahead of him. Button stopped as she reached the front door, and Wheeler opened it. He cursed as he saw the black Volkswagen people carrier turning into the driveway. 'My wife,' he said.

'I'm here to sell you health insurance,' said Button.

'We already have health insurance,' Wheeler hissed.

'I'm offering you a better deal.'

Mrs Wheeler parked the Volkswagen next to the Porsche and climbed out. She was as pretty as her photograph and wearing full make-up. Shepherd wasn't a fashion expert but he was fairly sure that her checked jacket was Chanel and the red soles of her high heels meant that they were Christian Louboutin. Her blonde hair was tied back in a ponytail and there was a slim gold chain around her neck.

Button strode towards Mrs Wheeler, her arm extended. 'So pleased to meet you, Mrs Wheeler,' she said. 'I'm Samantha Stanhope, I've been talking to your husband about health insurance. I'm sorry I didn't get a chance to talk with you, but we have two more appointments to make before lunch so we have to rush.'

Mrs Wheeler looked confused, but shook Button's hand nonetheless. 'Health insurance?' she said.

'I'll put some brochures and a quotation in the post,' said Button. She turned and waved at Wheeler, then crunched across the gravel to the Vauxhall. Button and Shepherd climbed in, and Button waved goodbye to the Wheelers before reversing into the road and driving away. The Lexus followed at a safe distance.

'You are good,' said Shepherd.

'Praise from you is high praise indeed.'

'I'm serious, Charlie. You are amazing. You couldn't have played that any better. You got everything you wanted and he gave it up willingly.'

'To be honest, he didn't have much choice. The stick is very real, the Russians would kill him and his family without a second thought.'

'It was interesting that he didn't know that Sasha was working for us,' said Shepherd. 'It was just the Russians wanting them both dead just because they'd been arrested. That means there isn't a bad apple in Lewisham police station. And from the sound of it, they're not getting information from inside Thames House. It's those Sandworm hackers, hacking into our databases. So we don't have to deal with moles.'

'Well, let's keep an open mind on that,' said Button. 'But yes, Sandworm are the cyberwarfare experts, which would explain their phone tracking and access to the DVLA database.'

She was checking her rear-view mirror and side mirrors, but there didn't appear to be a tail. If there was, the guys in the Lexus would spot it.

'It was interesting that he didn't seem to know your real name,' said Button.

'Yeah, I noticed that.'

'He knew you as Darren Griffiths and had worked out that you were undercover and probably a cop, but he doesn't seem to have made the MI5 connection.'

'So how did he come to send assassins to Battersea?'

'Exactly. Did you take the Darren Griffiths phone to Battersea?'

Shepherd nodded. 'A couple of times.'

'Maybe that's how they found you. They knew you'd been to Battersea, maybe they sent people to several locations where they thought you might be. The guys at Battersea got lucky.'

'Not so lucky considering what Lex did to them.'

'But you take my point, Dan. Max might never have found out your real identity, which makes your life easier moving forward.'

'It would be nice to finally have some good news,' said Shepherd. He wrinkled his nose. 'The deal you offered Wheeler, has Pritchard approved it?'

'No,' said Button.

'Do you think he will?'

'I won't be mentioning it to him. There is no deal, Dan. How could there be after everything he's done? No, it only ends one way for Wheeler.'

'So you lied to him?'

Button raised her eyebrows but didn't answer.

CHAPTER 58

Button received several text messages as she drove through London. She checked them but didn't reply. 'What are your plans for this afternoon?' she asked as she pulled up in front of Shepherd's building. It was just before midday.

'I'll probably hang out with Liam,' said Shepherd. 'I'll be steering clear of Thames House until this is over.'

'That sounds like a plan,' she said. 'Do give Liam my best. In the meantime, there's somebody I'd like you to meet.'

'Now?'

'He's waiting for us in the park. I think he'll be able to help us with Jafar Hosseini.'

'Were you able to get any intel on Hosseini?'

'Plenty, but nothing that connects him to the Russians. I was hoping that Wheeler would be able to tell us but I think he genuinely knows nothing about the Iranian connection. It's clearly all handled through the Russians. We know that Reznikov has been a regular visitor to Dubai over the past couple of years, but so far we have no evidence that he met with Hosseini and we're getting nowhere following the money trail. It's possible, of course, that Reznikov has been flying back with cold, hard cash.'

'That would make sense,' said Shepherd. 'The Iranians would prefer that there was no money trail, obviously.'

'We know that Hosseini is a bad 'un, no question of that,' said Button. 'He was involved in the planning and financing of the 2023 Hamas attack in Israel that killed more than twelve hundred civilians. He was in Tehran at the time but phone and email traffic clearly shows that he was involved.'

'How easy is it for you to do that?'

'Do what?'

'Get phone and email details?'

'It's all doable, providing you have the money. Emails are easier because we can use GCHQ, but the phone companies are getting increasingly problematic.'

'Amar Singh says that the official channels are backed up.'

'That's certainly true, but we never use the official channels, obviously.'

'Amar has contacts he can use that shortcut the process.'

Button smiled. 'There's every chance that we use the same people. But even using our contacts takes time. Whereas Sandworm can presumably access the data in real time using their dark arts. So, are you okay to meet this guy?'

'Sure,' said Shepherd.

They climbed out of the Vauxhall. The Lexus had parked further down the road. Two of Button's heavies had climbed out, sunglasses already in place. 'Are they for me, or for you?' asked Shepherd.

'Both,' said Button. 'Wheeler seems to be cooperating but there's always the possibility that he might have a change of heart.' She gestured towards the park. 'Shall we?'

Battersea Park was a two-hundred-acre green space on the south bank of the Thames, a short walk from Shepherd's flat. It was where he tended to exercise, usually running and stretching. In his younger days he had done his running with a rucksack filled with bricks wrapped in newspaper on his back, but those days were gone. These days a forty-five minute jog with a few sprints and stretches was his exercise regime of choice. The park was home to a boating lake, a running track – that Shepherd tended to avoid – tennis courts, cricket, and football pitches. In the middle of the park was the Pump House Gallery, an art gallery and gift shop, housed in a four-storey Victorian tower.

Button headed towards the gallery. The two minders were about fifty feet behind them, heads swivelling from side to side. 'There he is,' said Button. She gestured with her chin at a man who was sitting on a bench in front of the pump house. He was small, barely five foot six, with pointed features and a thinning black comb-over. He was wearing a black overcoat with the collar turned up and Shepherd realised why Button had brought him to the park. The man's name was Joel Schwartz and his official title was Public Affairs Manager at the Israeli Embassy, but his real job was working for Mossad, the national intelligence agency of the State of Israel. Mossad – AKA the Institute for Intelligence and Special Operations – was responsible for Israel's intelligence collection, covert operations, and counter-terrorism. It had a yearly budget of close to two billion pounds, employed seven thousand people and its director answered only to the Israeli prime minister. But Mossad was more than just an intelligence gatherer – it was the organisation which the Israeli government used to take revenge on its enemies. Mossad tended to describe revenge attacks as targeted killings rather than assassinations, but whatever the label, there was no doubt that Israel's enemies tended to meet violent ends. The Mossad killing machine had gone into top gear following the 2023 massacre, assassinating Hamas officials and sympathisers around the world, much as they did following the terrorist killings of Israeli athletes at the 1972 Munich Olympics. Under Operation Wrath of God, Mossad assassinated dozens of terrorists including members of the Black September group and the Palestine Liberation Organisation.

Schwartz stood up at they approached. 'Dan, this is Joel Schwartz, he works for the Israeli embassy.'

'Joel and I know each other,' Shepherd said. He held out his hand and the two men shook. 'In fact, the last time we met was here in this park.'

Button was usually expert at hiding her emotions, so Shepherd took some pleasure from the look of surprise that flashed across her face. She quickly regained her composure and smiled at Schwartz. 'You didn't mention that, Joel,' she said.

'I just assumed that you knew,' said Schwartz. 'Good to see you again, Dan. You're looking well.'

'So, you know what Joel does,' said Button. 'That's good. Saves any explanation.'

Schwartz waved at the bench. 'Please, sit,' he said.

He waited before Button and Shepherd had sat down on opposite ends of the bench before dropping down between them.

'I was telling Dan that you're interested in Jafar Hosseini,' said Button.

'His name came up as one of the financiers of the 2023 attacks about a year ago,' said Schwartz. 'We had his name but we weren't sure where he was. We thought he was in Iran, Tehran probably, but then we discovered that he was in Dubai. We have had him under surveillance since then.'

'With a view to what?'

'Hosseini was responsible for paying for much of the ordnance used in the attacks, and he paid for a number of training exercises, including the use of paragliders. He has Jewish blood on his hands, and there is a price to be paid.'

'So you'll be sending in a Mossad hit squad?' said Shepherd.

Schwartz smiled but didn't say anything.

'Joel, we believe that Hosseini has been funding assassinations in the UK, with Iranian dissidents as the targets,' said Button.

'I can believe that,' said Schwartz. 'The Iranians tend to farm out their dirty work. It's the coward's way.'

'The point I'm making is that we would be happy to co-operate with you on this.'

'That's very kind of you, but we tend to handle these things ourselves, Charlotte.'

'I understand, but we could help with intel and logistics. If we had time we could handle this ourselves, but we don't. We will be clearing up the UK end of his operation shortly, and the worry is that if we do that it might tip off Hosseini that we are onto him and he might go into hiding or even fly back to Iran.'

'So why don't you wait until we've taken care of him?'

'We are under a lot of pressure to get this resolved now,' said Button. 'There have been a number of killings in recent days and civilians have been hurt.'

'They shot my son,' said Shepherd.

'I'm sorry to hear that,' said Schwartz. 'Is he all right?'

'He was lucky,' said Shepherd. 'Just one round to his shoulder. But it could easily have been a lot worse.'

'We have to stop this now,' said Button. 'The assassinations are being handled through an agency in Birmingham, run by two Russians. Former FSB.'

'Can't you just arrest them?'

'We could. But the British government wants to avoid a trial, for obvious reasons.'

Schwartz nodded. 'Better to give them a taste of their own medicine. Plus, it sends a message back to Moscow.' He smiled. 'That is the philosophy that we follow, of course. Mess with the bull and you get the horns.'

'We want to wrap up the UK situation as soon as possible, but as I said, it's probably better if you take care of Hosseini first.'

Schwartz raised an eyebrow. 'You're looking to set a deadline for us?'

'Not a deadline as such, Joel. But we are in a position to deal with the Russians now, and the longer we leave it, the more likely it is they will realise what we're planning. These people have a first-class intel network.' She smiled. 'Not as good as yours, obviously. But we need to get this done sooner rather than later.'

Schwartz sighed. 'Very well, I will talk to our people.'

'It might be helpful if Dan goes with your team to Dubai. He is familiar with the city. And it would probably be better if I liaise with him rather than pestering you.'

'I will run that by my superiors,' said Schwartz. He stood up. 'I will get back to you later today,' he said.

'I'd be so grateful,' said Button. 'And if there is anything I can do to help, don't hesitate to let me know.'

Schwartz held out his hand to Shepherd. 'Good to see you again, Dan.'

'And you,' said Shepherd. The two men shook hands. There was an amused glint in Schwartz's eyes now. Button was justifiably proud of her intelligence network, but she clearly didn't know that they had met before and that when they had met,

Schwartz had given Shepherd an Israeli passport. The passport had been a gift, in return for what the Israeli government had seen as services to their country, though in fact Shepherd had only been doing his job. Shepherd had never used the passport, it was sitting in a safe deposit box in the Halifax bank's Oxford Street branch, but it was a useful safety net to have.

Schwartz nodded, shoved his hands into his pockets, and walked away, his head down.

'Well that went well, didn't it?' said Button, watching him go.

'He's not thrilled about you putting him on the clock.'

'No one enjoys being given deadlines,' she said, as she started walking back to the cars. 'But we don't have a choice. There's no sign of the Iranians letting up, there are presumably more assassinations on the way. And the big worry is that the Russians might start extending their reach. This is about causing the maximum embarrassment for the United Kingdom, so I wouldn't be surprised if they don't start offering their services to the likes of China and the Saudis, they both have plenty of dissidents in the UK that they'd like to see the back of. We need to nip this in the bud now.'

'That makes sense,' said Shepherd.

'And you're okay going to Dubai?'

'Sure. I can make sure that the job gets done and get straight on to you. The Israelis are our allies, but they do have a tendency to put their needs first. Who will you get to take care of the Russians?'

'I have a few people in mind,' she said. 'We'll need serious professionals because it's clear from what happened to Wheeler's people that it won't be easy taking them out. I was thinking of asking Lex.'

'I'm sure he'd jump at the chance of getting his own back,'

said Shepherd. 'He came very close to getting shot in the street when they attacked me.'

'I'll check through the drives that Wheeler gave me,' said Button. 'I'll have a better idea then.' They reached the Vauxhall, the two minders nearby. 'Well, I'll love you and leave you,' said Button. Shepherd wasn't sure how to say goodbye, but she solved the quandary for him by leaning forward and planting a soft kiss on his cheek. 'I'm glad they missed,' she said. 'I mean, I'm dismayed that they shot Liam, obviously, but I would hate to have lost you.'

Shepherd was surprised by the show of affection but before he could say anything she had climbed in and started the engine. One of the minders climbed out of the Lexus, jogged along the pavement and got into the front passenger seat of the Vauxhall. Button gave Shepherd a final wave and drove off. The Lexus followed. Shepherd watched them go then headed towards his flat.

CHAPTER 59

Shepherd was staring up at his bedroom ceiling, wondering whether he should get up and go for a run around the park when his phone rang. It was Charlie Button. 'Things are moving quickly,' she said. 'Can you get to City Airport?'

'Sure,' he said. 'When?'

'Now. Joel says there's a plane waiting for you. Our Israeli friends are flying out to Dubai and they are happy for you to join them.'

'I'll go right away,' he said, rolling out of bed.

'Don't forget your passport.'

Shepherd ended the call and shaved and showered as quickly as possible. Just over an hour after Button's phone call, he was getting out of an Uber at the Private Jet Centre at London City Airport in the east of London. A pretty blonde girl in a dark blue blazer and grey slacks was waiting for him. She checked his passport and led him out onto the tarmac where a gleaming white Gulfstream G650 was waiting with its steps down.

Shepherd thanked her and headed up the steps. There were two men and a woman sitting in the plane and they all turned to look at him. The woman was sitting across a table from a tough-looking man with a shaved head that Shepherd immediately recognised from MI5's Mossad files. His name was Gil

Stern, who was about to turn sixty-one. Stern's right cheek was a mass of scar tissue which according to his file had been caused by a grenade that had exploded just feet away from him twenty years earlier. Stern was a key member of Kidon – Hebrew for 'tip of the spear' – the department within Mossad that was tasked with the assassination of Israel's enemies. Over the years, Kidon had carried out targeted killings around the world but it had gone into overdrive following the October 7 attacks.

Stern stood up and offered his hand. 'I'm Gil,' he said.

'Dan,' said Shepherd. There was no point in using fake names, Stern would have checked up on Shepherd as soon as he was told that he would be joining them on the mission.

Stern gestured at the woman. She was in her late twenties with killer cheekbones and long legs, her fingernails painted a bright red that glistened under the overhead lights. 'This is Dinah.' Dinah nodded but didn't offer her hand. 'Dinah looks like a catwalk model but trust me, she's former IDF and a crack shot.' Shepherd also recognised her from the MI5 database. Dinah Klein.

Shepherd smiled. 'Good to know.'

'And this is Nathan,' said Stern, gesturing at the man sitting in a large seat on the opposite side of the plane. He was in his late twenties with tanned skin and a pair of Oakley sunglasses pushed back into black curly hair. He was wearing a vintage Rolling Stones T-shirt and faded jeans and strings of beads on his left wrist. He stood up and shook hands with Shepherd. His full name was Nathan Segal and according to the files he was an IT expert and skilled hacker.

Shepherd sat down in the seat on the other side of the aisle from where Segal was sitting and buckled his belt. One of the pilots appeared from the cockpit in a starched white shirt with epaulettes and immaculate black trousers. He pulled the door closed, nodded at Stern, and disappeared back into the cockpit. After a few seconds the jet's engines kicked into life.

'Our flight time is a little over seven hours,' said Stern, sitting down and fastening his seat belt. 'We plan to hit the ground running. We have a team watching Hosseini as we speak.'

The jet began to taxi.

'It's all short notice so we don't have a flight attendant but Segal popped into Marks & Spencer and picked up some sandwiches and drinks.' There was a green Marks & Spencer cool bag on the seat opposite Segal and he pointed at it. Stern gestured at the rear of the plane. 'There's a coffee maker there, and the toilets.'

Shepherd nodded. 'Great.'

'How much do you know about Hosseini?' asked Stern.

'Not much, to be honest,' said Shepherd. 'Just that he's an Islamic regime paymaster and that he's been funding assassinations of Iranian dissidents in the UK. His name only came up a few days ago.'

'You saw it on Layla Latifi's blog?'

Shepherd nodded. 'The blog and her website were both taken down after she was killed, but one of our techies managed to get a copy.'

'We saw it the moment it went online,' said Stern. 'It was a game changer. Everyone had assumed he was holed up in Tehran, then we saw him drinking champagne and fondling hookers in Dubai. We sent a team straight out there. We assume that he thought because of the ceasefire that he was somehow safe. Or perhaps he thought that Dubai was a safe haven.' Stern smiled. 'Big mistake.'

'He definitely helped plan the 2023 attacks?'

Stern nodded. 'Planned and financed it. Passed Iranian money to Hamas and directly funded several smaller groups, paying for weapons and ammunition. He was back in Tehran when the attacks happened but his fingerprints were all over it.'

The plane stopped for a few seconds, then the engines roared and it sped down the runway. Shepherd had been on private jets before but the steep angle of ascent always took him by surprise. Unlike commercial jets which rose sedately into the sky, the Gulfstream shot up like a rocket, pressing him back into his seat.

Once they had levelled off and were heading west, Stern waved Shepherd over to join him at the table with Dinah Klein. She produced a manila file and placed it on the table in front of Shepherd. He opened it. Inside were a dozen or so surveillance photographs and a head and shoulders shot of Hosseini.

'He has a waterfront villa in Palm Jumeirah, five bedrooms and is worth in excess of twelve million dollars. It's not in his name, it's registered through a Cayman Islands company, but he seems to have sole use of it. He has a driver, a team of maids, and four full-time bodyguards.'

Shepherd flicked through the photographs. There were pictures of Hosseini entering and leaving a large villa, getting in to a stretch Mercedes, and several photographs that had been taken in a bar, with Hosseini entertaining pretty girls.

'We should be arriving in Dubai at 8 p.m. local time,' said Stern. 'Hosseini tends to arrive in one of three bars he frequents at about 10 p.m. He usually spends two or three hours in the bar, then returns to his villa, usually with two ladies. They spend the night with him and leave at dawn.'

'He does this every night?' asked Shepherd.

'Every second night,' said Stern.

'He probably needs a day to recover from his exertions,' said Klein. Shepherd couldn't tell if she was joking or not.

'Time is obviously of the essence,' said Stern. 'Charlotte is keen to resolve the Russian matter as quickly as possible, and the worry is that if that happens and Hosseini becomes aware of it, he will flee to Tehran and we will never see him again. The plan is to take care of Hosseini immediately. If he follows his regular schedule he will be out tonight. We have someone outside his villa now and we will know if and when he does leave. When he visits the bars he only has one bodyguard with him, presumably so that he has the back of the car to himself. The bodyguard and the driver stay with the car in the bar's underground car park. We believe we can incapacitate them and replace them with our people. When he is ready to leave, our people will be in the car when it pulls up to collect him. We can send the hookers on their way and deal with him. Assuming it all goes as planned, we can leave Dubai tomorrow, job done.'

'Where will you do it?' asked Shepherd.

'Probably in the car,' said Stern. 'We can take the car into the desert and set fire to it.'

'Making it look like an accident?'

Stern shook his head. 'No, we want his associates to know that he was killed. That he got what was coming to him. And that they will get the same.'

'And what's my part in this?' asked Shepherd.

'So far as I understand it, you are an observer. You can confirm the kill and inform Charlotte accordingly so she can take care of the London end.' He smiled. 'Unless you'd prefer a more active role?'

'I'm happy to leave it up to the professionals,' said Shepherd.

Stern smiled at the compliment. 'Good to know,' he said.

CHAPTER 60

Arriving in Dubai was as easy as leaving London. The Gulfstream stopped in front of the private aviation terminal and within minutes an immigration officer wearing a gleaming white robe and ghutra headdress appeared. He was in his forties with a neatly trimmed beard and Ray-Ban sunglasses that he kept on as he entered the plane. Stern handed over the group's passports, including Shepherd's. The man sat at the table, examined them and stamped them one by one. Shepherd noticed that Stern and Klein were travelling on Irish passports and Segal's was Spanish. When he had finished, the immigration official flashed them a beaming smile and wished them a pleasant visit. He didn't look around the cabin or check their bags.

Waiting for them on the tarmac was a white Nissan Patrol four-wheel drive vehicle. The driver was a man in his mid-thirties with jet black hair and a black and white checked scarf loosely tied around his neck. He climbed out of the vehicle as Stern walked down the steps and embraced him.

'This is Micha,' said Stern, by way of introduction. Shepherd had already recognised the man from the MI5 database. Micha Abramov. Abramov shook hands with Shepherd. He had a firm grip and he looked Shepherd in the eyes as they shook. 'Micha, this is Dan.'

'The English observer,' said Abramov.

'Apparently so,' said Shepherd.

'Micha is one of our top surveillance guys,' said Stern.

Klein and Segal came down the steps and Abramov embraced them in turn, hugging them and kissing them on their cheeks.

Stern made a quick call on his mobile phone, then went over to Shepherd. 'Ben Elon, our other surveillance expert, is outside Hosseini's villa,' he said. 'He'll phone us when he's on the move. I suggest we go to the house we're using here and then Micha can take you to the bar so that you can see Hosseini for yourself.'

They piled into the 4WD and Abramov drove them through the city. Shepherd had been to Dubai several times and nothing had changed since his last visit, towering steel and glass skyscrapers, six and eight lane motorways filled with brand new top of the range SUVs and a smattering of supercars, and cranes clustered around new buildings that were going up everywhere. Shepherd had read somewhere that almost a quarter of the world's cranes were in Dubai.

The 4WD's aircon was on full blast, a necessity as it was over forty degrees Celsius outside. Eventually they arrived at an estate of near-identical pale yellow houses with flat roofs and double garages with white doors. The road was wide and spotless and there were palm trees dotted around the houses that Shepherd would have sworn were fake. Abramov used a remote control to open one of the garage doors and drove in. 'Home sweet home,' he said.

The garage door came down and they climbed out of the 4WD. They walked through a door into the house. The inside of the house was a comfortable twenty degrees. 'There are four bedrooms, all en suite, so help yourself to a shower if you want one,' said Abramov. 'The fridge is full of food and booze, and there are plenty of delivery services in Dubai. Talabat is the one we use. That's Tala*bat* and not Tala*ban*, obviously.'

Stern's phone rang and he took the call, spoke in Hebrew for a few seconds, and then put it back in his pocket. 'Rain check on the shower,' he said. 'Hosseini is on the move. He's got just the one minder with him so it looks like he's on the way to a bar. As soon as Ben knows which one, Micha can take you. Then we'll liaise with Ben and put our plan into operation.'

'Assuming it all goes well, when do we leave Dubai?'

'Micha and Ben will stay here and close up the house over the next few days, we'll fly back early tomorrow morning so we'll hopefully be back in London by tomorrow afternoon. But let's not go counting chickens, we'll take it one step at a time.'

He took them through to a large sitting room with two low sofas angled to face one of the biggest televisions Shepherd had ever seen. Stern picked up a remote control and turned on the television, flicking through the channels until he came to the Al Jazeera news channel.

'Anyone want coffee?' asked Abramov. 'There's a very nice Italian coffee machine in the kitchen.'

'Excellent,' said Stern. They all told Abramov what they wanted in the way of coffee and he headed to the kitchen.

Five minutes later, Abramov reappeared with a tray and five mugs of coffee. Shepherd had just started to sip his when Stern's phone rang. He had a quick conversation in Hebrew and then put his phone down on the sofa. 'You'll need to take that to go,' said Stern. 'We know which bar Hosseini is heading to.'

Abramov took Shepherd into the garage and they climbed into the 4WD. Twenty minutes later they were driving down into an underground car park below a towering five-star hotel. 'That's his limo,' said Abramov, nodding at a stretch Mercedes off to their left. An Asian man in a chauffeur's uniform and a bigger man in a black suit were standing by the side of the car, vaping.

Abramov parked some distance away and phoned Stern. He told him where the Mercedes was parked, then Abramov took Shepherd into the hotel and up to the bar. It was a huge room with grey walls and a glistening black floor and modern black light fittings that sent cones of light up to the ceiling. There were long bars at either side of the room, and between them were fifty or so round tables each with four stools. There were women at about half the tables, and about a dozen men, mostly Westerners, some on their own, others drinking with women. At the far end of the room were half a dozen sofas with small tables in front of them. Shepherd immediately saw Hosseini sitting on the sofa on the far right, a stunning blonde girl in a tight-fitting gold minidress next to him. A waitress was pouring champagne from a bottle.

Abramov took Shepherd over to an empty table and they sat down. Shepherd could see Hosseini from the corner of his eye. 'Just so you know, the bar is divided into three areas,' said Abramov. 'To my left are the Chinese hookers. To the right are the Russians. There's an imaginary line running down the middle and they stick to their own sides. If the Chinese want to use the toilets they have to walk around the bar next to the wall. The only circumstances under which they can cross is if, for instance, a customer wants a Chinese girl and a Russian girl, but they have to be invited and can only stay on the other side so long as the customer is buying them drinks. Every now and again a new girl will inadvertently step over the imaginary line and retribution is swift.' He grinned. 'It's a bit like North and South Korea.' He gestured at the area ahead of them. Very tall Asian girls, most of them with long, glossy black hair, were preening themselves at half a dozen tables. 'This area is where the transsexuals work. Most of them are Filipina and Thai. Now, if the transsexual is Caucasian, even Russian, they are allowed into that area. Gender trumps race.'

'How did you become so knowledgeable about this, Micha?'

Abramov chuckled. 'I've been here several times since we discovered that Hosseini was in Dubai. When he's here he always sits with the Russians. He seems to have a thing for a ménage à trois with a brunette and a blonde.'

'I guess he doesn't get much of a chance of that in Tehran,' said Shepherd.

A waitress came over and Abramov ordered a soda water with ice and lemon. It was always a good undercover drink because anyone watching would assume it was a gin or vodka and tonic. Shepherd ordered a beer. His undercover technique was to drink slowly, to sip rather than gulp.

'So, this is basically a pick-up place,' said Shepherd.

'One of the busiest in Dubai,' said Abramov. 'By midnight most of these girls will have been taken by clients and their places taken by the late shift. Some of these girls can earn in one night what they'd get in a month back in their own countries.'

'Prostitution is illegal here, right?'

Abramov nodded. 'Sure. But the authorities generally turn a blind eye provided it's kept out of the public eye. And there's no problem getting the girls in. UAE nationals are permitted a number of residence visas every year for domestic staff and the like, but a lot of people sell their surplus visas for up to ten thousand dollars a time to middlemen and they end up in the hands of prostitutes who can then stay in the Emirates for up to two years. The ones that can't afford the visa find agents who get them into the country on thirty-day tourist visas.'

The waitress returned with their drinks. Abramov paid. 'My treat,' he said.

'Cheers,' said Shepherd, and he sipped his beer. Out of the corner of his eye he saw a man stand next to Hosseini's sofa, and then sit down next to him. Shepherd glanced over. 'Shit,' he said. He quickly changed stools so that his back was next to the two men.

'What?'

'That's Boris Reznikov.'

Abramov frowned. 'Who?'

Shepherd moved his head closer to the Israeli's. 'He's one of the Russians we're looking at in the UK. He's the one arranging assassinations for the Iranian regime. We believe that Hosseini passes the details of the hits and the money to Reznikov.' He shook his head. 'I can't believe that he's here. He should have been under surveillance.'

'Is this a problem?'

'I'm not sure. Maybe. Maybe not. I need to make some phone calls.'

'Go ahead,' said Abramov. 'I'll mind the fort.'

Shepherd left the bar and went to reception. He found a quiet corner and called Button. 'Reznikov has just walked into a bar in Dubai,' he said.

'That sounds like the start of a bad joke,' she said. 'It's not good.'

'Weren't you watching him?'

'We've had his apartment building under surveillance for the last twelve hours.'

'But nobody checked to see if he's home or not?'

'I'll find out what happened, but what matters is where we go from here. Do you have any idea where Reznikov is staying?'

'I was hoping you'd know that. All I know is that he's sitting in the bar next to Hosseini.'

'We've left the Dubai end up to our Israeli friends,' said Button. 'We haven't looked there at all. The assumption was that he was in London and we'd be taking care of him as soon as the Israelis handled things in Dubai.'

'They can't do anything if Reznikov is here,' said Shepherd. 'If he finds out that something has happened to Hosseini, he'll tell Lazovsky. They'll know something is up.'

'Can you get the Israelis to wait until Reznikov has flown back to the UK?' asked Button. 'If not, you'll have to take care of Reznikov yourself. And as soon as it's done, we'll deal with Lazovsky.'

'Please tell me that you at least have eyes on Lazovsky?'

'I was told that we have, but obviously I will now check. I am sorry about this, Dan. But as you know, shit happens. What matters is how we deal with shit.'

She ended the call and Shepherd rang Stern. He quickly explained what had happened, and Reznikov's role in the grand scheme of things. Stern understood immediately. 'So, we either kill two birds with one stone, or we let him fly back to London and take out the target at a later date. How long will the Russian be here?'

'I don't know. Until he walked into the bar I didn't even know he was in Dubai.'

'It sounds to me as if Charlotte has dropped the ball on this one.'

'Things are moving very quickly,' said Shepherd. 'We're having to think on our feet.'

'I hear you,' said Stern. 'The problem is that our plan involves Hosseini getting into his car with two hookers. We can pay the hookers to leave and then we get Hosseini on his own. Two against one. The scenario changes if the Russian gets into the car. He's GRU, right?'

'FSB. But yes, I take your point. It could get very messy.'

'I don't see that we can deal with two of them at the same time, Dan. I'm tempted to say that we cancel tonight. Regroup first thing tomorrow.'

Shepherd sighed. Cancelling was the right thing to do. Rushing an operation was never a good idea. Reznikov would have undergone extensive unarmed combat training in the FSB and would be familiar with a wide range of weapons. He would be a difficult man to subdue. As much as he wanted to get back to London, it made sense to wait. 'I think you're right, Gil.'

'Can you tell Micha?'

'Of course. We'll keep them under surveillance.'

'We'll be ready to follow his car when he eventually leaves. But we won't be moving against him. We'll meet at the house later tonight.'

Shepherd thanked him and ended the call. He went back into the bar and brought Abramov up to speed. They sat and sipped their drinks, finished them and ordered another round. Three more girls joined Hosseini and Reznikov. The girls were drinking champagne, Hosseini stuck to his champagne and the Russian seemed to be drinking whisky. After an hour, Shepherd's phone buzzed. It was a message from Button.

'OK to talk?'

'I need to make a call,' Shepherd said to Abramov. He headed out of the bar, keeping his back to Hosseini and Reznikov. As soon as he was outside he called Button. 'Boris Reznikov is booked on Emirates flight EK3 leaving Dubai at fourteen thirty tomorrow and arriving at Heathrow at eighteen twenty,' said Button. 'We'll have him picked up at Heathrow. I need you to confirm that he is on the plane and fly back with him. We'll deal with Lazovsky while Reznikov is in the air. And our Israeli friends will deal with Hosseini at the same time.'

'That sounds like a plan but there's a good chance that Reznikov has seen my photograph. Wheeler recognised me so it's very possible that Reznikov will too.'

'I hear you, Dan. But Reznikov has booked first class so if you fly economy there's no way he should bump into you.'

'So I'll sit at the back near the toilets?'

'Apparently it's the safest place to be in the event of a crash,' said Button.

'That will be some comfort,' said Shepherd. 'Okay, all good, I'll call you from the airport tomorrow.'

'Safe travels,' said Button.

CHAPTER 61

Shepherd had been waiting in the departure area of Dubai Airport, sitting on a seat with a view of the London check-in area, for the best part of two hours before Boris Reznikov arrived. He was wearing the same suit he'd had on in the bar the previous night, and was pulling a Samsonite wheeled carry-on bag. He was greeted like a king at the first class check-in desk, then whisked off to the fast track lane and the champagne and smoked salmon that was no doubt waiting for him in the first class lounge. Shepherd waited until the Russian was out of sight before sending Button a message on WhatsApp.

'R has checked in.'

Button replied within seconds.

'See you soon.'

Shepherd put his phone away and joined the queue for economy check-in. Despite the long line he was checked in within thirty minutes and through immigration and security in another twenty.

He sat in a coffee shop until an hour before the flight was due to leave, then he walked to the gate and found a seat that gave him a decent view of the area where the first class passengers boarded. The minutes ticked by with no sign of Reznikov. Shepherd had bought a copy of the *Khaleej Times* as cover and he had it open in front of him as the flight opened and the passengers started queueing. The first and business class passengers boarded first, and when they arrived at the gate, there was no queueing for them. Eventually the economy passengers were allowed on and there was a scramble to join the queue. Shepherd looked at his watch. It was getting close to departure time. He was starting to worry that Reznikov had changed his plans but then he saw the Russian heading towards the gate, pulling his Samsonite case behind him. Shepherd raised his newspaper as Reznikov was ushered onto the plane, presumably where more champagne and canapés awaited. He took out his phone and sent a WhatsApp message to Button. 'R has boarded', then joined the economy queue.

CHAPTER 62

Harper checked his watch. It was just before noon. They had plenty of time.

'Right, let's do it,' he said. He was sitting in the front passenger seat of a grey Range Rover. Bob Hurley was sitting in the driving seat. Harper had worked with Hurley before and they had always got on well together. In a previous life Hurley had worked for Border Force, mainly interviewing passengers at Luton Airport, but had been caught accepting a bribe from a Bangladeshi businessman and after a spell in prison had found himself unemployable until a friend had introduced him to The Pool. Like many members of The Pool, Hurley had military experience, in his case five years with The Rifles, the British Army's largest infantry regiment. Hurley's Army record had been unblemished but he had always hated taking orders, a sentiment that Harper could sympathise with.

In the back seat were Keith Ingram, a veteran of The Pool, and like Harper a native of Liverpool, and David Butcher, a former Northumberland beat cop who had been drummed out of the force for allegations of brutality, which he had always denied.

They climbed out of the Range Rover. Harper and Ingram were both wearing suits. Harper's was a pinstripe that he'd bought in a charity shop on King's Road. Ingram's suit was his own but it was a size too small and his socks were visible below his trousers. Neither of them were regular suit wearers but they were supposed to be Met detectives so they had to look the part.

They walked slowly to the entrance of the building where Lazovsky lived. It was on Bayswater Road overlooking Hyde Park. Lazovsky lived on the eighth floor.

A middle-aged woman in a Prada coat was trying to tap in her entrance code to get access to the foyer while juggling a selection of bright yellow Selfridges carrier bags. Harper flashed her a smile and held the door open for her. 'There you go, madam,' he said.

She ignored him and hurried over to the lifts. 'You're welcome, madam,' said Harper to her retreating back.

Ingram, Butcher, and Hurley followed Harper into the building and he let the glass door close behind them. There were two lifts and they let the woman go up before getting into the second one and taking it up to the eighth floor. They were all wearing baseball hats with the peaks pulled down and they kept their backs to the single CCTV camera in the ceiling of the lift. The doors opened and they walked into the corridor and along to Lazovsky's flat. Harper and Ingram took off their baseball caps and stood in front of the door. Hurley and Butcher stood either side of the door, their backs pressed against the wall. They both took latex gloves from their pockets and put them on.

Harper pressed the doorbell. There was no response so he pressed it again, longer this time. Eventually they heard the pad of footsteps. 'Who is it?' growled a voice in a heavy Russian accent.

'Police,' said Harper. He took out a warrant card and flashed it at the peephole. He didn't intend to let Lazovsky take a close look at it. Button had obviously thought it funny to give them warrant cards in the name of DI Jack Regan and DS George Carter. Reznikov almost certainly wouldn't have ever seen *The Sweeney* so it wasn't a problem, but Harper would rather not take the risk. He put the card back in his pocket.

The door opened. Lazovsky was wearing a white bath robe and his hair was wet. 'We didn't interrupt your shower, did we?' asked Harper.

'I'm heading out,' said the Russian. 'Lunch at The Ivy. Not that that's any of your business. What do you want?' His accent was heavy and he spat the words out as if they were insults.

'This won't take long,' said Harper. He moved towards Lazovsky, forcing the man to step away from the door. Ingram moved to the left and grabbed the Russian's right arm.

'What the fuck?' said Lazovsky.

They were in a large sitting room with windows overlooking Hyde Park. The furniture was modern and expensive and there were large canvases on the walls that looked as if they had been splashed with paint.

Butcher appeared in the doorway. He moved towards the Russian, who began to back away. 'What do you want?' said Lazovsky.

Butcher grabbed Lazovsky's left arm.

Hurley stepped into the room and took Lazovsky's right arm from Ingram. The Russian struggled but Hurley moved quickly, twisting the arm around the man's back. Butcher did the same and together they forced the Russian's head down. He was grunting and cursing but the pressure on his stomach kept the noise down.

Harper and Ingram pulled latex gloves from their pockets and put them on, then pulled on their baseball caps.

Ingram moved quickly across the room and slid one of the windows open. Lazovsky saw what he was doing and yelled for them to stop.

'Be quiet, mate,' said Harper. 'Just take deep breaths, it'll be over soon.'

The Russian continued to struggle and shout as Ingram walked away from the window. He grabbed Lazovsky's legs and together they lifted him off the floor.

'Here we go,' said Harper. He reached out to seize Lazovsky's right leg as Hurley held on to the left one.

They rushed across the wooden floor, keeping a tight grip on the Russian's arms and legs, and heaved him through the window, feet first. Lazovsky screamed in terror as he fell and he was still screaming as Ingram closed the window.

'Right,' said Harper. 'One down, one to go.'

CHAPTER 63

A little over seven and a half hours after leaving Dubai, the Airbus A380 touched down at Heathrow. The flight had been easy enough, the food had actually been quite good and Shepherd had watched two half decent movies. Not that Shepherd was one to complain about flying economy – in his SAS days his main method of international travel had been strapped to the fuselage of an RAF Hercules, ear defenders protecting his ears from the roar of the four turboprop engines, with the toilet facilities shielded from the passengers by a flapping curtain. An Emirates economy seat was luxurious in comparison.

As the plane taxied to the gate, he switched on his phone and sent Button a WhatsApp message. 'Just landed.'

She replied after a minute. 'Lex will pick him up.'

After a few seconds, another message arrived. 'L resolved.'

Shepherd raised his eyebrows. If he was reading that right, Lazovsky was already dead. Button did not mess about. He called Harper's number. It rang for almost a minute before he answered. 'Welcome back.'

'Is everything okay?'

'Perfect. We'll intercept him and then take him home. He lives in a high-rise in Vauxhall. DAMAC Tower. Interiors designed by Versace, apparently.'

'I want to be there,' said Shepherd.

'The more the merrier.'

'Snag is, there's a chance that he might know me,' said Shepherd. 'I kept out of his eyeline in Dubai but he might have seen my photograph at some point here in the UK.'

'Not a problem. I'll have you met and you can cab it to Vauxhall. A guy called David Butcher – Butch. He'll find you.'

'See you later,' said Shepherd and he ended the call.

Shepherd knew of DAMAC Tower, it was a luxury development owned by a global property company run out of Dubai. There were fifty floors with views over the river and Shepherd was fairly sure that the north facing flats overlooked Thames House. He put his phone away as the plane arrived at the gate. The fasten seat belt sign went off and passengers jumped to their feet and started pulling their bags out of the overhead lockers. Shepherd stayed in his seat. He was in no rush.

CHAPTER 64

B en Elon sipped his drink. Two Chinese girls at a nearby table were trying to attract his attention, but he blanked them. Dinah Klein had already moved in on Hosseini and was sitting next to him on a sofa, sipping champagne and giggling at something he'd said. She was wearing a long blonde wig, a black micro skirt and a sheer black top over a white lacy bra and was made up to the nines. She was pretending to be Russian which wasn't difficult, she was reasonably proficient at the language anyway, but Hosseini spoke only English, Arabic, and Farsi. Getting Klein close to Hosseini had taken some arranging as the Russian hookers knew perfectly well that she wasn't one of theirs and they protected their territory aggressively. She had paid three of them a thousand bucks each to be allowed to sit at their table, which was only twenty feet or so from where Hosseini was sitting. She had made eye contact with him a few times, then she smiled seductively, then she crossed and uncrossed her long legs and eventually he waved her over. That was half an hour ago and now she was rubbing her hand along Hosseini's thigh and whispering in his ear. The plan was for her to persuade the Iranian to leave with just her. Elon wasn't sure what she was promising him but whatever she was suggesting had started Hosseini's left leg trembling.

Hosseini waved for his bill. An Indian waiter hurried over and Hosseini gave him a bundle of notes.

Elon tapped on his screen. 'On way.'

Stern messaged back within seconds. 'All good.' Stern and Micha Abramov had already seized Hosseini's stretch Mercedes and secured the driver and the bodyguard in the boot, both bound, gagged, and drugged. The driver and the bodyguard were Pakistanis, merely hired hands, and the Mossad team were planning to release them unharmed when the operation was over.

Klein had her arm through Hosseini's and she kept brushing against him as they walked towards the exit. Elon could see the Iranian's erection from where he was sitting and he smiled to himself. Klein knew exactly what to do to keep a man interested, he had worked with her on several honey traps over the years. What made her technique all the more impressive was that she was a lesbian. It was all an act, and a good one.

Elon had already paid his bill so he took a last sip of Coke and followed them out of the bar. He reached the lifts just as the door was closing on them and he pressed the down button, apologising in Arabic. He joined them in the lift and avoided eye contact as they headed down.

Klein was scratching her fingernails across Hosseini's groin. She whispered something in accented English and he grunted. He pulled her close and kissed her on the lips. She kissed him back and Elon had to admire her professionalism. She really seemed to be enjoying it and was moaning enthusiastically as if he was the sexiest man in the world.

They reached the ground floor and Elon held back to allow them out of the lift first.

Segal was in reception, faking a mobile phone call.

Hosseini and Klein walked towards the exit, arm and arm. Public displays of affection between non-married couples would draw the attention of the police in Dubai, but in the hotel precincts no one would say anything.

Hosseini's stretch Mercedes was waiting outside, the engine running. As he walked out of the hotel, Hosseini released his grip on Klein and they moved apart, just enough to be respectable, though it was clear to anyone who saw them that she was a hooker and he was the client. Elon and Segal followed.

Hosseini stopped at the rear of the car, obviously waiting for his driver to open the door. He stamped his foot in frustration.

Klein laughed and reached for the door handle.

'My driver is an idiot,' said Hosseini.

'Allow me, sir,' said Klein. She gave a theatrical bow and he laughed. He moved past her and started to get into the car, freezing when he realised that Stern was sitting in the back. Stern moved quickly, sticking the hypodermic needle into Hosseini's neck and depressing the plunger. The Iranian passed out immediately and went limp. Stern dragged him inside. Elon followed Hosseini into the car and pulled the door shut behind him.

Klein and Segal walked away, heading for their own car.

Stern used a thick plastic tie to bind the unconscious Iranian's wrists together. 'Let's go, Micha,' said Stern, and Abramov accelerated away from the hotel. The windows of the stretch Mercedes were heavily tinted so no one outside the hotel had seen what had happened.

Stern looked over his shoulder but no one was following them. The plan was to drive Hosseini out into the desert and deal with him there. There was no need to convey any message back to Hosseini's masters in Tehran, Mossad didn't want to claim the credit for the kill, they just wanted him dead.

Abramov kept to the speed limit as he drove down the E11 motorway, heading southwest to Abu Dhabi. The plan was to bury Hosseini in the desert closer to Abu Dhabi so that in the unlikely event that the body was discovered it would be the Abu Dhabi police investigating rather than the more efficient Dubai police.

Stern's mobile phone buzzed in his pocket. He pulled it out, looked at the screen, then took the call. He listened for a few seconds, then nodded. 'Okay. Well it's your decision obviously.' He ended the call and put the phone away. 'There's been a change of plan,' he said. 'Micha, take us back to Dubai.'

CHAPTER 65

'There he is,' said Harper, nodding at Reznikov who had just emerged from the doors leading to the customs area. The Russian was looking around, probably seeking his driver.

Ingram nodded. 'He looks Russian, doesn't he? Funny, right? You can always tell a Russian. The square jaw and the eyes close together. And the thick brow.'

'Bit racist that, mate,' said Harper.

'How is that racist?'

'How would you like it if someone said they could tell that you were from Liverpool just by looking at you?'

Ingram wrinkled his nose. 'I'd be more upset if they thought I was a Manc.'

'Fair point,' said Harper.

Harper moved to block Reznikov's way. 'Mr Reznikov?' he said. 'Boris Reznikov?'

Reznikov offered the handle of his luggage and Ingram took it. 'Where's Ivan?' snapped Reznikov.

'Ivan?'

'My regular driver.'

'We're not chauffeurs, Mr Reznikov. We're with the police. We need to ask you some questions.'

'I want to talk to my lawyer,' said Reznikov.

'I'm sure you do, but you are being detained under Schedule 7 of the Terrorism Act 2000. If necessary you will be arrested under Section 41 of the act. You can speak to your lawyer after we have questioned you.'

Reznikov gritted his teeth and nodded. 'Fine. I have done nothing wrong and my visa is in order.'

'We can take you to the police station to question you, or we can continue this at your home. Which would you prefer?'

Reznikov nodded again. 'Take me home.'

CHAPTER 66

Shepherd walked out into the arrivals area. He spotted Butcher immediately, mainly because he was holding up a piece of paper on which he had scrawled a cartoon spider. 'Butch?'

'I like to think so,' said Butcher. He grinned and offered his hand. 'Great to meet you. Lex is a big fan.'

Shepherd could tell immediately that Butcher wasn't former special forces. He was a big man, well over six feet tall, with broad shoulders and hands like shovels. He was clearly strong and could probably lift Shepherd above his head if he wanted, but a physique like that was counterproductive when it came to marching across the desert with sixty pounds of gear on your back. When it came to special forces soldiering, stamina, speed, and commitment were more valuable commodities than brute strength.

'We need to get a move on,' said Butcher. 'Lex is taking Reznikov to Vauxhall and wants you there ASAP. He's taken the car so we'll need to black cab it.'

They hurried to the cab rank and climbed in the back of a black cab. Butcher gave the driver the address and settled back in his seat. 'Should take us about an hour,' he said. 'I'll give Lex a heads up.' He sent Harper a text message.

Butcher clearly wasn't one for small talk and he spent most

of the journey looking out of the window. He didn't seem to be worried about the possibility of a tail, but Shepherd did enough checking for the two of them and reassured himself that no one was following them. They didn't speak again until the cab had dropped them down the road from DAMAC Tower. They waited until the cab had driven away before heading to the entrance.

'Lex and the guys should be inside already,' said Butcher. He pressed four buttons on the console by the door and they heard a ringing sound followed by Harper's laconic voice. 'Yeah?'

'It's us,' said Butcher.

The door buzzed and Butcher pushed the door open. They crossed the lobby to the lifts and rode up to the top floor. The fiftieth. Reznikov was in the penthouse. The door hissed open and they stepped out into the corridor. A door was open and Harper waved them over. He bumped fists with Shepherd. 'Better late than never,' he said.

Shepherd and Butcher followed Harper into the flat. There was another man standing in the hall. He had the typical SAS build, slightly less than average height, wiry and compact. Like Harper, he was wearing a baseball cap.

'I don't think you met Keith, he was with the Regiment, but long after you'd left,' said Harper. 'Keith Ingram, so we call him Mac Ten, obviously.'

'Obviously,' said Shepherd. He shook hands with the man. Ingram had longish black hair that he kept flicking away from his face, and had the look of a young Tom Cruise. 'Pleasure to meet you, Spider. You're a bit of a legend at Stirling Lines.'

'Good to know that I've not been forgotten.' He looked at Harper. 'All good?'

'We were just waiting for you, Spider. Otherwise we'd be out of here by now.'

He took Shepherd through into the sitting room. Reznikov was sitting on a low sofa. Standing in front of him was a man in a leather bomber jacket, black jeans and an Arsenal baseball cap, holding a Glock. 'This is Bob,' said Harper.

'Hi, Bob,' said Shepherd. He gestured at Reznikov. 'Do you know me?'

The Russian looked up at him and narrowed his eyes. 'Should I?'

'You sent someone to kill me.'

The Russian shrugged but didn't say anything.

'So, you don't know me?' asked Shepherd.

The Russian looked at Shepherd carefully, then shook his head.

Harper took a pair of latex gloves from his pocket and put them on. Ingram and Butcher did the same.

'Do you remember Sasha Zlatnar?' said Shepherd. 'You knew him as Stretko Divak. Stretch.'

'The Serb?'

'Yes, the Serb. You had him killed, for what?'

'The cops arrested him. He would have led them to us. Are you a cop? You don't look like a cop.'

Shepherd ignored the question. 'So, you killed Sasha? And Donnelly? And the two men in the car with them? And then you killed one of the men who followed your killers?'

Reznikov shrugged. 'I did not pull the trigger.'

'No, but you told Wheeler that he had to do it. You said you'd kill his family if he didn't.'

Reznikov smiled. 'Wheeler always needs persuading.'

'You think this is funny?'

Reznikov shrugged again. 'It is business, that's what it is.' He sneered at Shepherd. 'Do what you have to do. Arrest me and take me to one of your comfortable prisons with televisions and PlayStations and a well-equipped gym.' He stood up and held out his hands, expecting to be handcuffed.

Shepherd shook his head. 'You're not going to prison, my friend.'

Ingram and Butcher moved either side of the Russian, grabbing his arms securely, but not so tightly as to leave marks. Harper slid the French windows open and a soft wind blew in from the terrace, ruffling Shepherd's hair.

'There's something you need to know,' said Shepherd. 'The man you call the Serb, Sasha Zlatnar, was working for us. He helped us bring you down. It's because of him that you are in this situation.'

'Just arrest me and take me to the police station. That is your duty.'

'Because of what Sasha did, his wife and children will be given new lives in this country. We will take care of them.'

'You talk too much,' sneered Reznikov.

'When we have finished with you, I will be tracking down your family. Your wife, if you have one. Your children if you have them. Brothers. Sisters. Your parents if they are still alive. I will track them down and kill them.' Shepherd spoke quietly, with menace, and it was clear from the way the colour faded from Reznikov's face that the Russian believed him.

'You can't do this,' hissed Reznikov. He began to struggle but Ingram and Butcher held him firm.

Harper walked over and grabbed the Russian's left leg. Butcher stepped forward and seized the right leg. The four men lifted Reznikov off the ground. He bucked and kicked, grunted and cursed, but they held him firm, carried him through the window, across the terrace and tossed him over the edge. His limbs flailed and he screamed but then gravity did its job and whipped him away. His screams faded with the distance and ended with a wet slapping sound followed by silence.

Harper walked back into the room. Butcher, Hurley, and Ingram followed him.

'That was cold, Spider,' said Harper.

'He deserved it.'

'Are you serious about slotting his family?'

Shepherd smiled coldly. 'Of course not. But I wanted him to think that I was as he died.'

'Bloody hell, mate. Remind me never to get on the wrong side of you.'

'I will, mate. Don't worry.'

CHAPTER 67

Hurley drove Shepherd and Harper back to Battersea. As the crow flies it was less than a mile and a half from DAMAC Tower, but Butcher took the long way around, driving north across Vauxhall Bridge, west along Grosvenor Road and crossing the river again on Chelsea Bridge, giving them plenty of time to check that they weren't being followed.

As they pulled up in front of Shepherd's building, they all spotted the black Lexus. 'Looks as if Charlie wants a word,' said Harper. 'I'll leave you to it.' He patted Hurley on the shoulder. 'Cheers, Bob. Thanks for your help today.'

'All good, Lex.' He twisted around in his seat. 'Great to meet you, Spider. I hope we can work together again at some point.'

Shepherd nodded and smiled, but the last thing he wanted was to be doing The Pool's dirty work again. Reznikov had been a special case.

Harper got out of the car and headed towards the apartment building. Shepherd climbed out and looked over at the Lexus. Button got out and flashed him a smile as he walked over to join her. She started walking towards the park and he kept pace with her. 'How did it go?' she asked, even though Shepherd was sure that she knew exactly how it had gone because Harper had sent her a number of messages as they had left DAMAC Tower.

'Fine,' said Shepherd. 'I worry about the CCTV at the building,' he said. 'We kept our faces away from the cameras, but he'll be seen walking in with Lex and Ingram.'

'Not a problem,' she said. 'We have access to their security system and anything problematic has already been wiped.'

Shepherd frowned. 'You can do that?'

'We can do a lot of things, Dan. It's why we're paid the big bucks.'

'I've told Razor that he can let Ricky Lewis go so now the only loose end to deal with is Max Wheeler.'

'That's in hand,' said Button. 'We'll have our disinformation people out pushing the narrative that the killings were the work of the Kremlin. The fact that they went out of the windows will be enough to convince most people that Putin wanted them dead. And he's always keen to play the hard man so I doubt he'll bother to deny it. Not that anyone ever believes his denials anyway.'

She turned and started walking back to the Lexus. Their conversation was clearly nearing its end.

'What about Hosseini?' asked Shepherd.

'Ah, yes, apparently there's been a change of plan. The plane that flew you to Dubai has been repurposed as an evacuation flight and it left for Tel Aviv this morning with a doctor and two nurses and one of their citizens who is in a coma and is being taken to the Ichilov Hospital in Tel Aviv for emergency treatment.'

'Hosseini? They passed him off as an Israeli?'

'Indeed. They arranged a passport and the correct paperwork. Or more likely just paid off Dubai customs and immigration.'

'So they're going to do a deal with him?'

'I very much doubt it. Feelings are still running high about what happened in 2023. I think he's destined for a hard interrogation followed by an unmarked grave in the desert.'

Shepherd nodded. 'I certainly won't be shedding any tears for Hosseini, not after what he did.'

'Karma?'

Shepherd shrugged. 'What goes around, comes around.'

'Well on that thought I shall love you and leave you,' said Button. 'Do give my regards to Giles next time you see him.' She leaned forward and this time he was expecting the kiss on the cheek so he leaned into it. She gave his arm a soft squeeze as her lips brushed his cheek. 'You be careful, Dan Shepherd,' she whispered.

'You too,' said Shepherd.

She let go off his arm, smiled, then turned and walked back to the Lexus, her heels clicking on the tarmac. Shepherd watched her go.

'She fancies you,' said a voice behind him. It was Lex Harper.

'Bloody hell, Lex, will you not creep up on me like that.'

'I'm your guardian angel, where else am I supposed to be?'

'I don't need protecting from Charlie Button,' said Shepherd.

Harper reached out and patted his shoulder. 'I wouldn't be so sure about that, mate.'

CHAPTER 68

Maxwell Wheeler sipped his coffee and read through the *Mail Online* story. Two Russians, in separate parts of London, were dead after falling from their high-rise flats. The police said that both deaths appeared to be accidental and that there was nothing to connect the two men. Wheeler smiled to himself. Hopefully it would stay that way. The journalist who wrote the story seemed happy enough to repeat the police line, and it would take some considerable digging to link the two men, especially as the police had released their fake names and not their true identities. Wheeler scrolled down to the comments section. At least half of the comments had gone the conspiracy theory route, saying that the deaths were very much linked and that it was almost certainly the Russian president exacting revenge on his enemies.

Wheeler didn't believe for one minute that the deaths were accidental, but he couldn't work out what had happened. The woman who had called at his house had said that the Russians were going to be arrested. What had happened to that plan? The police in the UK didn't go around killing people, certainly not by throwing them out of high-rise windows. The addresses of the Russians had been on the thumb drives he had given her, along with details of the money The Office had received and of the contract killers who had been paid for their services.

The Russians should have been behind bars by now, not lying dead in hospital mortuaries. Had someone in Moscow discovered that the police were about to arrest Lazovsky and Reznikov and decided to have them killed? And did that someone know that Wheeler was involved? If they did, maybe his life was still at risk.

The door to his study was flung open and Wheeler flinched, but he relaxed when he saw it was Sophie, his oldest daughter. 'Dad, can I go to the cinema tonight with Debbie and Jennifer from school? I'll be done by eight.'

'What does your mum say?'

'Mum says it's okay with her if it's okay with you. She'll pick me up after Jeremy's flute lesson.'

'Then it's okay with me.'

Sophie smiled and held out her hand. Wheeler sighed and took out his wallet. He gave her a ten-pound note but the hand stayed out and the smile hardened a little. Wheeler gave her another ten-pound note and she hugged him. 'Love you, Dad.'

She disappeared down the hall and her place was taken by Emily, his younger daughter. 'Dad, can I have money for snacks?' she said. She had learnt from her older sister, smiling and holding out her hand. She was only nine but it was clear that she was going to break hearts when she was older. Emily was happy with ten pounds but no doubt that would soon change.

His wife Rachel appeared in the doorway. She flashed him a smile. 'Max, I'll need to fill the VW's tank and my credit cards are maxed . . . no pun intended.' It wasn't much of a pun but she did use it at least twice a week and had done so since they had married.

'No problem,' said Max. He pulled a fifty-pound note from his wallet and gave it to her. She laughed.

'When was the last time you filled up the tank?' she said. '1998?'

'Sorry,' he said and gave her another fifty-pound note.

'And I thought I'd get some nice T-bone steaks from Waitrose. The big ones that you like.' He smiled and gave her another hundred pounds. She blew him a kiss and closed the study door. He heard the clatter of shoes down the hall, the front door opening and closing, then the crunch of shoes on gravel. The VW started up and the tyres crunched as Rachel drove away.

He sipped his coffee. He always enjoyed the silence in the house when Rachel was on the school run, it was time that he could spend thinking and planning without being interrupted. He sat back and scrolled further down the comments. If he was lucky, really lucky, he might just get out of his predicament alive. The Office was finished, clearly, and he wasn't sure if his previous contract killings would come back to haunt him, but if the Russians were dead and if there were no repercussions from their deaths then maybe, just maybe, he and his family would get through this.

He jumped as the doorbell rang. One of the kids had probably forgotten something. He hurried down the hallway and opened the front door, his eyes widening when he saw the woman standing there. It was Samantha, the cop, but this time she was on her own. He looked over her shoulder just in case she had armed police with her, but there was just a car. It was a black Lexus, top of the range. He frowned. Last time she and her accomplice had been in a battered Vauxhall. Her clothes were different, too. She was wearing a Burberry overcoat over a dark blue dress that looked as if it was designer, and she had a Chanel handbag over her left shoulder. She couldn't have looked less like a police officer if she had tried.

'Are you here on your own?' he asked.

The woman looked around. 'It clearly looks that way, doesn't it?'

'So no SWAT team?'

'As I said, we call them ARUs. Armed Response Units. But no. No guns.'

'And what about Darren Griffiths?'

'Oh, he's busy doing something else. We're not joined at the hip. And today I'm very much flying solo.'

'What do you want?' asked Wheeler.

'What I'd really like is a cup of tea,' she said. 'Anything but Earl Grey, really. I can't abide Earl Grey. And then, over a nice cup of tea, I'd like to make you an offer you can't refuse. A last chance, you might say.' She smiled brightly. 'So, are you going to invite me in?'

THRILLINGLY GOOD BOOKS FROM CRIMINALLY GOOD WRITERS

CRIME FILES BRINGS YOU THE LATEST RELEASES FROM TOP CRIME AND THRILLER AUTHORS.

SIGN UP ONLINE FOR OUR MONTHLY NEWSLETTER AND BE THE FIRST TO KNOW ABOUT OUR COMPETITIONS, NEW BOOKS AND MORE.